Taryn Belle is the pe[...]
Canadian author who [...]
childhood in two men[...]
Nearly Normal—both [...]
is a former international model and a businesswoman,
running a swimwear company with merchandise
popularised by celebrities such as Jessica Alba and
Kate Hudson. She loves playing board games with her
husband and three children, hosting dinner parties in her
Vancouver home, and crafting out.

Margot Radcliffe lives in Columbus, Ohio, right now,
but surrenders to wanderlust every couple of years, so
it's hard to say where she'll end up next. Regardless of
location, her apricot dog will be by her side while she
writes fun romances that hopefully will make readers
laugh and space out for a bit, with heroines who aren't
afraid to take what they want and confident heroes who
are up to a challenge. She loves creating complicated,
modern love stories. She can be found @margotradcliffe
on Twitter and @margot_radcliffe on Instagram.

If you liked *Intoxicated* and *Sin City Seduction*
why not try

Sexy Beast by Jackie Ashenden
Burn My Hart by Clare Connelly

Discover more at millsandboon.co.uk

INTOXICATED

TARYN BELLE

SIN CITY SEDUCTION

MARGOT RADCLIFFE

MILLS & BOON

First Published in Great Britain 2020
by Mills & Boon, an imprint of HarperCollins*Publishers*
1 London Bridge Street, London, SE1 9GF

Intoxicated © 2020 Cea Sunrise Person

Sin City Seduction © 2020 Terra Rogerson

ISBN-13: 978-0-263-27754-8

MIX
Paper from
responsible sources
FSC   FSC® C007454
www.fsc.org

This book is produced from independently certified FSC™ paper
to ensure responsible forest management.
For more information visit www.harpercollins.co.uk/green.

Printed and bound in Spain
by CPI, Barcelona

INTOXICATED

TARYN BELLE

MILLS & BOON

To Nicole

CHAPTER ONE

THE BRIDAL SHOP was at the corner of Spring Street, conveniently located beside a bakery displaying a flower-adorned wedding cake in the window. Standing on the sidewalk stuffing the last of her street vendor veggie dog into her mouth, Laina Rose stared at the fluffy white dresses with loathing. It seemed like everywhere she looked these days she saw some sort of display of everlasting love, which she guessed came with spring everywhere, not just downtown Atlanta. Businesses trying to cash in on the illusion of forever, still pretending in this day and age that it could be a real thing.

It made Laina sick.

Sighing deeply, she opened the door to the bridal shop and entered. She heard a squeal, and then a bundle of silk chiffon and strawberry-blond hair was launching itself into her arms. "Banger!" Kiki shrieked.

"Mash!" Laina shrieked back, using the old nicknames they'd given each other during a high school trip to London. Just seeing her friend's beaming face was enough to make Laina's bad mood vanish. "You look amazing!" It was true—Kiki was lit with a glow from within that could only mean one thing. "Oh my God," Laina said as realization hit. "The adoption came through, didn't it? You're getting a daughter."

"Yes!" Kiki's eyes were dancing. "I still can't believe it—Dev and I go to China to pick her up in a month. Right after the wedding!"

Laina grasped Kiki's hands happily, her fingers closing around a large ring. She looked down at it and laughed. "Wow. All those climbers must be really disappointed that Mount Everest has been relocated to your finger," Laina said, lifting the impressive chunk of jewelry up to eye level. "Dev doesn't mess around, does he?"

"Nope." Kiki grinned back at her. Despite Laina's cynicism about marriage, she was truly thrilled for her best friend, who'd weathered more heartache on the path to happiness than anyone she knew: the loss of her mother, divorce, multiple miscarriages and infertility. The girls had met in ninth grade and become inseparable at their Atlanta private school, with their friendship continuing after Kiki moved to LA for university. Later, when Kiki had needed a getaway after a shattering divorce, Laina had offered her the perfect solution. Her parents owned a second home on the Caribbean island of Moretta, where Laina had spent her holidays growing up. Even though it had meant the unpleasant task of asking her parents for a favor, she hadn't hesitated in offering the estate's guest cottage to Kiki. It didn't take long for Kiki to decide she was staying on the island, finding a bartending job and moving into her own cottage. Eventually she'd met Dev, a fellow Moretta resident who also happened to be a chart-topping rock star, and now they were getting married on the island in just two weeks.

"So, what do you think?" Kiki asked, pulling Laina over to the dressing area and doing a spin in front of the three-way mirror. On closer inspection, Laina could see that the dress had a faint blush-pink hue—Kiki's signature color.

"It's perfect," Laina said, glancing at her own reflection over Kiki's shoulder. She'd been up for work since 5:00 a.m., and it showed. Her dark curls had escaped the loose bun she'd put in that morning, allowing errant springs of hair to dance around the neckline of her navy work dress. Up close she could see that she'd forgotten to put mascara on, not that it mattered much. With her roundish face and a mouth that always looked too wide to her, Laina didn't think of herself as particularly beautiful. But her eyelashes were her pride and joy, framing her large brown eyes in way that prompted friends to ask where she got her extensions done.

Kiki was twisting back and forth in front of the mirror, holding her hair off her shoulders in a mock updo. "You're really up for this? I still can't believe you're going to host a wedding on your parents' property."

Laina shrugged. "It was their idea, remember? They almost never use it anymore. Plus they adore you."

"They've met me exactly once."

"To know you is to love you."

Kiki dropped her hair and turned to face Laina with a look of concern. "Still… I know this must be at least a little uncomfortable for you. I mean, you haven't even stayed at their estate in what, ten years?"

"Twelve. Since I was twenty," Laina said more tensely than she'd meant to. She relaxed her tone. "But it's not like I'm staying at the main house— I'll be in the guest cottage. Besides," she added, lifting an over-the-top crystal headpiece and placing it playfully on Kiki's head. "My parents were right—if the press got wind that the rock god of the century was getting married, the paparazzi would be all over his house. Hibiscus Heights is the perfect decoy."

"Well, I hope you know how much we appreciate it."

"Of course I do. Just remember to keep my name out of it."

"Pinkie swear," Kiki said, and Laina grinned. She knew no further discussion was needed; Kiki had been there to nurse her broken heart several times when Laina had discovered that certain men were only after one thing. And it wasn't her body—it was what they assumed she had in her bank account.

"Listen," Kiki said, looking at Laina squarely. "I feel like I've been really carried away with the adoption thing and the wedding lately. I've hardly asked about you. I mean, how are things? How's work?"

Laina moved to a display of delicate necklaces and started fingering through them. "Well, let's see. I was up at five to finish a drawing for a client meeting this morning, I checked in on a condo project to find exactly *one* tradesman working, I spent an hour on the phone talking a client down from the ledge, and then I paid the bills and bought a veggie dog with my entire profits for the month. But I love it," she said, finishing with a grin.

Indeed, three years into setting up her own Leadership in Energy and Environmental Design—LEED—architectural firm, Laina's work often felt like a labor of love. Great progress had been made in recent years with green construction, but passive design was still in its infancy. Even though she'd done nine major residential projects since opening shop and won an award for the city's most promising architect, convincing clients that a LEED certification would save them more money than they could count in the long run was no easy feat—and her bank account showed it.

"Mmm. Sounds like you need an assistant," Kiki said, accepting a necklace Laina was holding out to her.

"I wish. Running a one-woman show isn't easy, but I keep telling myself it won't be like this forever. At least I'm my own boss—I wouldn't go back to working at a big firm for anything."

Kiki fastened the bow-shaped pendant around her neck and glanced in the mirror. "A bit too sweet for me, I think," she said, taking it off again. As she passed the necklace back, her eyes met Laina's. "Okay, I have to ask," she said with a sigh. "Do you ever hear from—"

"Asswipe?" Laina interjected. "No, never." As she flicked her eyes away from her friend, they landed on a row of dresses on display. A high-necked, sleeveless bodice with a full skirt of lace. A pale aqua strapless number that reminded her of a mermaid. And a soft, drapey column with sweeping layers—exactly the type of dress Laina would have chosen if she'd gotten married a year ago like she was supposed to.

It had been twenty-two months since Ward left

her, and though she didn't have a shred of feeling left for him, the memory of his departure still stung. To think she had actually loved someone who would be that cruel to her…it made her wonder if she could ever trust her judgment again. It wasn't enough that Laina had found her fiancé in bed—*their* bed—with another woman on a day she'd come home from a canceled lunch date. It was that after the woman had left, he'd acted like the whole thing had been Laina's fault. *I'm sorry you're hurt*, he'd said, as if that were any kind of apology, and then he'd shifted to a passive-aggressive stance. *I blame myself. I knew you'd only been with two other men when we met, but I guess I didn't realize that meant you'd only ever want to do missionary.*

Laina had slapped him across the face when he said that, shocking even herself. And it wasn't just because she'd been pushed to the depths of humiliation. It was because they'd started out so sweetly, with him leaving love notes in her pockets and cooking her dinner when she came home tired. Because she'd remained patient with him as she busted her butt to get her firm going while he stayed home "just waiting for the right opportunity to come along." Because they'd planned their wedding and talked about forever as if it were a done deal. And because what he said was true: she really *wasn't* that interested in sex, and she sometimes wondered if that meant there was something wrong with her.

But never again. She'd learned her lesson. Men were more trouble than they were worth, and her time and energy was much better put toward rewarding pursuits, like her career. And it certainly wasn't Kiki's fault that she'd introduced her to Ward and was now the one getting married instead.

"Seriously, though," Laina said, "you know how you're supposed to go through all those stages after a breakup? I'm finally at indifference. I feel like I could see him now and it would barely faze me."

Kiki bit her lip. "Well, I'm really glad to hear you say that, because…"

Laina stared at her. "What?"

"I've been dreading telling you this," Kiki said, dropping her face into her hands. When she spoke again, it was through her fingers. "First you have to promise me that no matter what, you'll still come to the wedding and be my bridesmaid."

Laina looked at her warily. "O…*kay*."

Kiki heaved a deep sigh. "Asswipe is going to be there."

Laina's heart plummeted. "You're joking."

"I *know*," Kiki moaned. "It's horrible. It's just… you know that his parents are my dad and stepmother's best friends. They were the only family he asked me to invite, and…my father's done so much for me. I just couldn't say no. I'm so sorry."

"I suppose he's bringing a date," Laina stated flatly.

"Yeah, he did check the plus-one box."

Lifting the trailing skirt of her dress, Kiki dropped onto a satin-covered bench. Laina sank beside her and took a deep breath. "You know what? It's fine. This is good, actually. I knew I couldn't avoid him forever, and I'll be so busy helping you I probably won't even…" She trailed off unconvincingly as Kiki's hand landed on top of hers.

They sat in silence for a few moments, and then Kiki turned to her with an excited expression on her face. "What is it?" Laina asked cautiously.

"I just got an idea. What would you say to a little revenge?"

Laina shook her head firmly. "You know me—not my style. I believe in karma, remember? It'll all come around."

"Oops, did I say revenge? What I meant was… *fun*. As in going to my wedding with the world's hottest guy. And just as a fringe benefit, making your ex wild with jealousy."

"When you say 'world's hottest guy'—"

"I mean my cousin James. Honestly, it's probably against the law to say this about a blood relative, but he's ridiculous. And single. And supersmart. And loaded—not that you care about that."

"So what's wrong with him?"

"Wrong? Um, nothing, as long as you don't let

him put you under his spell. Let's just say he's… got a way with the ladies."

"Ah." Laina rolled her eyes. A womanizer was the last thing she needed to welcome into her life right now, but showing up at the wedding of the decade alone while her snake of an ex flaunted his new girlfriend in front of her? Just the thought of it was enough to make her crawl into a hole. "Would he even agree to it? If he can have his pick of anyone…"

"Ha! If he sees a picture of you, I guarantee he'll jump on it."

Laina felt herself blushing. She couldn't help it— she just wasn't a seductress by nature, and the idea of being in the company of a man who was used to getting his way with any woman he wanted… It was *intimidating*.

But the alternative was even worse.

"Okay," Laina heard herself say. "But he has to understand it's just for show, okay? The last thing I need right now is some guy who thinks I'm going to fall at his feet for whatever he has in his pants."

"Oh, my God. It's beautiful," Jennifer breathed in wonder as she stared. "Bigger than I was expecting, but…perfect."

James grinned. "It always looks bigger in real life. Months of photos can't compare to the real thing."

"You're telling me. Makes me wish I could enjoy

it for myself. But I know for sure that it's going to make a lot of women extremely happy."

"My goal exactly," James said with a smile, looking around the space with satisfaction.

This was the moment he lived for, the unveiling of the result of years of work to a happy client. Three years ago he'd partnered with Jennifer Liu, a Hong Kong investor, to formulate the development of Revive Fitness Centers. The one they were standing in was only the first of eighteen that would be built across Florida and Georgia over the coming years, and he already knew the huge risk he'd taken to finance it with Jennifer was going to pay off in a big way. Much more than just a gym, Revive featured an Olympic-size pool, sauna, minispa, Keto-inspired restaurant, fitness shop and day care with complimentary childcare—like a county club that was exclusive to women. Membership wouldn't be cheap, but he knew the clientele would be able to afford it. He'd positioned his flagship center right in Bal Harbour, just blocks from James's beachfront home in one of the wealthiest neighborhoods in Miami.

When Jennifer turned to face him, a quick image of her naked body flashed through James's head. It had been five years since he'd slept with her—only once, and before they'd officially formed a business relationship. But from the way she was dressed—body-hugging dress, nude heels,

black hair swept back to reveal her slender neck—
he was pretty sure she was hoping for a repeat
performance. Jennifer was a beautiful woman and
he'd enjoyed their night together, even if he hadn't
given her a second thought outside of business
since. Not only were clients and business associates off-limits, replay encounters made things
complicated. And James did relationships only one
way: simple and straightforward with no expectations on either side. Somehow that didn't seem to
stop a lot of women from trying to be the one who
changed his mind, which James put down to his
unavailability. His work was his life, and though
many of his conquests showered him with com-
pliments on his looks, he supposed he just didn't
see what they did when he looked in the mirror.
With his sun-streaked hair, permanent stubble and
tanned skin, all James saw was the same kid who'd
spent his life at the pool, paying his way through
university with his lifeguard certificate.

"What about the cat story?" Jennifer asked, gazing up at him under lash extensions. "We're opening in a month. We don't need any bad press right
now."

James smiled reassuringly. Several months ago,
his workers had bulldozed a small section of naturally occurring vegetation to make way for the
center's planned outdoor gardens. But it turned
out that five stray cats lived in those bushes, and

the woman who fed them every day went ballistic, calling the press and raising a huge animal rights– and environmental-fueled stink. James got it; when he was little, he and his mother used to feed the stray dogs that hung around their concrete apartment complex, and he remembered crying when his favorite mutt failed to turn up one morning. After the woman complained, James had gotten his staff to take immediate action, turning the whole thing into a tall, cool glass of lemonade.

"It went away," James assured Jennifer. "I personally visited Mrs. Lopez with photos of the cats in their new homes. When she finally realized they were much better off, she took the protest signs down from her lawn and even called the *Herald* to share the story. It was the heart-warmer of the day."

Jennifer tilted her head at him. "And just like that, Ellison Enterprises was golden again. You must have the magic touch."

"I believe that would be you," James said sincerely. "Both projects I've done with you so far have surpassed our projections."

"Let's hope this one does the same," Jennifer said, glancing around. "As well as the Moretta project. When do you break ground on that one?"

James's smile didn't slip. "I think I mentioned that I'm still working out a couple of details. But I'm going there in two weeks, and I should be able to work it all out then." He searched his brain for a safe change of subject. The truth was that the Moretta project was currently stressing him out for a number of reasons, but that was information better kept to himself.

"I'm sure you will," Jennifer agreed. "You know me, James—I hate delays. Once I make a decision, I like fast and furious." She crossed her arms over her chest to squeeze her breasts together slightly.

"That I do," he replied, keeping his eyes on her face. He extended his hand to the side. "Would you like to see the restaurant?"

Jennifer ran a hand down her ponytail and glanced at her watch. "Actually, I was thinking that a celebration drink is in order."

James groaned inwardly, his brain scrambling to find an excuse. Just then his phone vibrated in his pocket. *Saved by the bell*, he thought as he glanced down at the screen: *Kiki Becker*. His cousin—nothing urgent, and he hated the rudeness of taking a call in the middle of a meeting, but right now he really needed an out. Excusing himself to Jennifer, he walked a distance away from her and picked up. "Kiki."

"Cuz. You still single these days?"

He grinned. Same old Kiki—no pleasantries, just a quick cut to the chase. "As if I'd have it any other way. What's up?"

"Just that I'm about to make your day. How

would you like to go to my wedding with the hot-test woman in Atlanta?"

"As in a blind date? No can do, cuz—you know that's not my scene."

"I'm betting you'll make an exception when you see her."

"You sound pretty confident."

"I am. Laina Rose—you can look her up. But before you do…"

"Yeah?"

"Unless she makes the first move, she's off-limits."

"Then what's in it for me?" he joked.

"Consider it a favor. She's my best friend from high school. Awesome girl—funny, smart, a bit of an activist. Actually, I kind of owe her my life, since she's the whole reason I moved to Moretta in the first place."

"You mean she lives there?"

"No, she's just…been there many times." James thought her tone was slightly evasive. "Anyway, she's had a rough go with her ex, and he's going to be at the wedding. I convinced her that a little arm candy goes a long way in a situation like that. So, yeah—I'm fully using you. Just so you know."

James shook his head affectionately. Blind dates definitely weren't his scene, but there wasn't much he wouldn't do for his cousin. "Okay, but we're talking a full week together here. What if she can't stand me?"

"That's a distinct possibility—"

"Gee, thanks."

"—in which case you're free to go your separate ways."

He hesitated. "Can I think about it?"

"Of course. I'll call you back in ten minutes."

"You're cute. Later."

After James hung up, a quick glance at Jennifer told him she was now on a call herself, so he used his phone to pull up Laina Rose's Facebook profile.

Her photo was taken from a distance in front of a mountainous background. It looked like she was dressed for a hike, and from what he could tell she was attractive enough—not that it really mattered, as he wasn't about to break his no-first-move word to Kiki anyway. He was about to turn his phone off again when he remembered his cousin's vague remarks about Laina's connection to the island. Curious, he pulled up Google and typed her name into the search engine.

A few minutes later, he looked up from his phone with a grin on his face. It was almost too good to be true, but why shouldn't he get something out of the deal too?

He fired a text to Kiki: I'm in.

CHAPTER TWO

As Laina drove her rented golf cart away from Moretta's open-air airport, she focused on trying to relax her body one muscle at a time. Her jaw felt tight, her arms were tense and her stomach was thudding dully. Part of her stress was the result of the long flight to Barbados followed by the tiny puddle jumper to Moretta, but she knew that more of it had to do with her destination: her family estate. Though Moretta was tiny—consisting of only ninety-two properties on three square miles—and Laina had come here to visit Kiki many times since she'd moved here, she'd always managed to avoid her childhood second home. Today she would be setting foot on the property for the first time in over a decade.

For as long as Laina could remember, this island had been part of her life. With its lush tropical vegetation, picturesque white sand beaches and clear turquoise water, it was impossible not to love.

Though Moretta was now established as a retreat for celebrities, it had originally been built up by a group of judges and high-ranking politicians who'd recognized its beauty early on and capitalized on it. Laina's paternal grandparents, both in politics, were among its earliest inhabitants and had constructed Hibiscus Heights, which they'd eventually passed down to Laina's parents. But her similarities with her family didn't extend far beyond their mutual love of the island. Laina had always been different from her parents and two older brothers, who embraced the enviable position they'd been born into and used it to their advantage. She didn't begrudge them that; she just didn't feel the same way. Introspective as a girl, she'd often pondered the issue of class inequality and wondered at its unfairness. Along with her other passion of environmental causes, she'd done school essays on the class divisions and delighted in arguing her opinions on social justice. Laina understood clearly how lucky she'd been to be raised with such privilege, but she'd desperately wanted to blaze her own trail in life—a trail her parents simply didn't understand. Which was exactly why coming back to Hibiscus Heights after more than a decade away made her feel like a sellout hypocrite, even if she was only doing so to help out a friend.

Laina could see the estate in the distance now, rising like a mirage from the top of the hill. As she pulled her golf cart into the long driveway that traversed the grounds, she had the eerie feeling that she'd never left. Everything looked exactly the same, tended by a team of staff that spent much more time at the estate than her family did. Memories lurked at every turn: the pool she'd learned to swim in, the front porch she'd built blanket forts on for her dolls, the palm tree she'd hauled out a ladder to climb when she was ten. Imagining it through a stranger's eyes, Laina knew the house was undeniably gorgeous. Placed among eight lush acres in the center of the island, its clean white lines, black pitched roof and majestic columns had been built in the French colonial style. A massive pool swept outward from the front terrace, bracketed by a pool house on one side and a guest cottage on the other, each a tiny replica of the main house. And all around, in every direction, were stunning views of the Caribbean Sea.

Though the wedding was still several days away, Laina could see that the planning team was already hard at work. A series of white tents had been set up on the expansive lawn, and rows of silver chairs had been placed before a massive archway beside the pool, where the ceremony was to take place. She couldn't help the small lift in her heart as she waved to the staff, driving her cart past a row of swaying palm trees to bypass the main house. A wedding was indeed a beautiful affair, even if Laina was quite certain she didn't have one of her own in her future.

As she parked her golf cart in front of the guest cottage and grabbed her suitcase off the passenger seat, Laina's thoughts turned to the evening ahead. Kiki's wedding was a five-day celebration and tonight was the first planned event, a sunset yacht cruise for all the wedding guests—which also meant Laina's first meeting with Kiki's mystery cousin. Remembering the ridiculous commitment she'd made two weeks ago, she kicked herself for not having called Kiki to back out. Ever since she'd agreed to the arrangement, she'd just tried to forget about it, refusing Kiki's offer to send her a photo of James or pass on his number so they could get acquainted beforehand. What had seemed like a good idea at the time had felt increasingly desperate and pathetic as the days passed. So what if her ex was going to be there? Laina couldn't care less what he thought of her, and she certainly didn't have to bring a blind date along to feel confident enough to face him. What had she been thinking?

She hadn't been thinking—Kiki had. But Laina had agreed to it, and now she had to be nice and social and thankful to some cocky playboy for acting the part for her. As the big day approached, she'd meant to tell Kiki to call off the blind date, but she'd been so busy with work that the intention had disappeared into the mad whirl of her workday. And now, with just three hours until the cruise, Laina had to choose between being rude and spending the week in excruciating discomfort.

Option two was worse, she decided as she rolled her suitcase into the bedroom. She would cancel, and in the end James would probably thank her for freeing him to pick up as many chicks as he liked.

Laina was digging in her handbag for her cell phone when she heard it ding. She extracted it from her bag's black depths and stared down at the text, which had come in from an unfamiliar number. A drink before the cruise? The Palms at 6 if you're interested. Room 418.

Laina's reticence was replaced with fury. His *room number*? Who the hell did he think he was—and who did he think *she* was? That did it—if she suspected this had been a mistake all along, this proved it.

Furiously, she typed back a message. Sorry, not in the habit of going to strange men's rooms. Have fun at the wedding, though! She punched the send button with a jab of satisfaction. The ellipsis activated, and then: So we're strangers now? It's Ward. New job came with new cell phone. Thought you might want a chance to make nice, but guess I was wrong.

She threw her phone across the room, where it thankfully landed on her pillow with a quiet thump.

Make nice? She felt like screaming. The fucking prick.

She needed to walk, get some air, blow her fury off. Slamming the door behind her, she left her cottage and headed across the lawn.

Her again. Jesus.

James started from the dream and opened his eyes to early-afternoon sunlight streaming into his hotel room. He hadn't meant to fall asleep, but after arriving on Moretta and checking into The Palms an hour ago, he'd laid back on his bed to go over a project report and dozed off. And he'd dreamed of her again: Laina Rose—the girl he'd never even met—for the third time in two weeks. Last night he'd been standing with her in the doorway of one of his half-constructed buildings while a party went on around them. It might have unnerved him if he didn't know better than to put any stock into the nocturnal tricks of the human mind. The reason for the dream was an obvious combination of three things that were stressing him out: his upcoming blind date, the completion of the property deal on Moretta and the dreaded wedding itself.

Weddings to James were like wet changing room floors to bare feet—to be avoided as much as possible. In fact, with all due respect to Kiki, he'd only accepted her invitation because it fulfilled another of his agendas on Moretta. James

didn't need a therapist to tell him he disliked weddings because his parents had divorced when he
was two and he'd never known his father. He also
realized that at age thirty-eight he should be wanting the happily-ever-after himself. He should have
found a woman he wanted to commit to, maybe
even started a family by now. It was what all of his
friends were doing, but the mere thought of it left
him cold—and he wasn't sure he liked that. Casual
encounters seemed fine until a certain age, when
they suddenly started to look a little pathetic.

Like Jennifer. He was still kicking himself for that
one. As determined as he'd been not to sleep with
her again, he'd felt obliged to accept her offer of a
cocktail. One drink had led to another and another,
and before he knew it she'd been sitting on his lap
in the lounge of her hotel room, and then...

James shut down the memory. It had been a
mistake, but why? Jennifer had the full package—
beauty, brains, drive, even money—so why wasn't
he interested? It was the same with every woman:
out of sight, out of mind. And he had no idea why.

Rising from his bed, he changed into a clean
T-shirt and put on his running shoes. Then he left
the hotel and started down the dirt road, taking in
the now-familiar sights of the island. He'd loved
this place from the first time he came here to visit
Kiki three years ago, and it had pulled him back
many times since. Growing up, he and Kiki had

lived polar opposite lives; while she was raised by her father and stepmother in a middle-class household, he was brought up in project housing by his single mom, who was the sister of Kiki's long-lost mother. Though the cousins had little in common, they'd formed a tight bond, probably because his small family was Kiki's only connection to her missing mom. Kiki had always made sure James was invited over for important holidays, where James remembered laughing with his mother around their dining room table. In fact, it was at that table that she had first announced to the family that she was sick.

James shook off the memory as he walked up the hillside, surveying the passing scenery through the eyes of a developer. Besides being idyllic in every way, this island—with a single hotel, one bar, a tiny grocery store, a gift shop and a post office its only nods toward commercialism—was also a world of untapped opportunity. As he climbed higher, barely breaking a sweat thanks to his regular workouts, James could feel a sense of power building with each step. Soon this place would transform for the better, and it would happen because of him.

Finally he stopped and turned to admire the view behind him. From up here he could see everything— the waves lapping against the white sand, the small town at the island's west end, and below him, several homes built against the cliffs to take full advantage of the panorama. It was a perfection that deserved to be appreciated by more than just the superwealthy of the world, and James already had a development planned for Moretta that would facilitate just that. He'd started taking meetings with the island's council members two years ago, and they had heartily agreed with him: it was time to expand—tastefully, of course, and at a pace that would hardly be noticed by their established residents. It was inevitable that change would eventually come to Moretta, and the council believed that he was the person to do it. James prided himself on doing things right. He had assured them that his structures would work with the lay of the land, taking cues from both nature and the surrounding buildings to create visual masterpieces that practically blended into the scenery. There were only two things keeping James from completing the deal, but he would soon have both of them in hand.

To his right, a grassy clifftop dotted with palm trees beckoned. He left the dirt road and started walking toward it.

Laina hadn't been sure where she was going when she started walking, but it wasn't long before she was pulled toward Pelican Rock. The high cliff was set near the edge of her family's property, and her parents had brought her here as a child to show her something amazing—a rare Caribbean brown pelican nest. Observing the nest of driftwood sticks on the ground from afar, she'd spent hours making notes and drawings in her sketchbook. At the time the birds were threatened, but their numbers had recovered since then due to conservation efforts, and the pelicans had continued to make their home here. In her teens, her parents had even had the council name the small area a parkland so it couldn't be developed.

And now it had been invaded. As Laina broke through the stand of palm trees into the clearing, she stopped short and froze. A man was standing with his back to her, taking photographs of the view with his iPhone.

Laina knew the flare of annoyance she felt was unjustified—this was public property, after all—but she couldn't help it. Locals mostly stayed away for the good of the birds, and even she rarely came here anymore.

She cleared her throat loudly. "Hello?"

"Jesus!" The man jumped and dropped his phone. It landed at his feet in a patch of scrubby vegetation and slid downward, stopping dangerously close to the edge. He pounced on it and stood up, inspecting the device for damage. Laina couldn't help the smile that came to her lips. *Serves him right.*

"Scare the shit out of people much?" the man asked, finally turning to face her with a look of annoyance that matched hers.

Laina blinked at him, rooted to the spot. Even

with thunderclouds on his brow, the guy was insanely gorgeous. His thick sun-streaked hair looked
freshly cut, and his green eyes stood out like laser
beams in his chiseled, tanned face. He wore shorts
and a plain white T-shirt, so she could admire the
lines of both his arm and leg muscles, which currently looked coiled and ready to strike.

He's like a dream come true.

She put her shoulders back and stood up a little
taller, making the most of her five-foot-six frame.
Then she glanced over at the empty nest at the edge
of the tree line. It was well-camouflaged. He probably hadn't even noticed the nest, but she didn't want
to draw attention to it. "Sorry, but this is private."

He raised an eyebrow. "Private property? Am
I trespassing?"

"Not like that, just—no one ever comes here."
His eyes were on hers, making her squirm. God, but
it was hard to stay angry with a man who looked
like *that*. "You surprised me, that's all," she added.

The man nodded, keeping his eyes riveted to
her face. Why was he staring at her like that? Like
he knew something about her that she didn't. No,
like he *knew her*. Then his gaze dropped, taking
a slow inventory of her entire body right down to
the silver Havaianas on her feet. Now what was
that heat she could feel rising from her belly to her
cheeks, and that unfamiliar flutter in her groin?
She'd never had a reaction like this to anyone,

much less some dude who'd invaded a sacred spot
to take photos like some tacky tourist.

When he met her gaze again, he looked slightly
amused. "I see. Then I apologize. I was just...
admiring the view."

Laina flushed again as she realized he was referring to her. Quickly she tried to remember how
she'd looked when she'd left the cottage, but she
hadn't glanced in the mirror since she'd stepped out
of the shower in Atlanta that morning. She was certain she looked travel-weary—bleary-eyed, static-
haired and swollen-ankled from the long hours of
dehydration. She tried to think of a snappy response
but came up blank. "Is that what the pictures are
about?" she finally asked, cringing at her stupidly
obvious question. "The view?"

That amused smile again. "Yes. This island is
incredible—it's a shame only the top point-one percent get to experience it."

The flutter in her belly gave way to discomfort.
The fact was that she agreed with him; part of the
reason she'd stepped away from her family and was
currently staying in the guest cottage rather than
the main house, was because the exclusivity of the
island irked her. But there were other things to consider that were even more important. Just who the
hell did this guy think he was? She knew almost
everyone on the island, and she'd never seen him
before—he was obviously some tourist who'd made

himself an authority on something he knew nothing about.

And just like that, her brain kicked into gear again. "Actually, it's for the island's own good," she snapped. "There's a reason only ninety-two homes are allowed to be built here—it can only support so much growth. Do you know what would happen to the ecosystem of a place like this if it were allowed to be overrun by tourists? Just look at a place like Boracay—it's a perfect example."

"You sound very protective."

"I've been coming here since I was two. I'm more than a little invested."

"So it seems." A smile played at his lips. Sure, they were sexy, but was she really imagining them on her neck, trailing down to her breasts, finding her nipples…she never had thoughts like this. So why was she looking for a wedding ring on his hand?

This wasn't good. In fact, it was ridiculous—and she still had a date she needed to cancel.

"Hey, you know what?" she said, holding up a hand. "I'll just leave you to it, but next time? This isn't a tourist spot, so please enjoy the view somewhere else." And with that she turned on her heel and left.

CHAPTER THREE

IT HAD BEEN HER, and she looked like an angel.

Strolling onto the pier and making his way to the luxurious yacht waiting at the end, James spotted her standing amid the circulating guests, engaged in conversation with another woman. She had that distracted look of someone occupying themselves while waiting for another to arrive, her eyes scanning the crowd every so often as she laughed with her companion. The top of her hair was swept up, leaving the rest loose down her back. She had just enough makeup on to bring out her gorgeous eyes and lips. And her body under that dress…

Seeing her eyes tracking in his direction, James ducked his head to avoid detection. If their first meeting was any indication, this was not going to go well. He knew he shouldn't have let her walk away. He should have told her who he was right then and there, getting the awkwardness over with, but it wasn't like she'd given him a chance. And it didn't help that James had been practically dumb-struck. Standing on the cliff in a tank top and denim cutoffs, she'd been a million times more gorgeous than her photo, even with no makeup on. And so unbelievably sexy. Dark, wavy hair that fell to her nipples. A youthfully rounded face that didn't detract from her enviable cheekbones, and a small dimple in her chin. At first he'd been stunned into silence by her beauty, and by the time he'd registered that it was *her*, she hadn't even given him a chance to make the connection aloud. Just like she had apparently dismissed his offer, through Kiki, to arrange a meeting before the wedding. He would have liked to take her out for a drink before the cruise, made sure she was comfortable with him, exchange some basic information so they could make their display for her ex believable—or at least have a phone conversation. But she didn't seem to care, which made him wonder why she'd agreed to the ploy in the first place. And now he'd somehow blown it before he'd even officially met her. Once she figured out her date was one and the same as her cliff invader, she'd probably call the whole thing off and spend the week ignoring him. And beyond wanting to jump her on the spot, James needed her for another reason. Not only would he have to win her over, he'd have to make her get past the fact that she already hated him.

Accepting a glass of champagne from a passing

waiter, James watched as Laina's companion gave
her a quick hug and moved on. Laina sipped her
drink, turning her back on him to take in the blaz-
ing sunset over the ocean—which was beautiful,
but nothing compared to her. Finally James could
allow his eyes to rove freely over her body. She was
wearing a shimmery pale yellow sheath dress that
just skimmed the tops of her knees, displaying her
firm ass to perfection. Spaghetti straps crossed at
her back, where the fabric plunged down to the in-
dentation of her spine at her waist. He felt a bolt of
heat shoot through his groin. He could imagine running his hands up that back, under the straps, slowly
pushing them down…he could practically feel her
satiny skin against his. She turned toward him again,
and he stole a glance at her face. There was that
beautiful mouth, those huge brown eyes under del-
icately arched brows, that cascade of chestnut hair
that he longed to wrap his hands in, claiming her
as his for the night. Or perhaps even the week—a
quick, sex-fueled fantasy in paradise that would dis-
sipate for both of them with their return to reality in
seven days. Then James would go home to his free-
dom with his goal accomplished. Perfect.

It was time to strategize.

Since she didn't know who she was looking
for, James still had the element of surprise on
his side—which meant he had to wait for just the
right moment to strike. A moment that would bind

them together in not only her eyes, but the guests', as well.

Through the crowd, he saw an underdressed man with a hipster haircut spot Laina and start making his way toward her, pulling his overly buxom date along behind him. When Laina spotted him, her face told James everything he needed to know.

This was his chance.

Moving along the edge of the crowd, he sidled up behind Laina and slid an arm around her waist. She turned to him with raised eyebrows, her mouth an O of surprise.

"Babe, I'm so sorry. That took forever," he said with a bright smile, holding her tightly. This close, he could smell the vanilla scent of her perfume. Just the curve of her waist under his hand made his libido rage. He switched his gaze to the couple. "Warning—if you need to go to the bathroom, leave a trail of bread crumbs behind you. That boat is like a maze! I don't think we've met. I'm James Ellison," he said, sticking his hand out to the couple.

The woman took it first, giving him a name he immediately forgot, and then after a heavy pause the man followed suit. "Ward Harris," he said with a curt nod.

"A pleasure." Keeping his smile on high-voltage, James turned toward Laina and circled his other arm around her, and then he reached up to stroke her hair. It was as soft as he'd imagined, taking his mind to thoughts of it trailing down his torso toward his cock. As her eyes met his, he felt another electric bolt to his groin. In his arms she felt amazing, firm and taut. And furious, like a cobra waiting to strike.

"I missed you," he said in a voice just loud enough for the couple to hear. "Ten minutes away from you...how is that even possible? I swear to God, I am the luckiest man on earth." He tipped her chin up toward his face and gazed into her eyes. "You. Are. So. Beautiful."

"Um..." she stammered, "thanks." Her cheeks were burning hot, but he could tell she was enjoying this. And was it his imagination, or was her body relaxing slightly in his arms? In any case, hipster dude looked like he wanted to kill—*perfect*. Mission accomplished. Even though he knew he should pull away from her now and sweep her toward the boat as a final touch, leaving the guy fuming in their wake, he didn't want to stop touching her. But he had to do something before his barely restrained cock made her think he was some goddamned pervert. He stepped away from her slightly to put the brakes on his arousal, but then she surprised him by yanking him back toward her.

"We should really get on the boat, darling," she said, finally falling into the role. "I can't *wait* to see what the staterooms look like." She nodded at the couple. "Have a wonderful evening." James re-

leased his grip on her, but not before her hand slid
down to give his rear end a playful squeeze. Then
she took his hand and pulled him down the gang-
way into the yacht.

"What the fuck?" Laina sputtered at him the second they were on the boat, ripping her hand out of
his. Her question was directed at the man who'd
just manhandled her in front of her ex—the same
guy she'd blown a fuse at on the cliff, no less—
but it might have been directed at herself. Her entire body had gone to mush the second his arm
had gone around her. After she got over the initial
shock of both who he was and what he was doing,
all she'd been able to think was that she wanted
more of him. Considering both of her encounters
with the man, it made absolutely zero sense. And
of course the whole thing had been nothing but a
role play anyway.

He was looking at her with that teasing grin
again. "Listen, do you think we could talk somewhere a little more private?" he said in a loud
whisper. "You're going to blow our cover." Without giving her a chance to answer, he took her arm
and steered her toward a bathroom.

Laina had been so distracted that she'd barely
had time to glance around, but as they cruised
through the saloon, she had a moment to absorb
her surroundings.

She'd seen plenty of luxury in her life, but she'd never been on a boat like this before. This room alone was as big as her entire Castleberry Hill condo back in Atlanta, and everything about it screamed *opulence*. The room was circular, laid with blond wood flooring. The furniture was all white leather and sparkling glass. Tuxedoed staff circulated among the guests with platters of gourmet appetizers. The stern side of the saloon opened onto a huge deck, where guests were lounging on outdoor beds or streaming toward the bar, which was framed in billowing fabric that fluttered in the wind. Above the bar was a silver sign with *Kiki and Dev* spelled out in pink lights. Laina took a quick glance around for the happy couple, not wanting to miss their entrance—she hadn't even talked to Kiki since she'd arrived on Moretta—but they were nowhere to be seen.

"In here," James said, pushing her gently through the bathroom door and shutting it behind him. She took in the large room quickly—polished ebony vanity, ornate gold mirror over a waterfall sink and a chaise longue sitting alongside a table displaying every toiletry imaginable. The word *head* just didn't seem right for luxury like this.

Laina crossed her arms over her chest and fixed her eyes on his. "Really nice way to introduce yourself," she said testily. "You might have told me who you were today when you had the chance."

"Chance? Is that what you call that nanosecond between telling me to get the hell off your cliff and dressing me down for taking photos on it?"

"Well, excuse me!" she said, throwing her hands up. "You could have, I don't know, gotten in touch with me afterward—"

"Exactly how? You wouldn't let Kiki give me your number, remember?"

"—or at least introduced yourself like a normal person just now, instead of...*pawing* me in front of my ex—" She was advancing on him now, hands waving wildly, but he wasn't budging.

"Aha! So it *was* him—I knew it!" He gave a self-satisfied grin.

She finally stopped in front of him, her toes inches from his. She could smell his aftershave now, woodsy, intoxicating...a smell that had her imagination going to places beneath his clothing. And the way he looked in his khaki pants and white linen shirt, sleeves rolled up to reveal muscular forearms...his eyes on her, those lips she longed to kiss—*good God*. Okay, so the guy was hot, but that was no excuse for such inappropriate thoughts. What was wrong with her?

"We put on a great show. Isn't that what you wanted?" he continued. "He bought every word. Not that I didn't mean them, by the way."

Laina felt a flush that moved all the way from her toes up to her hair...and she could tell he was enjoying her discomfort. Shit, but he was unnerving. Men didn't call her beautiful without an ulterior motive, and Laina was certain there was no way James could have one—she'd been too careful to hide her true identity. "Still," she said, softening a bit. "That didn't mean you had to get all handsy with me."

James lifted a hand to his chin, as if he were pondering her words. "Hmm. Okay, so what you wanted was a 'boyfriend'—" he added air quotes "—who politely stood at your side without touching you. Who made small talk with your ex instead of showering you with the attention you deserve." He shook his head. "Maybe you need to raise your standards a bit, Ms. Rose."

Laina could feel her face tighten with fury, and it wasn't because he was wrong; what did she know about choosing a man? She'd almost married a guy who'd let her pay all the bills and then cheated on her. All she'd cared about was that he didn't seem to care about her family fortune, unlike every other man she dated. She knew she had to hold out for more than that—but she wasn't about to admit that to the person who'd just called her out on it. "You don't know the first thing about me—or my standards," she retorted hotly.

He stepped a little closer to her, removing the last inch of space between them. She could feel his shoes touching the tips of her toes, the heat radiat-

ing off his body. "Maybe not, but I'd sure like to."
His gaze was steady on her face, his lips within
reach of hers. Her stomach flopped over. Did she
want him to kiss her? What would she do if he
did—pull away or kiss him back?

It depended on whether she listened to her brain
or her body.

Do it, she thought. *I dare you.*

Just then, she heard a roar go up from the crowd
outside; Kiki and Dev must have arrived. Reaching
his arm past her, James put his hand on the doorknob. "That must be the happy couple. Enjoy your
evening, Ms. Rose."

And then he was gone.

CHAPTER FOUR

JAMES STOOD AT the edge of the saloon, trading how-do-you-know-the-bride-or-groom stories with a circle of guests. But his mind wasn't on his cousin and her famous fiancé—it was on her.

He hadn't made the progress that he'd hoped to so far, but if he knew anything about women, he knew that to a certain type, unavailability was the ultimate aphrodisiac. And judging by his interactions with Laina so far, she was that type. All he had to do was bide his time circulating among the crowd and avoiding eye contact with her, perhaps engage in some mild flirtation with another woman when he knew she was watching, and *bang*—before he knew it she'd be stammering an apology, shortly after which she'd be heading for his bed. It was a no-brainer...so why was he feeling reticent?

Because she'd already had her heart busted by some asshole. Or because he could tell she wasn't a one-nighter kind of girl…in fact, judging by her refusal to play games and her discomfort with his flirting, she probably didn't have much experience in that department at all.

The problem was that that made her all the more appealing. When he thought about the things he could teach her and the pleasure he could give her, it was enough to pump lust through every cell of his body. In fact, just the thought of it—

"Cuz!"

James turned to see Kiki rushing toward him. She was wearing a body-hugging fuchsia number that ended at her slender ankles, a cascading diamond pendant and the biggest smile he'd ever seen. "You look gorgeous." He grinned, giving her a quick hug.

"Not bad yourself," Kiki said. She stepped a little closer and lowered her voice. "So have you met Laina yet? Has Ward seen you together?"

"I did. He has."

"And…?" she asked impatiently. "What did you think?"

"Bad haircut. And wearing jeans to an affair like this? Tasteless. Laina was smart to get out when she could."

"Not him, dimwit—*her*!"

"Oh, her. Well…" He shook his head. "Does it really matter? No first moves, right?"

"Right. But if I know you…"

"Maybe I'm not as bad as you think. Has that ever occurred to you?"

"Yes, you are," Kiki said. "And whatever happens this week, do not hurt her. I'll break your fucking face if you do."

Kiki scowled at him as Dev came up behind her. James watched as he slid a hand up Kiki's front, stopping just shy of her breast. James had met Dev a few times, and watching him and Kiki together, he hadn't been able to suppress the odd stab of envy. The couple had been together for two years, and it was obvious the heat between them was as searing as anything James had experienced during a one-nighter. To think that some people could sustain that kind of passion was both heartening and depressing, because James couldn't imagine finding any woman who brought that out in him.

"Hey, man." Dev stepped forward to give James a quick embrace, but not before landing a kiss on the back of Kiki's neck.

"Hey." James grinned, clapping Dev on the back. "Congratulations, my man. You've landed the sweetest girl in the western hemisphere." He shook his head at Kiki affectionately. "I hear a vodka soda calling."

Yes, getting some air would be good. He walked out to the deck and stepped up to the bar, scanning the crowd for her face, but she was nowhere to be seen. The boat was a good distance from

Moretta by now, cruising at a comfortable speed past a few smaller islands that looked straight out of *Cast Away*. The entire boat had been strung with white lights, lighting up its frame to a magical effect. With the sun having dropped behind the horizon, leaving behind an indigo sky and a crescent of moon, the setting was pure romance.

James accepted his drink and turned away from the bar—and came face-to-face with Laina. Her eyes widened slightly before she spun on her heel. That's when James noticed she had company; standing beside her was a man with thinning hair who gave him a challenging look and then hurried after her like a puppy dog. *What was that all about?* James wondered, and then he remembered that he and Laina were supposed to be together. The guy had probably had his eye on her on the pier and seen them embracing, and now that she was giving James the cold shoulder he considered her fair game.

Which she was, of course, because she obviously wanted nothing to do with him. Clearly he had been wrong—Laina Rose was *not* going to apologize to him and then beg him to drag her off to his bed.

He sighed and went after her, pushing past the man in hot pursuit. "Listen," he said when he reached her, touching her lightly on the arm. "Can we start over?"

She stopped walking and faced him as the man

caught up to them. He stood looking at the couple uncertainly until Laina gave him a smile. "Would you excuse us for a minute?"

The man shrugged and left them reluctantly.

"Thank you," James said. He smiled at her. "I'm James Ellison. Pleased to meet you."

She crossed her arms over her chest, clearly still annoyed with him. "The pleasure's mine," she said with touch of sarcasm.

"Let's get to know each other. What's your favorite color? Mine was blue until about an hour ago. Now I think it's yellow," he said, letting his eyes drop to her dress.

There it was, that blush again as her eyes flitted away. He may have gotten a few things about her wrong, but he would put money on her inexperience. Which equaled the very best kind of sex—the type where he was completely in control, where she would discover exactly how much pleasure her body could give her through his touch.

Anticipation burned hotly in his groin. He couldn't wait to hear her moan when he slid his hard cock into her…but not before he teased her nipples and licked her sweet clit until she came, burying her hands in his hair as she pressed his mouth into the best climax of her life. It was going to be amazing.

But of course he had to get her there first, and she wasn't an easy one to reel in. He was formulating his next move when she suddenly stepped toward him and put her arms around him, and then brought her mouth up to his for a passionate kiss.

What am I doing? Laina's brain screamed at her as James's mouth yielded to hers. She never did things this impulsive, but it was all because of Ward. When she'd seen him looking at her across the deck, she'd remembered exactly what James was supposed to be there for and decided to take advantage of it.

But wasn't that just an excuse to kiss him? Hadn't she been sorely disappointed that he hadn't done it when he'd had the chance earlier? And didn't she want him more than she'd ever thought it was possible to want anyone?

This was no time for self-analysis. All she cared about right now was the feel of his lips; as they parted and his tongue met hers, her knees went weak. She kissed him back urgently, wanting more and more…it was insanity. She could feel her nipples hardening, wetness between her legs—she wanted him to fuck her, she realized. Not make love to her; for the first time in her life, she wanted to be *fucked*. She wanted nothing to matter but the connection of their two bodies, the heat of the moment…the thing she'd heard friends talk about but had never experienced for herself.

And he wanted her too. His hands were on her

ass, pulling her hard against his groin. As their lips finally broke apart and they looked at each other breathlessly, she could feel him at her waist—long, thick, hard, and just for her.

"I've been wanting to do that since the moment I saw you on that cliff," James said in a thick voice. "God, I wish we could get off this boat."

She looked at him coyly. "Who says we have to?"

The sight of his surprised face gave her a bolt of satisfaction. He wasn't expecting that from her, either, and for once in her life she was being a little bit wild. For the first time ever, it occurred to her maybe she'd been boring in bed because the men she'd been with had bored *her*.

She was about to find out.

CHAPTER FIVE

THANKFULLY, THE STATEROOM they chose had a lock on the door. Sneaking in together while making sure no one saw them, James could tell Laina was having second thoughts.

"Feels like we're in high school, doesn't it?" he said with a laugh, and she gave him a quick grin. Shutting the door behind them, he took a look around. Since this was a rental yacht, he didn't have to feel bad about invading anyone's private space—this stateroom was like any hotel room, if you could ignore the luxury of it all. The all-white, king-size bed was lit by overhead lights reminiscent of stars, and beyond it a massive window afforded a view of the passing islands in the near-darkness. Outside, he could hear music mingled with the noise and laughter of the party guests, heightening his already intense anticipation. He loved the idea of bedding the hottest woman at the party with a boatful of people—including her dick of an ex—mere feet away.

James took Laina's hand and led her to the bed.

She sat down, smoothing her hands over the duvet cover. Then she picked up a small vase beside the bed, which contained a single lavender-colored rose, and inhaled its scent. "My favorite flower," she said, placing it down again. Her voice sounded nervous. "Whoever owns this yacht must have some serious clout, because they're impossible to get on this island." She glanced at him. "And I'm rambling."

He ran the back of his hand up her arm. "You're in charge, okay?"

She nodded, and then she suddenly leaned forward and reached for his shirt buttons. God, this woman was as unpredictable as she was beautiful. In a million years he couldn't have foreseen that first kiss on the deck. It had been even better than he had imagined, firing intense heat straight to his cock. Now that familiar pleasant ache in his balls was getting more urgent. He knew he had to take it slowly, but she was moving so fast; was it because she was nervous, or could he be wrong about her inexperience? He had to find out. Not once had he put a woman into a position where there could be potential for regret on her side, and he wasn't about to start now.

James caught her hands in his. "God knows I want you," he said, meeting her eyes. "But are you sure about this?"

Laina looked shocked. "Yes! I mean, I've never really felt…" She shook her head. "I want this. And

I know a lot of women want you, but that's okay—
I'm a big girl. I know what I'm getting into."

He grinned at her. "You've never done this before."

"I was engaged! You don't think—"

"No, I mean this fast. You're not in the habit of
having casual sex."

She shook her head. "Whatever you want to call
it—no. I've never, um, exactly had a raging libido
before."

He pushed her hair back with two hands, gazing
into those deep, dark eyes. "Maybe that's just because you haven't been with the right man."

"But you are. The right man—for this, I mean.
I don't expect—"

"It's okay," he said, stopping her chatter with a
kiss. "You don't have to say anything." He hooked
a finger around a spaghetti strap, trying to rein in
the charging need that was pounding through his
body. He'd been with inexperienced women before, but there was something about this one that
was messing with his process. He wanted to rip her
dress off, ravage that beautiful silky skin and sat-
isfy his aching need like an animal in heat. But he
owed it to her to take this slowly, no matter what
his cock was screaming for.

Sliding his hands to the place where her neck
met her shoulders, James brought his mouth down
on hers. Laina opened to him, her tongue sliding

against his with increasing urgency as he nudged her dress down to her waist. Then he drew back to look at her.

No bra. And so beautiful, two perfect breasts crowned with nipples that strained toward him hungrily.

His cock surged in his pants. "You're just full of surprises, aren't you?" he said, spiraling a fingertip around one areola. She arched backward and he took her in his mouth, flicking his tongue across her nipple.

"More," she gasped.

"*So* much more, don't you worry," he assured her, bringing his mouth back to hers to bite her lips gently. "Tell me what you want me to do to you," he whispered into her mouth. "Tell me what makes you come—I want to make you come harder than you ever have."

"I…whatever you want," Laina said, reaching for his shirt buttons again. James could see that her hands were trembling slightly as she unbuttoned his shirt and pushed it off. She gazed at him with big eyes, her pupils dilated. "Look at you," she breathed.

"I'd much rather look at you," James growled. "Among other things." Reaching under her dress, he found the lacy edge of her panties. He moved his hand in a slow circle over the thin fabric, palming her pussy. Her breath hitched as she pressed his hand tighter to her. Moving her panties aside under her grip, he found her wetness and drew it up to circle her clit. She let out a long moan, the sweetest music to his ears.

"Oh, God—"

Sliding two fingers inside her, James groaned himself. She was incredibly tight and wet, perfectly ready for his hard cock. He moved his fingers in and out, picking up speed as her eyes went hazy. "Please," she whimpered, lying herself flat on the bed as he swirled his fingertips around her swollen clit again. "Now...*please*."

He could barely take it anymore, but he had to. The most explosive rewards came with the longest tension—for both of them. "I haven't even seen you yet," he said, finally hooking his fingers around her panties and tugging them down. Her dress came next as he pulled it over her head. She looked up at him with those huge brown eyes, utterly beautiful and completely naked besides the delicate silver necklace at her throat. "You are amazing," he said hoarsely. Keeping his own pants on, he laid on top of her. "Feel that," he whispered to her. "That's how much I want you. Do you know how good that's going to feel inside you?"

"Yes," she gasped.

"I can't wait to feel your wet pussy wrapped around me," he teased, pausing to bite her lip. "I'm going to ease myself into you and move slowly until you beg me to go faster. And then I'm going to fuck you hard enough to make you scream. Are you okay with that?"

"Uh-huh," she managed to say, her breath coming out fast and hard.

He moved his hand downward, finding her clit again. "Do you want me to lick you first? Is that what makes you come?"

"I—I don't know."

He gazed down at her face as realization dawned on him. "You've never had a proper orgasm, have you?"

She shook her head.

Her first orgasm. *Jesus.* He'd just hit the jackpot.

Why did I have to go and tell him that? Laina wondered. She'd never revealed that embarrassing little item to a man before, and none of them had asked—not even Ward. And here she was telling a practical stranger…but maybe it was better this way. After all, this was just one night—what Kiki had always referred to as a hookup until she met Dev and got swept away by domestic bliss. Yes— she, Laina Rose, Little Miss Conservative when it came to sex, was about to have her first orgasm with a man who would likely kick her out of bed immediately afterward.

It was insanity.

But here she was self-analyzing again while he

was busy taking his pants off. She watched him slide his boxers over his hips and then stand up to give her a full view. And there it was—what she was aching for. What she'd never known she could want so desperately. It was perfect—long, thick and smooth, standing straight up with urgent desire.

James opened his hand to reveal a condom—where did that come from?—and before Laina could blink he had it on. Propping herself up on a pillow, she felt her hips gyrating toward him as if that could bring him closer faster. He kneeled between her thighs, hovering so the tip of his cock lingered at her opening. She couldn't take it. Animal lust pumped through her veins, taking her to a place she'd never been before. She arched into him, but it only made him smile and pull away. "Please... *now*..." she moaned.

He took hold of her wrists and put his lips to hers. "I'm going to let you feel me inside you first," he informed her in a hoarse voice. "And then I'm going to make you come."

"Yes, please." Her heart was pounding with delicious anticipation.

Finally, without moving his hands or taking his eyes off hers, she felt him slowly sliding into her. Being filled with his hardness felt incredible. He closed his eyes, and a low groan escaped his throat as he started to move. "So good..." he said, easing slowly in and out of her.

"*So* good," she agreed breathlessly. "But harder. Please, harder."

"Like this?" Rising up on his hands, he started driving into her, his skin slapping against hers. She threw her head back and moaned. It felt *so* amazing—

"Or like this?" Before she knew what was happening, James had grabbed one of her legs and wrapped it around his waist so he was thrusting into her from one side. The new position allowed him to fill her even more deeply and, judging from the look of pleasure on his face, brought him dangerously close to the edge. Her body broke out in goose bumps—she'd never known sex could feel like this.

Flipping her leg back and pressing it firmly to the mattress, he lowered himself until he was back on his hands above her and slowed his pace. Laina inhaled his delicious scent and pushed her hands into his soft hair, indulging in every erotic sensation. "Look at that," he whispered, pulling out of her far enough for them to see his glistening cock. "You are *so* wet. I think you're ready."

He brought his mouth down on hers again, filling her senses with the most intense kiss she'd ever experienced so that when he pulled out of her she barely noticed. All the same, she moaned in protest when he started moving down her body. "Nooo…"

"Shh. Just wait."

Then his mouth was on her nipple again and his hand was on her pussy. The circling of his tongue matched the rhythm of his fingertip on her clit, barely skimming it at first and then circling it faster. She could feel an unfamiliar heat start to grow in her pelvis, spreading down to her thighs and upward to her chest, making her heart gallop. "Ahhh—"

"That's it," she heard James say urgently. His fingers went inside her, and by the time he pressed his palm into her clit again she was ready. As she bucked against his hand with a helpless cry, she finally understood. Her climax exploded out of her, crest after crest of heat that she rode with an endless moan. Her hands fisted the duvet over and over again in an effort to control something—*anything*—in her body while this ecstatic feeling invaded every cell. It was unlike anything she'd ever felt before, and she wanted it to last forever, but it finally subsided. She collapsed back onto the pillow with a sharp exhale.

"Good?" James asked, moving up to her shoulders.

"Not good. Incredible," Laina responded, breathing hard. She turned toward him. He was lying beside her with his face close, his heart-stopping eyes pinned on hers. "How did you do that?"

"If I tell you that, then you won't have any more

use for me." He grinned. "And I don't know about you, but I'm not ready for this to be over."

God, but this man was so damned dangerous. Laina could only imagine the lineups of women he'd given pleasure to over the years, and now she had joined them, only one of many. But that was okay. This was her night to be wild, and she'd known what she was getting into. Just for now she was going to give her body over to him completely, absorb every little thing he could teach her and every drop of pleasure he could give her. He'd already taught her the most important thing of all— that her body was capable of absolute ecstasy. And that she *wasn't* boring in bed, if his stiff cock was any indication.

Laina slid her hand down between their entwined bodies and grasped him. Still rock-hard for her, just waiting to take her to new heights. "Now it's your turn," she said.

"I can wait. If I give you a few minutes, I bet I can make you do that again."

She ran her hand up his arm, cupping a muscular shoulder. She didn't want this to stop. She didn't ever want him to come, because that would mean this was over. And what would happen then—now that he'd had her, would he move on with someone else tomorrow? The thought gave her a sharper stab of jealousy than she liked, but she wouldn't contemplate that now. In this moment, the idea of feeling him inside her again, of having him chase his own climax as a result of his intense desire for her was too intoxicating to resist. And she was already burning for him again, feeling a low buzz in her clit that told her what had just happened hadn't been nearly enough.

"I didn't get enough of you inside me. You promised to fuck me until I screamed." The dirty words felt foreign and awkward coming from her mouth, but they also gave her a powerful charge she'd never experienced before. She *was* sexual, desirous and desired, and the discovery of that potential was worth any discomfort that might come over the rest of the week. "I don't want to wait," she said, reaching for his raging hard-on.

A second later he was inside her again, with his eyes on hers. His body sheened with sweat as he drove into her over and over again. She loved the slick feel of it on her skin... She pushed her hands up into his hair, feeling its dampness. All because of her, and being the recipient of his urgency was the most incredible thing she'd ever felt. She could tell he was close now as he pushed one of her thighs upward and quickened his pace. His breath came out in an urgent pant. She tightened herself around him.

"Laina—here I come—" His whole body shuddered as he emptied inside her, a low groan emitting from his throat. He rode out his climax with

his eyes fastened to hers, his face a mask of ecstasy,
until he finally collapsed on top of her.

She trailed her hands up his back. "Let's do it
again," she whispered.

CHAPTER SIX

JAMES COULDN'T SLEEP. From his bed at The Palms hotel he could see thin, early-morning light coming through the blinds, and from outside he could hear the soft calling of tropical birds. His room, with its white-canopied bed, massive whirlpool tub and expansive view to the ocean, was perfectly conducive to rest and relaxation. But it made no difference.

He couldn't stop thinking about her. And it wasn't just his mind—his entire body wouldn't stop yearning for her. He hadn't wanted to leave her after their time together on the boat. Three times last night they'd brought each other to heaven, and still it wasn't enough for him. He'd wanted to stay with her all night, doing it over and over again to tame the raging lust he felt every time he looked at her. He wanted to teach her everything he knew about pleasuring him, pleasuring herself, taking both of them to heights they'd never imagined. He wished she were here right now so he could put his arms around her, bury his face in her beautiful hair, and then pull her on top of him and enter her, hear her moan—*damn it*. He'd only had one night with her, and suddenly he was like someone possessed. James was a man who lived in the moment, moving on from his encounters within minutes of ending of them. The next morning, he never missed the women he bedded. He was always too busy with work, but somehow that didn't seem to matter right now.

Work. He had to get his head back into it. Rolling onto his back and giving his erect cock a light swat to tame it into submission, he pictured the blueprints of the resort in his mind. All of his projects started with a photograph in his head that he couldn't erase. When it was still hanging around in his head a month or two later, he knew it was time to act—and so far, he'd never been wrong. Sure, he'd thrown himself into a couple of developments that hadn't become roaring successes, but he'd never had a failure. Some of it was luck, he knew, but a lot of it was drive. He'd done his first project at the age of twenty-two, right after graduating from Georgia State—the best he could afford on his lifeguard wages—with a BA in business. Though Kiki's father wasn't a wealthy man, it was he who'd lent James the five thousand dollars he needed to finance his first commercial venture, a smoothie stand in a strip mall that he'd helped build with his own two hands. Back then James had been driven by fear, a desperate attempt to make enough money to save his mother before it was too late.

But she'd never seen the stand completed.

James had needed twenty-six thousand dollars for the experimental treatment. He hadn't cried at her memorial, but when he surpassed that number three months after her death, he spent a whole afternoon staring at the number on his computer screen with tears streaming down his face. And as the tiny business began to cough out more and more revenue, he buried his grief in a determination that had served him to this very day. He entered each new project with abandon instead of caution, optimism instead of pessimism, perhaps subconsciously honoring the spirit of his mother.

She would have loved Laina.

James jumped from his bed, almost physically shaken. Where the hell had that thought come from? He raked a hand through his hair, trying to clear his head. His phone dinged on his bedside table and he snatched it up, happy for the distraction. Jennifer Liu: All a go on Moretta?

James scrubbed a hand over his face. He didn't want to deal with this right now, but it was a fair reminder. He wasn't just in paradise for a wedding. He was here to get a deal done, and that was what really mattered. What *always* mattered. Yes—he had to get his mind off Laina Rose's smoking-hot body and get it back into what she could do for him.

Working on it, he typed back.

Glad to hear it. I'll expect an update tomorrow. The ellipsis spun, and then, I've been thinking about you.

No. James dropped his chin into his chest and let out a sigh. He had created this. He had slept with a woman he knew he shouldn't have, it had given her hope and now he hated himself for it.

And yet he had to be careful. Jennifer had many places she could invest her money, but she'd chosen James's projects four times because his deals were relatively fast and clean. This was the first time he'd hit a major hurdle on a project with her, but he knew better than to think she wouldn't pull out. And she had every right to, seeing as he hadn't filled her in on what the problems were. He could have a legal nightmare on his hands if he didn't figure this out, and now she wanted more personally from him on top of it all. He'd royally messed up. How the hell was he supposed to respond to a message like that when he didn't feel the same way?

Nice of you to say so, he finally decided on. I'll be in touch soon. He pressed the send button and squeezed his eyes shut. His phone dinged in his hand again, and he cautiously opened his eyes. Kiki Becker: Don't forget horseback riding at 10!

James groaned and slapped a hand to his forehead.

* * *

Placing her foot in the stirrup, Laina lifted her other leg and swung it over the mare's back, settling herself comfortably into the saddle. It was a perfect day for a ride, with just a few streaks of cloud above and an endless stretch of white sand before her. The waves lapped around her horse's ankles, but the mare barely seemed to notice. Almost all the horses on Moretta were accustomed to walking along the beach, often going into the water up to their haunches without fear—which was no small feat for their trainers.

Laina loved riding. It was one of her favorite things to do on the island, bringing her back to childhood memories of being sandwiched between her parents and brothers as they rode in a line through the hills near their home. They'd kept horses at the estate right up until Laina had stopped going there when she was twenty. Though she hadn't officially announced her decision to her family, her mother must have sensed it because Laina got a call from her not long after. *We're thinking of relocating the horses. Of course, if you think you might be spending more time here again...*

But Laina hadn't. The horses had gone to live at the corral managed by the island council, where they could be given more attention and ridden frequently. After that, Laina's mother had punished her by failing to send her a birthday gift a month later. Laina hadn't cared about that, but it was the lack of a phone call, email or even text acknowledging her twenty-first year that had stung. Showering their children with extravagant birthday gifts was a tradition with her parents, and the way she and her siblings received them said a lot about how different she was from them. While her brothers used to rip open their presents, leaving their cards abandoned and sometimes even unread on the floor, Laina had always cared about them more than what was inside the boxes. Rarely personalized, she'd nonetheless looked for clues within those Hallmark poems, some sort of proof of her value that she rarely got verbally. *To the best daughter in the world. From the day you were born, you lit up our lives. To someone who's special and wonderful.* She got only a few of those, but she never forgot them. More often they were of the generic variety—*To our number one daughter; Thinking of you on your birthday; May the year ahead be all you hope for!*

But Laina had stopped looking for validation from those cards, or from her parents, over a decade ago. Her mother and father had both made it clear they weren't in support of her choices, and Laina had come to accept that some people just didn't fit in with the rest of their family. She was one of them.

Laina's horse was raring to go. Talking to her softly, she held her in with the reins while the rest of the party mounted their steeds and got ready. But still no James.

Just the thought of him sent a sharp flutter to her groin, a heat to her cheeks… Against her will, she twisted her head around to look for him for approximately the fiftieth time. She had to stop. She'd known exactly what she was getting into yesterday, and it had been everything she could have possibly dreamed of and more. She'd discovered life-changing things about herself and climaxed not once, but three times under James's relentlessly pleasurable tutelage, leaving her completely spent at the end of the night and yet still yearning for more. Yearning for *him*.

But it was over, and she had no right to expect anything more from him. Even if the thought of spending five long days in his presence was torture, she could handle it. She'd keep herself busy by helping Kiki with the wedding and working on a housing project she was behind on. And she would *not* keep thinking about how amazing James had felt inside her, how hard his cock had been for her, how he'd pushed her hair off her face so he could see her eyes while he fucked her, how his ragged breath had sounded in her ear when he came, how his lips had felt on hers, biting her ravenously like he couldn't get enough of her—

"Tell me it was him who made the first move and I'll castrate him."

Forcing her mind back to the present, Laina turned her head to the sound of Kiki's voice. She'd brought her horse alongside Laina's while she'd been lost in her feverish daydream, and now her friend was looking at her as if she knew exactly what was going on in her head.

"What are you talking about?" Laina asked innocently.

"My dumb-ass cousin. If he hit on you—"

"No! It wasn't like that. I, um…"

Kiki gave her a slow smile. "You *um-ed*, did you? I see." Glancing over her shoulder, she gave her horse a pat on its side. "Well, have fun um-ing. Just remember what I told you, okay?"

Laina dropped her chin slightly. It wasn't like there was any possible way she could forget, and she had to admit it was a little embarrassing for Kiki to know she'd fallen under James's spell— exactly what she'd warned her not to do. But it wasn't like she could hide the truth from her friend, and Kiki knew a thing or two about falling for womanizers. Like Dev, former groupie-addict turned doting fiancé. "Don't worry about me, okay? I can handle this."

"I know you can," Kiki replied, lifting the reins and expertly circling her horse back toward Dev. "Have a great ride. Oh, and by the way? James is right behind you."

Laina's belly exploded into a flurry of butterflies. Slowly she turned her head in his direction, her brain immediately going numb when she laid eyes on him. Wearing jeans, a navy T-shirt and a smile just for her, he looked like some sort of cowboy fantasy—the epitome of sexiness and confidence. And he was walking directly toward her.

He stopped beside her horse and gazed up at her. "I'm scared shitless," he said.

It was as horrible as he remembered.

From atop his horse looking down, James literally felt queasy. Laina had assured him that the beach was the best possible place to learn to ride—if he fell off he would land in soft sand, she'd reminded him with a smile. Which did not help. The last thing in the world he wanted was to look like a fool in front of this woman, but he hadn't wanted to skip the outing, either. He needed her to know he was interested, and not showing up would have sent the wrong message.

He could feel his saddle shifting slightly as his horse walked. Was it on tight enough? He was certain it wasn't. The horse was going to bolt any moment now, and he would be helpless to stop it, sliding off to one side and hanging on for dear life until he fell off and got trampled under the beast's hooves—

No! He had to breathe, get himself under control.

"You're doing great," Laina said, catching up

to him from behind. "Just relax your hands a bit. Give the reins some slack—show your animal some trust. And when you want to slow him down, pull the reins up instead of back. That's a common beginner mistake."

"Up and not back. Gotcha." James nodded. He could see her looking at him from the corner of his eye. Despite his nerves, her cock-stiffening beauty had not been lost on him when he'd had a chance to observe her before panic set in. She was wearing those damned cutoffs again, which showcased her tanned legs to perfection. Her hair was swept back into a ponytail, with a few loose tendrils around her face. It had taken all of his strength not to yank her off her horse and kiss her right then and there, but he'd had to settle for a light brush of her thigh with the back of his hand. Her hand had settled over his for a moment, communicating what he hoped was an unspoken message: *Again.*

Shit, how he wanted her. Even in the middle of the hell he was in, he wanted her more badly than he could ever remember wanting anyone.

Goddamn it. James could feel his cock thickening, just what he didn't need right now. He focused on the scenery ahead, trying to stay upright in the saddle, and shoving all thoughts of her tight, wet pussy from his head.

From behind them, he could hear a horse approaching. He turned toward Laina and saw Ward

come into view on a white stallion. Ward gave
James a scathing look and then galloped away, leaving a trail of kicked-up sand in his wake.

Laina looked at James and burst out laughing.
"What was *that*?"

He laughed with her. "A one-up on me, I'm
guessing. It doesn't take much to see I suck at this."

Laina shook her head in amusement. "If only
he knew I wasn't keeping score. Or that if I was,
he'd always lose."

James hesitated. It was hard for him to believe
anyone could be engaged to a woman like Laina
and be fool enough to let her go, but he was hardly
an expert on relationships. Safer not to comment,
he decided—at least for now. "You're obviously an
excellent rider," he said instead.

Laina grinned. "I grew up with horses. Certain
things were expected in the Reinhard household."
She gave him a quick glance and then faced forward again. "Riding, piano lessons, a tutor twice a
week whether I needed it or not. Things like that,
you know."

He shook his head. "Actually, I don't. I think
we grew up in very different worlds. I take it your
family has money?"

When she didn't answer right away, James turned
to look at her face. She was staring straight ahead,
and her profile had a hardness to it he hadn't seen
before. Was it defensiveness? Guardedness? He

wanted to have this conversation—no, he *needed* to have this conversation, but maybe he was moving too fast. "You don't have to answer that," he said quickly. "Sorry. None of my business."

"It's not that," Laina said with a shake of her head. "Yes. My family has money, and they have pretty much since currency was invented. Which I guess makes me a first generation starving artist."

James grinned. "I wouldn't say that. An architect, and LEED certified, no less? I'd call that a rousing success."

She looked at him sharply. "How did you know that?"

He stared back at her. "You mentioned it yesterday."

"No, I didn't."

He sighed. "Okay. I might have Googled you."

She nodded slowly. "I see. And did you like what Google had to say about me?"

"I did. You're clearly very passionate about your work, and I find that very attractive. I checked out your projects—extremely impressive. Your parents must be very proud of you."

Laina snorted. "I wouldn't say that. They've never really understood my choices. It's like they expected me to go all granola on them or something, just because I care about the environment. I tried to show my father a set of blueprints I'd made up once, and he barely glanced at them. It was a good design too—something completely new in passive multiunit living. But my career didn't fit with their picture."

James kept his eyes on her. *Careful*, he thought as the sentence came into his head, but he had to say it. "I find it hard to believe that anyone wouldn't see how amazing you are."

Laina looked him sharply, and then her face relaxed again. "You're just saying that because…" When she trailed off, he grinned.

"Because it's true, and—" He was about to add something clever and suggestive, but just then his horse decided to veer toward the water. As it turned out, trying to ride an animal you had no control over made for very awkward flirtation. "Whoa!" he called out. "Lucky! Whoa! *Stop!* Not that way!"

Laina calmly pulled up beside him, and then leaned toward him and reached out to take his reins. Clicking softly with her tongue, she gently steered his horse away from the water and back on course. James let out a sigh of relief. "Thank you."

"I take it this is your first time," Laina said, guiding her horse around a large piece of driftwood lodged in the sand. They were at the back of the pack now, with the other members of their party starting to wind their way away from the beach and into the trees ahead of them.

"Second. The first time didn't go so well."

"No? What happened?"

He hesitated. He'd never talked to a woman about his mother before. In fact, his first and only real girlfriend had left him for more or less that reason—he was "too closed off"—and that had been it for him for relationships. Strangely, though, he hadn't made that connection in his head until just now.

He took a deep breath. "I went with my mother when I was twenty-one or so. My horse was okay, but hers wasn't. He was acting up from the very beginning, but the ranch hand kept telling her he was fine. And then something spooked him and he bolted. He went for the woods. She managed to hang on, but it scared the shit out of her and she got banged up by the trees pretty badly."

Laina shook her head. "God, that must have been horrible for her. For both of you—you must have been terrified."

"I was. I hadn't wanted to go in the first place, but…" He trailed off.

James felt her eyes on his face again. "But what?" she asked softly.

He sighed. "But I couldn't refuse. Horseback riding was on her bucket list."

Laina was quiet for a beat, and then said, "Oh, James. I'm so sorry."

"Me too."

They walked in silence for a moment, and then

she moved her horse in front of his with a quick dig of her heels. "There's something I want to show you," she called to him over her shoulder. "The others will never miss us. Follow me!"

CHAPTER SEVEN

THE RIDE UP the incline was longer than Laina remembered, but maybe it was just her nerves that made it seem that way. Winding through the trees with James following behind her, she tried not to think too hard about what she was doing. She'd never taken anyone to this place, and though she'd checked in on it a few times over the past decade, she hadn't really spent time there since her late teens. Like Pelican Rock, it was somewhat sacred to her, and what if James didn't see the magic in it that she did? She couldn't help it—no matter how strong her attraction to him was, she was certain it would lessen her opinion of him.

Laina knew they were getting close when they passed the iron gates of Ocean Lookout, the last property on the way up the path. Beyond it stretched the overgrown four-acre lot of Terrasse de Rêves with the house at dead center. After passing through a crop of fruit-bearing calabash trees, she drew to a halt.

It looked exactly the same as the last time she'd seen it. She stole a quick glance at James, who'd drawn his horse up beside hers, and she immediately knew that he got it. "Wow," he breathed. "That is crazy."

"I know," Laina said with a smile. She led James to a shady tree and dismounted, and then she waited for him to do the same. He cautiously swung a leg over his horse and then settled onto the ground.

"What is this place?" he asked, turning back to the ruins.

"It's called *Terrasse de Rêves*—that's *Terrace of Dreams*. But I call it House of Broken Dreams."

"How dramatic." James grinned. Laina took his reins and tied both horses to tree trunks where they could graze, and then she and James both walked toward the structure.

The house was both unfinished and decaying, making for a uniquely ambiguous effect. It was easy to see how the home, if brought to completion, would have been stately and impressive. Laina remembered the day she had discovered it. She'd been riding with her family, and while they rode right past it like it was nothing interesting, she'd stopped and stared. When questions about it to her parents went unanswered, she'd gone to the council on her own to find out what the story was. Decades later the home was still an unsettling sight in its failed grandeur. The grounds, which had once been clear-cut, were now grown over with enough trees and bushes to create a darkly haunting atmosphere around the house. The red brick walls had begun crumbling with age, and the expansive wooden porch sagged into the ground. But oddest of all were the unfinished roof, which consisted only of rotting plywood, and the empty holes for windows and doors.

"It *is* pretty dramatic, actually," Laina said. "The family who owned this place were some of the first outsiders to build on the island. The father was a respected judge from Montreal. While he was building this house, his wife left him for another man. A few months later, his young daughter was diagnosed with pancreatic cancer and died. He had a complete nervous breakdown—it totally destroyed him."

"Whoa. That *is* tragic," James said, walking closer to the structure. "I guess that explains why it was never finished."

Laina nodded. "He stopped construction of the house but refused to sell the land. When I was a teenager, I remember there being a big fuss about it—the residents were complaining and wanted the house torn down. I freaked out because it was my special place. I begged my parents to try to save it, and they went to the council and managed to talk them into it."

James raised an eyebrow at her. "Wow. It sounds like you have a lot of influence around here."

Laina looked away. That was the last thing she wanted him to think, and she was still angry with herself for her slipup back on the trail. She never told anyone her former last name, but judging from James's lack of reaction, he either hadn't picked up on it or he already knew; Laina was savvy enough to get that with some minor sleuthing it could be found out.

"I wouldn't say that." She brushed the comment off, turning back to the building. "But I was attached to this place. A house that had never become a home—it haunted me. I was always struck by how it looks like it's growing from the earth. I think it's what first lit up my love of architecture, and gave me the idea of combining progress with nature." She turned to James with a hint of challenge on her face. "You're a developer. Would you have built here if you had the chance?"

He looked taken aback. "Why do I get the feeling there's only one right answer to this question?"

She shrugged. "Not necessarily. We all have to live by our own code of ethics, and I'm not in the habit of pushing mine on others. Inform yourself and make your choices, is what I always say. I'm just curious."

He gazed at the house again. "That's a tough one. This island is so beautiful, and with property at such a premium… I'd be tempted to side with the residents."

"Well, I can't fault your honesty." She tore her eyes away from his face. She was disappointed in his answer, but not surprised…and it certainly didn't make her want him any less. They were standing side by side, his body inches from hers, and she longed to lean close to him and feel him take her into his arms. But did he want the same thing? Sure, he'd trailed his fingers up her thigh when he'd first walked up to her, nearly causing her to combust, but he could just be toying with her in the way playboys did. If there was one thing Laina didn't have experience with, it was navigating the subtleties of post-one-night stands.

She started walking toward the house, needing to escape the waves of electricity she felt radiating off her.

"So what were your broken dreams?" James said from behind her.

Laina stopped at the front porch, gazing into the gaping hole where the front door was supposed to be. Beyond it, she could see a majestic curved staircase, looking completely out of place in a framed room with no drywall. "Nothing big."

"I'd still like to hear them."

"Would you?" Laina was used to keeping her laments to herself. Growing up with privilege, she'd learned quickly that she wasn't allowed to have

complaints, at least in the eyes of people who hadn't
grown up in the same way. Everyone knew that
money could make dreams come true, even Laina.
It was only a problem if your dreams weren't material.

James walked up to her and searched her face.
Then he slowly reached for her hands, as if waiting to see if she would meet him halfway. Almost involuntarily, Laina felt hers rising. Before
they'd even touched, she felt a jolt of electricity
zap straight to her pussy. Their fingers entwined,
and then James pulled her forcefully toward him.
"Yes. I would."

His face was inches from hers, his eyes electric
on her, their torsos lightly touching. She stroked
her thumbs across his wrists. God, was she really
doing this? But it was like she was under a spell,
powerless to stop the irresistible pull of her body
toward his. She could already feel heat burning at
her center, reminding her of every amazing thing
she'd felt last night. "Well. You know what I'd like?"
she asked.

His pupils dilated. "The same thing I do. At least
that's what I'm hoping."

Disentangling one hand from his, Laina reached
behind him and ran it up under his T-shirt. Just the
warm, smooth feel of his skin had her knees going
watery. She lifted her mouth to his and brushed it
ever so slightly with her lips. "I want us to make

each other come again. And then I want you to teach me everything you know."

At Laina's words, James felt his cock go rigid. Oh, yes.

He wanted her—no, he *craved* her—and he'd missed his chance to have the conversation he needed to have with her anyway. She'd even offered him the perfect opportunity when she started talking about their careers, but his comment about her influence was as far as he'd been able to go. Clearly it was a topic she didn't like, and he could only imagine the horror on her face if he were to ask her the question that was burning in his mind. But it couldn't be avoided, and the longer he waited and the more physical they got, the worse it would become for both of them.

He had to ask her. He should stop this right now—simply step away from her, take a deep breath and spit it out like a big boy.

But he couldn't. Unfiltered lust had taken over his brain and his body, making him burn with a desperate desire that only *she* could quench.

James brought his mouth down on Laina's with an animal sound, feeling her tongue reach for him urgently. He took her lower lip between his teeth and sucked it gently, and then he brought his hands to her waist and slid them under her tank top. Releasing one breast from its bra cup, he felt her nipple stiffen under his palm. She moaned and collapsed backward with her hands on the back of his head, bringing his mouth down to her breast. When their eyes met again, hers were already wild with desire.

"Show me," she whispered fiercely.

Taking her hand again, James pressed it to his cock, now rock-hard through his shorts. Hot anticipation rolled off him in sweet waves. "You're going to bring me to the edge but not let me come," he said into her ear, holding her firmly against him. "And then it'll be my turn."

Laina moved with lightning speed, opening his zipper and yanking his shorts and boxers down his hips. They settled in a pool around his ankles and stayed there, evidence of the desperate need coursing through both of them as Laina lowered herself to her knees. When she looked up at James and licked her lips hungrily, he almost groaned aloud. *Jesus*—this woman was making him come apart in a way he never had before. He took her hands, wrapping one firmly around his shaft and the other around his scrotum. "I want to see your mouth on me," he said hoarsely. Her lips wrapped around his head, tentatively at first, and then she was taking all of him in. "Oh, yes. So beautiful. So sexy," he groaned. Her mouth felt hot and wet, and the sight of her—

He exercised control, knowing he could explode in an instant if he wanted to. Now that he was slick from her mouth, he took her hand and showed her how to work it up his shaft and over his head with her palm.

"Is that good?" she asked breathlessly.

"*So* good," he managed to say, his knees practically buckling. Her eager face, looking for his approval when she had no idea of the power she held over him—it was mind-blowing. "And I am so… *close.*"

When he felt her release him, he pulled her up, kicked his shorts and boxers away and pushed her back until she was up against a tree. "Let's see if you're ready for me," he growled into her ear, yanking her zipper down. She gasped as he grabbed one thigh and pulled it up and out to spread her open. The he slid his hand into her panties. "Absolute perfection," he said, bringing her wetness up to circle her clit.

"*James—*" Laina cried, bucking back against the tree. But he was only getting started, and already control was a line he was just at the edge of crossing. He never went beyond it. He conducted his sexual encounters like anything else in his life, orchestrated with a measured plan and process that never veered off course. But right now his mind was hazy with unadulterated wanting, and what he wanted was to do *everything* with this woman. To have everything *from* her, and suddenly he barely knew where to start or where to end.

Like her sweet pussy, for example. He'd been planning to get his mouth onto it, but the feel of her wetness was messing with his head. Slipping his hand out of her panties, he brought his fingers to his mouth. "You taste like heaven," he rasped, pushing her shorts down. "I can't wait to lick you, but I just have to fuck you first."

"Thank God," Laina panted. Her chest was heaving, her fingernails digging into his back with desperation. "I need you so badly. *Right now.*"

Keeping her pinned to the tree, James got the condom on and then lifted her thigh again. He pushed into her, wanting to prolong the moment, but Laina grabbed his ass to pull him in deeply. "Harder," she rasped, each small cry that ripped from her lips spurring him on further. *"Harder!"* James drove into her relentlessly, keeping his hand at the small of her back to save her skin from ripping apart on the tree trunk. Their urgent breath mingled in the warm air, two people in the throes of a passion so intense that every muscle burned as they raced toward their ultimate pleasure.

Restraint. Control, James chanted in his head, but it was hopeless. He needed everything she could give him, everything he could give to her. He growled and spun her around so her back was to him. Bending her forward by the neck, he entered her from behind in one forceful thrust.

"Yes, *yes, yes*—" Laina cried, meeting him thrust for thrust.

Looking at her tan-lined bottom and tapered waist, James suddenly felt like he'd entered a realm that he hadn't even known existed. What was happening to him? He'd had plenty of good sex in his life—even great sex—but nothing like this. Like if he couldn't have her he would die, like he'd compare every other woman to her from now on, like he wanted to *possess her.*

And now he was way too close for comfort and almost beyond caring. His release was so near, and he knew it was going to blow his mind. He wrapped Laina's hair around his hand and tugged her head back until his mouth was at her ear. "I can't get enough of you," he whispered to her, all hope of restraint shattered by the sheer force of their connection.

"That makes two of us," Laina said breathlessly. "Now *please* make me come."

Reaching under her, James found her swollen clit and worked his fingers over it. It didn't take much. He felt her pitch forward, and then her body shuddered as a long, animal moan escaped her mouth. Her pussy clenched his cock tightly over and over again, drawing him ever nearer—

And then he was falling over the edge himself, his entire body radiating with the most intense, white-hot pulses of pleasure he'd ever felt. When he finally collapsed on top of her, they were both breathing as if they'd run a marathon.

Finally James pulled her up, meaning to turn her toward him, but she stopped him by placing a hand at his waist. "Where do you think you're going?" she asked, looking over her shoulder at him. She looked incredible, her face flushed with heat and her hair tangled from their passion. Arching her back, she rolled her hips up and down, making her pussy squeeze around his still-stiff cock. "You still feel plenty hard to me."

It was true. Though he'd had an earthquake-worthy orgasm just a minute ago, judging by the state of his cock he would never know it. He groaned. "God, Laina. You're killing me."

"But you like it."

"No." He threw himself over her back and found her lips. "I love it."

She separated herself from him with a quick bump of her hips, and then she turned around to face him. Kicking her shorts away, she slid her tank top up to expose her bra. Then she ran a hand down her belly to cup her pussy, letting her eyes flutter shut as she moaned. James's cock lifted from half-mast to a full-blown erection as he watched her, awestruck. "So, do you want to fuck me again?" she asked, her breath already quickening.

His heart started to pound. "I think the correct

word would be *need*," he said, moving to close the gap between them.

"Then go ahead," she said, but she put a hand out to stop him. "On one condition."

"Name it," he said, licking his lips ravenously.

"That you take me into your bed tonight like a proper gentleman, and that you answer all my questions."

"That's two conditions."

"Take it or leave it."

"Oh, I'll definitely take it," he said, reaching for her.

CHAPTER EIGHT

"SO TELL ME," Laina began. She was lying on James's bed with her bra and panties on, thanking her lucky stars she'd thrown one matching set of lingerie into her bag when she'd packed. She'd chosen it, a silky white set overlaid with nude lace, to go under her bridesmaid's dress. James was stretched out beside her in navy boxers, kept on at her insistence. With the sky faded to a dark indigo beyond the hotel's windows, his room was in darkness other than a bedside lamp. "What position do you like best?"

James threw back his head and laughed. "My, my. What happened to that innocent creature I bedded only twenty-four hours ago?"

Laina grinned. Twenty-four hours—was that even possible? How could it be that only a day ago she was ignorant to the heights of pleasure her body could feel? It was like the doors to her world had been thrown open overnight. "I'm thirty-two years old. A late bloomer, which means I don't have any time to waste. You need to tell me everything you know."

"I'd rather show you."

"Later. Now answer the question."

"Fine. Favorite position? We haven't tried them all yet."

It was Laina's turn to laugh. There was something undeniably sexy about knowing James had been with so many women and only wanted her—at least for now. But she wasn't about to fool herself into thinking that meant it was going to be anything more permanent, even if she had to admit that her desire for him was more than physical. There was something about him—the softness beneath the commanding presence, a vulnerability she sensed that he kept deeply buried—that made her want to explore his depths. She loved the way he threw his head back when he laughed, the way he looked at her like he wanted to devour her, and the way he touched her even when they weren't having sex, soft caresses that he seemed to find any excuse to give her. But Laina knew well this was a line of thinking that could lead to her ruin, so she was determined to keep her mind on one thing only: the amazing, breathtaking, earth-shattering sex. "Then use your memory," she said. "I'm sure you've got plenty of experience to draw on."

"Funny, but I seem to be drawing a complete blank right now."

"Come on, you promised."

James ran a hand slowly up her arm, making her shiver. "I promise to let you know once we've worked our way through the entire *Kama Sutra*."

Laina shook her head. The thought of having James to herself that long was intoxicating, but totally unrealistic. "Fine, but that's your only gimme. You have to answer the rest."

"Yes, Your Grace."

"Your first time?"

He grinned. "Seventeen years old, her dorm room. She was older and much more experienced."

"Longest you've gone without?"

He looked sheepish.

"Don't answer that," she laughed, wishing she had the nerve to ask the real question that was boring into her mind: *How many?* But she didn't dare.

"What's your favorite way to come?"

He looked down at himself. "Would you stop? A man can only take so much of this kind of conversation."

She glanced at the bulge in his boxers and then drummed her fingers on the bed. "I'm waiting."

"Okay, okay. I'd never say no to your mouth, but face-to-face—it's hard to beat the classics."

"Best sex ever?"

He ran a hand up the curve of her waist. "Let's do it right now, and then I'll tell you all about it."

Her belly flopped over. He was teasing her, of course. It was pretty obvious that he was enjoying their arrangement as much as she was, but this was all part of the game. Heating each other up with dirty words and utterances that made the other person feel special. She may not have much experience, but she knew better than to fall for it…even if it did sound amazing to her ears.

"Okay. Last question…" She trailed off, plagued by second thoughts. Was she really going to ask him something so embarrassing? Despite his reputation, there was something about him that made her want to trust him, which was undoubtedly reckless and stupid. But she was living in the moment, she reminded herself. This was her chance to learn about something she'd been missing out on for far too long, and even when they said goodbye to each other forever on Monday, she'd be walking away with an arsenal of experience and knowledge that she could use with the men in her future. Not that *that* idea appealed to her in the least right now.

"Come on, don't be shy," James prompted softly.

Laina took a deep breath. "Okay. Why did I never have an orgasm until you came along?"

To her surprise, his face remained serious. "Because you've been lied to."

"Lied to?"

"Yes. Every woman has. Movies and books will have you believe that if you're aroused enough, it'll just happen. A little pumping action on the guy's end and you're off to the races. There's probably a small percentage of women who are built that way, but for most it's a matter of direct stimulation and the right touch at the right time. Also—" he took on a reporter's voice "—studies show that in long-term relationships, most women can only climax if they employ fantasies."

She stared at him. "You mean, like, role play?"

James shook his head. "Not necessarily. I mean up here." He tapped his head.

She let out a sigh of relief. "Good. Because I don't think I'd be into that."

"It's not for everyone."

"Is it for you?" she asked shyly.

"It's nothing I need. But…"

Her heart skipped. "Yes?"

"There is something I think you might like." His hand moved to the fabric of her bra, where he starfished his fingers to spread over her nipple. She pressed into him, helpless to control her reaction to his touch. "Will you trust me?" he asked.

Laina hesitated. God, but this was a bad idea. Whatever he had in mind, she knew it was going to blow her mind yet again. But that was what she was here for, right? "Nothing painful?"

"Not even close."

Laina found herself nodding.

By the time James was in the bathroom checking through the selection of mini hotel-supplied toiletries, his cock was already starting to strain against his boxers. Just the thought of what he had in mind...

And Laina. Not only was she a sex goddess and as intelligent, passionate, kind and independent as they came, he was blown away by her maturity. Most women he'd known would never be secure enough to broach the topic of his past lovers, and he loved how open she was to talking about sex. To learning more about her body and how to please him—it was a rare quality.

Yet as mature as she was, there were things about her that reminded him of a little girl that he wanted to protect. And Jesus Christ if he wasn't getting in over his goddamned head because of it. Each round of their passion was sinking him deeper into a place he wasn't sure he'd able to return from. Tonight, when he'd been anticipating her arrival, he'd been as excited about having a conversation with her and just feeling her close to him as he had been about the sex. And that was not only completely unfamiliar to him, it was downright terrifying.

But he could worry about all that tomorrow, James told himself. Because right now there was no way in hell he was going to walk away from what was about to happen between them.

Picking up and discarding the mini bottles one at a time, he grinned when he found what he was looking for. Pure aloe-vera gel, great for sunburns and mind-blowing sex.

When he returned to the bedroom, Laina was lying back against the pillows on his bed with her phone in her hand. "Mood killer," she said, putting it aside when he walked up to her. "Sorry."

"No problem. Nothing urgent, I hope?"

"Just my mother." She grinned. "*Serious* mood killer."

He sat down beside her and put a hand on her forearm. "Anything you want to talk about?"

It wasn't just a polite question. If there was something upsetting her, James not only wanted to know about it, he wanted to help her fix it. *So* terrifying…and extremely bad news considering what her reaction would likely be when he finally got around to asking her for the favor he needed. Mood killer indeed; he pushed the thought from his mind.

"It's not important," Laina assured him. "Now, where were we?"

James pushed her hair back from her face. Those deep, dark eyes, that sexy mouth—*Christ*. "You were going to trust me," he replied. "But it's nothing that can't wait. Are you sure you're up for this?"

"Are you kidding?" Circling her arms around his neck, Laina brought her mouth close to his. "Always," she whispered, pressing her body into his as she kissed him.

Always. Why did that word sound so amazing coming from her lips? Better not to think about it. Better to just let this happen, enjoy it for all it was worth, and let the rest take care of itself. Laina's hands were at his waist now, tugging at the elastic of his boxers, but he caught them in his. "Later," he said softly. "Right now, it's all about you."

Laina could hear the blood rushing through her ears as James placed the tie over her eyes and fastened it at the back of her head, leaving her in complete darkness. What was she getting herself into? She'd never read Fifty Shades of Grey, but she'd heard enough about it to know that the kind of sex that went on in those pages was definitely not her thing. Handcuffs, spanking, bondage, nipple clamps—no, thank you. But she also knew there was a big difference between a serious fetish and a little playful fun.

"Just relax." James's mouth was at her ear, his sweet breath sending a shiver down her spine. "Trust me," he said again, and something about those two words sounded extremely erotic to Laina. To put herself at the mercy of this man, despite all her cautions against him, made her feel cared for and reassured and aroused all at the same time.

So dangerous.

She felt her hand being lifted and laid against the cold bedpost, and then the silky touch of a tie securing her wrist.

"Don't worry," James said as he started on the other hand. "If you don't like it, we can stop."

But she *did* like it. His lips were on her neck now, his tongue dipping into the hollow beneath her jaw and sending goose bumps across her skin. Her bra clasp was released behind her, and then her nipple was in his mouth, being pulled to the back of his throat. "You are so beautiful," he said hoarsely. "You have no idea what you do to me." Those words…so addicting each time he said them, pulling her further and further into a vortex of desire that she wasn't sure how long she'd be strong enough to swim up from. She verbalized her response with a soft moan, afraid of her own voice.

James was pulling her panties down to her ankles. She could feel the heat building inside her already, that sensation that was still so new to her. She wished she could reach for him, touch him to see how much he wanted her, but being at his mercy was almost just as intoxicating.

When his fingers went to her pussy and pushed inside her, Laina gasped. His hand was warm and slippery, coated with something that made each stroke feel more intense than she'd ever thought possible. He moved his fingers to her clit and built her fervor with expert strokes. Up, up, up her desire spiraled, intense enough to make her breathing turn ragged in minutes. "I'm already so close," she gasped. "That feels so good."

"This will feel even better," James promised. And then—*oh, yes*—his warm mouth was on her swollen clit, sucking and licking her relentlessly toward explosive pleasure. She'd only had this done to her a few times in her life, but it had never felt anything near to this. Like her whole body was being washed in warm sensuality, like she'd do anything in the world to keep that perfect mouth on her until she reached her release.

"Do you know long I've been wanting to do this?" James rasped as he moved his fingers inside her. "To taste your sweetness on my tongue?"

"How long?" she gasped.

"Since the moment I saw you."

His tongue latched on to her again and within seconds she was there, hit with the force of a tsunami, pure ecstasy saturating every cell of her body. Her hands strained at the ties as she practically levitated from the bed. "Yes, yes, *yes*!" she cried as the incredible feeling finally subsided.

Laina's body felt like it had been singed with heat, hypersensitive and yet still wanting, ready for so much more. And James must have known it, because he was far from finished with her. His lips were on hers now, pushing her mouth open as far as it would go as his tongue probed her deeply, a guttural sound coming from his throat. The way he kissed her—like he wanted to possess her, like it meant something beyond what either of them wanted to acknowledge—clawed at her chest. Animal heat ripped through her as she felt him bite her neck, her shoulder, her breast. She could hear his breath in her ear, his audible desire for her already pushing her past raw need.

He spoke to her softly, with barely restrained urgency in every syllable. "Laina, I am so hard for you."

The torturous visual filled her mind. "Let me feel you. *Please.*"

A second later she felt him settling between her thighs, and then his cock was lying on her belly, long and hard as he rocked it against her. It felt wet and slightly sticky to the touch—with the same thing he'd used on her pussy. His voice was above her, inches from her face. "Do you know why my cock is slippery? Because I've been stroking myself as I watch you. I can't handle it, Laina. You're too amazing."

"Let me see," she demanded, so firmly within the grip of desire she felt like she'd kill for a glimpse. That part of him she was so addicted to after only two days—it was madness. "I have to see. *Please.*"

The blindfold was ripped off, and her eyes were filled with the sight of James straddled across her thighs. His cock was in his fist, his face a mask of lust as he moved his hand firmly up and down. It was the most arousing thing she'd ever seen in her life. "Oh, James…" Her hips gyrated beneath him, desperate for pressure. His hand, his mouth, his cock—anything to quench her aching need. Her heart was pounding through her chest, beating to the force of her insatiable hunger.

James leaned forward and pulled the tie on her right hand. "Touch yourself," he commanded in a thick voice. "Let me see you touch yourself, and I promise to fuck you."

Laina proudly didn't miss a beat, though she'd never masturbated in her life. The thought of it had always seemed morbidly embarrassing to her, but right now it sounded like the best idea she'd ever heard. Because it was with James, the man who'd completely turned her world upside down in just twenty-four hours. "Before or after we come?" She could barely get the words out.

"You come," he panted as he continued his stroking. She could see his balls pulled up tight, ready to explode. "I'm going to save myself for your beautiful pussy."

"What if I want to see you come on me?" *Who was she?* Laina Rose did not say things like that, did not do things like this. But thanks to James Ellison, Laina Rose had officially turned into a sex maniac.

"Stop talking like that, or I *will* come right now. And you want to feel this inside you, believe me."

He grabbed her free hand and clamped it down on her pussy. "Now let me see you touch yourself."

Laina laid her hand flat over her mound and slid it slowly downward, letting her body's response guide her pleasure. She sunk a finger inside herself and drew it out again, circling her clit, and was surprised when a whimper emitted from her throat. It *did* feel good—not as good as when James touched her, but having his eyes fastened on her every move like a predator in heat more than made up for it. The wild look in his eyes drove her forward as she reared her hips up from the bed, consumed with reaching that beautiful point of no return. Knowing she was safe to climax because James would bring her back yet again after she did, ready and aching for more of this, more of *him*. He was under her skin so far now it was pointless to try to deny it. She never wanted this feeling to end, and whatever that meant on a practical level didn't matter.

Her fingertip swirled her clit once, twice, three times, and she moved her finger inside herself again as she moaned. James looked like he was dangerously close to combusting, but she was almost there. She was gasping for breath now, so close to ecstasy and yet never wanting it to end. She finally fell over the edge into bliss with a sharp cry, rocking side to side with her head thrown back into her still-bound left arm.

When she came back into her body, James was

releasing the tie on her wrist, then flipping onto his back and reaching for a condom. His heavy breathing and erotic words had been replaced with a focused silence that was no less arousing. Laina could see that it was taking all of his strength to keep himself together, and the knowledge that it was she who had taken him to that agonizing place was so sweet it almost hurt.

James was prone on his back now, his hand spread wide at the base of his sheathed cock to hold it upright. Laina licked her lips at the sight of it, miraculously still aching for him. Still yearning for more.

James's voice was barely controlled when he spoke. "Do you think you can come again?"

She nodded—unbelievable but true. Her clit was so sensitive now she feared it might hurt if she did, but she knew it would be a good pain.

"Good," James said calmly. "You're going to sit on my cock, and I'm going to fuck you until I come. It won't take much, I'm warning you. Make yourself come at the same time, and squeeze my cock as hard as you can when you do."

Laina scrambled over his hips, dying for the feel of him filling her. She positioned herself over him, and he grabbed her hips. This time there was no slow entry, no watching him ease into her one sweet inch at a time. There was only raw power and an impossibly forceful thrust into her as James's consuming need broke like a dam. Holding her hips immobile, he began to drive into her, making her head flop forward as goose bumps broke out across her body and she lost all sense of time and place, anything beyond this room and this man and the incredible feeling that was welling up in her yet again.

"I'm going to come so hard," James groaned. "Squeeze my cock."

Laina did. She would have done anything for him, anything he asked, as long as he was taking her to that incredible place she wanted to go again. She felt warmth radiating upward, from her pussy into her belly, until she was once more balancing on the brink. And then she was toppling over, feeling him thrust upward one last time as groan and after groan ripped from his throat.

As they rode the crest together, Laina knew that she needed him, every part of him, and that it was already painful to think of a tomorrow without him.

CHAPTER NINE

On my way to the spa with Kiki, have fun with the guys! See you this afternoon xx

AS JAMES LOOKED down at the text from Laina, a war of emotions tore at his gut. At the top was his insanely heated craving for her, along with a mind-bending urge to pull her closer to him than physical limits even allowed. A terrifying, vulnerable, deep feeling that informed him he was past the point of no return with her. It made absolutely no sense that he should feel this way after only two days, but telling himself that did nothing to change the facts. He would never find another woman like Laina. She was hotter than a million casual lays, better than anyone he could have imagined inserting into his world, and the thought of going back to a life without her made his chest ache with emptiness.

And at the bottom of his gut was raging regret for letting things go this far.

Damn. Ever since yesterday he'd been ignoring work calls and emails, not to mention trying to forget that Jennifer Liu had the power to put the Moretta project on the chopping block if he didn't come through. Knowing how skittish his partner was about certain things, he'd let her come in on the deal without divulging a couple of major snags, confident he could iron them out without her ever knowing. But it hadn't been as easy as he thought, and the truth was he knew better than to do business like that. He'd come under the spell of the island and, if he were completely honest with himself, his own greed. He'd seen an opportunity he wanted to jump on before anyone else could, and he'd needed Jennifer to make it happen.

And now he needed Laina to make it happen. Damn it—how had he let things go this far without talking to her? He should have done it right when he met her, gotten it out of the way before they got involved personally. Not that he'd had a chance, seeing as they'd gone from enemies to lovers within about one second flat. That first kiss on the deck had led to more so quickly…

Tossing his phone onto his bed, James dropped his boxer shorts and walked naked into the bathroom. Laina had left around midnight, but the truth was that it had taken all of his strength not to invite her to stay. He never let his conquests sleep in his bed, but Laina was more than that, and he'd known it. If she'd been disappointed, though, she certainly hadn't let on. Even though he'd insisted on driving her home to the point of getting himself dressed, she'd vehemently insisted on driving herself, leaving him with a lingering kiss. And now the hotel room still smelled like her. *He* still smelled like her. And even the thought of the heavenly bliss that had gone on between them last night had his ravaged cock lifting off again.

He had no choice—he had to get it over with. He'd practiced the lines in his head and there was no easy way to ask her the question, no way to sugarcoat his words without disclosing his full intentions. He needed to come clean, come what may.

A dark sense of dread filled his head as he slid the shower door open. He could lust after Laina all he wanted, could even fool himself into thinking she might be important enough for him to make a serious change in his life. But the truth was that they were on an idyllic island for one week where romance took on a falsely shiny optimism, and that nothing would change the fact that on Monday they'd both return to their real lives—whether Laina was willing to help him or not. The bottom line was that he had to get the conversation over with so he and Jennifer could move ahead with the project. Now. This afternoon. He'd do it when he saw Laina later today, he decided. Even if the thought of it made his stomach clench like a fist.

He stepped into the shower and turned the cold water on full blast.

* * *

"Are you sure you don't need any help?" Laina asked Kiki, facing her sideways on the massage table. "I haven't done a single thing since I've been here. Aren't I supposed to be making party favors or something?"

"I just asked her that this morning," Kiki's second bridesmaid, Nicola, who'd arrived for the wedding the night before, piped up on her other side. "But you know Kiki. She's so organized—or at least she is since Dev came along."

"You noticed that too?" Laina grinned. "You should have seen her in high school. She was an executive functioning nightmare, and yet somehow she managed to score straight A's. And become an executive assistant, of all things—go figure."

"Try having her for a roommate," Nicola said. Her face was turned into the cutout on the massage table, making her voice come out muffled. "I remember this one time—"

Kiki cleared her throat loudly. "*Excuse* me for interrupting, ladies, but are you two sure you've never met? Because you're like a couple of peas in a pod."

"It *is* hard to believe," Laina laughed to Nicola. "I've visited Kiki here so often, but I guess I missed the time you were living with her."

"I know." Nicola turned to face Laina. "I thought I'd be staying here a lot longer, but then I met Alex and he swept me back to LA."

Though the two women had met only two hours ago, Nicola had already filled in Laina on the odds she'd faced to find true love on the island with Alex, and to Laina it all sounded like a modern fairy tale. Knowing Kiki and Dev's story too, she couldn't help wondering if this island had a magical taming effect on certain alpha men.

Which was exactly the kind of dangerous thinking that would lead her directly into shattering heartbreak, Laina reminded herself. She knew better, and she'd do not well to forget it. No matter what kind of otherworldly encounter she and James might have had last night.

"Would you two please stop talking?" Kiki sighed. "You're supposed to be relaxing."

Laina tried. Closing her eyes, she attempted to succumb to the massage therapist's kneading strokes down her back, but it was no use. Her head was a hot mess. She'd managed to deal with a few work emails this morning and even put an ad in for an assistant—Kiki was right, she really couldn't continue without one—but she'd failed to respond to her mother's text from last night asking Laina to call her. Not that the timing had been ideal, with James just appearing in the bedroom to tie her up for the most intense experience of her life.

At the memory of it, a small moan nearly escaped her lips. The way he'd made her feel—her entire body broke out in goose bumps just thinking about it. A low buzz vibrated in her pussy, making even the pressure of the massage table something she longed to grind into just to quench the aching desire she now lived with constantly. And she was sore down there today, another new experience for her, but it was an exquisite pain. A pain that reminded her of James and everything that had gone on between them over the past few days, and of everything she knew they were still going to do. But she feared for her mind, which was filled with thoughts of him that bordered on obsessive. All she could think of was *him*—his touch, his smell, the boundless magic he'd unlocked in her body…and the questions that kept burning at the back of her mind. Was this more than just sex? Was she special to him, or was he like this with all his conquests, making each feel like she was the only woman on earth who mattered right up until the moment he moved on to the next one? After all, he hadn't invited her to stay last night.

Laina tried to remember whose idea it had been for her to go home—had she brought it up or had he? She was pretty sure it had been her, and then he'd offered to drive her home—like she was ever going to let him see where she was staying—but he had eventually let her go. Laina may not have had much experience with sex, but she did know that a man who let you leave his bed after a full night of earthshaking pleasure didn't usually have long-term potential. It was a thought that brought an arousal-killing punch to her gut. Despite what had happened with Ward, she had pretty healthy self-confidence, but she knew that if James discarded her, it would hurt more than she cared to admit. Even more than Ward, she realized.

And that was when she knew she was in way over her head.

"So," Kiki said to Laina, flipping onto her back so her massage therapist could start working on her neck. "I'm assuming you found your way back to the stable yesterday? If I didn't know you were such a good rider, I'd have been worried you got lost." She turned to her with a raised eyebrow.

Laina felt her cheeks tingle. She should have known better than to think her friend wouldn't notice what was going on with her. "I thought you wanted silence."

"I do—right after you tell all."

"There's not much to tell."

"Liar."

"What are we talking about?" Nicola asked.

"Nothing," Laina insisted.

"Come on," Kiki urged. "I know you're dying to tell us."

"About *what*?" Nicola pressed again.

Laina heaved a sigh. "Fine. It's just… I kind of have a blind date for the week. Long story. And, well…" She gazed straight up at the ceiling to avoid her friends' eyes. "We may be having a really amazing time. And I may be *extremely* confused."

There was a beat of silence before both women started making cheering noises. Laina laughed. Anyone who thought women didn't indulge in locker-room talk didn't know the half of it.

"Well, who is it?" Nicola asked when they finally settled down.

"That's the weird part. It's Kiki's cousin. She thought it would be a good idea to—"

"Do you mean James?" Nicola asked.

Something in her voice caught Laina's attention. She lifted her head. "Yes. You've met him?"

She watched Nicola exchange a quick glance with Kiki before she answered. "I have. He came to visit Kiki once while we were living together—but he stayed at The Palms," she added quickly.

Laina could feel her gut twisting. *No.* But she already knew. "And?" she asked, trying to keep her voice light. "What did you think of him?"

"He was nice," Nicola said before turning away again.

Laina dropped her face back down. "Oh, my God. He hit on you, didn't he?"

Nicola shook her head quickly. "No! I mean, yes, but—he didn't know I had a boyfriend. Alex was back in LA, and—it was so not a big deal, I swear. He was a total gentleman when I shut him down."

Laina hated the churning in her belly. She hated

the raging jealousy she felt streak through her as her mind immediately filled with the picture of their naked bodies together—which had never even *happened.* So he had asked another woman out—so what? He had been single, Nicola was as gorgeous as they came—it made perfect sense and there wasn't a thing wrong with it.

Except that it reminded her that she was only one of many. And that maybe there wasn't anything special about her at all.

"Listen," Kiki said, breaking the uncomfortable silence. "I've never known James to have a relationship, but that's not to say it couldn't happen. I mean, look at Dev—the number of groupies he slept with before he met me? *Horrifying.* But I know with everything in my heart that those days are over for him. I think it can happen to any man if he meets the right woman. And I can't imagine a better one than you." She ended her comments with a smile.

Laina tried to smile back, but she knew it looked forced. *The right woman.* What Kiki said may be true, but where did Laina get off thinking that could be her? Very likely, *every* woman who slept with James thought she could be the one to win his heart. Even if James had done nothing wrong, she felt humiliated by her own naivete and fragile hopes. A man of thirty-eight didn't just suddenly decide he wanted his very first relationship when he'd spent a lifetime choosing whoever he wanted whenever he wanted.

Laina closed her eyes, trying for an indifferent tone. "You know what? I'm really not looking for anything like that right now, anyway. And seriously, Kiki—I insist on helping you. Isn't there anything I can do for you this afternoon?"

By the time James was walking downstairs to the lobby of The Palms to meet Laina, he'd come up with a plan that he thought was half-decent. The first part of it involved making sure they didn't end up in bed again before he accomplished his mission. If they did, James knew he'd just fall deeper into the hole he'd already dug for himself, not to mention probably spend the rest of the day having sex like the world was coming to an end. No—James would begin by taking her to the site of his planned hotel and describing his vision to her, and then he'd invite her to be a part of it. He'd even managed to convince himself that he might be stressing out for no reason. Why wouldn't she agree to what he needed from her? It wasn't like she had nothing to gain from the deal. Maybe it would all work out just fine, and they could finish the day together doing something a lot more fun than discussing business details. His cock twitched hotly in his pants at the thought of it.

With a lift in his step, James continued down the

stairs and turned the corner—and almost bumped right into Laina. Her eyes went wide when she saw him, and then she took a quick step backward. She was standing between Kiki and another woman who looked vaguely familiar.

"Ladies! How was the spa?" James asked with his eyes directly on Laina. Despite planning and building the flagship Revive spa in Miami, he really had no idea what actually went on behind those mysterious doors, but whatever it was had made Laina more beautiful than ever. Her nails were polished in a soft pink, her hair was still damp from a shower, and her skin, free of makeup, was glowing as if she were lit from within. She was wearing white terry-cloth shorts that showed off her legs, and a tank top that revealed a narrow slice of her flat tummy. She looked good enough to eat…but that didn't explain the urge James felt to possess her with his entire being.

"Um, it was good," Laina said, but her gaze was on his chest. He tried to catch her eye, but she turned to look at Kiki. "Right, Kiki?"

"Right. You remember Nicola?" she asked him, gesturing to the third woman. As he greeted her, he did remember; he'd met her once when visiting Kiki, and had even asked her out for a drink, which she'd declined. But that was ancient history. It couldn't possibly be the reason Laina was acting strangely with him right now.

He clapped his hands. "Well, I hate to break up your party, but Laina and I—"

"Actually, Kiki needs my help this afternoon," Laina cut in.

His smile faded as he flicked his eyes to his cousin for confirmation.

"*Actually*, I don't," Kiki said firmly.

"Not true," Laina responded. "The wedding is in two days. I'm sure there are a million things to do. And that's what I came here for, after all." Her eyes held a touch of defiance. What the hell was going on?

"Laina, could I speak to you for a moment?" he asked. She looked like she was about to refuse when the other two women stepped away. He put a finger under her chin and forced her face up to his. "What's wrong?"

"Nothing. I came here to be Kiki's bridesmaid, and I got distracted."

His stomach rolled over sickly. "Distracted? Is that what you call the last few days?"

Laina turned her face away stubbornly, forcing him to drop his hand. "I realized I need to be a better friend, that's all."

"That's not what Kiki seems to think."

"She's just being nice. She knows I like you, so she's trying to play cupid."

"And that's a bad thing because…?"

"Because it's not going to work." Laina shook

her head. "Look, James. I've had an amazing time with you, okay? But I'm not going to fool myself. I know you're not a one-woman kind of man. Not that I'm necessarily looking for a commitment, but this? I—I just really don't know how to do *this*." She dropped her arms to her sides, suddenly reminding him of a little girl who'd decided to drop out of the school play because she didn't think she could act. Her authenticity was disarming. James was used to head games—women playing hard to get, trying to make him jealous, showing up for sex at unusual times or places to try to make themselves memorable. None of it worked with him. "I thought I'd be okay with just…sex," Laina continued in a lowered voice. God, even the word made her blush; how could someone so innocent tip his desire off the Richter scale the way she did? But of course that was all part of it—her total oblivion to the power she held in her hands, her body, her mind. "But I'm not."

James's head was spinning. He and Laina had charged past the casual hookup line the moment they'd entwined their hands in front of Laina's beloved crumbling house. Maybe even before that, if he were honest with himself—that first night on the boat, her body had met with his in a way he'd never come close to experiencing with another woman. Laina deserved a hell of a lot more than a relationship that was defined purely by sexual encounters—she deserved a man who would worship the ground she walked on. But until just two days ago, James hadn't even considered a lifestyle any different from what he had. And no matter how addicted he'd already become to her body, he would not break her heart with a promise he wasn't 100 percent sure he could deliver on.

"Laina, I…" He raked a hand through his hair, wondering what to say. He needed time to think, that was all, get his head wrapped around the possibility of leaving behind something he never dreamed he wouldn't want. Of devoting himself completely to her—because if he was going to do this, that was how it would have to be. She was too special to think about any other way.

Laina's deep eyes finally met his. "I know," she said softly. "And I don't want you to feel bad about it. I mean, we never expected this, right?"

James's chin dropped. She knew exactly what was going through his head, and that only made him feel worse. She cupped his jaw with a hand. "I want you to know that I had the time of my life with you, and I don't have a single hard feeling. You taught me things…" She shook her head. "The most amazing things ever. I'll never forget you," she concluded.

James's chest tightened painfully. The thought of never touching her again, of her taking what she'd learned from him to use with another man—it was

beyond torturous. "Laina, this is just—I'm so sorry."
He shook his head. "This is all new to me, and I
can't… I mean I would never want to play with
your heart. You deserve so much—*everything*—"

She pressed a finger to his lips. "Don't. Your
honesty with yourself is just as important as your
honesty with me." Moving closer to him, she took
her finger away and replaced it with her lips for a
soft, but much too brief, kiss. Then she turned away.

The tightness in James's chest expanded to his
belly. Jesus Christ, was he going to cry? Even as
his feet stayed rooted to the spot, his mind lunged
after her. But he didn't dare act. Not yet, anyway—
not until he was absolutely sure.

But then he remembered something. "Laina."

She turned back to him with a question on her
face.

"What about your ex? Do you want to keep it
up? I could be a total gentleman."

Laina gave him an ironic smile. "You know, it's
funny—I'd completely forgotten about him until
you brought him up. It's hard to believe he could
have been so important to me once. But I always
wondered, you know?"

"Wondered what?"

"Why I never dreamed about him. Isn't that
weird? That I dreamed about you last night, but I
never once dreamed about the person I was supposed to marry?"

James stared at her as the memory took shape in his head: the dream he'd had about her on the night he'd arrived here. Laina give him one last sad smile and walked across the lobby back to her friends.

CHAPTER TEN

I DEFINITELY DID the right thing. Definitely.

Laina repeated this in her head over and over again as she lay in bed staring at her iPad screen. It had been six hours since she'd walked away from James in the lobby of The Palms, and she'd been able to think of nothing else. Memories of their bodies moving together, of the glimpses she'd gotten into the man she'd come to care about so quickly tortured her. In her mind she'd had distractions planned for this evening—a swim in the ocean, a try-on of the bridesmaid dress Kiki had handed over to her today, dinner at Pablo's with some of the other wedding guests—but she wasn't able to do anything except sit here with her heart heavy in her chest. She'd spent the past hour searching *Ellison Enterprises* on her iPad in the perverse hope that her decision today would be backed up by what she found. And it had been.

Like most developers, James prioritized progress over sustainability. The few news stories she'd

found about his company were seemingly insignificant and in line with issues almost every developer faced—small areas of vegetation bulldozed,
old-growth trees felled to clear a lot, a sewage
line that had accidentally leaked into the ocean,
a condo development built on a floodplain that
had displaced grassland birds. Each of the stories
came with a mollifying statement from the company: the stray cats displaced from the vegetation
had found homes; the trees, removed in the name
of safety, would be replanted; the sewage line had
been capped immediately upon discovery; the
grassland birds were plentiful and nonendangered.

It was exactly the type of thinking Laina hated:
that repairing and replacing was just as good as
leaving well enough alone. She'd also perused photos and public reports on James's developments,
mostly luxury hotels, spas and condominiums. And
while she couldn't help admiring their designs—
many of them took cues from nature for a green-
looking effect—it was obvious to her that they
made almost no effort to reduce their carbon foot-
prints. Again, this wasn't a big surprise, but Laina
knew that everyone had the power to make a difference, and that someone in an industry like James's
had an even greater opportunity to do so. Over her
years of designing LEED homes, she took reassurance that she'd helped reduce energy and water
usage as well as greenhouse gas effects, and saved

her clients countless long-term dollars. It could be
done, but not without a dedicated desire to do the
right thing—which James clearly didn't have. No
matter what power he held over her body, no matter how much she enjoyed his company out of bed,
he was just like all the others. Her decision to walk
away was in line with both her good sense and her
moral compass. So why didn't she feel any better?

Because the decision wasn't in line with her
heart.

A thick feeling clawed at Laina's throat. She
swallowed hard, determined not to give in to the
tears that had been threatening all day. To find
someone like James again, someone who could
shake her world like an earthquake—it was rare,
maybe even once in a lifetime. And as ridiculous
as it might seem to become attached to someone
after only three days, Liana knew that what they'd
had was magical.

She stood up, opened the door to her cottage
and stepped outside. She had her bikini bottoms
on under her shorts; maybe a swim would help to
clear her head. But as she rounded the corner to
the pool area, her breath caught in her throat. She'd
been so distracted by everything that was happening with James that she'd barely paid attention to
the ongoing wedding preparations. Now, with the
wedding only a day and a half away, the grounds
looked absolutely stunning. In the dusk, two staff

members were still working to string the last of the lights around the pool. Then one of them threw a switch and the entire area lit up.

The decor was luxurious elegance with a nod to rock and roll. Beyond the expansive pool deck, Laina could see the lawn dotted with rectangular white tables surrounded by silver chairs. A pergola that was draped in greenery and hung with a variety of crystal chandeliers had been built over each table. Tall candleholders topped with pink peony posies acted as centerpieces. Beyond the dining area was a large stage for the band backdropped with black velvet, flanked on each side by a white tent draped in pink tulle and white fairy lights. The massive poolside archway had been covered in pink and white flowers, untamed strands of greenery and crystal teardrops. Each silver chair set before the archway was wrapped with a black tulle sash. And the entire pool had been floated with clear balls filled with flower petals and fairy lights.

It was beautiful to behold, but it also shook something loose in Laina. She *did* want the happily-ever-after. Just because she'd chosen poorly once didn't necessarily mean she would again. She wanted this for herself someday, and James Ellison obviously didn't. She would not be one of those women who hung on to a noncommittal man with hope and a prayer, managing to fool herself into believing he'd change his mind one day while she watched the years tick by.

Her phone dinged with an incoming text, causing her heart to skip a beat. Damn it—she hated herself for wanting it to be him. She reached into her shorts pocket and pulled out her phone. Mom: Is the place still standing? How are you? Send me photos of the wedding and tell Kiki we wish we could be there. And call me.

Laina sighed. Small talk. Surface questions. Why did her parents have to be so distant from everything that mattered to her? Not that she expected deep conversions via texting, but was it too much to ask for at *some* point in her life? What she wished for more than anything was something real from her parents—for them to show an interest in what she did, for example. But she knew that was a pointless dream, because Laina's career choice had actually coincided with the moment she knew she had to separate herself from her family.

She'd just arrived on Moretta for a summer vacation after her second year of university, and she wanted to show her father a set of blueprints she'd created for the final project of her design course. She was excited about the project, which she'd scored an exceptionally high mark on, and was planning to announce to him that she was pursuing a career as a LEED certified architect. Laina found her father in his office, but she'd barely un-

TARYN BELLE   129

rolled the blueprints on his desk when he dismissed
her for an incoming call from his investment manager. She left with her papers gripped to her chest,
trying to fight back tears, and that was when she
knew: she may have a family in theory, but she was
on her own. That was the moment she decided to
stop staying at the family estate.

No—a conversation with her mother was not
what Laina needed at the end of a day like this.
Without responding to the text, she tucked her
phone back into her pocket.

"...she bent over right in front of me! I looked
down and saw that her shoelace wasn't even un-
tied, and that's when I knew I was taking her to
the Caribbean with me."

Across the table, James watched as Ward snaked
his arm around his date's neck and dropped his
hand to her breast. She gave him a drunken smile.
"Best second date *ever*!" she said, slurring her
words, then reached for her cocktail.

James turned his head away, searching for the
waiter. Pablo's was packed, as it was nearly every
night of the week, and as he scanned the room, he
picked out several celebrities seated nearby. Wondering how they'd react to his planned resort, he
suddenly felt a flicker of guilt. Celebrities were
people with problems just like everyone else in the
world, but they had the added challenge of often liv-

ing them out in the public eye. Moretta was one of the few places they could get away from all of that, and in a sense James would be taking that away from them with an influx of more tourists. But still, it didn't seem fair that any place in the world should be available only to the superwealthy—so what was the right thing to do?

More important, James thought, *who fucking cares?*

James was in a foul mood to end all foul moods. Ever since Laina had walked away from him, his body had been assaulted with a crawling sensation that made him want to rip right out of his skin. All that filled his head was *her*—the soft feel of her hair, her deep eyes on his, her sweet moans of desire for him in his ear. Coming out for dinner tonight to try to distract himself had been a mistake, and as luck would have it, he'd landed right across the table from the most obnoxious prick in the room.

"The thing I love most about Roxy is she knows better than to ask me, 'What does this mean?'" Ward went on in a simpering imitation of what James guessed was, to Ward, a typical female. "She just goes with it. Don't you, baby?" He yanked her toward him and kissed her with his tongue in full view.

Suppressing a shudder, James looked down the table at Kiki and Dev. The contrast between the two couples was glaring. While Kiki was engaged in an animated conversation with a guest, Dev was watching her face as if there were no one else in the room. James knew exactly what Dev had been like before he met Kiki—womanizing and noncommittal, but he was like another man now. A happier man. A better man.

Giving up on the waiter, James took out his wallet and laid two fifties near his plate. Ward was yammering on about his date's wealthy family now. To think that this douchebag had once had Laina in his bed—had lived with her, even, and hadn't even known the treasure he had—made him sick.

But was James really so different?

The thought was gross enough to propel him out of his seat and through the door into the evening air. Palm trees loomed against a yellow sky, and when he turned toward the ocean, he could see another fiery sunset painted over the water. A small group of wedding guests was gathered outside, talking and laughing, but James walked swiftly past them toward the beach. He felt like royal shit. He'd let Laina go, let her walk right out of his life, and why? Because he'd been afraid. Because with his casual hookups and zero expectations policy, he wasn't all that different from her ex. And now he'd messed up with the best woman he'd ever had.

His phone dinged in his back pocket and his pulse quickened; could it be her?

Jennifer Liu: I was expecting a report by now. Anything you're not telling me?

James puffed his cheeks out, releasing a long sigh. Until this very moment, he'd forgotten that he'd meant to talk to Laina about the project today. But right now that seemed like about the least important thing he could think of.

Ignoring Jennifer's text, he pulled up Laina's number and typed her a message. I messed up. I need to see you.

He pressed the phone to his chin, daring himself to hit the send button. If she took him back, what then? Did it mean their affair would extend beyond this week and this island? If so, he had better be good and sure this was what he wanted—because if it wasn't, he'd end up hurting her. And he'd rather dig his own heart out with a dull stick than do that.

Don't be hasty. Give yourself some time to think.

Shoving his phone into his pocket, James strode back to his empty hotel room and his infuriating self-reflections.

CHAPTER ELEVEN

"LAINA."

"James. Wow. Hi."

As they stared at each other across the sand, Laina tried to dislodge the hot bud of desire that bloomed in her clit. God, but she couldn't wait for this week to be over, because seeing him without being able to touch him was pure agony. She'd come to the beach this morning specifically to avoid him, but she hadn't even gotten as far as the water when she'd heard him call her name. And now she was staring down at him, sitting on a lounge chair with his iPad in his hands and his red-hot body on full torturous display. She tried to keep her eyes from roving over his muscular arms, the abs that had clenched with each thrust into her, that ruinous bulge in his swimming trunks—

Stop it already. It's over.

James got to his feet. "I was hoping to run into you," he said.

"Were you? It's kind of early for the beach, but

I like to get here before it's too hot," Laina bab-
bled over the pounding of her heart. "I was actually going to go for a swim in my pool, but it's full
of flowers." She clamped her mouth shut. God, she
really wasn't any good at this. Not only was she
completely undone by the sight of this man, she'd
also just revealed that she was attached to the wedding location. Not that it mattered now—they were
over, and whether he knew her family was worth a
fortune or not really made no difference.

But James didn't seem to have caught her slipup.
"I missed you at dinner last night. And at breakfast
this morning."

Laina licked her lips. Her mouth was cotton dry.
"I guess I wasn't hungry."

"Neither was I."

"No?" She cringed; couldn't she think of *anything* intelligent to say? She crossed her arms over
her chest, suddenly aware of her near-nakedness.
Did he still want her? And so what if he did? It
wasn't like she could act on it anymore, even if she
could feel that aching buzz in her body again just
from standing near him. "So what did you want?"

"Want?"

"You said you were hoping to run into me," she
reminded him, shifting her weight. God, she was
a mess—she wanted to run away from him, she
wanted to clamp his hand to her pussy and beg

him to lock her up in his room. No commitment after that, just three more days of hot, blissful sex.

Which would ruin her even worse than she already was.

"Oh, yeah." He took a step closer to her. "I wanted to ask you something."

"So did I."

"Really?" His face lit up a bit. "Okay, you first."

She drew herself up. "Do you ever lose sleep over your developments?"

He blinked at her. "My developments?"

"Yeah. I took a look at them, and I wasn't impressed."

"You weren't?" He tilted his head at her. "But I get my designers to take their cues from nature. I'd think that would appeal to you. A lot of the buildings practically blend in with their—"

"Yes, I noticed that. Rather ironic, because you do almost nothing to minimize your environmental impact. I couldn't leave the island without asking you to at least consider that. I'd be happy to give you the name of some green building consultants in Miami," she concluded in a steady voice. Despite her strong beliefs, voicing her convictions wasn't something that came naturally to her.

James still looked taken aback. "I—okay."

"Okay you'll consider it, or okay you'll call them?"

"Okay I'll call them." He shook his head. "Laina,

look. It's not like I haven't been trying. My investors like to keep their costs down, and if I don't make them happy, I don't get the contract."

She laughed dryly. "Of course they do. But short-term savings don't always translate into long-term ones. You can actually save a lot of money in the long run by building green. And plus," she pointed out, "you're the boss. You say it's going to be done a certain way, and they can take it or leave it. I know your company's net worth. Even if you never did another development in your lifetime, you'd be fine."

"Believe it or not, it's not about the money for me."

She cocked her head at him. "Bullshit."

He grinned. "Okay, maybe it is a little. But building is my life. Ever since—" He stopped himself.

Laina waited, refusing to press him. After coming this far, she wasn't going to buy into whatever excuse he might offer—even if it was a tragic one, which she sensed coming.

"Since my mother died," he said with a sigh. "When I was little, all I wanted to do was play with my Legos. My mother used to bring bags of it home from garage sales, and I had this entire city sprawled over my bedroom floor. I remember she read me this book about a castle in the sky—she loved that book. I used to tell her that I was going to build her a real one someday. And then she died, and… I guess I'm still here, trying to build it."

Laina dropped her chin. His story was as good as any film tearjerker, but it was real. She couldn't imagine what it must have been like for him, losing his only parent when he'd just entered adulthood. And the image of him as a little boy, trying to make his mother's dream come true—it was heartbreaking.

But she wasn't going to be sucked in. "I'm really sorry," she said finally.

"It's no excuse," James replied with a shake of his head. His eyes met hers, and he looked like he was going to say something more when he suddenly glanced over her shoulder and groaned. She followed his gaze and saw several wedding guests heading their way, including Ward and his insipid date.

"Quick, ground, swallow us up," James joked, looking down at his feet.

Laina laughed. And then, before she could think too much about what she was doing, she gestured toward the palm trees. "Come with me."

James stared at the small stretch of beach. "You're telling me no one knows about this?" he asked incredulously.

Laina shrugged. "I'm sure some of the locals do. But it's hard to get to, so no one ever comes here."

"Then how did you discover it?"

"I was a curious kid, and I loved nature. While my family was picnicking on caviar, I used to go exploring. One day I discovered this cave and went inside, but it was actually a tunnel. Who knew this would be at the other end?" She lifted her arms to the scene before them: a perfect expanse of white sand surrounded by rocky cliffs. Waves lapped at the shore while a tortoise made its way across the sand. In the quiet, they could hear the music from Pablo's mingled with the calling of gulls.

"You really know this island, don't you?" James said.

They dropped onto the sand. James kept his body parallel to Laina's, gazing out at the ocean to keep his eyes off her. Her near-nakedness had nearly undone him when he'd first seen her, resulting in an embarrassing response that he'd had to hide behind his iPad. It was torturous. Though Laina had put on her cover-up for the short walk here, its mesh fabric was useless at hiding what was beneath it. But if he stood a chance at winning her back, he needed to do this right. No touching. No sex. Just straight-up honesty that was about to lay him bare, which he had zero experience with.

He was terrified.

"So, what was your question for me?" Laina asked, letting a handful of sand sift through her fingers.

"That day at the old house. You never told me what your broken dreams were."

Laina gave him a sideways glance. "That's it? Nothing more interesting than that?"

"No," he answered firmly, and it was true. At around 2:00 a.m. last night, after waking from yet another agonizing dream of her, he'd made his decision: he would not involve her in his development. He would find another way to get what he needed. He had no idea how, and it could quite possibly mean the death of the project. But he'd felt oddly at peace with that this morning, and then his decision had been confirmed by the conversation they'd had on the beach: she would never help him with something like this. He still had to break the news to Jennifer, who would surely make his life a living hell over it, but he could deal with that. In fact, he felt like he could deal with anything as long as he had Laina by his side.

But first he had to win her back.

Laina resumed sifting sand. "My broken dreams. Hmm." She shrugged. "Nothing important, really."

"I keep hearing that from you." When she didn't respond, James went on. "Laina, do you not see how incredible you are? Why do you dismiss yourself like that?"

The last of the sand drained from her fingers, and she stared out at the ocean. "Rich kids aren't allowed to have broken dreams—I learned that early

on. Money is supposed to be able to buy us anything we could possibly want, so we better not expect any sympathy from the world if it doesn't. The
problem is that my dreams didn't have anything to
do with things." She sighed. "What I wanted most
of all was a close family. We were once—at least I
think we were—but it all changed. I don't even exactly know when. All I know is that one day when
I was about fifteen, I realized that I was spending
more time at that broken-down house than at my
own. I was different from my parents and brothers.
It's a strange kind of loneliness, to have this family that looks so perfect to everyone else but feels
so distant from me."

"You're speaking in the present tense."

"Yes. It hasn't changed much. When I was
twenty, I did something—something they didn't
agree with. At the same time, I stopped coming to
our home here. The two events drove a wedge between us, and it's never been the same since."

"Have you tried to make things better with
them?"

"Not really. It's not that I don't love them or
know how lucky I was to grow up the way I did.
And it's not like we don't have a relationship—we
do, on the surface. It's just that to me, embracing
them means going back to everything they have and
represent." She grinned. "Do you know what I did
when I was sixteen? Got a summer job at Wendy's.

It paid less than half of the allowance that landed in my account each month for doing exactly nothing. That was the first year I refused to spend the summer in Moretta. I told them to go without me, that I was old enough to look after myself. At that point my mother tried to make a deal with me—that if I got a 'more respectable' job at their golf club, she'd let me stay home for the summer. We got into a huge fight—I told her that if I didn't do it on my own, it didn't count. She used to get so exasperated with me."

James chuckled. "It sounds to me like you were just fiercely independent. I love that in a woman."

To his shock, Laina gave him a scathing look. "Do you? Well, then, it's a good thing there are a lot of us out there." She jumped up, ripped off her cover-up and headed for the water. With his mouth gaping, James watched her dive in, and then he went after her. The water closed over his body, warm as a tepid bathtub.

"What did I say?" he asked as he caught up to her with powerful strokes.

She swam away from him, shouting over her shoulder, "Don't worry, it's my bad. I was about to get sucked in again."

"I am *not* trying to suck you in—"

"Of course you are!" she sputtered furiously, standing up in the waist-deep water. "Someone like you doesn't change his ways overnight! Why not try your luck for one more roll in the hay before we go home? Don't shower me with false flattery—it won't work!"

He shook his head, walking toward her slowly. How had this gone so wrong so quickly? "False flattery? That is not what this is about! Jesus, I hardly slept last night—"

"Then you're obviously not thinking straight!"

"Laina—" He reached for her arm.

She yanked it out of his grip and turned on him, wet hair whipping across her face. "You need to stay away from me! Do you know how long it took me to get here after Ward? He just *threw me away*, and you know what? I thought I deserved it! My life has been easy, so I thought he was my payback! And now I almost did it again—let myself fall for someone who only has a limited time use for me! So just leave me the hell alone!"

"But I can't leave you alone!" James slapped his hands on the water in frustration, making it splash up between them. "You've changed *everything* for me! I started thinking about my life last night, and all I could think of was how it'll never be the same now that I've been with you. And I—I don't *want* to go back to being the person I was before you!" He stopped, searching his brain for the right words to continue. Laina was looking at him with an un-readable expression, water from her hair dripping down her face. She looked more beautiful than he'd ever seen her, raw and perfect. "Look, I admit it. This was not in my plans—meeting you, reexamining my life. And I don't just mean the way I was handling my personal life—I mean everything. I feel like...like I've been in this numb place. Work, make money, sleep with whoever I want, and don't feel a thing. Don't question the ethics of what I do because I might not like the answer, and that would mean I need to change things. My whole childhood was about change—new apartment, new school, my mother's new jobs. And then she went away, the only constant in my life. And ever since, I just keep doing what's working because it's safe." He shook his head. How was it that he'd psychoanalyzed his entire life in just one minute? Because he was finally seeing things clearly—thanks to this woman he was indescribably crazy about. "My mother died seventeen years ago," he continued, his voice cracking with emotion. "That's seventeen years of being numb. And then—and then you come along, a woman with the face of an angel and the body of a thousand wet dreams. And I'm only just getting to know what's in your mind and heart, but I want all of it, Laina. I want all of it, because you make me feel so *alive*. I may not have experience with relationships, but I want to try. And the only person on earth I want to try with is you."

James was breathing hard by the time he finished, and Laina was still staring at him. He inhaled deeply and closed his eyes, unwilling to watch the rejection come over her face. *I tried. I did my best*, he thought.

"I want you too, James," he heard her say. Warmth bloomed in his belly. He opened his eyes to see her closing the gap between them. She looked up into his face. "I keep telling myself how dangerous you are, but it doesn't make any difference. It's like—it's like the only thing in the world I want is to belong to you. The way you make me feel, I couldn't even imagine it a week ago. It's like I was dead inside before you. The way we are together… I don't know how to live without it now. And it's not just the sex, it's *all of you*. You're like a dream come true."

James felt his chest expand almost painfully. Laina's eyes were shiny with emotion as he brought his hands up to push her wet hair back from her face. "I'm not a dream, Laina. I'm realer than real, and I want you so much."

Her hands slid around his waist. James looked into her face, absorbing every beautiful detail, and then his lips found hers. She opened her mouth immediately, and he lost himself in the sweet slide of her tongue against his. It was better than their first kiss, because it held the secrets of everything they already felt for each other. Connection. Need. Endless possibility and impossibly hot longing. He bit her lips, sucked them, kissed them some more.

Laina pulled him tighter to her, hard enough to make James's lungs squeeze. It wasn't nearly close enough. He wanted to pull her into him, hold her inside him, keep her safe, make her his and his alone. Make her feel the same yearning that was driving him forward like a derailed freight train.

Between their bodies, his cock was already hard. "Feel that," he whispered into her mouth, grabbing her hand and wrapping it around him. "It's all yours. And this pussy is *mine*." He found her with one hand, clamping it over her bikini bottom. She rolled her hips forward, bucking into the heel of his hand. He pulled the tie at the back of her top and yanked it over her head. Then he attacked her erect nipple with a guttural sound, catching her around the waist as she threw herself backward. His cock was straining painfully at the netting inside his trunks, so he ripped them down to free himself, watching Laina's ravenous eyes take him in.

"James," she breathed, grinding her pelvis into his erection. "Oh, God, James—touch me. *Please.*"

He moved her bottoms aside and found her wetness, sinking his fingers in as far they would go. Pressing them forward, he watched her face collapse with lust as he hit that sweet spot inside her.

"More," she panted. "Don't stop."

James had no intention of stopping. He kept his thumb circling her clit while he moved his fingers, massaging the inside of her until she turned liquid in his arms. The water lapped around her waist, dancing with her movements. She was gasping for breath now, letting words out in a nonsensical string. Listening to them was looking into a window to her deepest desires. *Harder. Faster. Need. Want. Never stop. Pleasepleaseplease—*

He watched her, fully consumed by the intensely pleasurable world he was creating for her. Head thrown back, slender neck exposed, wet strands of hair across lips that were still swollen from their passionate kisses. At his mercy. It was the hottest, sexiest, most beautiful thing he'd ever seen.

She came on his hand with a cry he was sure could be heard on the next island. An endless breath whooshing out of her, every muscle in her entire body straining toward her pleasure, her pussy contracting on his fingers over and over again. His arousal was at a fever pitch, that place he'd only ever been to with her where he felt like he would kill for release. His cock at maximum erectness, his balls so tight they were crawling back into his body, visible drops of his desire already glistening at his tip. Aching to be lost in her slippery heat. "I have to get inside you," he groaned.

"Yes, you do. *Right now*," Laina said. With her orgasm behind her she looked flushed, practically delirious, but ready for so much more.

The twenty steps it would take to lie her down on the sand was like a trek across the desert, so James lifted her onto his hips instead. "Hang on to me," he said. Laina's arms went around his neck as he shoved her bottoms aside again. He got his cock into position and was about to enter her with a gratifying thrust when he stopped. *"Noooo!"* he roared.

Laina drew back to look at him in shock, still breathing hard. "What?"

"No condom."

Laina groaned as if she were in physical pain. "Oh my God. I completely forgot."

"Me too. And that right there is what you do to me," he said, letting her slide back down to the ground. Reality invaded the perfect erotic bubble that had contained them, assailing James's senses with bright sunlight, crashing waves and circling gulls.

"This is literally the worst thing that's ever happened to me," Laina said. "We have to get to your room."

"In this state?" He looked down at himself. "There's no way in hell."

"It's not all bad," she crooned, stroking him slowly. "Just think how good it'll feel when you finally come. In fact, the thought of that is making me even wetter right now."

He groaned painfully. "You're not helping matters."

"How about if I suck you off?"

His cock surged upward. Those dirty words coming from that sweet mouth—he couldn't get enough of it. "That'll do in a pinch," he joked. "But, Laina…" He pushed into her hand, desperately seeking pressure. Sure, he was brain-meltingly horny from interrupted desire, but it was more than that, something James couldn't even fully describe. His intense need to be inside her, to be one with her, to meld his body with the only woman he wanted to join with in that sacred way, was driving him as much as anything. "I've been dying for you for two days now, and I am going to fuck you if it's the last thing I do." He grinned. "Come on. You can block me while we make a run for my hotel room."

She licked her lips. "We could. Or…"

"Or?"

"Or we could not."

He shook his head. "I don't follow."

"I mean I'm clean. How about you?"

A fresh wave of lust fired through his body. What she was suggesting… "Totally. I've never not used a condom in my life."

She tilted her head at him. "Wow," she said slowly. "So you mean you've never actually felt…"

He shook his head. "Never."

"Holy shit."

"I know. Poor me, right?"

Still stroking him, Laina looked into his eyes and cupped his jaw with her other hand. "Then I'm going to be your first," she said softly. "Right now."

James's cock jerked in her hand. It was too

amazing to believe. This was a missing aspect of
sex he'd resigned himself to long ago, a trade-off
that came with choosing hookups over relationships. But that was before Laina. Before the woman
who'd completely turned his life upside down inside
a week. And now he was going to know what she
really felt like, an experience that would bond him
to her in a way he'd never expected to be bonded
to anyone. And he was *so* ready for it. "I'm in your
hands," he said. *"Show me."*

Propping herself up on her elbows, Laina slowly
spread her legs in the sand. James, who was kneel-
ing between them with his cock in his hand, looked
like he was going to combust. Her breasts were already heaving as she imagined the ecstasy that was
about to wash over both of them. The idea that she
was going to introduce him to something new, his
first time with no barrier, feeling how much she
wanted him for real…she was so wet with anticipation she wanted to rub against him like a horny
teenager. She loved this feeling, so close to the edge
and filled with hot promise. And after the way he'd
already undone her in the water… God.

No matter what James said, he *was* a dream come
true. That she could have gone through her whole
life never knowing what this felt like…it was unbearable. The words he'd said to her had seared into
her soul, made her see the vulnerability beneath his

strength, and she wanted to take that part of him and lock it away for safekeeping in her heart.

But right now, she needed to blow his mind.

She batted his hand away from his erection. It stood straight up, too hard to fall forward even an inch. "You are not allowed to touch yourself," she said. "This is all about feeling *me*." She spread her legs wider, watching his eyes on her. Seeing his pupils dilate with heated need. She leaned back. "I thought you might want to see how wet I am first."

His tongue darted out. "You're killing me. Please, Laina—"

"Please?" She brought a hand to her pussy. "How much do you want this?"

"More than I've ever wanted anything. I'd kill to fuck you right now."

Another band of heat seized her pelvis. This felt too good to be real. Never in a million years did Laina think she'd be a girl who got off on talking dirty, but that was James Ellison for her—he'd turned her into a freaking sex goddess. And she was going to keep the torture up for all it was worth. "Do you have any idea how amazing you feel inside me?" she asked him, trailing a fingertip from her pussy up to her mouth.

"I think so," he said in an unsteady voice. He was breathing hard, coiled to strike, a fully cocked trigger ready to blow.

And completely at her mercy.

"Tell me and I'll let you touch me."

"Rock-hard. Long and thick and smooth. Every thrust feels like heaven."

"That's right. And if you're going to feel my wet pussy, you're going to describe every little thing to me. Now get ready."

"Thank Christ," James said thickly, lowering himself on top of her. She raised her knees and grasped his cock, then teased his head at her opening. "Laina, *fuck*—" He slammed into her with a guttural sound. Anchored deep inside her, his eyes fluttered shut and then opened again. Then he started to move, building their mutual heat at breakneck speed. She pushed her hands into his soft hair, met him thrust for thrust, watched his face contort with need for her.

It was paradise.

"How does it feel?" she demanded.

There was already sweat collecting on his brow from his fevered restraint. "Like the first time," he gasped, fastening his green eyes on hers. "But so much better because it's you."

Paradise. Goose bumps danced across her skin. Her heart was slamming in her chest, driving her toward a point of no return so explosive it was almost frightening. "Tell me more. Tell me everything."

"So, *so* good," James panted as he drove into her. "Better than heaven. Wet—so slippery and wet. And so warm and tight. Jesus, Laina, I'm going to die if I don't come."

She was barely under control herself. The feeling of him filling her over and over again on the firm sand, making his thrusts even deeper…she was becoming completely undone. But his words were too arousing to let go of. "How long do you want to fuck me?"

"All day. All night. Forever." Sweat dripped off his brow onto her lip.

She darted her tongue out to taste its saltiness. "I'm not letting you come until you make me a promise."

"Anything." His voice was tortured, agonized, barely intelligible.

"That we'll do this again today."

"Yes. *Yes yes yes—*"

"Now come in me, James. I want to feel you explode. I want every drop of you inside my pussy."

Like a man possessed, completely unhinged, James rose on his hands. He drove into her once, twice, three times, pausing between each thrust before pulling out almost completely and driving into her again. It was brutal, almost violent, and the most incredible thing she'd ever felt. Her climax built to the point of no return. Just before she fell over the edge, she heard James cry out her name as he emptied into her with all the force of their combined passion.

CHAPTER TWELVE

JAMES WAS DREAMING.

He was standing at the doorway of the smoothie stand he'd built to try to save his mother, looking up into a clear blue sky. There was a hill ahead of him, and on the hill was the castle he'd built for her. Her castle in the sky. As he looked at it, tight grief filled his lungs. *Where is she?* he thought in panic. *Where is she?*

She appeared beside him, looking like she did the last time he'd seen her: wasted in her hospital bed, hooked up to tubes whose purpose he didn't even want to try to understand. But she was standing, and she was smiling.

James pointed. *Look. I built it for you.*

His mother clapped her hands like a delighted child. *It's perfect. I knew you'd do it.*

He put his arm around her, but his grief didn't subside. It didn't make sense. He'd kept his promise, made her happy. But the feeling stayed firmly lodged in his throat, even when he clawed at it like he was choking.

You didn't need to save me. You were everything I ever needed, his mother said wordlessly. *You built it for her.*

James looked. There was Laina, sitting cross-legged on the lawn of the castle like a little girl. A light glowed around her as if she was otherworldly. His heart swelled as a feeling of peace washed over him. His belly fluttered with a thousand butterflies, the warmest, lightest feeling he'd ever known.

Go to her. Go to her. Go to her...

James drowsed slowly to wakefulness, opening his eyes to the early-afternoon light slanting through his blinds. He was lying on his bed naked with the sheets tangled in his legs, and she was beside him. Laina. She was awake, turned toward him on her side with her hands tucked under her cheek like a prayer. That innocence. That angelic beauty. His chest opened as he looked at her. Wordlessly, he reached for her and pulled her close to him. He could feel her heartbeat next to his. She looked up from his chest and pushed his hair away from his face. He smiled down at her, tracing a finger over her lips, but suddenly her eyes flooded with tears.

No. "What is it?" he breathed.

She shook her head, tucking her hand under her chin again. "Nothing."

"Tell me," James said urgently. What was it?

God, after everything that had gone on today, if she was having second thoughts...it was unbearable. "You can tell me anything, okay?"

"Just...this," she said, hooking her finger around his. "What I've always wanted. What I never thought I'd have."

Relief flooded through him as he wiped a tear away with his thumb. "You have me," he said, his voice thick with emotion. "And I am so unbelievably lucky."

"I'm the lucky one. James..." A sob tore from her throat.

"What is it?"

"Just... I need you."

James felt a tight ball in his belly. He'd never seen anyone shed tears of happiness before, and he felt like the most honored man on earth to be in this moment with her. To be the reason for her joy. And that ball in his belly was happiness, blended with the excruciating possibility of what might never have been.

Laina rolled on top of him, straddling her legs over his hips while she lay flat against his chest. For once, his cock didn't go instantly hard, but it wasn't for lack of want. The intoxicating addiction of her had swept over him as powerfully as a tsunami after their time together on the beach. He'd come apart at the seams at the feel of her, and like a junkie desperate for his next fix, he'd been hard again within minutes. He'd laid her out on a boulder on the walk back to his hotel so he could feel her again. He'd brought both of them to climax when they were back in his bed. He'd fallen asleep still hard inside her, hardly daring to breathe for fear of breaking the dream. He was a man possessed and obsessed. He wanted her, he needed her, he craved her like a drug.

He brought his hands up into her hair and pulled down slowly, feeling it slip through his fingers. He pushed his palms over her cheeks to wipe her tears away. She closed her eyes and caught his fingers in her mouth, sucking them gently. She brought her hands over his, moving them down her neck, her breasts, her belly, and then up again. Something ignited in his body, something more precious than lust and more acute than need.

Love.

He knew it in that moment. He loved her. It was relief and terror to admit, but it was the most beautiful thing he'd ever known.

Despite the ravages of the day, his cock had hardened. Laina reared her hips up and slowly sank onto him, enveloping him completely. She stayed there with him buried deep inside her, her eyes luminous and her lips parted, rocking back and forth with gentle movements. He wanted to say something to her, but when he opened his mouth no words came out. They didn't have to. Everything they needed to say to each other was spoken through their bodies, and through the perfect clarity of that moment.

CHAPTER THIRTEEN

LAINA SLIPPED INTO her shoes and looked into the mirror, holding her hair off her neck as she turned from side to side. No bite marks. She'd found one on her breast when she'd been changing, and the sight of it had triggered an inhalation of breath so sharp she'd hardly been able to contain it.

It was perfection. She wished for more of them, along with the red marks James's stubble had left on her belly and chin. Scratched, marked, bitten—she loved it. It meant she carried him with her everywhere, on every part of her…especially her heart.

She sank onto her bed, her knees almost too weak to hold her upright. She was so exhausted she wasn't sure how she was going to get through this night, and it was an important one—the rehearsal dinner. She knew she hadn't been eating enough on the lovesick diet. And even though James had slept briefly today, Laina hadn't been able to. She'd lain awake watching him, just feeling the pulse that beat at her core over and over again. All for him.

Every part of her so exposed to him that it took her breath away. And when he'd opened his eyes, Laina had known: she loved him. With all of her heart and soul, with every part of her being, she was madly and deeply in love with him.

And yet she still hadn't told him the truth about herself.

She stood up again, planting her feet steadily to keep her undernourished, oversexed body from collapsing. With her hair and makeup carefully done, she didn't think anyone would notice her state. Her dress was turquoise silk with small fluttery sleeves and an asymmetrical hem that ran from midthigh to past her knee. She'd accessorized it with high black slides, long crystal drop earrings and a matching bracelet. She'd had visions of an old Hollywood hairstyle, but it had been all she could to aim a blow-dryer at her hair.

She glanced at her watch. Six o'clock, almost time to meet James. After he'd offered to pick her up for tonight's party, she'd sidestepped it by suggesting they meet for a drink at The Palms before dinner instead. She'd regretted it as soon as it was out of her mouth, because there was no good reason she shouldn't tell him the truth: that a decade ago she'd become Laina Rose, dropping the wealthy Reinhard surname to use her middle name as her last, and that the estate the wedding was taking place on belonged to her family. But old habits died hard, she supposed. Since she'd changed her name, she hadn't told any man her secret other than Ward, and the way that had ended had been enough to put her off men for good. Laina knew that his wandering ways had been more a result of her admission to him than her skill in bed. She was pretty sure it wasn't a coincidence that just a month after she'd told him she'd renounced her family's fortune, she'd found him in bed with someone else.

But to compare Ward to James wasn't even in the realm of sanity. She'd fallen for him completely, and even if they hadn't said the words yet, she knew it was in both of their hearts. James deserved her trust and she would give it to him, no matter how much the Reinhard name on her lips made her cringe.

Grabbing her sequined evening bag, Laina left her cottage and walked toward her golf cart. The air was warm on her skin—the perfect evening for the event, which was to be held in the estate's tents. In the distance, she could see an army of staff taking care of last-minute preparations.

Her phone dinged. James: Come up to my room when you get here.

She almost groaned aloud. Even if his intentions were pure, she knew it was impossible for them to be in a room together without getting naked, and she actually wasn't sure if she could handle another session today. More than anything, she wished she could just fall asleep in his arms right now, and sleep until the morning light. But that would happen later—she was sure of it.

When the knock sounded at his door, James took one final glance around his room. Everything was in place, and he couldn't wait to see Laina's face when she laid eyes on it.

On his way to the door, he caught a glimpse of himself in the mirror and stopped. He barely recognized the man that looked back at him. Sure, he'd dressed up for the occasion a bit, but it was his expression that had stopped him in his tracks. Just like the town fool, he couldn't wipe the goddamned smile off his face. He'd had no idea anything could feel this good. And even if he and Laina were too exhausted and sore to do anything tonight, he didn't care. He just wanted to hold her close to him, feeling her heart beat with his. For the first time in his entire life, James was inviting—no, *insisting*—a woman stay in his bed all night.

It was going to be magical.

He pulled the door open just enough to see her, blocking the room from her view. She smiled at him, so beautiful even when she was dead exhausted. "You look amazing," he said into her mouth as he kissed her.

"And you...holy shit." She hooked a hand into his waistband and gave it a little tug.

"You're killing me," James groaned.

"I'm already dead. Were you planning to invite me in?"

"Sure." James threw the door wide open.

Laina inhaled sharply as her eyes flew open. "Oh. My. *God!*"

He smiled as he watched her face. The entire room was filled with lavender roses. They spilled out of vases on the desk, the bedside tables, even on the floor.

She shook her head. "Where did you—"

"I had them brought in from Barbados. I called the flower store at three and they were here by five. Now that's service."

"No, it's insane. Do you know how rare these are?" She plucked a single rose from a fishbowl-shaped vase and sniffed it.

"Do you know what they symbolize?" James asked.

She shook her head. "I've always just loved them for the color."

He watched as she took in the rest of the room— the tray holding a bottle of Veuve and a silky lingerie set on the bed, the soft music in the background. "What—what is all this?" she asked, turning to him.

James circled his arms around her. He'd never felt more sure about anything...and this was only the beginning. "I want you to spend the night here with me. After the dinner. And the night after that, and the night after that and after that."

Laina's eyes reached into his. "That's four nights. We'll be back home by then."

He bumped his forehead to hers. "I know."

He heard her breath hitch. "James. Oh, my God."

"I don't ever want to be away from you," he whispered fiercely. That amazing feeling was welling up in him again, saturating his cells. He blinked as his eyes went shiny. "Whatever that means, however that looks. I know we live in different cities right now, but that doesn't matter. We'll work it out. I just want *you*—in my bed, by my side, in my life. Starting right now."

"I—this is the best day ever," Laina said. She looked as though she was going to burst, but instead she just kissed him breathlessly. And then her mouth opened slowly, almost like it was happening against her will. Her tongue reached for his, and then she sighed against his lips. "I can't believe I'm saying this, but…how long do we have until we have to leave?"

CHAPTER FOURTEEN

"...SO PERHAPS IT all began that Christmas, when I traded Dev my guitar for the video camera our parents had gotten me. Little did I know that I was in for two years of wearing earplugs to bed. Dev's room was right next to mine, and let me tell you, he did not have a natural talent for that instrument."

The crowd laughed appreciatively. Up at the podium, Dev's brother Alex was just finishing up his roast to the groom. Naturally, Kiki had played the wedding by her own rules, doing most of the speeches tonight "to get them out of the way" and inviting not just the wedding party, but all of the guests to the rehearsal dinner. Laina and James were seated at a table across from Kiki and Dev, who was shaking his head good-naturedly at his brother's jabs.

As Alex finished up his speech, Laina glanced around the room. It was breathtaking, with a variety of both white and black crystal chandeliers hung at different lengths throughout the tent. The soft lighting cast a flattering glow on the guests. The pale pink tablecloths had been set with white dinnerware and black glassware. Each round table featured a massive spray of pink peonies enmeshed with fine silver wire that sprung from the center of each bouquet like a cascading water fountain. If this was only the rehearsal dinner, she couldn't wait to see what was in store for the actual wedding tomorrow.

As Alex took his seat between Nicola and Laina, she watched Dev and Kiki kiss. Catching her glance at them, James squeezed her hand. Was it a silent message that he wanted the same for them someday, or was she reading too much into it? It didn't matter. There was plenty of time for that. All she knew for sure was that she was completely head over heels in love with him, and she couldn't wait to find the right moment to tell him.

She turned to watch James's profile as he chatted across the table with Kiki. She'd been so blown away by his rose-filled room—and what had come after—that telling him about her family had completely escaped her mind.

Or had it? She could have told him on the drive up here, but it had been so short that she hadn't wanted to start the conversation. And now she had to face the undeniable weirdness of the situation. Here she was, sitting in a tent on her family property as if she *hadn't* spent practically every summer and Christmas here from age two to twenty. She would tell him eventually—of *course* she would—but there was something very appealing about living in a bubble that excluded her family. It made her feel capable and independent, like she'd built the life she had without any help. Because deep down, she knew her family would always be a safety net for her. And going through life with a safety net meant that her struggles didn't really count.

"A match made in heaven, I'd say," Kiki stated.

Laina reeled herself back into the conversation. "What is?"

"You and James, of course."

Laina felt herself blushing. The embarrassment she'd once felt at succumbing to James's charms was gone, and for the first time it occurred to her that if everything worked out between them, Laina and Kiki would become part of the same family. She glanced at James, wondering if he'd had the same thought, but he had an odd expression on his face. Slightly sheepish. Her brows drew together.

"Sure," Kiki continued, toying with the stem of her wineglass. "You bring in the money, and Laina draws up the plans."

Laina shook her head in confusion. "Um. What are we talking about?"

Kiki blinked at her. "James's development."

Laina fastened her eyes on James, who was tapping his knuckles on the table distractedly. "What development?"

"Wait," Kiki said to James. "You mean you haven't told her?"

Laina was beginning to feel sick. James's elusiveness, that look on his face… "Told me *what*?"

Kiki fell silent, and then James cleared his throat. "I've been meaning to tell you. It's not like it's a secret or anything, but I know how you feel about this place, and rest assured, you've convinced me to be a lot more environmentally responsible—"

"And he will be," Kiki piped up. "James is a man of integrity. Always has been."

Laina's heart was thumping. "Okay. But what are you talking about?"

James tapped a finger on the table. "I'm planning to build a hotel here. A resort, actually. I've already received approval from the council."

"I see," Laina said. Though her first reaction was to reject any kind of commercialism here, she also knew that her island couldn't be protected from change forever. And if James was the developer, she could help him do it right. So that was what Kiki had been referring to—not them as a couple. She couldn't help a jab of disappointment. "Where will it go? Beachfront, I assume?"

"Actually, I want to take advantage of the views. The beach is such a short walk away no matter where you are on the island, and the resort will be less obtrusive in the hills."

The hills. She could hear blood rushing through her ears. "So…where then, exactly?"

"That's the crazy thing," James said. "Would you believe right here? I already have accepted offers to the properties north and south. The only holdout is this very estate."

Laina felt a prickly, sick heat sweep up her torso. It couldn't be—but of course it made perfect sense. He'd done his research before he'd met her and discovered who she was. Or maybe he hadn't—maybe he'd only figured it out that day they were riding when she'd let it slip. How thrilled he must have been at the convenience of it all—here he was, already fucking the woman whose family happened to own the estate he needed to buy. All he had to do was bring down her defenses by making her think he was falling for her, play like he didn't know about her attachment to the property, and then marvel at the coincidence of it all while he convinced her to get her parents to sell. Hadn't she known all along he was too good to be true? He was just like all the other men who'd chased after her for what they thought she had in her bank account. In fact, the only difference between he and Ward was that while Ward had taken nearly a year to convince her he cared for her, James had only taken four days.

"You're kidding, right?" she finally managed to say. Her head was swimming. Her voice sounded far away, like it was coming through a tunnel. Her eyes moved from James's pretend-stunned face to Kiki, who was looking at her with concern.

"Laina, what's wrong?" James asked as she pushed her chair away from the table. Just as she stood up, James's phone lit up with an incoming text. She glanced down at it.

Jennifer Liu: Are you avoiding me?

God—it was even worse than Laina had thought. She felt like she might pass out. She took a stumbling step backward as Kiki came rushing toward her. James was on his feet now, hands raised in defense as he shook his head. "Laina, please don't get the wrong idea! Jennifer is just—"

"Stay the hell away from me," she said in a quavering voice, and then she rushed out of the tent.

"Laina! Laina!"

She was gone. It was beyond belief, but she was nowhere to be found. He'd been only steps behind her out of the tent. Kiki had intercepted him for a moment, trying to get him to give Laina a little space, and when he'd looked past her again she'd disappeared into thin air.

"Goddamn it!" he roared up at the starry sky. What the hell had just happened? What had he said? He knew she might not be crazy about the idea of

the resort, but this? It was as if he'd told her he was planning to bulldoze the entire island to build a freaking parking lot.

Raking his hands through his hair, James paced back and forth on the lawn. Desperation clawed at his throat, but he pushed it away—he had to stay calm right now, think straight, work out his options. He could talk to Kiki to see if she had any insight, but that was a grossly unfair thing to do on the eve of her wedding. He could drive the golf cart down the hill, calling for Laina all the way down as if she would actually answer him. Or he could go back to his room and hope she came to her senses and got in touch with him.

His room.

Just the thought of it brought James's fists down on his thighs. All those flowers. The champagne. The night he had planned for them, the perfect moment he was going to tell her he was madly in love with her—*ruined*. Gone. And he had no idea why.

"Just give her some time."

James whirled around to see Kiki standing near the entrance to the tent. "Jesus, Kiki, are you *smoking*?"

She shrugged. "I quit the night before I got married to my first husband. I figure I'll change my luck for sure if I start up again the night before I marry my second one."

James shook his head. "I don't think you need any luck. Dev's wild about you."

She grinned as she bent down, knees sideways to accommodate her skintight black dress, and elegantly snuffed out the half-smoked cigarette on the grass. "Good thing. I've lost my taste for it. So you going to tell me what that was all about?"

James threw up his hands. "I wish I could. Honestly, I don't have a goddamned clue. All I said was that I was hoping to buy this estate. Everything was—*gahh*!" He let out a sound of frustration. "It was going so perfectly between us!"

"I know. I've never seen you like this with a woman, and she's crazy about you too. Whatever went wrong, I'm betting it'll be worked out with a little trust."

"Trust? Sorry, cuz, but you sound like a cheesy greeting card right now."

Kiki shrugged. "Those cards say what they do for a reason. We all carry our pasts with us into new relationships, and it's easy to go back to our go-to responses, to things that have gone wrong before."

"You should have been a psychologist."

"Nah, I'm not nearly empathetic enough."

"Good thing, because I don't have a clue what you just said. You want to try some specifics?"

"Not really."

James shoved his hands into his pockets. "The crazy thing is that I was going to ask her a favor.

Before I met her, I mean—I Googled her and saw that she was a LEED architect. I wanted to build on the cliff where the pelicans nest—the view there is the best on the island. The council vetoed it when I approached them last year, but I thought maybe with her influence here we could change their minds. She's a change maker, people listen to her. I thought if we could come up with a plan to relocate the birds, and I brought her in on the deal…" He shook his head. "It was stupid. Some lines in nature shouldn't be crossed, and I've always tried to blur them in my favor. I see that now, so I decided not to ask her. Screw the panoramic view and the extra millions in revenue—those pelicans are way more important."

"You should tell her."

"If she ever talks to me again, which doesn't seem too likely right now." He forced a smile. "But I'm keeping you from your special night. Go in there and have some fun, and I'll see you at your wedding tomorrow."

"Remember. Trust," Kiki said, and then she yanked her bandage-wrap dress down her thighs and went into the tent.

James waited for a minute, and then he tried one last time. *"Laina!"*

She could hear him calling for her. Let him.

Sitting on the sofa in her cottage with the lights out, Laina reached for another tissue. She had to stop bawling and get herself under control—she was going to look and feel like hell tomorrow if she didn't, and that was totally unfair to Kiki. She knew her friend; no matter what was happening in her life, she never stopped caring for her loved ones. Even ten minutes ago Kiki's main concern had been Laina, not her own party that she'd been forced to leave behind. Laina had made Kiki promise not to tell James about her connection to the estate—she would *not* give him the chance to put on a fake surprise face for her friend and deny he knew anything about it. And Laina wouldn't pay her friend back for her loyalty by ruining her wedding photos with puffy eyes and an expression of sheer misery. As Kiki was about to walk down the aisle, Laina didn't want the bride to ask under her breath if Laina was okay. She wanted Kiki's focus to be on no one but herself, because she deserved to have a perfect day more than anyone Laina knew.

But who was she fooling? This kind of heartbreak was way too powerful to control. Her body collapsed into itself, and she rolled onto her side in a sobbing heap. In truth, she wasn't sure what she was angrier about—James's deception or the text. Are you avoiding me? There was no excuse for it. Even if there was a perfectly good explanation for a woman sending him a text with an extremely personal ring to it, even if she was a former conquest that Laina couldn't fault him for, it showed her that he wasn't dealing with her. He was letting her hang. Like insurance, backup, plan B if things with Laina didn't pan out. It was disgusting.

If only, Laina thought regretfully. If only she hadn't fallen for James, hadn't slept with him, hadn't said yes to the blind date with him, hadn't gotten engaged to Ward and wanted to make him jealous in the first place. How far back could her regrets go? Further than she cared to think about. Back to the way she'd treated her parents, dismissing them along with their surname, carrying a chip on her shoulder because she'd wanted to be raised middle-class while the rest of the world wanted what she had.

She suddenly felt ashamed, and completely disassociated from her family's world. Her parents would never sell this place, would they? But what did she know? Considering the way she'd behaved over the past decade, it's not like she had the right to any say in the matter.

And she hadn't even bothered returning her mother's texts.

Opening her evening bag with a shaky sigh, Laina took out her cell phone, glanced at her watch and punched in her mother's number. After a few rings her voice mail picked up.

"Mom, it's me. Sorry I've been out of touch," Laina started, hoping her voice sounded steady. "You're probably at your bridge night, so don't worry about calling back. I just—the place is great. You should see it, all done up for the wedding. It's gorgeous. And I, um…" She adjusted the phone on her ear. She was an emotional wreck. She should just hang up. She wasn't thinking clearly—or was she? It had been so long since she'd allowed herself to show any emotion at all around her parents; maybe it was just what she needed. She cleared her throat. "I'm thinking I might like to spend some time here again. With you and Dad, I mean. Not just at the cottage." She dropped her chin. "Okay, well, gotta go. Love you." She hung up, pressing the phone to her forehead.

James. The love of her life. Over.

A fresh flood of tears washed down her cheeks, but she wiped them away impatiently. She'd been fine before him, and she would be fine after him. He might be near impossible to get over, but she had to believe that somewhere out there was a man who didn't give a flying fuck about who her family was or what they thought she could do for them. She'd be able to trust them. And that was worth everything, even if she didn't feel half for them what she felt for James.

CHAPTER FIFTEEN

SATURDAY. A CLOUDLESS blue sky, sun streaming through James's window, the perfect day for the wedding of the decade.

A room that still held the presence of roses, even though he'd asked for a garbage bag at the front desk last night.

Laina looking at him in horror, stumbling away from him, hating him.

Stirring awake, James's reality crashed over him like waves on the loneliest shore. It was the same way he'd felt on those first mornings after his mother died—disorientation followed by a moment of denial, and then the slow downward spiral into grief. The only thing that had given him comfort was knowing he'd never have to go through it again. His only parent was dead, he had no siblings and he would never marry. Even then he'd been sure of that, and it looked like he'd been right. The only woman he'd ever fallen in love with was lost to him.

But why? *Why?*

If he didn't do something to work this burning, toxic frustration out of his system, he was going to lose his mind. Today was going to be near impossible to get through. He had to do his best to put on a happy face for the wedding, and he knew that seeing Laina would be pure torture. She was in the wedding party, which meant she'd be standing before him with her beauty on full display. He had to find a way to talk to her beforehand, try to get to the bottom of her fury so he could at least find out what he was dealing with.

A run, he decided—maybe that would clear his head. Swinging his feet the floor, he couldn't help doing a quick check of his phone. He'd sent Laina a text when he got back to the room last night, but unsurprisingly, it had gone unanswered. He tapped on his messages and pulled up the one that Laina had seen from Jennifer. Just a single line, but he could understand how it could have been misconstrued. And it served him right—he *had* been avoiding his business partner, dreading breaking the news to her that they would no longer be building on the island's prime spot. Not that any of it mattered if he couldn't get the owners of Hibiscus Heights to sell. The whole thing was a mess, and if he was smart, he would just cut his losses and scrap it. But he couldn't, and it wasn't about the money. This was going to be his mother's castle in the sky. He had promised it to her, and breaking that promise felt

like breaking the thread that still kept them teth-
ered together across the border of life and death.

You're right, and I'm sorry. Call me anytime, he
typed back to Jennifer. Then he yanked on his
shorts and T-shirt, pocketed his phone and left for
his run.

It was pure fantasy, but Laina hardly noticed. Making her way across the grounds of the estate to the
main house, she missed the words Kiki and Dev
spelled out in eight-foot flower-petal letters on the
lawn, the towering white cake in front of a tempo-
rary waterfall. But she stopped at the head table to
do a check of the place settings. She'd put in a last-
minute request for she and James to be separated,
and she felt a mixture of agony and relief to see that
he'd been moved to the far end of the long table.

Laina's feet weighed a thousand pounds as she
made her way across the lawn. She knew her face
was a puffy mess, and she'd hardly slept a wink.
Just the thought of James was enough to make her
certain she was going to vomit. It was going to be
the longest day of her life.

When she got to the dining room, Kiki and Nicola were already gathered around a fruit platter.
Through the door to the kitchen, which was bigger
than Laina's entire condo in Atlanta, she could see
an army of cooks preparing the wedding feast. She
held her hands up in front of her face as she came

in. "Can we make a deal?" she asked her friends quickly. "And just not talk about it?"

"Are you sure?" Nicola asked.

Laina nodded. "I don't want this day to be about me—it's about Kiki," she said, giving her best friend a brave smile.

Kiki waved a pineapple slice at her dismissively. "Please—this whole princess-for-a-day thing is already giving me hives. Everyone keeps telling me to enjoy it, that as soon as I become a mother I won't have a minute to myself. But you know what? I'm okay with that. I've done me for long enough now." She placed a croissant on a plate and slid it toward Laina. "Eat something."

As Laina looked down at the pastry with distaste, Nicola laughed. "This reminds me of when I was going through all that stuff with Alex. Kiki kept trying to force food down my throat, but I was so upset I couldn't eat a thing."

"I'm like that too," Laina said.

"I think you might be like me in more ways than that."

"What do you mean?" Laina asked with a raised eyebrow.

Nicola shrugged. "Just that my triggers were buried in my insecurities. When I met Alex, I was really trying to protect myself from getting hurt, so it's almost like I was looking for an excuse to send him packing. So when I heard something questionable about him, I jumped all over it before I even knew what the full story was." She paused, fixing her aquamarine eyes on Laina. "Do you know what James's full story is?"

"I don't need to know," Laina said, raising her chin. "It's obvious he was using me."

"How can you be sure he knew your connection to this estate?"

"Because it's easy to find out! He even admitted he Googled me, and I let it slip a couple of times—"

"What if he wasn't looking for that? What if he actually has no idea?"

"As if! He's, like, this cutthroat developer. His projects are worth billions—someone doesn't get to a place like that without stepping on a few heads."

"Maybe you should ask him about the pelicans," Kiki cut in, smearing butter on her croissant.

Laina stared at her. "What are you talking about?"

"The pelicans. Just ask him." She glanced at her watch and picked up her plate. "Now, I really do have to get ready. Nicola, would you mind?" She gave Laina a wink. "Take a moment. Join us when you're ready."

Laina watched them retreat upstairs to the bedrooms, and then she looked around the room. She'd been so engrossed in her misery that she'd forgotten to stress out about entering this house for the first time in years. Trailing her hand along the mahogany table, she thought about all the dinners she'd had with her family over the years. Everything had always been so perfect, from the formally laid table to the centerpiece of cut flowers, a fresh bouquet each day. There was the staff who waited on them hand and foot, and the pleasant and supportive dinner conversation. Never any conflict. Even behind her parents' closed bedroom door, Laina had never heard a raised voice, even if she knew it wasn't possible that her parents never fought with each other or with their children. It was a kind of perfection that was intimidating, sure to make her feel like a failure when she felt emotions of her own that she couldn't contain. She remembered wanting to scream and curse sometimes, but even imagining her parents' reaction was enough to stop her. Laina hated conflict, so she'd separated herself from them. And now here she was again, avoiding conflict instead of demanding an explanation from James.

But if he was who she was certain he had to be, he didn't deserve that chance.

Completing his route from the beach back to The Palms, James headed for the main road through the island, his breath labored as his feet pounded the dirt. He'd been jogging for nearly half an hour, but he didn't feel any better. The perfect weather and postcard view hadn't budged his mood. The music coming from his earbuds couldn't even dis-

tract him; annoyed, he ripped them from his ears
and shoved them in his pocket as he ran.

Laina. He was so miserable that he'd lost her,
and now he'd have to see her again in just one short
hour. Nothing would ever be the same again. Even
though they lived in separate cities, every single
day for God knew how long, he would be searching crowds for her face. Looking at diners in restaurants, people on park benches, women browsing
in shops. Since they had Kiki in common, he'd get
news of her every now and then whether he wanted
it or not. One day his cousin might even tell him
that Laina had a new boyfriend—or worse. The
thought was nearly enough to make him dry heave.

This is pointless, James thought. Stopping suddenly in his tracks, he leaned forward onto his
knees, breathing heavily. Sweat beaded on his forehead as he stood up again and started walking in a
circle to cool down. That's when he noticed two men
in the distance behind him. They were running side
by side, but their eyes were on him. He stood solid
as they approached, and then he suppressed a groan
when their faces came into focus. One of them was
Ward—just what he really did not need right now.
James prayed he'd pass by him, but no such luck.

"Glad I caught up with you," Ward said as he
pulled up in front of him and stopped with his
buddy in tow. "Seems running's more your speed
than horseback riding."

"I guess I prefer to carry my own weight."

"Good for you," Ward replied with an artificial smile. "Then I guess Laina is the perfect girl for you."

James's face darkened. "What's that supposed to mean?"

Ignoring the question, Ward gazed out at the ocean. "Wow. This place is paradise, isn't it?" Stretching his arms back and forth to show off his biceps, he switched his gaze to James. "Look, I've been getting the vibe you're not my number one fan, so I just wanted to set the record straight. I'm not sure what Laina's told you about me, but I'm guessing it wasn't flattering."

James arranged his features into a puzzled expression. "Actually, she's hardly mentioned you."

"Is that right?" Ward said, and then shrugged. "Hey, man, you know what? I was just trying to save you a little pain. But if you're not interested—"

James clenched his fists. "That's pretty funny, considering the amount of pain you caused her."

Ward took a step closer to him. "She misrepresented herself, man. That kind of shit ain't okay. I found out and broke up with her, that's all."

James felt a hit to his gut. *Misrepresented?* "What are you talking about?"

"So she suckered you in too, huh?" Ward shook his head and exchanged a look with his buddy. "You know she only stays in that cottage because her parents let her."

James's mind raced. *That cottage?* He hadn't even seen where Laina was staying. The one time he'd asked, she'd told him she was in a guest cottage, and he hadn't thought anything of it—they were all over the island. But come to think of it, she had refused all of his offers to go anywhere near it.

James threw his hands out. "Okay, you got me. I have no idea what you're talking about. Inform me."

"For realsies?"

God, but he was annoying—like a ten-year-old who'd connived himself into a man's body.

"For realsies," James agreed, patronizing him.

Ward heaved a great sigh, as if he were dealing with a slow child. "The estate? The one her gazillionaire family owns? Don't let her tell you she stands to inherit—"

James stared at him. "Estate? What estate?"

"Seriously?" Ward looked genuinely shocked. "Where the wedding's being held. It belongs to her family. The Reinhards?"

Reinhard. James knew that name. It finally clicked: they were like Atlanta royalty. But that wasn't all, he realized. When James had put his offers in to the three Moretta properties, only Hibiscus Heights had declined. The name on that contract, the very people he was still trying to convince to sell to him, was Reinhard.

Holy shit.

"Reinhard. The estate that wouldn't sell," James said to himself as two and two finally came together.

But Ward wasn't finished. "That whole changing her last name thing is just an attention grabber, if you ask me. It took her about ten minutes to tell me who she really was. What she conveniently left out was that she renounced any claim to her parents' estate years ago. Not just the house here, but all of it. So, yeah—no money on that train. Kind of need-to-know information if you're planning on marrying someone, don't you think?"

James turned away from Ward's smirking face to keep from punching a hole through it. His ears were ringing. It explained everything: Laina's reticence toward her wealthy family, her reaction to him telling her he wanted to buy Hibiscus Heights, even her mysterious disappearance last night—she must have been staying in the estate's guest cottage.

He had to talk to her.

Glancing at his watch, he calculated. Forty minutes until the ceremony started. She would be helping Kiki get ready, unable and unwilling to see him or take his call. He'd have to wait until the reception, but that was okay. He'd talk to her, explain everything, and she would see that he'd had no idea who she was.

It was all going to be okay.

Thank you, Ward Harris, you dumb asshole, he thought gleefully as he jogged toward his hotel.

CHAPTER SIXTEEN

FIFTEEN MINUTES UNTIL she saw him.

As Laina hurriedly left her cottage to go and join Kiki and Nicola in the main house, she tried to tame the uncontrolled drumming of her heartbeat. The thought of standing up there for the entire ceremony, knowing his eyes were on her...would she even be able to handle it?

Yes. She would. She'd made up her mind—she was going to talk to him at the reception. Even if it achieved nothing, she had to know she'd tried her very best. Nicola was right, she realized; she needed to give him the benefit of the doubt. Someone like James was too amazing to just let go of without a fight, and she would even walk straight into conflict to do it.

But that didn't change the fact that right now she was a mess. Sure, her hair had been smoothed into a jewel-adorned updo, her makeup had been done by one of New York's makeup artists to the stars, flown in especially for the occasion, and her show-stopping dress had been accessorized with a real diamond choker gifted to her by Kiki this morning. But she could feel sweat beading on her upper lip, and her whole body felt woozy. Her normally organized brain suffered from distraction and lack of sleep, sending her back to her cottage three times to pick up things she'd forgotten—her evening bag, her heels, the high school ring she'd meant to slip over a flower stem on Kiki's bouquet for her "something borrowed." She'd finally remembered to grab her cell phone this time, and saw that she had two missed calls from her mother—not that she could do anything about that right now.

As she made her way along the pool, she could see that most of the ceremony viewing seats were already filled. Her heart gave a lift as she saw everyone decked out in their best outfits, all here to celebrate her best friend. The mood was celebratory but also tense, just as it should be for a wedding this special. But was *he* here? Scanning the crowd quickly as she passed, she was relieved not to find him.

"Lains!"

No. Ward was the only person on earth who called her that, even though she'd asked him a hundred times not to when they'd been together. His voice had come from behind her, so she hurried on without turning around. Surely he would get the hint and leave her alone.

"Lains. *Hello!*" he said into her face. He'd rushed past her to get in front of her, his breath slightly boozy from the empty glass of champagne he held in his hand.

She couldn't even look at him. "What is it, Ward?" she said to the palm tree over his shoulder. "As you might imagine, I'm in a bit of a hurry."

"And looking white-hot while you're at it, I might add," he said. It was impossible to believe that she'd once found that shit-eating grin charming.

She glanced pointedly at her watch.

"Hey, I can take a hint. I just wanted to be the bearer of good news, that's all."

Laina looked skyward. "Okay, fine. I'll bite. What good news?"

"Just that I know how *paranoid* you are about evil men going after you for your money." A waiter passed by, and he grabbed another glass of champagne off the tray. Judging from his slurred voice, Laina guessed it was probably his third or fourth. *Same old Ward*, she thought—the wannabe rich guy who never missed a freebie. "So I took care of your date for you. What was his name again? It doesn't matter. Don't worry, I don't expect a thank-you. Consider it atonement for my little… indiscretion."

Laina kept her face neutral. "I'm not sure I understand."

Ward took a swig from his glass and shrugged. "You don't need to worry about him anymore. Of course I hated to rain on his parade right before such a joyous occasion, but when he came up to me and asked if I might try to convince you to sell Hibiscus Heights…well, I just couldn't keep my mouth shut. I made sure he understood you have no pull in your family's estate. The look on his face…well, let's just say shock would be an understatement."

Laina felt a muscle in her cheek twitch. Ward may be a pretentious self-centered prick, but how else would he know James wanted to buy her family's property if he hadn't told him so himself?

She felt like she was going to be sick. To think she'd been planning to give him another chance, when meanwhile he'd been appealing to her ex to collude with him? How low could he possibly go?

Turning away with tears in her eyes, she walked to the main house as fast as her heels would allow.

If James had disliked weddings before he met Laina, the feeling was intensified a hundredfold as he sat in his aisle seat fiddling with his program. A classical trio was playing fun takes on old rock songs and the atmosphere around him was festive, but it couldn't tame the sick thud in his gut. Any moment now Laina was going to be right in front of him, a full display of everything he'd had and lost. It was going to be his worst nightmare.

But he would turn it around—he had to.

The music changed to a classical rendition of "Here Comes the Sun," and a hush fell over the crowd. He had to admire his cousin's creativity and irreverence. Turning with the rest of the guests, James saw Nicola walking slowly down the aisle toward him, followed by Laina.

How does she do that? James wondered as he watched her walk right past him, almost close enough to touch. Her face looked as peaceful and happy as it was supposed to on a day like this. Didn't she feel anything? Wasn't she upset at all by what had happened between them last night? Was she really able to move on so quickly?

It didn't matter, because it didn't change how James felt about her one bit. Just as he'd known she would, she looked like a goddess. Her body-skimming silver dress, which reached to her ankles, fell open from spaghetti straps into a draped neckline. A diamond necklace, resting at the hollow of her throat, glittered as it caught the sun. Her hair and makeup made her look like she'd stepped from the cover of a magazine. And in her hands she held a loose bouquet of pink and white flowers. He wanted to try to catch her eye as she took her place under the archway, but the crowd was already standing up. James joined them and turned to look at his cousin.

Despite his foul mood, he couldn't help the

smile that came to his lips. Kiki was truly a sight to behold. Her strawberry blond hair had been left down and swept to one side, and there was no old-fashioned veil for her—instead she wore a bejeweled headpiece of crystal and pearls that looked like it had been woven into her hair. A double strand of something glittery, probably diamonds, hung from her neck. Her dress was a simple scoop-neck sheath in blush-pink silk, sweeping down to a long train in the back. On her feet she wore crystal-studded high-heeled sandals to boost her petite frame, and in her hands she carried a bouquet made from a riot of black and white flowers.

He watched her take her place beside Dev, who was looking like he might actually bawl, and then he switched his gaze to Laina again. His breath caught in his throat as a strange sense of déjà vu swept over him.

She looked exactly like his vision from the dream he'd had when he first arrived on Moretta. It hadn't been a doorway she'd been standing in, he realized now—it had been an archway. She and James had been standing side by side, and she had been wearing a long, pale dress.

The party that had been going on around them had been their own wedding.

To laugh with and cry with. To dream together and parent their children together. Kiki and Dev had written their own vows, and the words were still ringing in Laina's ears three hours after they'd exchanged them. The ceremony had been perfect—short, heartfelt and humorous in all the right places. Just the kind of wedding she would love to have one day, if she could ever find a man she could trust.

James fucking Ellison. Laina had felt his eyes on the side of her face the entire time, but she'd refused to look at him. He may have played her for a fool once, but never again. She knew exactly what would happen if she allowed him to talk to her—he'd suck her in yet again, feeding her his lies and proclaiming his innocence when she'd been nothing but a means to an end for him the whole time. That was what infuriated Laina most of all—that she'd fallen for it. She knew she wasn't the most experienced woman on earth when it came to navigating sex and relationships, but she'd truly thought she had better judgment than that.

It was enough to bring tears to her eyes as she walked toward the cake stand. But at least the formal part of the reception was almost over, and she'd miraculously been able to avoid him so far. Not that it had been easy. She'd busied herself with mingling among the guests during the cocktail hour, and then she'd spent the dinner chatting with her seat mates and listening to toasts. She'd even made a short one herself, which she thought she'd be nervous for, but it turned out that anger had a calming effect on her.

Twice during dinner she'd seen James get up from the other side of the table to approach her, but she'd hurried off to the bathroom both times.

Now all that was left were the cake cutting and the dancing, which Laina already knew required no formality. At that point, with her bridesmaid duties over, she could easily go back to her cottage to sob her eyes out again.

Kiki and Dev were already standing before the waterfall with the cake knife in hand. Up close, the confection was even more stunning than it had been at a distance. Edible white flowers spiraled up the six tiers, and now Laina could see that a subtle music note pattern had been embossed on them.

"He wrote that song to win her back, you know."

Laina spun around and came face-to-face with James. Her heart drummed in her chest. *Damn it.* She'd barely let her eyes flit his way all night, but despite everything, she couldn't help her body's magnetic pull toward him—*still*. He looked amazing in a lightweight grey suit that set off the green of his eyes. He was freshly shaven for the first time since the yacht party, making her want to feel that smooth cheek trailing down her belly.

But she had to hate him.

Laina took a step backward. Around her the crowd was cheering as Kiki shoved a piece of cake into Dev's mouth. James moved closer to her to fill the gap. "Kiki told me the story," he said. "He wrote it for her while they were broken up, and look at them now." He gestured to the happy couple, who was now kissing to wild applause.

"That's not the story I heard," Laina retorted. "He wrote it before that while they were together. On the night he played it on the piano for her, he asked her to marry him."

"Hmm. Funny how stories can get twisted when you don't have all the facts."

"Or how some people can change them after their lies have been uncovered," Laina threw back.

"Laina—" James reached for her arm, but she pulled away. "I'm sorry," he said, lifting his hands. "I just—I can't believe how wrong this has all gone. Can we talk? Away from this noise, I mean?"

She lifted her chin, standing her ground. "Not a chance."

"Okay. But you have to believe that I never knew who you were. I promise." He looked at her pleadingly. "I did want something from you—I admit that. The pelicans. I wanted to build on their cliff, and I thought that with your influence we could convince the council to relocate them, and—"

"So you weren't taking tourist pictures that first day," she said flatly.

He shook his head guiltily. "No. I kept meaning to ask you, but then we got involved, and…" He trailed off. "But I didn't ask you. I couldn't—"

"Why? Because asking me two big favors might have looked suspicious so you chopped it down to one?"

"No! I already had a meeting set up with the Reinhards—I mean *your parents*—before I even came here. I'm supposed to meet with them in Atlanta on Tuesday."

"Oh, yeah? Well, don't you dare think of asking me to help you out on that one! Or calling me when you're in town!"

"Of course I wouldn't ask—"

"Besides, they'd never sell this place," Laina cut in, though her voice quavered slightly with uncertainty. "And what you say proves absolutely nothing. I don't fool myself about my name change—anyone with half a brain could figure out who I was in about ten minutes. You made the connection before you came to Moretta, and then you used me." Her voice was rising as her anger built. She started stalking away from him to avoid a scene, but he hurried after her as she hammered her accusations home. "I bet you couldn't believe your luck! What a bonus! Some naive chick you could use to your advantage *and* have fun with on the side!" She stopped at the edge of the pool deck to turn on him.

James was shaking his head rapidly. "No! That's not at all what it was!" He threw his hands up. "And did it ever occur to you that *I'm* the one who should be upset here? We were a hot and heavy thing, Laina, and you didn't think to tell me you were staying at the very estate the wedding was being held at? That your family *owned*?"

"Don't you try to put this on me!" Her eyes flashed at him. "What about Jennifer? Who the hell is she? To think that I actually came to my senses about your playboy ways long enough to kick you to the curb, and you reeled me right back in! Or maybe I should be thanking you for that one— yes, lesson learned, so thank you very much!" She started marching away again.

"Laina, Jennifer is my business partner!"

"Is that right? So mixing business with pleasure is just par for the course? Does *she* know that?" A new thought nearly knocked her sideways. *No condom. Damn.* "Do I need to get tested for anything?" she asked in a terrified voice.

He squeezed his hands to his head. "*No!* God, Laina! What we did—don't you know how much that meant to me? You were my *only one*." His voice hitched with emotion.

Her stomach was roiling. He was saying all the right things, bringing her back to all their beautiful moments together.

But she couldn't afford this. Her heart wouldn't take any more heartbreak from him, and that was all she could see. "Why should I believe anything you say?"

James stopped in his tracks. They were far from the crowd now, close to her cottage, but there were still enough guests milling around that they were drawing attention. He lowered his voice. "Listen. I'm not going to lie, because guess what? *I'm not a liar.* I did sleep with Jennifer once—no, twice. But that was before I met you. I never led her on afterward. She was asking me if I was avoiding her because of the development. I wasn't making any progress here, and she likes things to move fast. So I didn't return her text. It wasn't the man-up thing to do, but I was…distracted. By you."

Shit, Laina thought, *is he going to cry?* He was good—but not good enough. "You mean by waiting for just the right moment to strike," she said, clarifying. "Which would have been at the rehearsal dinner if I hadn't finally clued in to what you were up to."

He groaned. "God, Laina, *no*! Isn't there anything I can do—"

"Do?" She glared at him in the fading light. In the background she could hear the band starting up their first set with "White Wedding." She stepped closer to James so he could hear her. Her nostrils filled with the scent of his aftershave mixed with musky sweat, reminding her of their bodies moving together. She still wanted him as much as she had every single second since she'd met him; how was that even possible? "Sure, there's something you can do. You can take me to my cottage right over there—" she gestured toward its darkened shape in the background "—and fuck me. See what it feels like to have sex with someone who cares nothing for you, just like you did to me. How about that?"

As James stared at her, she was still trying to get over what she'd just said. Was she actually serious? And what if he said yes?

But he dropped his chin into his chest and shook his head sadly. "Laina. If that ever happened between us again, I wouldn't be fucking you. I'd be making mad love to you."

Then he shoved his hands in his pockets and went back to the party, leaving her staring at his back with her mouth hanging open.

CHAPTER SEVENTEEN

"MY GOODNESS, HONEY, are you all right?" Laina's mother, Beverly, asked her over the phone. "I can't say as I've ever heard you this upset before."

"You've never heard me upset, period!" Laina couldn't help shouting back. She was sitting in the windowless bathroom of her cottage with the door closed against the noise of the ongoing party.

"I really don't think—"

"It's true, Mom! Everything is always so—*perfect* in our family. When do we ever communicate like normal people?"

"I don't think there is such a thing as normal, dear."

"Yeah, but still!" Laina took a deep breath, forcing herself to calm down. She'd reached out to her mother for two reasons, and calling her out on thirty-two years of repressed emotions wasn't one of them. "Listen, I don't want to argue, okay? I just want to know—" She took a deep breath. "You and Dad would never sell Hibiscus Heights, would you?"

There was a beat of silence. "What gave you that idea?"

"Long story. Would you?"

Beverly sighed. "I've been trying to get in touch with you all week. I wanted you to know that your father and I have an appointment with an interested party on Tuesday."

Laina inhaled sharply. "But...why?"

"*Why*, darling?" Her mother gave a humorless laugh. "More like why not? We hardly go there anymore. Paul and Wesley use it every now and then, but it's a family home, meant to be enjoyed together. And ever since you stopped going, that's all fallen apart."

Laina felt her blood pressure rise. "So it's *my* fault?"

"That's not what I meant at all," Beverly said. "I meant that you were the one who held us together."

Laina was sure she hadn't heard right. How could *she*, the black sheep who'd always wanted to be different from everyone in her family, be the person who kept them unified?

Her mother continued. "When you were around, you forced everyone to look at the world around them. To enjoy the little things and see what was really important. You were the grounding force. Without that, we've all floated off into our separate universes."

Laina's head was spinning. Was it possible she'd

been seeing things the wrong way this entire time? And why was her mother suddenly engaging her in the deepest conversation of their lives right now?

Okay, but you can't do it. You can't sell to him, she wanted to say to her now. But she had no right to. After over a decade of making sure her parents understood she wanted nothing to do with their estate and little to do with them, she couldn't just step in now and dictate what they should do because she'd had a sudden change of heart. It was their property, and they could do what they wanted with it.

But she still needed something else that she'd never asked for before. She took a deep breath. "I need a favor."

James stared at the vodka soda sitting at his elbow on the bar. He picked up the drink, took a small sip and set it down again with a sigh. Even if his body might feel like getting completely obliterated, his brain—or some other vital organ—apparently did not. The alcohol sat at the top of his stomach, making him feel nauseous and solving nothing. He'd been working on this same drink for over an hour, ever since he'd walked away from Laina, and his mind was in hell. He wondered when he could gracefully exit the reception, knowing his goodbye to Kiki would almost surely invite questions he didn't feel like answering. He wondered if he should try going after Laina again, even if it was obvious she was done with him. He wondered what he could possibly do to win her back.

The only thing that was keeping him sane was the thought that he still had one more chance. Both he and Laina were due to fly out Monday morning, which meant he still had tomorrow—and he was certain she wouldn't be able to avoid him all day. He would keep a clear head tonight and figure it out, just like he always did, and tomorrow he'd find a way to win her back.

His cell phone rang in his pants pocket. He fished it out and looked at the screen. *Jennifer Liu.* Shit—he may as well end the second most miserable day of his life on an even lower low. "Jennifer, I'm glad you called," he said when he picked up.

"Really?"

"Yeah. I'm sorry I took so long to get back to you." He walked across the lawn, leaving the sound of the band and the partiers behind. He stopped around the corner of the main house and took a deep breath. "Listen, it's not good news. I haven't been completely upfront with you—I hit a snag with the Moretta project a year ago, and I haven't been able to resolve it."

"What kind of problem?"

"I can't secure the location I promised. Part of it is on public land, and I thought I could sway the council, but they aren't budging."

A beat of silence, and then, "Anything else?"

He hesitated. "Yes. One of the homeowners doesn't want to sell."

Jennifer sighed. "This isn't good, James."

He scrubbed a hand over his face. "I know."

"But these things happen."

His hand stopped. *These things happen?* It wasn't exactly the ream-out he'd been expecting. "You mean you still want to go ahead with it?"

"Without a doubt," she replied, and then lowered her voice slightly. "As long as you're onboard with me, that is."

James felt his heart sink. Christ. Was she saying she wanted to continue the business deal because she wanted *him*? He couldn't be sure. Asking her to clarify would be monumentally awkward. The easiest thing would be to go along with it, claiming to have missed her double meaning if and when it ever came up again. By then the project would likely be well underway, leaving her no choice but to see it through.

It was exactly what the pre-Laina James would have done.

He squeezed his eyes shut. "Jennifer, listen. You're a beautiful woman, but if we move forward together it's going to be as business partners only. I made a mistake by letting us get personal a few weeks ago, and it's not going to happen again. I apologize if what I did gave you the idea that we might have any kind of future together." He finally stopped and opened his eyes, preparing himself for the worst. Far across the grounds by the dance floor, he could see Kiki breaking away from the crowd and heading toward him. *Shit.* "Jennifer, are you there?" he asked quickly.

"I'll take your statements under consideration and get back to you," she said flatly, and then the phone went dead in his hand. He shoved it back into his pocket as Kiki marched up to him. She'd changed into a cocktail-length orchid-pink dress that matched the angry flush in her cheeks. Once more, James braced himself.

Kiki fixed him with a square look and placed her tiny fists on her hips. "So here's the deal, cuz. Since I've just gotten married, I'm having the best day of my life, I'm a little drunk, and I think you've had enough for one day, I'm going to spare your life. But make no mistake about it—tomorrow over a hangover breakfast, you are going to explain to me exactly why my best friend just left on the last private plane off the island."

James gaped at her. *"What?"*

"You heard me. She said goodbye to me twenty minutes ago, and I've been hunting you down ever since."

"Jesus." He raked a hand through his hair and shook his head wildly. So much for his chance to turn things around tomorrow. "I'm sorry Kiki, but I have to go."

He turned and jogged toward Laina's cottage, but he could already tell by the darkened windows that he was too late. When a knock on the door went unanswered, his gaze settled on a golf cart parked nearby. He ran over to it and, seeing the key in the ignition, started it up and drove toward the main road. Had he noticed a plane fly overhead earlier? He hadn't been looking for one, and the reception had been noisy enough to mask the sound. Maybe he wasn't too late.

"Fuck!" he roared into the darkness, pounding a fist on the steering wheel.

CHAPTER EIGHTEEN

"THANK YOU AGAIN for meeting with me," James said as he stood, extending his hand first to Beverly and then to Conrad. "And also for your cooperation. I'm sure you won't regret it."

Conrad smiled at him, and as James shook his hand, a regretful feeling came over him. Even though he and Laina hadn't been together long, it was very possible that this man could have become his father-in-law. He couldn't help wondering for just a moment what it would have been like to look up to him like the father he'd never had, and to have a mother figure in his life after so many years without one.

But of course he knew that could never be. Not only was Laina distant from her family herself, James had blown his chance at any future with her. There was almost zero hope that this well-dressed, gentile couple would ever be anything more than passing business associates to him.

Walking across the graceful white lobby of

Atlanta's St. Regis Hotel toward the valet desk, James took a moment to reflect on the meeting. It had been a success. He'd gotten everything he'd wanted out of it, and now he just needed to make a couple of phone calls to set the wheels in motion. But he still needed one thing from Laina, and getting it wasn't going to be easy. Since he was certain she wouldn't take his call or answer his text, a face-to-face visit was the only way to go. But he only had her work address, where she would easily be able to avoid him or maybe even have him hauled off by security. He'd briefly considered asking her parents for her home address, but squashed that thought when he imagined what a creep he'd sound like.

The valet brought James's rented Land Rover to the curb and opened his door for him. James pulled away from the hotel toward Piedmont Heights, scanning the streets as he drove. He'd left Atlanta for Miami when he was twenty-three, and he'd only returned here a handful of times since. A lot had changed in fifteen years. The streets were mostly strange to him now, full of memories that no longer matched their surroundings.

Or did they?

On impulse, James turned off Peachtree Road toward a nondescript strip mall twenty blocks east. When he arrived, he pulled into a parking space beside a pickup truck and stared straight ahead.

It had barely changed. Same narrow storefront, same long lineup of customers, same retro-looking pink-and-green sign with the name painted across a smiling takeout cup. Sally's Smoothie Stop, named after his mother. James had known it would be here. He no longer ran it, but he still owned it, even if he hadn't visited it since shortly after his mother's death.

He would still build her castle in the sky, even if it would look different from what he'd always imagined.

Taking his phone from his pocket, he pulled up the name he'd gotten from Laina's parents and typed it into Google.

Locking her office door behind her, Laina left the building and took the stairs down to the parking garage. Coming in to work today had been a mistake. This morning she'd been driven in by the guilt of two projects she'd fallen behind on because of her week on Moretta. But after staring blankly at her computer screen for most of the day, she'd finally given up and left. Life without James not only felt miserable, it made everything else she used to take pleasure in feel pointless—her work, her goals, even her friends. She was shrinking inside her clothing and lying awake for most of the night. And the worst part was she didn't even want life to get back to normal again, because she didn't want the normal she'd had before him. At this point, the best she could hope for was that one day, if she was really lucky, she might be able to get back to a dating life filled with lackluster connections and tepid sex.

She'd thought that leaving the island early would help, but if anything it had only made things worse. As the plane lifted off on Saturday night, all she could think of was whether she was making a huge mistake. Whether she was being too stubborn, whether she should have given him the benefit of the doubt. His last sentence to her rang in her ears over and over again: *I'd be making mad love to you.* The words had punched into her gut, stamped her soul with eternal hopeless yearning. But was it the truth or just more manipulation?

At three o'clock in the afternoon, traffic was horrible. It took Laina an hour to fight her way across town into the heart of Lenox Park, but by the time she arrived at her parents' house she couldn't recall a minute of it. She'd driven on autopilot, her brain clattering with thoughts of James in her city. Today, meeting with her parents. It was unbearable.

As she drove into the circular driveway of her childhood home, she tried to remember that last time she'd been there. Christmas, probably, when she'd attended the obligatory family dinner. She felt slightly ashamed as she remembered sitting at the table with her parents and brothers, hating the happy pretense and wishing it all away. How could she have been so unappreciative when someone like James had no family at all?

James. It always came back to him.

"Laina," her father said when he opened the door. She stepped forward and gave him a quick embrace. "This is a surprise. It's good to see you," he said, kindly not mentioning how long it had been.

"You too, Dad. Where's Mom?"

"Out shopping. She'll be sorry she missed you."

Laina nodded as she slipped out of her flats and wandered into the sitting room. Everything was familiar—the Queen Victoria furnishings, the Persian rugs, the original art on the walls. Like a museum.

"I won't stay long. I just…" *Just what?* Wanted to grill you about James Ellison? Because that was why she was here, wasn't it? To feel a little bit closer to him because he'd crossed paths with them today? It was pathetic. "I was surprised to hear you were thinking of selling Hibiscus Heights. Why did you take so long to tell me?"

Her father looked shocked. "I'm surprised it matters to you. You always stay with Kiki when you visit Moretta."

Laina nodded. "I know. But this last week… I guess I realized what I've been missing."

He nodded slowly. "Well, your mother and I love that house, but things have changed. We don't use it as a family anymore. When a developer approached us last year, it got us thinking. Bev and I have always thought that more of the world should be able to enjoy the island. James Ellison—he does a lot of work in Florida. He looked like he had the right idea. Nice fellow."

Nice fellow. Laina didn't know whether to laugh or cry. "I get that change will come to the island eventually, Dad. But it should be done by someone with a record of environmental responsibility. James Ellison might have the right intentions, but if you sold to him—"

"Hang on, honey. I didn't sell to anybody."

"You didn't?"

"No."

Laina shook her head. "But…you *did* meet with him today?"

"Yes, though I must say your mother was more excited about the food than the actual meeting. You know how she loves the lunch menu at the St. Regis—"

"Dad, can we stick to the topic?"

"Of course. No deal was made. In fact, he rescinded his offer and withdrew his development proposal altogether."

Laina's mouth fell open. "*What?* Why?"

"He really didn't say. But I was going to ask how you know this fellow. Because he seemed to know an awful lot about you. In fact, he was asking me some rather odd questions."

Her heart skipped. "Such as?"

"He was very interested in some blueprints you made up sometime ago. The ones for your final project at Spelman. I told him the units looked a little large for what—"

Laina held up a hand. "Wait. You mean you actually remember those blueprints?"

"Of course."

"But—but you never said anything! If I remember right, you took a call while I was showing them to you, and then you never brought them up again."

Her father leaned forward, clasping his hands together. "Listen, honey. I just—passive housing, it seemed so pie-in-the-sky to me. But I didn't want to be unsupportive, so instead I said nothing."

"No conflict, right?" Laina said quietly.

Her father shook his head. "We just wanted you to be happy, honey—all three of you. But I see now that trying to fit you into a mold wasn't fair to you. I guess back then I thought a lot of your interests would change—"

"And become more like yours?"

He laughed. "Or at least like Paul and Wesley's. But I'm glad they didn't. And now, what do you know? Green construction is all the rage!"

"Dad—" Her voice caught.

"Yes?"

"Just—" Laina took a deep breath. "I wanted to say thank you. You and Mom gave me so much when I was growing up, and I guess I never really appreciated it."

Conrad chuckled. "I'd say that makes you like about ninety-nine percent of offspring out there."

"I know, but still… I've acted like a spoiled brat. Changing my name, refusing to stay at the estate. I guess I was able to fool myself into thinking that even though I was still going to the most exclusive island on earth, it didn't count because I was saving for the plane ticket all year and staying at a friend's staff cottage. Now that I think about it, it was actually kind of insulting to all the people out there who really do struggle." She shook her head. "I wasn't trying to hurt you, I just needed to make my own way. And I didn't know how else to do it."

"Honey…" Conrad grasped her hands. "Listen to me. I am so proud of you. You've always known who you are and what makes you tick, and you've always stayed true to your convictions." He sat up straight. "Which gets me to thinking. If that James fellow is so bad, why don't you teach him a thing or two? I have his number—I could set up a coffee date."

Laina almost laughed out loud. "Thanks for the offer, but I don't think so." She stood up. "I should get going. But it was great seeing you, Dad."

"You too," he said, standing with her. "Next time not so long between visits, okay?"

She slipped out the door and closed it behind her, and then she stood on the marble landing for a minute. There was so much to process. Her father's approval, James rescinding his offer to buy Hibiscus Heights, her blueprints. Why would James probe for information about them? Did he want to try to make things up to her by using her idea for his resort? But he'd never even laid eyes on them, and how would he complete his project without owning Hibiscus Heights? And did he *ever* stop trying?

No, Laina realized. James hadn't stopped trying to win her back since she'd unleashed her fury on him at the rehearsal dinner. Now that he no longer had any vested interest in her or her family, he'd proved his sincerity. But what if he'd been sincere about his ignorance the entire time, but had finally given up on her because he simply couldn't take the rejection anymore?

Laina pulled her phone out of her handbag and gave it a quick glance. Of course there was no message from him—she'd made it clear she didn't want to hear from him. So he'd listened to her, and who could blame him? After the way she'd treated him, she deserved it.

Oh, God. What have I done?

Propelling herself off the landing, Laina ran to

her car and pulled the door open. This was a conversation she needed to have in person, and with a
little luck he was still here. Where had her father
said they met today? The St. Regis.

She turned her car toward downtown and hit
the gas.

Standing at his darkening hotel room window holding his cell phone, James stared down at the passing pedestrians on the street below him. It was a
ridiculous way for him to spend his time, looking
out for a face he knew he wouldn't see, but he'd
made himself a deal. Here in Laina's city, tonight
and only tonight, he would allow himself to remember her. He would relive every detail of their
magical time together—that first kiss on the boat,
their earth-shattering encounters in the forest, in
his bed, on the beach, and the moment he'd known
he was deeply and madly in love with her.

And then, when tomorrow morning came and
he got on a plane to head back home, he'd force
himself to forget her forever. He'd get on with his
life and somehow find meaning in it without her.
He knew the truth now, even if he didn't accept it:
Laina was never coming back to him.

It had been three hours since James had climbed
the steps to Laina's office and found the door
locked. He'd known she worked on her own, but he
hadn't realized that really did mean *on her own*—

she didn't even have an assistant. He'd waited over
an hour for her, tolerating furtive glances from
passing strangers. At one point he'd stepped into a
neighboring business to ask about the usual opening hours of Rose Architecture, but they'd claimed
ignorance. Finally, as the other offices began to
expel their staff at the end of the day, he'd written her a note on a Post-it and stuck it to her door.

I'm sorry I missed you, but I had to try you
in person. Please call me. There's something
I want to do, but I need your permission first.
James

James looked down at his cell phone for the hun-
dredth time, as if a message from her may have ma-
terialized from nowhere. Then he hurled it across
the room onto his bed. This was fucking stupid. So
he'd done the right thing—rescinded his offer to her
parents, scrapped the development, and even ended
his partnership with Jennifer for good to avoid
any crossed lines in the future. It was nothing he
shouldn't have done a long time ago. And it didn't
change the fact that Laina wasn't going to call him,
that his shiny new idea wasn't going to win her
back, and that there was no reason for him to wait
around here any longer like a goddamned fool.

He was never going to see her again.

He looked at his watch, and then he walked over

to the desk and grabbed his iPad. There were still plenty of flights back to Miami tonight, and nothing was holding him here. He booked his flight, hurriedly packed his suitcase and left his room.

As he strode down the hallway toward the elevators, the last line he'd written on his note to Laina blinked in his head like a siren. How long had he stood there debating back and forth before finally going with his heart and scribbling it down?

PS I dream about you every night.

CHAPTER NINETEEN

LAINA WAS DREAMING.

She was lying on a bed in the middle of a room filled with lavender roses, and James was trailing kisses up her leg. From her ankle all the way to her thigh, his heavenly tongue teased her with what was to come. Her entire body was already throbbing with want, her pussy so wet as she waited for that delicious first sweep of his tongue. It made her cry out when she finally felt it. His fingers went inside her, massaging that magical spot while he sucked her clit softly, firmly, softly, firmly until she was rushing toward her climax so fast, so hard. She buried her hands in James's soft hair, not daring to look down at him. Knowing that if their eyes met while he had her under his power in this beautifully intimate moment, she would come apart.

"Laina, you taste so sweet," he murmured, opening his mouth wide so she could feel his warm tongue pressed flat to her. Her hips bucked up, a silent plea for more. More pressure, more of that slippery sensation, more of those perfect, intoxicating words that filled her body and heart with a feeling she was helpless to describe. So much more than lust, so much more than love. The most soul-saturating, passionate, excruciatingly beautiful emotion that existed. "I'm going to taste you like this forever. I'll always be with you. I love you so much I can't even see straight."

She had to see him. Had to look at him between her legs, worshiping her like that, loving her like that. His eyes fastened on hers, and her groin fluttered with the emotion of connection so intense it stole her breath. She reached for his hands and entwined them together, squeezing his tightly as the heat built to an inferno.

She fell over the edge, rocking her hips back and forth on the mattress, every muscle in her body tensed toward her pleasure, her pussy contracting sweetly on his fingers, crying his name over and over again. When she came back into her body, he was straddling her hips. His beautiful, rock-hard cock was straining upward, aching with desire for her. The fire that had just been sated inside her relit, hotter than ever, desperate for the feel of him inside her.

Her swollen lips were already open when James's mouth came down on hers, his tongue slashing her wide as an animal sound ripped from his throat. *"Everything,"* he said fiercely into her mouth.

"Every part of me belongs to you. Feel it. *Feel it.* Feel how much I need you."

He entered her with a thrust so deep and sweet it turned her body to liquid. Paralyzed with exquisite sensation from her head to her toes, Laina lay help-lessly under him as he drove into her. His breath turned ragged as he grabbed her thighs and shoved them upward mercilessly, laying her bare. Claim-ing her. His mouth coming down on her neck, on her breast, biting her there until she cried out from the perfect blend of pain and pleasure. She thrust herself into his mouth, wanting more of it, more of him, more of that savage need. She was already spi-raling upward, the heat in her clit growing again.

His eyes fluttered shut with sheer ecstasy as he quickened his pace even more, and then he opened them and fixed them on hers. "I'm so close," he panted. "So close because I love you so damn much."

Then the bed shook with the power of their com-bined climax, her shattering moan mingling with his guttural release, both of them lost in a moment so perfect it could never be repeated. Could only lie alongside all the others before and after, each a unique expression of an eternal bonding love for each other, made so much more exquisite from the power of knowing all they had almost lost.

It was real. So real, and Laina was crying.

As she emerged from the intimate space that had

contained only the two of them, her surroundings returned to her. The only piece of furniture in the room a gorgeous four-poster, the sheets tangled on the floor from the intensity of their passion. The floor carpeted in a sea of vases containing an entire garden of lavender roses, James's re-creation of the night eight months ago that they'd never had together. The walls plastered and ready for paint. And the view beyond their window of the calabash trees backdropping a partially framed cottage, alongside a massive hole in the ground that would soon be a saltwater pool.

Laina buried her face in James's neck as he stroked her back. She knew he didn't need to ask her why she was crying. Even months after they'd reunited in his Atlanta hotel room with the fierceness of two colliding trains, these moments still came upon her. The idea that this could have never happened. That they could both be leading their separate lives right now, scorched by the pain of indescribable loss, moving through the world like zombies.

She pulled away to look at James's face, and he traced her tears with his thumb. "I wish there were better words," she whispered. "I can't…"

"Shhh… I know," he said soothingly. "I know everything." He locked his eyes on hers as he cupped a hand around her cheek. "I want to show you something."

She stirred. "Does that mean I have to get dressed?"

"Absolutely not." He reached down to the floor and picked up two sheets, which they wrapped around themselves. Then James plucked a single rose out of a vase and reached for her hand. "Follow me."

He led her down the stairs with the sheets trailing behind them. As the burning intensity of her experience receded, real life returned. Laina walked through the living room with a critical eye, observing the new hardwood flooring, the stained-glass windows with the original owner's initials in them that had been installed just yesterday. It was going to be perfect. Not just because it had been James's idea, and not just because their collaborative effort was bringing her beloved crumbling house back to life. Because it, along with the six guest cottages built on the property, would be shared with the people who needed it most: those with limited incomes dealing with a terminal illness in their family. The project honored James's mother, Laina's passion for social justice, even the house's former owners with its final completion after all these decades. *House of Dreams*, her and James's castle in the sky.

As they walked across the newly restored front porch, James pulled Laina close and covered her eyes.

"What are you doing?" she laughed.

"The sign was installed today. I wanted to surprise you with it."

Laina's heart leaped. She'd put her heart and soul into redesigning this place, using all of her skill to create the lowest environmental impact possible, and each new detail that came to life was cause for her celebration. She felt James stop beside her and turn her back toward the house. "Are you ready?" he asked.

"So ready." She smiled. He moved his hand away from her eyes.

All Laina could do was stare. Her mouth fell open as the impact of what she was seeing hit her fully, and a bubble of emotion burst out of her in a gasp. "*Oh my God!* James, what—"

He took her hands. She looked from him back to the sign, unable to believe her eyes.

Instead of the words *House of Dreams* in the font she'd chosen, *Will you marry me?* had been printed across the arched wooden slab.

And now Laina could hardly breathe, because James was dropping to one knee and looking up at her rapturously. She brought a hand up to fan her face, so overcome with emotion she couldn't think straight. *Was this really happening? Was she dreaming?*

"Laina," James began as his eyes filled with tears. "My life is nothing without you. You are my heart, my breath, my everything."

Laina's eyes welled up as James held the single lavender rose up to her. "I asked you once what this symbolizes. It's love at first sight. And I know now that I've loved you from the moment I saw you on that stupid cliff in those damn cutoffs."

Laina was laughing and crying at the same time, shaking her head and nodding all at once. James opened his hand to reveal a diamond ring. Her breath hitched as he took her left hand, holding the ring at her fingertip. "Make me the happiest man alive, Laina. Tell me you'll love me forever."

"I—of course! Oh, my God! *Yes yes yes!*" She was vibrating with excitement, her body too full to contain any of it—him, their dreams, their future, the indescribable love she had for this man. He slipped the ring onto her finger and stood up to take her in his arms. Both of their sheets fell away and pooled on the ground as James lifted her off her feet and buried his face in her neck.

She loved him eternally, intensely, madly.

He was a dream come true.

* * * * *

SIN CITY SEDUCTION

MARGOT RADCLIFFE

MILLS & BOON

To Catfish.

For being just the right amount of withholding.

CHAPTER ONE

PARKER JONES LOVED her job. Didn't just tolerate
it like some of her friends whose chosen careers
made the Sunday scaries look like a slasher film,
but really loved it and couldn't imagine doing anything else. Except possibly swimming-pool-raft
model; those people always seemed super happy,
and lounging in water with beverages was a skill
she'd be happy to cultivate on a professional level.
In reality, however, she was a food writer for the
online magazine *Gastronomic*, so her days out of
the pool were spent traveling and eating delicious
food across the country, her current city being Las
Vegas.

And as she watched Hugh Matteson, ex-NFL
quarterback and owner of the restaurant she was
currently reviewing, saunter across the floor of his
extremely successful barbecue joint, Blue Smoke,
she couldn't help but add another bullet point to
her gratitude list.

Decked out in a deep violet suit with a white

shirt, lavender pocket square and no tie, he looked like he had the world on a string, a confident smile curving his firm lips as if he'd never not had a reason to be happy. Medium brown hair, clipped short, was pushed back and sideways away from his forehead and was just basic-bro enough to ground him in the realm of the living. His jaw was square and strong, the likes of which would compel Gaston to take up facial exercises. Sharp hazel eyes (she'd googled him, obviously, because research) were lit with an enterprising spirit she recognized in her own.

One of his big paws was casually shoved into a pants pocket, sure and easy as if everyone he spoke to was a friend and not a complete stranger. Straight white teeth completed the picture, but she knew that one of his incisors was crooked. A pale white scar, nearly two inches long, was etched across his left cheek and another jagged one separated his right eyebrow into two parts. In some of the photos she'd seen of him he'd worn a steel bar with a screwdriver piercing in the space between the sections, but it was absent today. Apparently, that's what his former teammates called him, the Screwdriver, because he never stopped driving. She didn't quite get it, but apparently, football or whatever.

He wasn't handsome; that was a silly, pale word to describe the sheer mass of man and the obvious contradictions that made up Hugh Matteson, ex-athlete, successful businessman and, lest she forget, tabloid fodder. Even before her research, she'd recognized his name from the constant press coverage his breakup had received. Several years ago, his fiancée dumped him. Not such an extraordinary story, but the timing was unforgettable. The breakup came shortly after his career-ending injury and mere weeks before their wedding day, and then was brutally followed by said fiancée's elopement to this very town with the guy who replaced Hugh as the New York Comets quarterback. It would have broken lesser men, but no one looking at Hugh now would ever guess that he'd once been the most pitied man in sports.

He exuded sheer magnetism and Parker felt an electric pull in the pit of her stomach that she rarely, if ever, felt. Part of why she loved her job was because it freed her from her responsibilities home in Chicago, also known as her father, who was still recovering from the fact that his wife (and Parker's mother) walked out on them nearly fifteen years ago. Her life on the road was hers and hers alone. The fact that Hugh wasn't relationship material wouldn't stop her from having fun with him. Because he looked like he could be a veritable Disneyland in bed.

As a rule, all her relationships ended the next morning anyway, because she was on the road most weekends and rarely home, but also because attachments weren't really her thing. When your own mom walks out on you, it tends to shake your faith in the reality of commitment.

Returning her attention to her plate of barbecue, she had to admit that she was tragically underwhelmed by the food. So having fun with the owner, who, considering his lackluster food, was the only smoking-hot thing in this particular barbecue joint, was probably a bad idea. There was an air of the generic everywhere, in fact. The floor-to-ceiling wood paneling and sunbaked longhorn skulls perched high on the walls screamed typical roadhouse decor, but it was something she could forgive because it was Vegas, the city that had invented camp, forgotten it, and then invented it again. It was better than the sports theme she'd expected at any rate, so points for that.

Pulling out her tablet, Parker began typing her initial thoughts for the review she'd write later. She'd ordered nearly everything on the menu, including two sampler platters consisting of sausage, brisket, ribs, pulled pork, salmon and chicken along with corn bread, collards, baked beans, and mac and cheese. The different barbecue sauces themselves were bland, which was downright heresy for a barbecue place. The smoke on the meat was just enough, but it was obvious that they used the same kind of wood to smoke all their varieties of meat, which was such a cop-out.

She managed to type out a few notes, but kept getting distracted. Hugh was working his way around the perimeter of tables that ran along the outside wall and eventually she abandoned even the pretense of working to watch him. Smiling at a blue-haired woman in an I Heart Las Vegas sweatshirt who had reached out and taken his hand, the corners of his eyes crinkled and lit up his whole face, which without the smile tended toward menacing. Her breath stopped at the sight, not quite a catch because she was a grown woman, but edging in that direction. His free hand abandoned his pocket and covered the woman's hand in his, a warm two-handed grip, before he crouched to get down to her level so he could hear her better. Parker had no idea what the woman was saying, and her expression was serious, but by the end of the conversation they were both laughing.

Then as if in slow motion, Hugh rose from his crouch, turned and caught Parker right in the act of blatantly staring at him. Turning back to her food would have been the best thing to do, but instead she held his gaze, because, hell, she wanted to. After a moment she looked away because staring was rude, but that look had communicated what she'd wanted. That, yes, she agreed with America that he was aesthetically advantaged, and also yes, she'd like to explore that advantage in a behind-closed-doors type of situation. Because that was what her work life was about. When she was on the road, she could be herself instead of her father's caretaker or the girl her friends still coddled because her mom ran out on them for a flashier life.

Then he was coming her way, making a beeline through other hopeful diners whose yearning eyes followed him as he passed them by. Her throat tight, she inconspicuously slid her tablet off the table and back into her bag so he wouldn't have another reason to be suspicious. Except upon further thought she should have acted like she was reading a book. No one ate alone without a buffer of some kind and here she was with half the food in the restaurant in front of her. Nervous and hating it, she took a drink of beer, one thing she couldn't complain about. From a local brewery in town, the light hoppy effervescence was the perfect fit to wash down rich, smoky barbecue.

Wiping the foam away from her mouth, she looked up to see him standing there and her entire body froze, with the exception of her wet hand sliding over the paper napkin spread across her lap.

"Enjoying your meal, ma'am?" he asked, an amused eyebrow raised, the one with the scar. His voice was grumbly and rough as he eyed the pile of food eclipsing the surface of the scarred oak table.

"Indeed," she got out, having second thoughts about engaging with him. Either he'd clock her as a reviewer right off the bat or he'd assume that she was the lone competitor in a food-eating contest.

Either way, she'd feel guilty for the unflattering review she'd ultimately be writing.

He held out his hand, but then thought better
of it when he saw that her fingers were caked in
barbecue sauce. "I'm Hugh Matteson, the owner.
Just wanted to make sure we were taking care of
you tonight."

Looking up into his eyes was an epically bad
idea, because she'd love to be taken care of by this
guy. He was even better up close, dark scruff shad-
owing that movie-star jaw; hazy green eyes ringed
with brown were clear and amused, hands so large
she bet he could hold a toddler in his palm. He was
also imposing, well over six foot five, and smelled
like a man who took care of himself—musky cologne hung on the air like a summer's breeze over
a marsh, intriguing and mysterious. She fantasized
about forgetting the article altogether and taking
him back to her hotel room for the night.

"I'm Parker Jones," she finally said, starting and
stopping again around the bubbly catch in her throat
from the beer.

"Were you expecting someone else?" he asked
pointedly, his gaze cataloging her many entrées.
"Or a group of people?"

"No, it's just me," she admitted, giving him what
she hoped was a cheeky smile. Like "I'm just a girl
who couldn't decide," not "I'm writing an article
about your mediocre food."

Part of her wanted to admit who she was, because she'd never been shy about writing unfavorable reviews before, but she wanted to flirt back with him even if it wouldn't amount to anything. He was, after all, a famous athlete, and she was a woman with barbecue sauce already crusting around her fingernails.

"I just really like barbecue," she added when he still hadn't responded.

That caught him up and he laughed, eyes crinkling, dimples in all their glory, that lickable crooked incisor up close and personal. His voice was lush and deep, plunging like an ocean wave pulling away from shore. An answering pull in her middle had her shifting in her seat. This was probably the reaction he received from every woman he met, which was just the reminder she needed to stop her X-rated thoughts right in their tracks. He was the kind of guy who could ruin her life, and it still wasn't quite put back together after the first time.

"I can see that," he finally managed, that amused grin still firmly in place. "But I've always been partial to a woman who could eat."

She laughed. "Oh, don't worry, I can eat."

"Apparently," he said, leaning back just slightly on his wing tip's heels.

They smiled at each other then in a moment of shared amusement and she felt the bubble of anticipation in her stomach grow.

"Parker Jones," he repeated, the words rolling off his tongue experimentally. "That name sounds familiar for some reason. Like Lois Lane or Jessica Rabbit."

Shrugging, she met his eyes again. "Sorry, don't know. To my knowledge I've never been a comic book character, and we've definitely never met."

"No, I would have remembered you," he agreed.

"Are you sure? I'm not always surrounded by tables of food."

He smiled again, their eyes still locked as if glued to each other. Breaking contact, she shoved a forkful of brisket in her mouth, nearly choking at the amount and the fact that it was far too dry.

Seeing her distress, he took a seat in the round wooden booth, his arm poised to make contact with her back, but she shook her head vehemently as she swallowed. "I'm fine," she choked out, reaching for her mug of beer.

Guzzling it down, she felt his eyes on her, saw him gesturing to a nearby waiter who wasn't hers. "Can we get two more of whatever she's drinking? Quickly, please."

"Oh, that's too much," she rasped, waving the request away.

"One's for me," he stated simply, as if she'd invited him to sit at her table.

In fact, once she'd fully caught her breath again, he decided to help himself to one of her ribs as

if they were old friends having dinner together.
Watching him chew was like a porno, that tight
jaw, gnashing and grinding. She really needed to
reevaluate her choices if this was the kind of thing
she'd been brought to, getting turned on by a man
eating. Honestly, it was too much, and yet admittedly, also very on-brand.

"Are you from Vegas or just visiting?" he asked,
throwing the clean rib into the basket already half-
full of them.

"Just visiting," she informed, taking another sip
of beer. She wasn't eating any solid foods until he
went away and it was safe to chew again.

"Where are you from then, Parker Jones?"

The waiter set down two frosty mugs of beer, the
foamy white heads just barely not running down the
sides, and she wondered exactly what she should
say. Revealing too much about herself would be a
problem. It wasn't outside of the realm of possibility that as a restaurant owner, he'd read her stuff.
"Chicago."

"And you're in Vegas by yourself, or just this
dinner?"

"Vegas."

He seemed to consider that for a second. "Business or pleasure?"

Shit. She didn't want to lie, but he was going to
ask her what she did and she wouldn't have a good

answer. Unfortunately, she was a terrible liar, so it would have to be the truth. "Business."

"Let me guess," he said, looking over the wealth of food again. "Soup kitchen director?"

She laughed, not expecting a joke. At least not a funny one. "Nope. Though I have volunteered at plenty of them."

"Good for you," he said, his eyes sliding over her face and down her chest. She wasn't wearing anything revealing, just a pair of jeans and a black V-neck T-shirt with a fitted burgundy blazer. All choices designed to hide any sauce or grease stains she might incur during the sampling process.

Nonetheless, his gaze stopped on her cleavage, and those tingles of anticipation rolled over her skin like a long-lost friend knocking at her front door after an extended absence. It'd been a long time, but she remembered them like it was yesterday. He quickly collected himself, straightening in his seat and meeting her eyes again, vaguely apologetic. If he hadn't just tried to save her life when she was choking, she might have given him a hard time about it, but she also didn't want to draw out the conversation considering what she was hiding.

"And you own the Blue Smoke Restaurants," she filled in. "And used to play some kind of sports game?"

That got him smiling that shy, humble smile again, his eyes drifting downward and his tongue sticking in his cheek. "Football," he supplied, eyes dancing with amusement. "The sport, that is."

"Gotcha," she said. "The one with the ball."

"Yeah, that one," he replied, shaking his head at her playful obtuseness. "So what do you do?"

She took a deep breath, having spent their entire conversation trying to figure out the answer to this very question. "I write for a lifestyle magazine." Not technically a lie, so: points.

"That's pretty cool," he said, his thoughtful gaze catching hers again.

Those hazel eyes were intelligent and sharp, at turns making her feel as if she were the only person in the room, but she knew at the same time they were evaluating his waitstaff and his diners' satisfaction.

"Yeah, it's my dream job."

"A lifestyle magazine," he repeated. "So, like, laundry tips and stuff?"

She shrugged, the anxiety crawling up her back. "I'm not too into laundry," she hedged. "It's more like menu planning and leisure activities." *Like where to eat*, she thought guiltily. Where was that waiter with her check and please don't let him ask the name of the magazine.

"Ah," he said, grabbing the platter with the chicken and sausage. "You mind?"

She shook her head.

"Thanks," he said, unrolling the extra setting of silverware the waiter had left, probably anticipating another person after all that she'd ordered. "I haven't had dinner yet and I don't know that we have enough take-out boxes for all this anyway."

Her eyes shut. Dear God. She knew he was just joking but still struggled against the embarrassment climbing up her neck. Oh, it was so, so bad.

"I just wanted to try a little of everything," she explained lamely, not ready to give her cover away regardless of how it might look. She didn't care what he thought of the amount of food she'd gotten. "It all sounded so good and I'm only in Vegas for a couple of weeks."

"Your first time?"

"No, I've been several times."

"I've never been a huge fan of it," he admitted, "but it's home for now. My real one is a ranch in San Antonio where I grew up."

"San Antonio is great, though the tiny Alamo was a bit of disappointment."

He laughed again. "Yeah, well, I think that's the point. The little guys lost the battle, but Texas came back to win the war. Think about how small the actual building is, and they defended it to the death against a larger and more powerful Mexican army. They knew they would die and did it anyway."

"Fair enough. Disappointment retracted," she said, holding up her hands in supplication. "I should know better than to disparage Texas in the first place."

"Texas forever." He grinned, repeating the popular catchphrase and holding up the longhorn steer sign on his hand, pointer and pinkie stretching up proudly.

She rolled her eyes, watching as he chewed on a piece of sausage, his expression turning thoughtful.

"Parker Jones, lifestyle writer in Vegas on business alone. You got any other plans besides eating the best barbecue in town tonight or would you wanna get out of here?"

And then Parker thought she might choke on just actual air this time.

She didn't choke again, but came damn close. Holy shit. Was this really happening? A one-night stand with a famous football player? One-night stands never gave her this much agita and she knew it was because this one was different. She was already enjoying herself and could actually fall for him. Her heart beat a chaotic jangle in her chest and sweat coated her palms. Rubbing them discreetly on her jeans, she met his eyes and her shock must have shown.

"I don't mean for that," he said quickly, holding up a hand. "I mean, not that I wouldn't. Hell, of course, but I just meant I could show you around. You know, as a local. I'd hate to think of you doing this whole trip alone. Besides, I don't meet many women who can eat this much, so I feel like this is my opportunity to get to know the kind of girl who at least gives it a shot. There are a lot of points on the board for making the effort."

It was a joke she couldn't *quite* laugh at, but she appreciated it and she wanted to stay with him. Didn't want the warmth of his body heating her left side to suddenly vanish without her really memorizing it to take out at a later date when she was back home, a place she was always slightly miserable if she were being honest.

"Sure, I just have to pay the check and we can go. Since apparently I can't box this stuff up."

Chuckling at the throwback to his previous joke, he stood, holding out his hand to help her from the booth. "How about I have the leftovers sent to where you're staying."

"But the check," she pointed out.

"It's on me, sweetheart. Keep your per diem for the next place you visit."

She bristled at the patronizing endearment and the per diem crack, as if she couldn't afford to go out to dinner on her own. Like she was just some girl who couldn't make it in the world and had to depend on her job's petty cash to buy her enough food to eat for an entire month.

Suddenly, it felt like she had rocks in her mouth, dry and crackling, and she wanted to grind them between her teeth until they were dust.

He must have read her displeasure because he held up a hand. "We can have the bill sent to your hotel, okay? I was just trying to be nice. If I can't buy a girl dinner at my own restaurant, I don't know when I can, you know?" His tone was overly conciliatory, which only served to irritate her more.

"Maybe I'll just wait here for the check. I have an early day tomorrow and I'm very tired," she backtracked, yawning to make it more believable.

Hugh crossed his big arms in front of his gorilla-wide chest, the tailored fabric of his suit pulling over the bulging muscles outlined underneath. Although it looked like it, he wasn't trying to be intimidating; she thought it was just his way of digging into his stance, which was obviously going to be to try to get her to go out with him. "Ms. Jones, I'm sorry if I offended you, but we've been looking at each other tonight the same way I hope people look at my food when it comes to their table. I don't pick women up in my restaurants ever and I'm interested, so I'd be grateful if you'd give me another chance and come grab a drink with me."

As far as apologies went, it was pretty good, but she'd already made up her mind not to do it since it was a bad idea for a lot of reasons. If things had been different and she hadn't been intending to write a review of his restaurant, she would one-night-stand the shit out of this guy, but alas, life was only that simple for the pool-raft models.

"Listen," he began just as she opened her mouth to tell him the aforementioned resolution. "I haven't been on a real date in years, not one with a woman who minds if I pay a check or not anyway, and I know we literally just met, but you seem pretty cool. I have it on good authority that I'm not great at this shit, so if you could cut me some slack I would really appreciate it."

She smiled; she couldn't help it. He didn't have to be vulnerable with her but he'd gone there, and it took guts to do that with a complete stranger.

"Whose authority?" she asked idly, still deciding what to do. "Who doesn't think you're good at picking up women in your restaurants? Seems like that would be pretty easy."

His lips thinned at the playful jab and his look was bland. "Well, my ex-fiancée for one."

"Did you call her 'baby' and try to put her in a corner?"

His thick eyebrows came together at the old movie reference. "No, that doesn't even make any sense."

"Well, you called me sweetheart and I hated it, just like I would hate to be called baby. And your offer to pay for my meal put me in a corner, metaphorically, if you know what I mean. So if you think about it, it really works on a lot of levels."

Hugh stared at her, a corner of his mouth twitching.

"You know what we call this entire conversation in football?" he asked, arms still crossed and that meaty thumb drumming impatiently on the upper bicep of his opposite arm.

"A touchdown?" she tried.

"Nope, intentional grounding. Where you try to kill the play before it even begins."

"It sounds like your words are saying you didn't like my joke, but your face is saying that you did."

He laughed for real then, the sound rich and deep, warming her belly more than his food had. "Yeah, I fucking liked it. I like you, too, so will you forgive me for trying to get what I have to assume is one of the largest meals ever ordered in my restaurant taken care of?"

She met his eyes, shaking her head at his food crack. "One drink and then I really do need to get home."

"Fair enough." He waved over a waiter to explain the situation about her leftovers and check.

"What hotel?" he asked.

"Halcyon."

"That's a good one," he approved.

"It's pretty for a casino in Vegas," she admitted, finally rising from the booth.

He offered her his arm and she slipped her hand through, trepidation filtering through her body along with just plain anticipation.

"And your fiancée might be right that you're bad at the pickup, but your follow-through is exemplary."

"You have no idea just how accurate that statement is," he told her, his tone edged with a delicious dash of danger and irony.

CHAPTER TWO

HUGH DIDN'T GET nervous as a rule. He'd faced down the largest men in the country running at him at speeds only athletes conditioned over the course of their entire lives could achieve, so a girl in his restaurant shouldn't have made him as edgy as he was, but Parker Jones was doing it. And not just because she had a chest not even his famously large hands could get around, though that was a huge plus.

He hadn't been interested in a woman beyond sleeping with her in a long damned time. If that was a commentary on him as a person, so be it, but after the hell he'd been through with his ex he hadn't trusted his own judgment to pick women. The scandal was long gone, but he'd never really gotten over being the nation's poster child for cuckolding. Nor the fact that Amanda was happily married with the family they'd dreamed about. He'd thought he'd have three kids by now, but the thought of finding someone who wanted him for him and not who he'd been as a player was too much work.

So the fact that Ms. Jones gave him some butterflies didn't mean much. She didn't even live in
the city, and a little what-happens-in-Vegas action
was just fine with him. It didn't matter that when
he'd caught her staring at him earlier, something
inside him had flickered on. She was beautiful with
cool blond hair and warm brown eyes, curves that
lasted for days, and expressive lips that he'd wanted
to lick his own barbecue sauce off of. And now he
also knew she was sarcastic and fun as hell.

He held her hand, small and soft nestled in his
long-fingered grasp, wondering when was the last
time he'd done something simple like that for a
woman and coming up short. Maybe he really had
taken himself out of the game for too long, like the
guys said, but every time he thought about really
giving a woman a chance he remembered all that
bullshit with his ex. If girls didn't want to be with
him for the money and notoriety, then they really
wanted to be with him because they felt sorry for
him. He honestly didn't know which was worse.
But already Parker didn't seem to care about either
his money or his past, which felt good. The sympa-
thetic head tilt was usually the first thing women
gave him, whereas she'd just lit him up and thrown
his money back in his face. Already, a small piece
of him felt liberated.

"When did you retire?" Parker asked when they
got outside, a gentle breeze blowing a lock of pale

hair across her face. His yellow McLaren was sitting in the first spot near the door.

"Six years ago."

He guided her toward the car, but she resisted, pulling her arm and breaking their forward momentum. "I assumed we were walking somewhere."

"We can if you want, but all the bars around here on the Strip are pretty much tourist traps."

At her raised eyebrow, he gestured to his car. "I'm not going to kidnap you and take you back to my place against your will. This is not that, I promise. Just a drink, like we agreed."

She didn't look completely convinced, white teeth chewing nervously at her dark pink lip. If she'd been wearing lipstick it had worn off, probably during her meal.

"But if it did end up being more, would that be the worst thing?" he threw out because fuck it, they were adults. "I mean, like, as long as we both want to."

She shook her head and he shoved his hands into his pockets. Hooking up usually wasn't this hard for him. Most girls would have asked to drive his car by now, and he couldn't even get Parker to have a drink with him.

"We can have a drink on the Strip if you want. Totally innocent and you'll be close to Halcyon. The problem is that I'll be bothered by fans at those kinds of places and we won't actually get to talk."

She considered him and he waited as patiently as he could. "Okay," she finally said, her tone still dubious.

"The place I have in mind would be private but it's too far to walk, so if I don't drive we'll have to use an app and ride in some guy's car."

"I had a lovely minivan experience on the way here," she claimed primly. "He even had a candy bowl, so I bet you feel foolish for being so snobby about ride-sharing now."

She pulled her phone from her bag and started tapping away. He accepted what was happening because after a moment of surprise that she'd easily wrested control from a situation he thought he'd been manipulating masterfully, he realized he actually kind of enjoyed not being in charge. It was a theme that ran through his entire life. He made his own decisions, the decisions for his parents, he'd managed his team on and off the field, he was always in charge of what he did on dates, he managed an entire chain of restaurants, but now here he was in the parking lot of his own restaurant waiting for someone else to decide his fate tonight. He hadn't known it was a thing that he'd enjoy, but he didn't hate it.

"I got the luxury option for you," she told him. "Whatever that means for a person who drives a car for a living. The app says a black Acura sedan."

"I'm sure it'll be fine."

"You're suddenly amenable to the car?"

He shrugged. "No, but I'm not going to argue with you."

Their eyes met in a benign challenge that he found oddly exhilarating, like when he was on the sidelines watching the other team play just waiting for his turn to go back out on the field. Only instead of the playing field being full of elite athletes, it was a single woman with a body designed to make men crumble before they could even attempt a play.

"Good," she told him, a corner of that full mouth raising in a playful smirk. "I hate difficult people."

He snorted because they hadn't been together for more than a half hour and he knew she wasn't exactly easygoing. And neither was he, for that matter. His own baggage was so heavy only a man of his imposing stature could carry it. He didn't fault her for knowing what she wanted and doing what she needed to do to get it.

"What?" she asked, reproach in her tone when he didn't follow up his snort with an actual response.

"Both of us are difficult, sweetheart. It's why we're standing here on the street together waiting for a car we don't need instead of me finishing the night talking to my guests and you eating your weight in barbecue. We like it."

Just then the black Acura pulled up, the familiar emblem of the car service on the windshield.

"Not bad," he told her, and she just rolled her eyes. Taking one last look at his own car that he loved and cherished, he helped Parker into the back seat of their ride, his fingers itching to cup the ass he could barely take his eyes off of as she bent to get inside.

"So where are we going?" she asked, oblivious to the fact that he was seconds away from completely mauling her.

"Oh, did you not want to choose?" he asked, meeting her eyes in the relative darkness of the back seat. The blue lights of the restaurant's sign shone onto her face, highlighting her pursed lips, which only made him want to kiss that know-it-all expression off of it.

"It's your town," she argued.

"Structure," he instructed the driver, a young man in his twenties who was more or less indifferent to their presence. He had a dirty-blond man-bun and beard that looked like it was taking its time filling in.

The kid pulled away from the curb, and because Hugh had become intensely private about what he shared with the public, he stayed silent for the short five-minute drive to Structure. The bar was on the top floor of the Crown Royale casino and had breathtaking 360-degree views of the city, but mostly he'd chosen it for the privacy. Because he wanted privacy with Parker. Every single dirty thing he wanted to do to her demanded it.

They rode the elevator to the club's entrance,

where they were enthusiastically greeted by Jesse. He requested one of the semiprivate spaces.

"Nothing but the best for you, Hugh," Jesse breathed, her eyes going dewy and sentimental. "And thank you again for that little loan. It really helped me out."

"Loan implies I want it back, sweetheart," he told her, giving her a wink. "I don't. Consider that car a gift from me to you."

She leaned up to give him a kiss on the cheek, her long blond ponytail swaying back and forth behind her. "You're the best, Hugh."

Jesse was a young girl in her twenties, but had a broken-down car and a small child she needed to provide for, so he'd provided the money to replace it. Structure was one of his favorite places in the city and he'd gotten to know the employees very well over the years, and when she'd needed help, he helped. He would have done it for anybody really, and often did. It was part of the reason he didn't have relationships. Everyone wanted a piece of him and the only pieces he was willing to give any woman nowadays had dollar signs on them.

He felt Parker's eyes on him and knew she could be thinking any number of incorrect scenarios. But he'd never slept with Jesse. Not that he wouldn't, but he hadn't. That said, he'd given cash gifts to a lot of women he'd slept with, not because he'd felt strongly about them, but precisely because he didn't. Relationships weren't gonna happen again as far he was concerned. He'd loved Amanda and she'd made him the literal laughingstock of America, which meant that now, if he had to pay women to leave him alone, he'd do it.

Following Jesse, Hugh led Parker through the club, which was comprised of small rooms and nooks furnished with couches and easy chairs. The decor was Vegas-style Roman, weathered columns reached from the floor to the ceiling and created an intimate space. Dim lighting threw shadows on the paintings of nude women and men on the walls enjoying life's baser pleasures. Gold-leaf ceilings and bloodred furniture gave the place a lurid feel, like just being there was the first step in finding Eve's apple and getting to sin for all eternity.

Jesse led them to a small corner room, cordoned off in case people like him showed up, with two red velvet couches and a single gold lamp with a deep red shade that cast the whole space in a muted, sensual glow. A gold coffee table sat in between the couches and he held open the red velvet drape for Parker to enter.

He sat next to her on one of the couches and fought the urge to take her hand again, wanting to feel her skin, to learn it, feel it warm up in his until they were sharing heat.

"I've never even heard of this place," she said, taking in the decadent room.

"It was the only bar we could go and actually hear each other," he explained. They were far enough away and enclosed so that the music from the bar was a dull rumble in the background instead of a roar. But that wasn't the only reason he'd chosen this particular place. He only did what he wanted now and he didn't want to take selfies or answer questions about his glory days—he wanted to flirt with a girl.

"It looks expensive," she observed, playing with the gold tassel on the lamp.

He shrugged. "I don't know what expensive is anymore," he told her honestly. He was also done pretending he was some "aw shucks good ol' boy" so people liked him. He was a multimillionaire, closing in on nine digits, and he wasn't going to apologize for it.

Her eyebrow raised and that corner curved up in her signature smirk again. "Look at you," she purred. "Mister big football man."

"That's right," he said, inching just the slightest bit closer to her as the waitress arrived to take their drink order. He rattled off his favorite red wine, feeling Parker's eyes on him.

"Maybe I didn't want wine," she said when the waitress had left them alone again.

"You should have spoken up then. It's not like you've had a problem with that so far."

She laughed, shaking her head at the truth of his statement. "Were you sad to retire from football?"

Getting comfortable, he stretched his arm across the back of the couch until he could almost touch her long blond hair with his fingers. "Yeah, the first couple of months were fucking devastating. It was the thing I'd done my entire life. I literally didn't know anything else outside football, but I had a business degree from UT so I thought I might as well use it."

"What did you injure?" Her eyes involuntarily scanned his body for what might be out of place.

Damn, he did not want to talk about this shit. Not right now. It was not at all sexy, but Parker was the long game. He already recognized that even if *long* in this case meant however long she was in town.

"It was late in the fourth quarter against the Steelers, a really physical defense, and I got tackled head-on. I had a compound fracture in my leg, which isn't too big a deal when you're a regular person, but the NFL was over for me. The recovery alone was nearly a year, then the conditioning to get back into shape would have been another. I would have been over thirty by the time I could even think about returning to the game, and no one ever has after that kind of injury."

"So you like running the restaurants?" she asked, changing the subject, which he was really thankful for.

"Hell yeah, I love eating and building something of my own. And I'm in charge, just how I like it."

She rolled her eyes at his pomp, but then gave the hand resting on the back of the couch a quick squeeze. "I'm sorry about the injury," she said, her voice steady and earnest. "Do you live with pain?"

He shook his head, but it wasn't the entire truth. No one left the NFL without some measure of pain management. It was the nature of the job.

The waitress brought them their wine and two glasses, and Hugh poured them halfway full.

"Pinot noir is my favorite," she told him before taking a small sip, those fuck-me lips closing over the delicate rim of the wineglass. His cock twitched with the X-rated visual of what they'd look like closed around him, her guarded eyes looking at him with want and need and completely lost to lust.

"After the accident, I toyed with buying a vineyard and bottling my own wine, but decided I was more of a smoked meats kind of guy."

"Definitely seems more on-brand," she agreed, a corner of her mouth lifting.

"You like making fun of me?" he asked, calling her out on the smug smile.

She shrugged. "Was I?"

Their eyes met, heat darting between them until finally he took a drink of his wine.

"What? A football player can't be into something highbrow like wine?"

"I didn't say a word," she claimed, even though she'd said enough without any words at all. "I think you're very sophisticated. Your car probably costs more than my house, so I wouldn't presume to make those kinds of judgments. Plus, this was a deep-cut wine choice. I'm impressed."

"Do you cover wine in your lifestyle magazine?" he asked, hoping to find out something of substance about her.

"Sometimes, but I'm actually a trained somme-lier," she revealed, and he raised an eyebrow in surprise.

"What? A girl who eats unlawful amounts of barbecue can't be into something highbrow like wine?" she asked, throwing his own words back in his face.

Damn, he liked her. Liked getting as good as he gave. His ex had wanted him to tiptoe around her feelings like they were Tiffany glass, whereas Parker could dish it out and take it with a smile. It was sexy as hell and his cock throbbed again, com-ing to life by slow but unstoppable degrees.

"Which leg?" she asked when he didn't have a response right away. He'd been too busy fantasiz-ing about fucking her on the gold coffee table be-side them. Hell, probably the Persian rug would be good enough for the filth he had in mind.

He stretched out his left leg, the one on the out-side of the couch, far enough to nudge her foot with his own. It was an innocent touch, just his wingtip nudging her black canvas sneaker, but he felt it in his dick and the back of his head which was clouding over from lust.

"Sorry," he got out, kneading his leg the slightest bit. "It's a little stiff."

She looked suspicious at first, and rightly so, because it was a major line of bullshit. It'd been the other leg in the first place, and in the second place that leg didn't hurt at all.

"Do you need a hot compress or something?" she said, raising an eyebrow.

"Might be nice if you could massage it for a minute, just to warm it up."

She laughed, the sound high and incredulous. "You've got to be kidding me."

"You're not going to just let me sit here in pain, are you?"

"Don't you have something you could take?"

He shook his head. "I don't like pills."

He jerked at his leg without even an ounce of shame. He wanted her and knew she wanted him, too, from the lingering looks, the jumping pulse at her throat when he touched her, the way she worried that lip. They were two strangers who liked each other; it wouldn't be a big deal if they saw it through. It was the very tagline of Vegas, for fuck's sake. He would be doing her a disservice not to offer her that kind of opportunity on her visit.

"Maybe I should go," she suddenly said, standing up. "Seems like you need to tend to that leg anyway."

He shot up then, too. "Please don't. I was just kidding about the massage."

"What are we really doing here, Hugh?" she asked. "It's not like we came out together to form a lasting friendship. I'm only here for a month."

"I just want to get to know you." And a month was a long damn time.

"Or you want to fuck me," she said baldly, the words shooting straight to his groin.

He didn't bother to deny it. "Of course I do. Look at you, and you've been riding my ass all night. We've been fucking each other with words since the moment I sat down at your table. But I get it, it's too soon and you want to go, but can I please have your number? Because I'm serious about wanting to know you."

Her mouth opened, ready to stick him with whatever accusation might render the truth of his statement null and void. But instead, she just murmured, "Fuck it," and pulled all two hundred and fifty pounds of him to her.

His lips met hers in surprise, but it didn't take him long to shift to straightforward lust. Once he got his bearings he took control from her, crowding her into the dark corner of the room where they blended in with the black around them. Hidden from all the dirty shit he wanted to do to her.

She pulled her mouth from his and glared at him. "And if you pay me for this, I swear to God I will claw your eyes out. I don't need to be taken care of."

The words were clear and a corner of his mouth lifted. No, he didn't suppose she was. "Noted."

So he yanked up her T-shirt, running his hands across the smooth skin of her sides and back, diving into the kiss again, coaxing her mouth open wider this time. Her little whimpers of pleasure drove him beyond madness, and he slipped one hand from under her shirt to tunnel back up into that silky halo of hair, adjusting her head so he could go even deeper, their tongues feasting on each other, excavating their secrets with desperate curiosity.

Sticking his knee between hers as an invitation, she didn't leave him hanging, riding hesitantly at first, but then moving her hips in earnest. It was the sexiest thing he'd ever seen, ever been a part of. "You're sexy as hell, Parker," he breathed hotly against her lips, swallowing another one of her greedy moans. "Ride me, sweetheart. I want to see you come."

So saying, he flicked open the placket of her jeans as his other hand drifted from her back to her breast, testing the heavy weight in his big hands. He wouldn't have cared if she had small breasts or large breasts—frankly he was more of a big-picture person—but fuck if that flesh didn't overflow in his meaty hands, making his cock throb a bass beat under the metal zipper of his pants. His hips started moving in time to hers as she rubbed over his leg, her hands grasping the lapels of his coat, tugging him against her but in turns pushing him away as she arched into him.

Sliding his hand in her pants, he found her slick and hot. He'd give a lot to be able to see her, to lick and suck until she was screaming louder than the music on the dance floor, but this was what they were doing right now. And then later he'd ask her to come home with him, so they could do this right and he could make her breakfast in the morning and then whatever the hell else she wanted. Hell, maybe even an actual date at some point.

She threw her head back, pale neck arched in pleasure as he ran his thumb over that sweet, lust-soaked nub. Changing the tempo and the pressure, he learned what she liked, what sent her closer to the edge, could feel the muscles in her abdomen tense against his arm. "Come on, baby," he whispered in her ear, his thumb pressing on the verge of pain just to torture her. "You know you want to come. No one can hear you, no can see you, but you know they're all there, just down the hall, don't you?"

She whimpered against him, bucking hard against his leg, and he let his hand move farther down, pumping two fingers inside her, agonizing over his own arousal as her moans got lower, more guttural, as if the sensation was coming from deep inside her.

"Fucking touch me," he commanded, unbuckling his belt and dealing with the zipper. He couldn't handle it anymore. He wanted to slide his cock into that dripping pussy and fuck her in front of every single person in this bar, wanted them to see him give her pleasure. The music was quieter in their private corner room, but it pounded through his veins like the downbeat to his own racing pulse.

Her cool hand weaved inside his boxer briefs, pulling his thick cock out, the tip already leaking. Their eyes met as she lifted her hand and licked her palm before running her thumb down the underside, teasing, testing, gauging his reactions. He pumped harder inside her, using three fingers now, stretching and exploring, loving her gasp and her involuntary squeeze on his cock in answer. She regained herself, straightening her back and taking his mouth again as her hand flew over him. He grunted against her mouth as they got each other off with the entire world down the hall. It was indecent, erotic, lewd, and it was only a hand job. He'd had his first in middle school, and yet nothing he'd done since compared to the heat in his stomach, the pooling of energy in his back, electric tentacles grabbing his insides up in a rough, greedy fist of passion so tight he could barely breathe.

Frantically, he pulled her shirt up under her bra

because he was going on her stomach—that was the only option at this point.

They were in a rhythm now. He was back on her clit rubbing in time to her quick, staccato strokes, designed to drive him insane with the featherlight abrasion of her hand. "Harder," he instructed, his thumb on her clit following suit.

"You're bossy," she breathed, taking his order, her hand clasping around the base of him and dragging up slowly and firmly. He couldn't get enough of that measured climb.

"Don't know why you'd think otherwise," he growled as her hand ran over the tip of him, lubing her up again to better handle him, to deliver even more mind-bending pleasure.

"I didn't say I didn't like it," she gasped, giving one last good tug before her head fell back and she cried out her orgasm. He swallowed the sound with a kiss, knowing that while they were unlikely to be discovered, the possibility existed.

Coming down, her eyes glazed in the dim light, she squeezed him again, pumping like mad until all his muscled contracted at once and he let go, spurting onto her stomach in thick bursts as his knees grew limp and worthless.

He met her eyes, working for his next breaths, and was stunned by what had just happened. The hottest moment of his life with a woman he barely knew in a club he knew too well begat a feeling of serenity he hadn't felt in years. Maybe the sense-lessness of it was what he needed, a fling with someone who normally wouldn't give him the time of day. Parker wasn't a football groupie or some-one who just wanted his lifestyle; she was someone who'd nearly fucked him in a public place just be-cause she liked him. He really hadn't known how powerful that would be.

He reached into his jacket pocket, pulling out the two-hundred-dollar silk pocket square, and cleaned her stomach off, going against his cave-man instincts to rub it into her skin so he was part of her. He'd save that for another time, because after discovering this kind of chemistry, there was no doubt that there'd be another time.

Gently pulling her shirt back down and dealing with her jeans, he dropped a light kiss on her fore-head, brushing his thumb across the apple of her cheek. "That was fucking crazy," he told her, help-ing her down from his leg, making sure she had her balance before taking her hand.

She just nodded, still dazed by what had hap-pened.

Looking up at him, her mouth opened and then closed again. Before finally she said, "I need to go to the restroom. Sorry."

And then she was rushing up the hallway.

CHAPTER THREE

PARKER CHANGED HOTELS the second she got back to Halcyon so that Hugh wouldn't find her, which she regretted. Not for giving Hugh Matteson a hand job in a bar, because that had been pretty epic. And running out on him at Structure was equally crappy of her, but in light of her article it would have been a major mistake to sleep with him and she definitely would not have been able to resist doing that if she'd stayed. The night had been world-shaking and they hadn't even had sex, so yeah, she'd needed to get the hell out of there.

Because she wasn't *not* going to write a truthful review of his restaurant. Hugh was a nice guy and she'd already lied to him. It sucked, but it would have been way worse if they'd actually had sex. Especially because her boss had published the review on their website as a teaser for the ten-page Las Vegas spread that would be in next month's physical issue. Because his name was attached, the story was already quoted all over social media, which meant the chances of her getting another opportunity to sow her wild oats with the Greek god of restaurant investors were pretty dismal.

She had a very real fear that Hugh was out there, even now, looking for her. When she'd called Halcyon to see if she'd left her toothbrush in the room, they'd sent over a message from him. An envelope with his phone number. Nothing else. So yeah, she knew enough about him to know that he wouldn't have taken being walked out on very well. She'd be livid if he'd done it to her, so she could only imagine how someone with that much pride would feel.

She flipped through program she was holding, vowing to stop thinking about Hugh. Which was difficult because she was getting ready to judge a barbecue competition for the Las Vegas Food & Wine Festival. For over a year she'd been scheduled to be a judge and it was generally one of her favorite things to do. She loved encouraging amateur chefs and often found a lot of amazing talent who ended up going on to really successful careers in the industry. Now it was just a reminder that she wanted to have sex with a local barbecue restaurateur.

Another plus to judging, she'd get to be inside an air-conditioned tent soon, because the heat was killing her. She'd spent the morning walking around the festival, chatting with vendors and chefs, trying not to feel miserable in the intense desert heat.

Her phone rang just as she was about to make her way to said air-conditioning. When she saw it was her dad she held back a sigh, but knew she had to take it. Leaning against a bushy green golden rain tree, she answered.

"Hey, Dad," she greeted, idly watching crowds of festivalgoers wander from one vendor to the next.

"Parker, honey," he responded, "I miss you."

"I miss you, too."

Parker loved her dad. But she spent most of her time at home making sure he went to work, making him dinner, generally being kind of a mother to him. All because her own mom had run out on them.

"How's Vegas?" her dad rasped, his voice sounding like he'd just woken up. It was a bad sign that he was sleeping so late in the morning. She knew from experience that it was usually when the depression crept in. "You put my money on twenty-seven?"

She forced a laugh she didn't quite feel. "No, not yet," she told him. "I haven't really had a chance to gamble yet." *Because on my only free night I gave a former NFL quarterback turned restaurateur a hand job in public* was what she didn't say. Her dad was a football fan, sure, but obviously not that much of one.

"I will before I come home, though," she promised. "How's everything up there?"

She thought she heard a sound in the background and then her dad was clearing his throat. "Everything's good up here," he assured.

"Is someone there?" she asked, putting a hand on her other ear to block out the music being pumped in from the overhead speakers.

Her dad coughed. "Nope, just me here. Probably hearing the television or something."

"Okay," she said slowly. "Well, just remember to get to work soon and call me if you need anything, okay?"

"Will do," her dad said. "Miss you, sweetheart. Hope you come back soon."

"Miss you, too, Dad," Parker returned, holding back a sigh. Her dad never outright asked for her help, but he had a way of making her feel like she needed to be home. It was why she loved her job so much. Sometimes she just needed space from her dad to be herself instead of the good daughter who took care of her father and didn't make questionable decisions. Her life on the road involved a lot of decisions the Parker at home wouldn't make, but ones that kept her sane. Her mom had run out on her, too, something her dad often forgot. Parker wasn't going to be like her and leave her dad alone, but sometimes she had to admit that she thought about it. Fantasized about being free to do what she wanted.

Parker ended the call to her dad and shoved the phone into her purse, glad that everything was okay at home.

Leaving her spot on the tree, she went in search of Karen, the fiercely competent organizer who'd contacted her about the festival in the first place. When she found her, juggling a tablet and two clipboards, she checked Parker in and led her to the judging tent. Set up with five chairs at a long table covered in white linen, the tent was dark and cool, and Parker couldn't have been more thankful if someone had also handed her a cold beer.

"Thank you again, Karen," she said when the woman showed her to her seat, which happened to be next to one of her personal heroes, Michael Barton. He'd been at the forefront of the farm-to-table food scene that was now exploding on a national scale and they'd become close acquaintances over the years. "I really love being a part of these festivals."

Karen smiled, her brown eyes warm as more judges entered the tent. "No problem, honey. I love the magazine. And Michael recommended you himself, in fact."

"I appreciate that," she told Karen. "I'm looking forward to the food. I feel like I should be paying someone for the opportunity instead of the other way around."

Karen laughed, her eyes drifting over Parker's shoulder to where Michael was making his way toward them, his pace speeding up when he saw her. But it wasn't Michael who caught Parker's attention; it was the man who appeared in the open doorway that had effectively shoved her heart in her throat.

"Fuck," she whispered under her breath. Of course Hugh would be a judge for this kind of event. He was a local celebrity. Fuckity fuck fuck fuck. She should fake an illness and bow out. That was the only option.

Michael's brow furrowed. "Here I thought you'd be happy to see me, darling," he pouted, kissing the top of Parker's hand. It was shocking how little chemistry or attraction there was in the gesture, considering the man who was now checking in with a festival employee could inflame her with a single brush of his finger.

"I am so glad to see you, Michael," she apologized, the words coming out on top of each other as she gave him an air kiss on the cheek as was their custom. "But I need to use the little girls' room before we get started. Please excuse me."

Then she booked it out of the tent, giving Hugh her back before he could have possibly seen her. She kept moving, past Michael's seat to the other end of the table, nearly tripping in her haste to escape.

She pretended to go to the restroom she didn't need and then wound her way back to the judge's tent, peeking inside to see if everyone had been seated yet. Her plan, if it could be called that, was to wait until everyone was in place and then surreptitiously take her seat. With any luck, his chair would be far away and she could completely avoid him. Then she could sneak off afterward and never talk to him again.

She watched as everyone took their seats, Karen standing in the middle of the tent scanning the area for Parker. Her time was nearly up.

Spotting her name card on the table, she bit back an audible curse. The whole bathroom charade had been for naught because on the other side of her empty chair sat Hugh Matteson, looking like an Adonis in his matching baby-blue pants and vest with white shirt and navy tie. There'd be no stroke of luck for her this time. She'd be sitting next to not only the very guy she'd walked out on after a public sexual indiscretion, but the guy who owned the restaurant she'd reviewed only days earlier.

Basically, it was going to be a really bad afternoon. Because while she'd sat beside plenty of people she'd given bad reviews to and not batted an eyelash, she hadn't almost slept with any of those people. Nor had she lied to them about what she did for a living.

With exaggerated slowness, as if she were going to face her execution squad, she slithered to her seat like the serpent-ish creature she was, nodding to Karen on her way.

She pulled out the folding metal chair beside him, but Hugh didn't even glance her way. He'd obviously figured out who was sitting beside him, considering the big white placard with her name printed on the front and back sitting on the table. Which meant the anger she could feel pouring off him as tangible as the chair in her hand was not imagined.

Luckily, Michael hopped up to help her get seated before she could even acknowledge Hugh. Small blessings and whatnot.

"Darling," Michael began, the warmth in his voice reminding her that she wasn't a completely horrible person. "Where are you staying? Let's go out after this. It's been too long since we caught up."

Crap. If she told him, she was going to have to switch hotels *again*. A fact that was driven home by the fact that Hugh cleared his throat ever so slightly beside her. The heat of him was radiating outward in waves and she was disturbingly aware of every single bit of him, from his putty-colored suede shoes to the way he'd rolled back the sleeves of his dress shirt to show off the finest forearm to ever grace certainly a food and wine festival, if not the universe itself.

"Let's definitely catch up," she told Michael, trying to focus but feeling like she was failing. "And I still need to review Toast and Jam. You know I live for a good lunch spot," she said, changing the subject from her hotel for obvious reasons.

Michael waved his hand as if dismissing the idea. "I would love it, of course, but it's very ca-

sual and probably not worth the travel time. But my
new place will be opening in Chicago by the end
of the year, so you will be the first on that, I hope."

"Oh." She involuntarily clapped her hands together, her voice a little too squeaky from the shred-
ded nerves of sitting by Hugh with so much unsaid.
"That's so exciting! Chicago has an amazing food
scene, but it's light on that magic you make with
vegetables. I didn't even like artichokes before I
had your soufflé and now I sometimes find myself
daydreaming about them."

She could have sworn she heard a snort coming
from Hugh's direction, but Karen took to the mi-
crophone to announce that judging would begin
and the conversation with Michael was cut short.
Karen went down the table introducing each judge,
one of whom was a local food critic and another a
local famous chef. She and Michael were the outsiders of the group.

When she was finished and Michael was distracted by the judge on the other side of him, Hugh
finally spoke.

"You're a good writer," he said, his voice deep
and only loud enough for her to hear. She could feel
his eyes on her but refused to look at him. Could
not look at him, in fact, due to crippling mortifica-
tion the likes of which no mortal person should ever
have to experience. "Maybe you should try your
hand at fiction, too, since you're so good at lying."

"I didn't lie," she gritted out of the corner of her mouth so that Michael couldn't hear.

"You have got to be shitting me. You told me you wrote for a lifestyle magazine. *Gastronomic* is a food magazine. Food is right there in the damn title, darling." He bit off the word like an insult, clearly mocking Michael's earlier familiar endearment.

"Food is part of life," she threw back, but knew it was lame. Knew all of it was futile. She deserved whatever he gave her, which taking in his tense shoulders and locked jaw was going to be even more unpleasant than she'd anticipated.

He was fully glaring at her now, but she ignored him and kept her gaze straight ahead.

"For all I knew, you could have been dead," he growled as Karen finished up and the first contestant plates were passed out. "I almost called the police until the hotel told me you'd checked out."

"I'm sorry for scaring you," she admitted, her tone low and earnest. "But surely you realize now why I had to leave. It was a conflict of interest."

His snort was 100 percent real this time. "Yeah, so you could write your shitty review about my restaurant?"

"If anything, my review was more complimentary because of what happened between us," she said, knowing how idiotic the words were as soon as they left her mouth. What had been her purpose? To curry his favor by insulting his livelihood but giving a backhanded compliment to his sexual prowess? Had the situations been reversed, she would have punched him in the face. "I don't mean that," she backpedaled, finally turning to see his face.

It was a mistake. A big one. The revulsion in his eyes was so naked that her breath caught. Running out on him had really hit a nerve with him, she realized, then understood, duh, it was pretty much what his fiancée had done to him. Unfortunately, it was pointless to try to explain to him that she actually resented how loyal a person she was, so instead she would stop being such a whiny baby and simply atone for her behavior.

"Hugh, I really am sorry. I know what I did was shitty," she entreated, still whispering so that Michael wouldn't hear. "But I had no idea you would be at the restaurant that night, had no idea you'd talk to me or that we'd have a connection. I tried to end it before we left your restaurant, but you were persuasive and I liked you so I went along with it and by then it was too late to tell you about the article without looking like an asshole. I don't think either of us expected it to go longer than one night, so I went for it."

A little anger did clear out of his hazel eyes, but they were still wary and not at all happy. Instead of feeling like an unwanted rodent in a sewer, she'd at least graduated to a well-regarded lab studies rat. She'd take it. Anything to get through the rest of this day. They had over fifty barbecue entries to sample and she'd never had less of an appetite.

Michael must have heard them talking because he craned his neck over the table so he could see both of them.

"Hi there, Hugh," Michael said. "Congratulations on your restaurant. I'm hearing great things, which isn't always the case for celebrity places."

"Thank you," Hugh said, his voice subdued as he watched Michael with hooded eyes. "I appreciate that."

"You know, Parker here knows barbecue inside and out," Michael informed Hugh, unable to read a room, or tent, apparently. "She quite literally wrote the book on it. You should have her check out Blue Smoke."

For fuck's sake.

"Oh, she came," Hugh said, leaning into the double entendre with a pointed look in her direction. "But apparently wasn't impressed."

"My review for Blue Smoke came out a couple of days ago," she informed Michael, whose kind green eyes widened with understanding.

"Ooh," he finally said, leaning back to mouth the words *I'm sorry* to her.

She shook her head. It wasn't his fault the tension between her and Hugh was a living, breathing monster, slobbering its displeasure all over the judging panel.

Suddenly Michael stood up, hastily tucking his scorecard under his arm. "I'm going to go speak to Karen about..." he started. Paused. Then, "Something. See you two in a jiff."

She watched as Michael took his plate to a seat farther down the table and away from the two of them. She didn't blame him and would have done the exact same thing.

Instead of sparring with Hugh, she took a bite of the rib Karen had put in front of her. After another bite, she started scoring.

"Your review was wrong," Hugh grumbled, finally breaking the tense silence. She pushed her rib to the front of the table, where there was an industrial-size garbage can waiting for it.

"Hugh, maybe it was, but I'm entitled to my opinion. It's my job. And Michael is right—barbecue is my specialty."

"I'm from Texas. I think I have the upper hand in barbecue," he challenged, voice snide.

"If you'd bothered to read my bio or book, you'd know that I grew up working in barbecue restaurants. Then I spent an entire year traveling across the country learning barbecue from the most renowned and decorated pit masters. I got my first job as a writer calling out other magazines for not giving barbecue its due, so if I know anything about food, it's what goes on a grill."

Hugh's hazel eyes narrowed, and she looked away again because he was too intense and she was too on edge. She had angered a beast and had no idea what to do. She was from a family who didn't talk about their feelings, just bottled them up and pretended they didn't exist. So being on the receiving end of Hugh's out loud and proud ones was like trying to navigate a map in a foreign language.

"If you know so much then why don't you open your own restaurant instead of crapping all over everyone else's hard work?"

"First of all, I did not crap on your hard work. And I like this job because of the travel and the writing. I get to try the best food in the nation. It's an amazing opportunity. I have no desire to run a restaurant where I'd be burned out and miserable within a year."

Hugh wasn't impressed with the answer, but she didn't care.

One of the contest employees set another plate in front of them and she tasted and rated.

"No one else has given me a bad review," Hugh finally responded. "I can't help but think it was retribution for what happened between us. Maybe you were embarrassed or something."

That got her back up. "What would I have to be embarrassed about? We got each other off in a club.

It was probably one of my poorer decisions in terms of possibly getting arrested for public indecency, but I'm not embarrassed by it. We were hot as hell for each other. It happens."

He laid a hand on the back of her chair, that long arm and tan hair-dusted forearm catching her attention as he leaned in so no one else could possibly hear what he said. "It doesn't always happen and you know it. We went at each other like animals, you ghosted me, and then stabbed me in the fucking back. If we weren't already over, I would drop you so fast your head would spin."

She could feel his breath on her bare neck, goose bumps lighting up her skin as she sucked in a breath at the insult.

"I didn't stab you in the back," she whispered, but it was faint and sounded lame even to her own ears.

"Why did you run?"

"I told you. It was a conflict of interest."

"It was already a conflict of interest before you ran off. Try again."

He eased up when someone came by with the fourth sample, but when they left again he leaned in close enough that her ear grew damp under his breath.

"Try again, Parker Jones. I knew your name was familiar. I've even read your book, you know? Granted, I revisited it again this week just to make

sure it was the same person, but there was your picture right on the jacket."

"I didn't lie," she insisted weakly.

"No, you're right, I should have put it together
just by the amount of food you ordered, but I liked
you so I ignored it. Why did you run?"

She desperately tried to think of an answer.

But then he decided to continue. "I'll tell you
why I think you did. It's because you're a coward
who hides behind her little computer and judges
everybody else before anyone judges her. When
have you ever had anything you've made judged?"

She rolled her eyes. "Every day for two years in
culinary school and then every day for three more
years in Manhattan working for some of the best
chefs in the country. I've been judged, Hugh, and
I know how to critique food fairly and honestly.
If you have a problem with my article, take it up
with my boss."

Turning, she met his eyes, soul-deep irritation replacing her embarrassment. "You know what really
bothers me? In fact, it pisses me off. That I had to
go through years of grueling training, both physically and mentally, and still have my expertise constantly questioned by restaurateurs who don't know
a damn thing about food. You're just some ex-jock
who thinks he can throw anything together and call
it barbecue just because he's from Texas and has
grilled out for Sunday dinner. The rate of failure

for celebrity-owned restaurants is incredibly high for one reason: people come initially for the novelty and then they don't come back because the food is shitty. Maybe people have told you your barbecue is good because they want to kiss your ass, but that's not really my thing. So maybe you need to check yourself before calling out real professionals."

With that, she shoved a huge bite of rib into her mouth and ignored him. She was so livid she could barely breathe.

She filled out the scorecard, making a real effort not to let her foul mood skew her ratings. Then she shoved the plate of food into the trash.

"I usually played ball on Sundays, so there wasn't really time to grill."

She glared at him, sucking in air, her eyelids fluttering in irritation. "You know what I mean."

He studied her, not looking upset by her pointed outrage, but almost thoughtful. "So you ran away because my barbecue was bad?"

"Hugh, your barbecue is not bad. That is not what my review said. I just thought it wasn't remarkable. For a lot of restaurants that's exactly what they want, but I'm picky about barbecue and my readers want food they can't get anywhere else. I don't know that Blue Smoke qualifies, and that's the whole story."

His tongue pressed into the side of his cheek as he sat fully back in his seat, his hand finally, *finally*, falling from the back of her chair.

Relieved, she chewed on a palate-cleansing cracker and sat back as another plate was put in front of her.

"Why don't we put our skills to the test then?" Hugh said, regarding her thoughtfully. "We could make this interesting."

"This cooking competition?"

He shook his head. "We could have one of our own. You and me."

Her brow furrowed. "What do you mean?"

"I mean we'll each make a plate of barbecue, have it judged impartially and see who wins. If you win, it'll be a great story for your magazine, and if I win, you'll know I'm better."

"No way," she said immediately. She was not spending any more time with Hugh Matteson. He would devour her whole. One hand job and she'd been ready to give him five stars and the gold medal for barbecue; no way was she sticking around for some bootleg competition with him that he'd probably rig.

"You scared you'll lose?" he taunted.

She took a bite of the pork, shaking her head. "I just don't want to spend more time with you."

He laughed at that, that wolfish grin with the crooked incisor giving her the shakes. He leaned in again and that deep rumbling voice taunted her. "You are such a chickenshit. What's the matter? Know you can't keep your hands off me? Even though I want to, I know I can't keep mine off you.

I've relived what we did in that club every hour of every day since it happened. Truthfully, sometimes more than that."

Parker swallowed, her breath stuck in her throat and her eyes closed against the wave of prickling anticipation that swept over her body. She shook her head, wanting it all to stop, yet knowing she wanted it to continue more.

At his low, knowing chuckle, she snapped back to reality.

"Fine," she bit off. "I'll do it, but if I win you have to sell *my* barbecue sauce in your restaurant and online store."

"Done," he declared, his grin triumphant. "And if I win, I get one night with you."

She snorted. "I'm not cattle, Hugh. I won't barter away my body for a barbecue competition. If you want me, you'll have to win me on your own wits. Unfortunately for you, I'm a lot more complicated than barbecue."

She shoved another plate in the trash.

But he wasn't finished, apparently, because he moved his chair closer to her, leaning in all the way so it looked like he was going to kiss her neck, but it was really just a distraction because in the same moment he put a hand high on her thigh, where a rush of heat surged.

"Better watch out, Parker," he murmured. "You just accepted a challenge with the only man in

Vegas who has always been the odds-on favorite to win."

She closed her eyes and nodded. She hadn't needed the warning; she was already well aware that she was in very deep trouble.

CHAPTER FOUR

"HAVE YOU DECIDED what you want if you win?" Parker asked Hugh, standing in the middle of the deserted kitchen of Blue Smoke.

It was late and Hugh was tired after the long day of judging at the festival, but he'd convinced Parker to come and see his kitchen under the guise of fair play for their competition. A competition he didn't exactly want to participate in, but it had been a good way to prove that she was wrong about his barbecue. It didn't mean he was quite ready to forgive her lie, because he was still pissed about that, but he believed her reasoning. That said, lying wasn't something he ever tolerated.

Ordinarily, he would have walked away and never given her a second chance, but the reality was that he hadn't been able to forget her. He'd been with a lot of women and nothing compared to what they'd had at Structure. He still felt her touch on his skin, smelled her citrus scent on the air, and he knew he wasn't going to let go that easily. He at least wanted her in his bed before he moved on to the next.

She was wearing some kind of flowy peach skirt that ruffled out above her knee and a white T-shirt that emphasized a chest he'd been remembering on a loop since that first night, too. Her long blond hair was pulled up into some messy knot on top of her head, with more and more strands falling onto her face and neck as the day had gone on. Despite the relative coolness the tent had afforded, they'd been sitting in one-hundred-degree heat eating barbecue and he'd spent most of it imagining himself licking up the single droplet of sweat he'd seen rolling down the back of her neck. He'd almost just done it, too, until she'd wiped it away with a napkin.

So, yeah, he was going to pursue this as a physical relationship, but that's where it would end. Parker Jones could not be trusted.

Of course, right at this moment she was the one who looked low-level pissed that he'd dragged her to a restaurant kitchen after hours when no one was around. He'd been maneuvering her all day, simply because she deserved it. He could give a shit about the review, but that she'd been operating on a lie of omission dug deep into him in a way he couldn't shake. Seeing her order that night, his first thought had been that she was a reviewer anyway; he didn't see what the big deal would've been if she'd just told him the truth. It wasn't as if she was held to some kind of food journalist code of ethics where his knowing she was a critic would somehow corrupt her review. It was just scared bullshit because whatever this was between them was combustible and she knew it, just as he did.

"I'll tell you if you admit that you writing that review wasn't the only reason you left," he said, baiting her.

"First of all, you're going to tell me anyway because I'm not agreeing to a competition unless I know what you're getting if I lose," she challenged, like the boss she was. "But since you want to be cute and hassle me first, I will admit that had I planned to write a positive review, I would have admitted what I did for a living."

That unintentional tell had him smiling. "I get it," he drawled, rocking back on his heels. "You didn't want to hurt your chances of a one-night stand with me by telling me the truth. It had nothing to do with journalistic integrity."

Parker shrugged. "So what? You hit on me first."

"No problem," he clarified, "just making sure I understand. And then you felt so guilty for using me for my body even though you were writing a crappy review, you cut out on me."

"I wouldn't say guilty," she said. "I don't feel guilty about writing the review."

"Of course not," he snarked. "Why would you feel guilty about that?"

"Because your food is fine, but it's not upscale," she told him, standing right in the middle of his own restaurant's kitchen. She might be a liar, but she also didn't pull her punches.

"I never said it was upscale," he told her. "Those were the words of another food writer, so hate to burst your bubble there. Furthermore, the people who come to a restaurant associated with me aren't coming for upscale barbecue. I know exactly who my customers are and sales just keep going up."

"Your price point is not at the family-friendly restaurant level," she argued, arms crossing under that magnificent chest.

He stretched his neck, trying to keep from reaching for her. Regardless if Hugh the person was still pissed at her, his dick had already forgiven her, bought her flowers, and was ready to move in together. "Are you going to keep droning on about business or are you just going to admit you were wrong and take your clothes off?"

"Excuse me?" she choked, and the satisfaction of catching her so off guard was very deep.

"I mean just what I said. We both know that regardless of the content of your review, which for the record I'm fine with, you owe me an apology for lying. So let's have it."

Her brown eyes narrowed. "I already apologized at the festival."

"Did you?"

She nodded her head and he smiled. "Well, I don't think I heard you, so maybe you should try it again. Maybe it'll stick this time."

"I'm out of here," she said, glaring at the command and grabbing her canvas bag from where she'd tossed it earlier on one of the stainless steel worktables.

"I thought something really bad had happened to you, Parker," Hugh reminded her. And this was a true fact, because he had honestly been concerned for her welfare, especially when he'd thought she'd passed out in the bathroom or something. The thoughts that had spun in his mind, like if he'd actually been taking advantage of a sick or drunk person, for instance, had been monumentally shitty. She'd appeared to be in possession of all her faculties, but when someone disappears like that anything seems possible. "You could at least acknowledge that. I mean, I called your damn hotel to make sure you were okay. And then you didn't even text me at the number I left the concierge to let me know. Do you know how much of a risk it was to leave my phone number with someone? The last time I gave it to a woman in a bar, she sold it. One thousand times. Made nearly a hundred grand. Yet I gave it to a random hotel employee just so I could know you were okay."

She regarded him, those warm brown eyes shrewd and assessing, as if he were lying. He didn't know what it said about him, but he was getting off on her skepticism of him. Being who he was, most girls just gave him what he wanted either because he was rich or they felt sorry for him. While he wasn't complaining, he was also very aware that his most distinguishable trait was that he was a workhorse. Fed off the drive, the goal, the raw, unfettered grinding toward what he wanted. If she thought that her back-off attitude was pushing him away, she couldn't be further from the mark. It only made him want to work harder.

Then she blew out a breath, a piece of blond hair alighting from her face and then plopping back over her eye. "I meant I was sorry when I said it earlier, Hugh," she repeated. "I have felt guilty for days about it and I don't know how else to get you to believe that, but it's true. I was afraid because we'd already made out and I hate lying, but that's no excuse for being a coward, which is what I was. It is, in fact, the only reason I've agreed to this ridiculous, and pointless I might add, contest."

He leaned back onto one of the big industrial ovens. "That was a lovely apology, thank you," he grinned. "I accept your prostration."

She rolled her eyes, still holding on to her bag.

"So you think it's going to be that easy to beat me, do you?"

Shrugging, she met his eyes. Not saying anything, but her meaning was clear. She wasn't worried about it at all.

"You know, I won't be using the recipes I use for the restaurant."

Still, she didn't look bothered. Fuck, not for the first time, he wanted to kiss that smug smile off her face. But he'd settle for needling her instead.

"Where are you staying now? Just in case you decide to wimp out of this competition, as well?"

"Do you want my blood type and Social Security number, too?" she asked, hands poised testily on her hips. "I'm not telling you where I'm staying so you can have access to me whenever you feel like it."

"Hotel staff isn't allowed to just give anyone your room number, Parker."

"Yes, but you're—" she waved her hand up and down in his direction "—you, so they'll do anything to please you."

That was probably true and why he'd asked for her hotel, but it wasn't as if he was going to stalk her there.

"You have a pretty low opinion of me if you think I'm just going around Vegas browbeating innocent hotel employees into letting me into women's rooms. If you want to know the truth, I could be single-handedly causing the plastic garbage heaps in the ocean for all the room keys I've had slipped in my pocket over the years."

It was the wrong move. He saw it as soon as the words left his mouth, but fuck it, he wasn't going to hide the truth of who or what he was.

"I'm sure lots of women do give you their room keys, but I'm not going to be one of them."

"But if you hadn't written that review, we both know we were headed back to one of our places."

"You don't know anything like that," she insisted, glaring at him openly.

He ran his tongue across the back of his teeth, watching her. She was bald-faced lying to him.

"We both know that night was off the charts. I don't know why you're trying to deny it now. I was fucking there and I remember every second of it," he said, his voice low as he took a few steps toward her. He wasn't going to get in her space. He didn't need to. He was big enough that getting closer drove his argument home. Case in point, she took a couple of steps back. "I have relived it too many fucking times to count. Even after I knew you'd written that review where you called my food, what was it? Ah, yes, 'lacking substance.' Even after that, I couldn't stop thinking about that night. Couldn't stop finishing it in my head. So don't fucking tell me you haven't. You've already lied to me once. Don't do it again, Parker."

He'd really done it now. Her eyes were shooting fireballs right at his face and her hands were clenched at her side, the knuckles stark white against her tanned skin.

But then after a moment she blew an audible breath through her nose, closed her eyes, then opened them again, her fists falling open at her sides. When she met his eyes again, she was calm.

"Are you going to show me where I'm cooking for the competition or are you just planning on hitting on me this whole time?"

"Ideally, hitting on you," he admitted, unashamed. "But I can show you around, too. Just to make sure you don't call foul play when I blow your shit away."

A corner of that cute bow mouth quirked, but she didn't take the bait. The confidence in her belief that her barbecue could beat his was sexy as fuck, and honestly, he didn't care if she beat him. He was a businessman and football player before he was a master of barbecue. He'd never fashioned himself otherwise. The food in the restaurant was good and designed for mass production, because his goal had always been a national chain. If he'd wanted a single restaurant of critical acclaim, he would have built one, but being adored by a few was never his thing. He went big. Always.

"Not gonna crack, are you?" he taunted with a good-natured smile. "Admit you want to punch me a little."

She rolled her eyes again and pulled out her

tablet from her gray canvas bag. Tapping it, she brought up a notes app and starting typing something. "Walk me through the kitchen?"

He shoved his hands in his pockets because apparently playtime was over.

Pointing to the oven, he said, "This is the oven."

Her lips pursed. "Just show me the smoker, please. And do I need to buy all my own ingredients or will we be working from the same basic ones?"

"You can use whatever's here, but I imagine we'll both want to use specific brands or types of stuff that aren't in the kitchen, as well. We'll check out the pantry after I show you the smoker."

"Great," she said, her smile more of lips being pressed together instead of genuine pleasure.

He laughed, shaking his head as he led her out to the back where six stainless steel smokers, each the size of a large refrigerator, sat on the cement floor of the outdoor kitchen extension. The area was covered, but also ventilated, because the smoke had to go somewhere. In the corner was a mobile smoking unit for when they went on the road to different area festivals or food truck rallies.

Parker went to work, taking pictures of the smokers, noting how many racks each one held. He explained how they worked and had to admit that she asked intelligent questions. Not that he'd thought she wouldn't. Her article had been thoughtful and thorough, after all.

"So mesquite is the traditional Texas wood used in barbecue, but it tasted like you chose hickory to smoke yours. Why is that?"

He raised an eyebrow, impressed that she'd noticed. "I use hickory for pork, mesquite for beef, maple for poultry."

Small white teeth appeared, worrying that puffy bottom lip. He felt a jolt in his dick, remembering those teeth on his tongue.

"I don't think whoever was smoking that day did that. I tasted hickory on everything," she told him, meeting his eyes.

He shrugged. "I do random checks every so often to make sure food is being made the right way. Other than that, there's not much I can do. Sometimes people forget, maybe the wood was out of stock, any number of things could happen on any given day. I'm more concerned with the quality of the cooking and the consistency of the service. No typical customer will ever know if something should have been smoked with mesquite instead of hickory."

The unspoken part was that she had. But Parker was no typical customer. The reality of a restaurant on or near the Las Vegas Strip was that it didn't really matter what your food tasted like as long as it got to the table fast, it was reasonably priced, and there was a lot of it. His place was better than most as far as quality so he wasn't going to sweat a few mis-smoked meats every now and again.

Parker seemed to accept this and went ahead with her perusal of his smokers, turning knobs, sniffing inside for some reason, asking about the speed at which the trays inside rotated. Seemingly satisfied with his answers, she scooted past him to look at the wood piles and he got a whiff of sweet citrus, like how lemonade tasted on a hot summer day.

"Are you finished?" he asked, crossing his arms over his chest, hoping the stance would hurry her along. While he was amused by her copious note-taking, he had a real agenda here, which was to get her into bed, and he wasn't sure helping her beat him in a competition was going to make that a reality.

"Getting scared already?" she quipped, the first real smile he'd seen from her all night. She must really have a true affinity for barbecue because for the first time today she seemed completely comfortable.

He smiled back, meeting her crinkled eyes. "Sweetheart, I couldn't care less if you beat me. I'm not a chef, I'm a businessman. And if your sauce is good, I'll be happy to sell it for you."

"You still haven't told me what you get if you win," she reminded, brow furrowed.

He thought about it, not really sure there was

anything he wanted that he couldn't just get on his own. "If I win, you work for me."

A light eyebrow rose. "I'm not a waitress or a chef, pal, and I don't need a job."

"I know, but I have a lot of chefs on my payroll to add input to the menu, make tweaks, offer suggestions, and I'm opening new restaurants all the time. It'd be a good business move to bring another on board for free, especially since you're so knowledgeable about barbecue."

In the back of his mind, he also knew it was a reason to stay in contact with her after she left Vegas, and he mentally reined himself in. He'd more than learned his lesson in ignoring the warning signs in women. Amanda's treachery had started with little white lies. Then the big stuff had crept in, no sex for months, going out with the girls every weekend and having no time for him, only wanting to be seen with him at team events where her lover also was, generally being annoyed with every single thing he did. He should have known, but he'd been so busy and had thought it was just a phase or stress about the wedding. Then the injury happened and he finally had the time to figure out what the hell was going on.

The news made it seem like Amanda had left him, but that wasn't the truth, though if he weren't a true gentleman, he'd have told them the real story. That first time he'd found the text messages between them and believed her lies that she and Todd were just friends. It wasn't until he saw it with his own two eyes, the two of them fucking in his own god-damn bed, that he kicked her out. She'd apologized and even wanted to go forward with the wedding, claiming that she loved him and had made a mistake, but he wasn't an idiot.

As if the situation couldn't get more fucked, in the middle of all of it, she'd found out she was preg-nant with Todd's baby and he decided to marry her. Hugh didn't know what the lovebirds were up to now and didn't care. But he wasn't going to ig-nore that kind of shit in the future. Parker had lied once. He'd give her a pass for sex, but he needed to be firm on not letting things with them go any further. Sex with her was already too close to the fire for his comfort.

"Sure, I can be in your consultant pool, but you only get a year of free service."

She clapped her hands together. "Now can you show me the pantry?" she asked, nodding at the back door of the restaurant. "I need to get back to my room. I have an early breakfast tomorrow."

He opened the restaurant door for her and let her pass through back into the kitchen. "So if you're not going to tell me where you're staying, at least give me your number so I can reach you."

"Why? Now that you know my last name, you can DM me on social media."

He rolled his eyes. "I'm not going to slide into your DMs, Parker. Do me a solid, make me a contact. I deserve at least that much for all my worrying."

Lips pursing, she motioned toward his pants pocket. "Well, hurry up and put it in before I change my mind."

He couldn't help it; he snorted. "I feel like I'm getting a preview of what would have happened the other night if you'd stuck around."

Her eyes rounded in surprise and then immediately narrowed in disgust. "Oh my God, you're awful."

And then she was leaving him in the doorway and heading back to the main kitchen area.

"Pantry's this way," he called, still laughing at himself.

He heard her huff, but then she appeared in front of him again.

"Rule number one of this contest," she announced, spearing him with a glare, "no inappropriate comments. The physical part of our relationship was an anomaly and we will not be repeating it."

He crossed his arms over his chest and gave her a glare of his own. "I'll agree to the inappropriate comments, but there's no putting the physical part of us in a box. It is what it is."

"That's nonsense," she clipped. "Rule two is that Michael will be one of the judges."

"It isn't nonsense. You know what's between us.

I'm hotter for you than my fucking smoker right now."

This seemed to irritate her extremely.

"I'm fine with Michael being a judge," he told her, throwing her a bone. He was just trying to remind her how good that night had been, not drive her away. That said, he wanted her clear on what it meant to him and that he thought they should do it again as soon as possible. "But let's also get someone local."

"And probably a third person, too. Someone completely impartial."

He shrugged. "To be honest with you, you'd really have to look under a rock to find someone who wouldn't want me to win a contest. I'm pretty famous in case you didn't know."

Parker snorted. "I guess we'll just have to find someone who you've already slept with. I'm sure they're vaguely disappointed."

He smiled slowly. "That's a population who unquestionably knows I'm a winner."

"You're an idiot," she muttered, pulling open the door to the pantry.

She stepped into the room, which was just as large as the kitchen itself, filled with enough food for an entire week of operation as was custom. Scanning the contents, she looked no-nonsense again as she wrote down what was on each shelf for her own esoteric purposes.

"Meat locker?" she asked.

He led her out of the pantry and down another hallway to the double doors of the meat freezer. He was running a barbecue place, so he'd spared no expense on where he kept his meat. It was a big enough place to store the huge monthly shipments of meat from Texas.

Opening the door, she peered in. "Holy shit," she breathed. "That's a lot of meat."

He couldn't help it, he chuckled again, but she didn't seem to mind this time. Stepping farther into the space, she looked around at the hanging sides of beef in awe. "This is awesome," she breathed, and he cocked his head.

He'd never shown a woman his meat locker before, but maybe that had been a mistake, because Parker was mesmerized by it, her eyes darting around in wonder. Hell, he was kind of jealous she wasn't looking at him that way. It really brought a whole new angle to feeling like a piece of meat.

But then she was shooing him out of the room. "It's freezing," she claimed. "Let's go. Should I get my own meat then or should we use the same?"

He led her back to the kitchen, turning when they'd reached her bag. "You're welcome to my meat anytime, Parker."

"Honest to God," he heard her mutter, her arms crossed over her chest and her head down.

He was smiling, but then her arms dropped and

he saw her nipples through her thin cotton shirt, hardened from the freezer. Damn it, that comment had backfired on him, because now his own figurative meat was as hard as those frozen sides of beef.

"When do you want to do this thing?" she asked, her eyes on his, ready to get back to business. His mind was anywhere but.

"On a Monday when the restaurant is closed makes the most sense."

"Great, let's plan for Monday," she said, clapping her hands together. "That's two days for you to pretend you can beat me. I can hardly wait."

He ignored her trash talk and pulled out his phone. "Your number, Parker," he reminded.

She rattled off some numbers with a Chicago area code he recognized and he went ahead and called her right then to make sure she wasn't lying. Her phone echoed in the empty space and she looked annoyed. Then she stuffed her tablet back in her bag and headed for the door out to the dining area.

"Parker," he called when she'd reached the door. "I may lose the cooking competition, but that other part we discussed, where I need to win a night with you on my own wits? Just be warned, that's one I won't lose."

He watched with satisfaction as she absorbed the words and left him alone in his kitchen, more determined than ever to live up to his own words.

CHAPTER FIVE

PARKER HAD NO doubt that she would win the competition with Hugh. She'd been perfecting her barbecue sauces for over ten years, making friends and renowned chefs taste countless iterations until finally calling them perfection. However, the industrial smokers in Hugh's restaurant were the wild cards. In the past two days she'd been researching like mad to figure out the ratios of wood to meat in one of those suckers. She'd even talked Hugh into letting her have two practice runs with them before the competition.

Thankfully, he hadn't been there when she'd done so, but he was here in the flesh now. Standing mere feet away from her at his designated oven, he was stirring a pot of sauce on a burner. In a pair of cotton black shorts and a light blue T-shirt with the Blue Smoke logo on it, all those muscles swelled out, their remarkable peaks and valleys on full and proud display. So distracted by thick calves that could crush a metal barrel, she could almost forget they were competing against each other.

"Are you ready for this?" she asked Hugh, checking her stopwatch to see how much time her ribs had left in the smoker.

"Yeah, I'm more than ready to be done with this, if that's what you mean. It's fucking nine hundred degrees and we could be making out in my pool, but instead we're doing this cooking bullshit."

After a grueling day in said heat, Parker's hands flew straight up in the air. "You're the one who ordered the competition! I was fine without it. But your pride was hurt by my review and here we both are, sweaty and hot, and not in a fun way."

His shoulders shook with laughter. "I don't give a fuck about my pride. But you deserved it for lying to me and making me worry."

"We both know that's not true. Quit yammering and cook. I have stuff to do," she ordered, pointing her spoon at the pots on his stove top. "And that gas is too high. You're probably burning your sauce."

He rolled his eyes. "Mind your own sauce, lady," he complained. But then, avoiding her gaze, he turned down the gas on his burner.

The timer on her phone went off and she went out to the smoker patio to get her ribs. Opening the double doors, she took the internal temperature of the pork and, satisfied, transferred them to the grill for a couple of minutes until they got a light char, and then returned inside.

Hugh spared her ribs a glance, but didn't say anything. Parker scooped some of her sauce into three spouted dishes and arranged everything on a platter. The sauce needed a second to cool down anyway before it could be served. She was ready for the first judging.

After a few minutes, one of Hugh's waitresses, a petite redhead, popped in to collect the ribs for the judges. Another Hugh admirer that Parker ignored. If anything happened between them, it would just be sex, and it didn't matter if she was the only one or if he had someone else the next day. Which he probably would.

Shaking the unpleasant thought from her head, Parker got back to work on her other sauce for the brisket.

She noticed that Hugh was leaning against his oven, watching her again.

"Are you not cooking?" she asked, putting her hands on her hips. Only ten minutes left until she needed to get the brisket out of the smoker.

"Yeah," he said, gesturing to his stove top. He ran a white towel over his forehead, collecting the moisture there. A bead of sweat slithered down his golden neck and into the open vee that revealed the start of an impressively defined collarbone, and she thought she might faint from the pure indecency of it, but he wiped that away with a towel, too, grinning knowingly at her.

"I don't have time to flirt with you," she barked, turning away from him to splash a bit more hot sauce into her pot.

"That's a damn shame," he said, his eyes on her chest. She knew there was a ring of sweat around the collar of her shirt. Felt it like a warm, wet hand around her neck, but there was nothing she could do about it. It was Las Vegas in summer, and even though the kitchen was air-conditioned to high heaven, she was still standing directly in front of three open flames and going outside every twenty minutes to check on the smokers that were baking in the sun. There was no getting away from the heat, literally or figuratively.

"Give it a rest, will you?" she begged. "I'm not going to sleep with you."

He stopped stirring and watched her add a bit of salt to a sauce. "I'm confused about why that is again?"

"Because I don't want to," she told him. Of course, she wanted nothing more than to sleep with him, but perversely, she also didn't want to give him what he wanted more.

"Liar," he laughed, brushing his big body past her on his way outside to the patio.

She blew out a relieved breath. Being in the same room with him all day was hell. All she wanted to do was rip his shirt off and jump him, contest be damned. He could put her on his payroll all day if he wanted as long as she got to finish what they'd started that first night.

Her phone dinged. She rolled her eyes at Hugh's text message.

Get out here! Your chicken is on fire!

Laughing, she texted him back a thumbs-down for his lame attempt to get her out to the patio again. He'd been doing it all day. Earlier he'd texted her that he saw a puppy, which had been a struggle not to verify.

When it was time, she did go out to collect her brisket. She'd made three and put them on completely separate racks just to account for any uneven cooking that might occur in the smokers. Basically, nothing was being left to chance. That just wasn't who she was. Not in the kitchen and not in life.

However, one thing she had not planned on was Hugh lounging in a plastic chair, naked from the waist up and fanning himself with his shirt. He was such an ass and totally doing it on purpose to drive her bonkers—and it was so working. Between the heat, the pressure of the competition and resisting him, it was just too much. She was only one freaking woman.

"You are shameless," she accused, pointing a finger at him.

He peered at her, still waving his shirt as he regarded her with slit, lazy eyes. "Pardon?"

"If you were that hot, you could have gone back inside," she pointed out, yanking open the doors to her brisket. She would not look at his bare chest; he didn't deserve it. If he wanted to sit over there looking like a sweaty Adonis, good for him. She wasn't having it. She was here to win a contest and then…well, and then maybe she'd let herself ogle his bare chest. Because it was really something to behold. Out of the corner of her eye, she saw the eight-pack carved elegantly into his tanned flesh, corrugated like tough steel and covered with rough velvet. Dark hair covered his chest, thinning out to a perfect line that disappeared under his shorts.

"I could have gone in," he admitted. "But I need to be out here to make sure you're not turning up the heat on my meat. My ribs got too hot and you were the only person who could have changed the temperature."

She rolled her eyes. "I did not turn up the heat on your meat," she gritted, turning to him. But then she saw his eyes glittering and that he was once again teasing her, goading her into saying the ridiculous sentence about his meat.

"You're a child," she complained, sitting the last brisket on her tray before closing the smoker doors.

Glaring at him, she left him on the patio to glory in his own juvenile antics.

Within a minute, Hugh was back in the kitchen as well, with his shirt intact, just in time for the red-headed waitress to collect their new plates. Parker started cleaning up her space.

The waitress came back in to let them know they had ten more minutes until the chicken tasting, so Parker and Hugh returned to the patio to get their chickens. Once back inside, Parker immediately started shredding hers with two wooden devices that looked like large combs. Trying the meat, she was satisfied that it was tender and flavorful. She could taste the sweet smoke from hardwood coals permeating the meat and it was going to be delicious with the tangy mustard sauce.

Taking a deep, relieved breath that it was all over, she put the last of the sauce onto the judging tray, confident that she had it all in the bag.

As the waitress left the kitchen, Hugh threw his towel on the counter.

"Hell, yeah!" he hooted, shoving his fist in the air. "We did it!"

His deep voice echoed in the empty cement room and she laughed at him. "You tired?" she teased. "I was barely getting started."

"You're so full of shit, Parker."

He tossed a juicy slice of brisket into his mouth and stared at her as he chewed, that strong jaw gnashing and grinding. It was hot as hell, nearly as hot as she was. "That's damn good," he said, drenching another piece of his beef with sauce and stuffing it into his mouth. "I don't think you're gonna be able to beat that dry rub."

She shrugged. "We'll see."

Flipping off all the burners, she started washing the utensils she'd used.

"Fuck that," he barked. "Cleaning crew will get the washing."

"It's not a big deal," she told him. His employees had volunteered to work today for time and a half, but that didn't mean they wanted to. Plus, it gave her something to do besides watch Hugh eat in the sexiest way possible. This whole day had her strung out, and she was ready to go back to the hotel and jump in the cool hotel pool with an ice-cold margarita.

But then Hugh was beside her at the sink, helping her wash dishes, and the very thing she'd been avoiding all day was right up against her. She knew he was doing it on purpose, getting in her space, making her all too aware of how she'd been wrapped around him in the dark room, riding his leg until she came.

Taking a few steps away from him, she started drying what she'd washed, creating enough distance between them that she could no longer be taunted by the lingering fresh scent of his deodorant still alluringly present underneath the overwhelming smell of woodsmoke.

"Whoever wins," Hugh eventually said when he'd washed nearly all of the remaining dishes, "we'll go out for a celebratory meal."

Parker looked at him speculatively. "You'll keep your shirt on?"

"No promises," he grinned, that crooked incisor melting her.

"Then my answer is no."

He laughed. "I've never met a woman so scared of my bare chest. You must be two seconds away from clobbering me."

"In the face," she muttered.

He was still laughing when Michael entered the room. "Guys, a decision has been made."

Parker met Michael's eyes and he smiled, so she knew she had it in the bag. Pulling out the front of her shirt and fanning herself with it, she realized she probably wasn't presentable for the judges. Her back was soaked in sweat; her hair was a limp mess on top of her head, damp strands falling down her neck. Making a quick stop in the bathroom, she ran cold water over a bunch of paper towels and freshened up. Redoing her hair and reapplying a bit of makeup was all she had time for, but it at least made her fit for the public eye.

She and Hugh made their way into the dining area where the judges were stationed, him accidentally bumping her as they tried to go through the doorway at the same time.

"Ladies first," she scolded him.

"You were going too slow," he accused, a corner of that wide mouth lifting as he looked down at her from his significant height.

"My legs are short," she informed. "I'm not a giant like you."

"Those legs are just right," he said, and she rolled her eyes at his incessant flirting. It was almost too much to even be true now.

In front of the judges, Hugh was even worse, chatting to all of them like they were the best of friends. Parker wondered if it was all an act, the gregarious football star shtick. Was the confidence so innate in him just covering up something soft and fragile? She wouldn't be the one to find out anyway, so she should probably put the curiosity away. Being curious about Hugh would lead nowhere good.

Fortunately, none of his schmoozing mattered in the end.

Michael stepped forward with the scores. "The rib round went to Parker, brisket went to Hugh, and chicken went to Parker, with Parker's averaged score being nine-point-five out of ten and Hugh's being eight-point-five. It was a great afternoon of barbecue, but that makes Parker our winner!"

Parker grinned at Hugh, whose thick arms were

crossed over his chest as he read the anonymous score sheets the judges had displayed on the table.

"This is hogwash!" he bellowed, pushing the sheets aside and giving the panel his best glare. But she knew he wasn't really upset, just playing it up. He pointed to the man-bun reporter for the newspaper, whose face froze in fear. "You better make it clear how close of a contest it was, pal."

"It wasn't a close contest, though," Parker pointed out, enjoying putting her hand directly over an open flame. "I wiped the floor with you and your weak barbecue."

His tongue shot to the inside of his cheek as he regarded her. "A lightning round. You and me, no smoking, no studying or working ahead, just us at the grill."

She rolled her eyes. "Fine. Far be it from me not to hand you your ass again if that's where you want it."

A thick eyebrow shot up, but she ignored him and his rude behavior. "You guys mind trying a burger?" she asked.

Everyone nodded their heads and she slapped Hugh on the shoulder. "Let's go, big guy, so I can beat you again. Triumph suits me."

He just grinned at her and it was trouble.

To Hugh's credit, he fired up both grills without a problem and they were able to get to work. He'd chosen to use already ground beef while she located the equipment to grind up sirloin and a little bit of pork butt. It would make for a more tender and flavorful burger. She made sure he didn't see what she was doing, though. And to top it off, she also added a crapload of butter to the mix because fat was what made burgers great. Then she hand-whipped some homemade aioli with tons of garlic and hot sauce, and caramelized some Vidalia onions until they were crispy and sweet. There was no way he was winning this, either.

However, as she stood in front of the grill in stifling heat that was over one hundred degrees, sweat pouring down her body, she had to wonder if it was worth it. She'd already beaten him at the main competition; this was all just to soothe his wounded ego. Again.

Flipping the hamburgers over, she placed a slice of smoked gouda cheese on top.

"Gouda?" he scoffed, his crooked nose wrinkling. "Miz Fancy-Pants over there."

"What are you using," she threw right back, "American? Just remember to take the plastic wrapping off."

"Smoked cheddar," he clarified, looking smug. "And there's nothing wrong with American cheese."

"Except that there's no food in it," she pointed out.

"What do you call all that cheese flavoring then?" he asked, grinning stupidly at her, clearly enjoying their non-argument argument. And that's when she realized that she actually liked Hugh Matteson. Not as some dumb hot jock who would be good in bed, but as a live human person who could make, and more importantly, take a joke. It wasn't good news for the no-strings-attached kind of affair she'd planned on.

She took her patties off the grill, along with the buttered and toasted sourdough buns, and went off to construct the burgers. Slathering either side of the buns with the aioli and same thick sweet barbecue sauce she'd used on the brisket, she added the onions, a couple of pieces of crunchy bacon and a juicy slice of tomato.

Hugh, on the other hand, just breezed into the kitchen, slapped the standard toppings on his burger, including squeeze bottle mayo, lettuce and tomato, and seemed to call it a day.

"You don't actually want to win, do you?" she accused.

"I just don't need my burgers to be precious is all," was his gruff retort. "Not every damn thing needs a fancy-ass mayo. You got truffle oil in there, too?"

"Nooo," she drawled. "I don't mind food trends, though. Bringing new foods and ideas to the forefront is exciting."

"That's all well and good, but a burger is a burger. It doesn't need to be gussied up."

"I know you're purposely trying to irritate me."

"Well, if you'd had to watch sweat dripping down your cleavage all damn day, you'd be fucking testy, too," he bit off, staring at her T-shirt pointedly. "Now let's get this finished so I can get myself into a cold shower."

That got her blood boiling. "You're the one who suggested this burger insanity!" she shouted at him, her nerves and patience shot. "We could already be in cold showers!"

His tongue slid to his cheek again as he met her eyes. "Yeah, but then I couldn't see you all sweaty." Then he winked at her and she swore if he were just a little bit closer she would have punched him right in the face.

He sauntered out into the dining area again and she nearly stomped after him, fuming all the way.

That is, until she won that contest, too.

She didn't bother to gloat, though, just smiled sweetly at Hugh as she bid Michael and the other judges goodbye.

Finally, it was just the two of them left in the restaurant and she returned to the kitchen to collect all the gear she'd brought, bearing the heat again when she went outside to get her utensils and the rest of the wood she'd brought for the smokers. She knew she was soaked, but it was over and she could finally hop in the hotel pool.

"Listen," she told Hugh when she got back to the

kitchen, "you don't have to bottle my sauce. This was fun, but I think I proved my point. I'm more than qualified to make a judgment about barbecue."

He faced her straight-on, hands on his hips. "I never thought you weren't, Parker. But lying pisses me off and you lied straight to my face even as you were coming apart on my leg. I didn't deserve it and I didn't like it." He said it all without his normal bluster and dramatics. Just a simple statement of how he felt, which she took in.

However, as she stared at his mulish expression, she realized that it had all been just punishment to him. He'd found her guilty and had handed down his sentence. She wasn't sure she liked it. It meant that they were involved in something together when she needed this to be physical attraction only.

"Come on," he said, waving her toward the other end of the kitchen. "I have an idea to cool us down."

She followed, a little trepidatiously, because now she didn't really trust him.

When he stopped in front of the meat locker, her gaze flew to his and all her conflicting feelings took a back seat. "You're a genius," she breathed.

He nodded, hoisting open the thick door and ushering her through.

"Oh my God," she breathed as the cold air hit her flaming skin like aloe on a sunburn. "This... is paradise."

Hugh flipped up his shirt and groaned. "I've been waiting all day to do this."

Parker swallowed hard because despite being inside an actual freezer, Hugh's abdomen got her heated.

"And, Parker, we're doing the sauce. All of them were goddamn delicious."

CHAPTER SIX

HUGH FELT ALMOST ashamed of how easy it had been to get Parker into the freezer with him. It wasn't entirely selfish, because his internal body temperature was at boiling from standing by the grill for that final burger and he imagined she was no different. He'd suggested the last burger challenge with every intention of getting her in the freezer afterward.

And it had been a good idea on his part, too, because she was looking at him as if he were Santa Claus and the Easter Bunny rolled into one.

"Good, huh?" he asked.

She nodded her head vigorously, holding her arms out from her body and fanning her shirt, the same way she'd been doing all damned day, driving him insane as the thin cotton caught at her chest and allowed him tantalizing peeks at creamy bare skin that were everything and not at all enough.

"Why haven't we been doing this all day?" she asked, her voice breathy with pleasure.

A good question, but mostly because his whole plan had been to seduce her with cold air, which he was rethinking now as goose bumps popped up over the bare skin of her arms and legs. She'd be ready to leave anytime now and he'd be right back where he started. His seduction game apparently needed some work, because he'd been doing a lot without much success. Or maybe what he was pursuing was different. He'd never had much interest in complicated women before, but Parker was bringing it out in him. He hadn't realized how much he liked to work for a woman in his bed, so it was a novel experience.

"I didn't want to interrupt the contest," he said instead. "You looked very intense."

"I was chill," she argued with a goofy smile that had him fighting his own.

Instead he snorted. "Yeah, chill," he mocked. "You barely knew anyone else was in the room. And you weighed your spices, for Christ's sake. I've never seen anyone do that in the history of my life."

She shrugged unapologetically. "My recipe is very exact."

"Well, now it's mine." The words were out of his mouth and he realized by her startled glance that she hadn't thought about that yet.

Her eyes narrowed dangerously and he felt it in his dick. What the hell was happening to him that he liked her anger? "Did you throw the contest just to get my recipe?"

"No, I certainly did not. But after tasting your sauce, I have to admit that it's better than mine and since you're a known entity in the food world, it doesn't hurt to have you featured in my restaurants."

"Oh my God," she drawled, pointing an accusing finger at him. "You did lose on purpose!"

"I did no such thing." And he hadn't, but it had occurred to him that bottling her sauce and adding another one to his restaurant could never be a bad idea. He liked to rotate them out anyway, and having a food critic create a sauce did give a kind of respectability to the operation that as a former sports figure he lacked.

She met his eyes, fire sparking in the ice-cold air. "I don't believe you. I retract my terms. I don't want to give you my recipe."

"I know, sweetheart, but a deal is a deal. It's in the newspaper and everyone is going to want to try the new sauce. Which one do you want to do, the Carolina mustard sauce? That would be a brand-new addition to my lineup, so it's what I'd prefer. And it's fucking legit dynamite."

The compliment seemed to take the wind out of her sails.

"You're much smarter than you look," she grumbled.

"I hear that a lot," he said, chuckling. "What's got your panties in a bunch, anyway? You'll get all the money without any of the investment, just like you planned in the first place when you made that your prize."

She pulled out her mass of hair from the elastic band, combing her fingers through it and grabbing the loose strands back up before anchoring it on the top of her head again. All that was well and good, but what it did mostly was draw his attention back to her chest arching out, stretching that Cubs logo to new proportions, hard nipples at full attention. He was in major trouble if he didn't get his hands on her soon.

"Yeah, but this whole thing is your doing," she pointed out with a deep frown. "You goaded me into a competition. Possibly just to get my sauce."

"Wait a second," he said, raising his hands up as if to ward off her inaccuracies. "I may have suggested the contest to show you a thing or two, but you dictated the terms of your victory. Don't blame me for turning a potentially bad situation into something profitable."

She stared at him, brows still drawn together in frustration, but her eyes met his and he knew she'd accepted that he was right. For what it was worth, he understood her irritation. She was giving up something incredibly valuable in her sauce recipe. But if anyone wasn't going to screw her over, at least not figuratively, it was him.

"I'll have a lawyer draw up my terms," she told him finally. Then she ran her hands up and down her arms. "Man, this feels so good."

"I know," he agreed, wondering how he had a full hard-on in a deep freezer with no less than twenty sides of beef and pork hanging from the ceiling on thick meat hooks. It wasn't a romantic setting but he had it bad for her. The cutoff shorts that barely covered her round ass were sending jagged bolts of lust straight to his dick. He wasn't much of a baseball fan, either, but from now on the Cubs were his number one team. She did miraculous things for T-shirts.

"I had fun today," she said, meeting his eyes again. Hers were warm and melty, not that she meant them to be in the context of their current conversation, but just in general. Parker was a badass, but her eyes gave away the fact that she was also sensitive and he felt that now as he watched her. Felt closer to her because he had shields up, too. "You're a pretty good trash-talker."

He laughed. "Yeah, I typically tone it down for the ladies, but we got pretty creative on the field."

"What was your favorite insult?" she asked, eyes sparking with curiosity.

"It's not for public consumption," he said, not going to say any of that shit out loud. No damn way.

"Oh, come on," she taunted. "I'm not a child, Hugh. I can take a little trash talk."

He thought about what he could possibly say that wouldn't have her thinking he was a cretin. "Guys would call each other's moms all kinds of stuff that was not nice, so those had to be the worst. And I'm not going to repeat them because I have a mother and she deserves better."

Parker crossed her arms over her chest, staring him down.

"You can glare at me all you want, but I'm not sharing," he dug in. "Let's just leave it at, I'm good at trash talk."

She looked like she might not let it go, but then her eye caught on a slab of beef. "You really have this shipped in from Texas?"

He nodded. "I own a ranch, remember? I supply my restaurants."

"So you have, like, actual cowboys on your ranch?" she said, eyebrows raised in interest as she moved in between the rows of meat.

His lips thinned. "Yes, there are cowboys there."

"But you don't do that?"

"I've been known to rope a bull or two," he admitted. "Why? You got a thing for cowboys?"

She shrugged. "I don't know, I've never really thought about before, but I probably could have one."

That made him smile. "Oh, yeah? What else could you probably have a thing for?"

Their eyes met and she shook her head, coming out from behind a side of beef to stand in front of him again. "Nope."

"What?" he drawled innocently, knowing exactly what she meant, but wanting her to say it out loud.

"I've never had a thing for football players."

"Good thing I'm not a football player."

"You know what I mean."

"Sure do," he agreed. "You don't want to admit you have a thing for me."

She raised an eyebrow. "I have a thing for you? You're the one panting after me all day like a starving dog."

He laughed. "I mean, characterizing me as a dog is a little harsh, but I concede your point. But then, I don't have any problem letting you know I have a thing for you. As I've mentioned, that seems to be your problem."

She didn't look impressed, so he continued, taking a step toward her. She took a step back, straight into the beef, and let out a high-pitched scream. The sound was muted in the soundproof space. Nevertheless, it was funny as hell.

"Don't worry, it's already dead," he informed her, laughing his ass off as she wiped at her arm where it had touched the raw meat. Any parasites had been killed off in the initial freeze or else he would have suggested a joint shower for her to get properly sanitized.

"Okay, I think I've cooled down enough," she declared in a huff, marching toward the door.

He stopped laughing and everything in his being wanted to just block her path, but he was a big guy and his size was intimidating so he was very cautious of using it like a weapon. He stepped aside, allowing her to pass, but before she got to the door, he said, "So when are we going for that celebratory dinner?"

Turning on her heel, she speared him with a serious gaze. "You know it's not a good idea."

"Is it because you kind of work for me now?" he asked, just to send her off again. He wasn't ready for her to go yet, enjoying their game.

"I do not work for you at all," she growled, her head tilting forward in irritation.

"Sure feels that way to me," he continued. "I'm making your product. I'm selling it and giving you money. Is that not how business works?"

"You're the worst," she muttered, her hand on the doorknob. "And FYI, that actually makes it sound like you're working for me."

"And I'm glad to do it," he told her. "I'll stop teasing if you agree to dinner with me."

"It's not even worth it," she grumbled to herself, head down.

Then facing him head-on, she pulled off the T-shirt of his personal mental torment, treating him to a strip show he would have paid good money for. "You want me, Hugh? Come and get me. I honestly don't know why I'm resisting anymore other than the fact that you're an impossible human being."

He got caught up staring at the two glorious mounds of flesh pressing out of her sheer, pale yellow bra. He was definitely going to lose his mind if he didn't touch her as soon as possible.

But then he saw her shiver and jolted into action.

"Come on," he growled, grabbing her hand and her shirt from the floor, "you're going to get hypothermia."

He led them next door to the pantry and snatched his own shirt off as well, tossing it carelessly to the floor.

Her eyes locked on his chest, she fanned herself. "Maybe we left the freezer too soon."

"This up to your standard?" He was messing with her because he knew exactly what he looked like. And worked out nearly every day to get there.

"On closer inspection, your abs could use a little work," she told him, meeting his eyes again.

"Get over here, Parker," he ordered. "I've been waiting too long to get my hands on you again."

She slowly made her way toward him and he braced himself for what was to come. He could easily take charge of this whole thing, but he had a girl who'd just stripped in a meat locker so despite the fact that he couldn't trust her, he quickly decided that he was going to do every damn thing to make this a regular event until she left.

"You are sexy as hell," he said, finding it hard not to watch as her breasts jiggled the slightest bit with every step she took.

The pantry was dark, just a hanging trio of shaded lights over a steel table in the middle of the room, but he could see everything he needed to. He hoped to hell the table was sturdy because as soon as Parker got close enough, he scooped her straight up in his arms and sat her down on it.

Maybe it was wishful thinking to imagine he could let her be in complete control. Next time. And he would make damn sure there were some next times.

She leaned in and dropped a kiss on his collarbone, making him shiver against his will. "You're sexy, too," she said, her voice soft. "An ass, but also sexy."

"Aw, sweetheart," he purred, "you're too nice to me."

And then he finally took her mouth, those sweet bowed lips softening under his own. He tangled his hands in her hair, the strands on her neck slightly damp, which really got his dick pulsing with need. He hauled her closer, her legs wrapped around his back, and he pressed into the waiting warmth between her thighs. Heaven was in his pantry, he swore to God.

Her tongue breached his mouth and he grunted, grinding his hips against her. Their fire was rising fast and furious, her nails biting into his back as she explored his mouth. He let her, loved feeling her small tongue against his, the sensuality of it, the intimacy. He'd missed that a lot since his breakup, being part of someone. She tasted like sweet diet soda and smoky barbecue, the perfect summer combination, and he pulled on her, egging her on and bringing her deeper into him so they didn't know where one ended and the other began.

"These fucking shorts have been driving me nuts all damned day," he growled against her mouth when he finally came up for air. He gripped her sides and lifted her so she could slide off the cutoff jean shorts that should be outlawed on her, they were so absurdly fitted. "Take them off. Take it all off."

He could feel her heart beating against her ribs and her eyes locked with his as she slid the jeans off onto the floor, along with her yellow bra and panties. "That's right, sweetheart," he murmured, not quite ready to look down at what she'd uncovered. "You like doing what I tell you?"

Her eyes flared, but he just raised an eyebrow because they both knew the truth. "You can tell me what to do, too," he taunted her, biting down on her tender earlobe. "I promise I'm very obedient."

She snorted and he sat her back on the table, taking her mouth again. He allowed her no room to think, took her over, inhaled her, ate at her mouth until she was limp in his arms, yet still pulling at the hair at the base of his skull.

Reaching into his pocket, he took out his wallet and dropped the condom on the table, meeting her eyes. If she wanted to stop this, now was the time.

Instead she rocked against him and he fucking loved it.

"How do you like it, Parker?" he murmured, gaze sliding down the sickest fucking body he'd ever seen. Her waist was pinched and it flared out into hips that were made for his big hands to grip. He pulled her closer into his waiting cock, grinding against her until her wetness darkened the front of his shorts.

He cupped her perfect globes in his hand, leaning down to take an unimaginably soft nipple into his mouth, sliding his tongue in circles around it until gently sucking the tip, the quiet sound erotic in the silent pantry where nothing else existed besides them.

"Gentle?" he suggested when she didn't respond to his question, running a thumb whisper-soft over her nipple.

"Or not?" he posed, giving the nipple a good twist, her whimper of pleasure making his cock throb spastically against his pants.

Switching nipples, he took the beaded tip into his mouth, sucking ever so slightly on it, barely running his tongue over it, her hips grinding into him to get closer.

And then he pulled it hard into his mouth, feeding off her groan.

"Hard it is," he murmured, applying the same treatment to the other nipple.

She reached down and unbuttoned his shorts, pulling him out of his underwear.

Parker watched as he got larger with each stroke, the flesh hardening in her hand. The feel of her around him was so damned good, he wasn't sure how long he could make this last. Taking her nipple again, his tongue explored every ridge of her, the smooth skin of her breast, tugging and shaping the elongated point, gently nibbling at it until she'd abandoned his cock and was digging her nails into his back.

Wrapping his hands in her hair, tugging just the slightest bit, he tilted her head down as his other hand ran down the middle of her stomach and into the silky folds he'd been sense-remembering on his fingers since their night at Structure. He held her there, wanting her to see every bit of it.

Their eyes were both focused on his finger as he slowly slid it inside her, watching it disappear into her soft channel. He crooked it and she shivered as he found that rough patch there, rubbing tenderly over it because his control was ready to snap. Two fingers were next and he pumped them inside, loving when her hips began to move and her breathing grew audible in the room.

Spearing three fingers inside her, he leaned down to take her mouth, swallowing her little moans of pleasure. She tasted like smoke and sugar and he was near bursting. "Tell me what you want now," he ordered, running a thumb over her budding clit. She was close to the edge, he knew that much. Her legs were locked tight around him and her breathing was tense and short.

Watching her, but still tilting her head down, he ran his hand up and down her slit, bathing it in her arousal. Then he gripped his cock, coating himself in her as he stroked himself.

Her intake of breath was satisfying and she grabbed back at the condom, but he shook his head. "Tell me what you want."

Eyes clear, she matched his gaze. "I want you inside me right now."

Smiling, he grabbed a kiss and then stepped back from her.

"Too bad," he told her, raising an eyebrow. "Because I want you to suck me."

If he thought she'd be irritated with his purposeful about-face, he was wrong, because she immediately slid off the table to her knees in an effortless move.

Cupping his sack, which alone had him locking his knees for support, she licked up the underside of him from root to tip, the vision of that pink tongue driving him to the brink. When she pulled his tip into her mouth his hand shot out to grip the table, his knuckles going white as she took the rest of him into her mouth. She was so fucking good at it, tugging and sucking with alternating pressure and contact, sometimes sliding him all the way out so just her tongue was tracing the slit, lapping up his pre-come.

"I want to do filthy, unspeakable things to you, Parker," he growled, pulling her up before he came. He was going to be inside her when that happened.

Her smile was feline and satisfied. "Good."

He picked her up, loving her yelp of surprise, and laid her out flat on the table with her legs dangling over the edge, all of her bared to his gaze at once.

"Arms up," he commanded, watching as she obeyed, her fingers curling over the edge of the steel.

He ripped open the condom and rolled it on, not sure if he could wait any longer to be inside her even though the need to torture her mindless was also powerful. In the end, though, he couldn't wait.

"You ready?" he asked, placing himself at her entrance, his hips moving of their own volition as he pushed just the merest fraction of an inch into her.

"Do it, Matteson," she demanded, hips lifting.

A smile on his face, he slammed into her, praying she could take it, waiting for and reveling in her grin as she did. She was liquid heat around him, living, breathing sex made for him. Every move she made, every sound that left her mouth, enveloped him like a lasso of dirty lust and desire, pulling and tugging on his insides as he pumped into her.

With every stroke, his sack tightened up, that knot in the small of his back gathering pull as he slid in and out, her satin muscles clinging and clamping over him, expressly designed to drive him to the pinnacle of pleasure.

"Fucking hell," he gritted, running a thumb over her clit, the resulting jerk of her hips a counterpoint to his thrusts. "You're so damned tight."

They went at each other then like animals, bucking and grinding, but he held her hands down the whole time, needing the anchor, wanting her to feel the full force of what they were together, which was a conflagration unlike any he'd ever experienced. She let go, her back arching and her insides gripping him until he exploded, darkness shuttering his eyes as all his muscles tensed up and then relaxed, a wave of relief and bliss washing the urgency away, leaving only gratitude and intimacy in its place.

Their breathing was the only sound in the quiet room as Hugh slowly returned to earth.

Eventually, he leaned down to drop a soft kiss on her lips. "I think that makes us both winners today."

CHAPTER SEVEN

"YOU WANT ME to do what?" Parker barked into her phone at Hugh.

"Two of my head chefs are sick and the other two are out of town," he repeated. "I need your help."

"You want me to cook at your restaurant to-night?" she asked again, because he could not be serious.

"Yeah, I'll pay you whatever you want for the night. I just need someone and I know you can cook."

"You seriously don't know anyone else in this town who could cook for you? There are tons of other barbecue places."

"Listen, Parker," he said, sounding stressed and agitated, "if you don't want to do it, that's fine. But just tell me because I really need to find someone for tonight before dinner begins and I'm totally fucking screwed."

"Why can't you do it?" she asked, pressing her luck.

"Because I'm a goddamn restaurant owner, not

a chef!" he bellowed, which should have made her scared but instead had her grinning. She liked it when he went all quarterback on her.

She just couldn't cave too easily, not after last night in the pantry where he'd completely blown her mind. If she wasn't careful, he could have her doing literally anything for another taste of him. And it wasn't even because his body put those of all other men to shame; it was because he was thoughtful, creative and just Hugh. Maddeningly bossy, fun as hell and too clever by half.

"I'll do it, Hugh," she finally relented. "But you have to be there with me. I'm not going in blind or alone."

"You got it, Parker," he said, breathing a sigh of relief. "Don't take this the wrong way, but right at this moment, I've never loved a human being more."

She laughed. "No problem. I'll head over there now to get a handle on what to do. I assume the meat has at least been in the smoker for the day?"

"Yep, it's all ready to go for a regular opening time," he confirmed.

When she got to the restaurant, it was true that the meat had been smoked, which was a load off her mind.

Hugh made his appearance in the kitchen wearing another mouthwatering suit. This one beige with peach threading, paired with a white shirt and peach tie. As usually, he looked cool and confident in a suit that on another man would have looked like he was trying too hard.

His gaze raked over her with so much heat she literally thought she might catch fire. The dude did not hide how he felt about her physically. All bets were off since last night, too. His texts were outright pornography and this morning he'd tried to initiate videophone sex, which she'd turned down because she'd had a brunch and also, what person looked their best first thing in the morning? That said, she felt the same way he did. Her thoughts were only about him. Much to her dismay, because she could not get involved with a man like Hugh who would break her heart faster than one of his quick grins. Just remembering the way he'd completely ignored that Jesse at Structure was in love with him. That's how she'd look one day if they kept sleeping together, like a lost puppy lapping up his measliest of affections and still begging him to love her. Jesse seemed like a nice enough girl, but Parker had no interest in being one of his castoffs or charity cases. That was for her regularly scheduled life, thank you very much.

"Why no phone sex?" he demanded, stopping in front of her, eyes still hooded. "Do you know the kind of painful morning wood I woke up with after reliving last night probably a thousand times over in my dreams?"

"Well, we could be repeating that right now, but

apparently I have to cook for however many people want a taste of your food tonight."

He ran a hand through his hair, clearly frustrated by it, too. "Usually the manager handles this kind of shit, but apparently one of the chef's parents died, which is why two of them are out of town at the same time."

"You don't have to keep apologizing, Hugh, but my payment will be high."

He crowded her against the long stainless steel table, identical to the one he'd had her on last night. "Tell me last night is what you're thinking about right now," he murmured, setting his lips against hers.

"It's one of the things," she admitted when he let up.

"Are you against phone sex in general or just today?" he asked. "Because it's very important to me."

She shook her head. "You're cracked."

His lips went fully in then, taking hers in a searing kiss that had her leaning against him on tiptoes. He picked her up and sat her on the table again, but she immediately slid off and gave him a speaking glance.

"Your employees will be here any second," she reminded him, and even though she wasn't an actual employee she wasn't going to just make out with him where anyone could see.

"I'm the boss," he continued without a shred of embarrassment, "and I like access." He nudged his mouth against hers again, waiting for her to grant him said access. Then he nuzzled her cheek until his lips reached her ear. "And by that I mean, I want video access when I call."

"I'm not your sex dummy, just available to fornicate whenever you please," she informed him, her head bending back to glare at his eyes. He was very large and sometimes she forgot, but crowded against the table she couldn't even see beyond his wide shoulders, which was grounding.

He ignored her, leaning down to nuzzle her neck again, and she couldn't help bending to the side to give him just want he wanted, better access. Lazy tingles of pleasure rose up on her skin like happy reminders of what he could do to her body.

"I don't want a sex dummy anyway," he murmured against her ear, his breath warm. "I thought one night would do it, but I was wrong." He drew small kisses back down the side of her neck.

"Come over tonight," he coaxed, his hand running up her rib cage.

She was definitely in danger of getting addicted to him, alarm settling in her belly at the thought. His big hand spanned her back as he gathered her into him and she would have given him whatever he'd asked. Luckily, what he wanted was something she wanted, as well.

"Yeah, I'll come over," she told him. "But it'll be nearly midnight before I get out of here. Are you sure you're up for it?"

"Are you insinuating I'm too old to be up that late?"

She shrugged. "I would never."

"You better be ready, sweetheart, because you'll be tired, but I'll still be demanding."

"So will I," she said, pushing at his chest as an employee entered the kitchen, but he didn't let go of her. It was as if he was already staking his claim and it sent shivers but also more trepidation sliding through her. The kid waved and then made his way to the employee lounge to clock in.

"That's my girl," Hugh murmured, the hand on her back drifting down to give her ass a powerful grip before letting her go completely.

"Excuse me," she choked, staring threateningly at him.

He just stuck his tongue in the side of his cheek and lifted one Hercules-esque shoulder in an unconcerned shrug. "Couldn't help it." He grinned. "I like that ass."

"Just go get the stuff I need for prep," she ordered, pointing an authoritative finger to the pantry.

He waggled his thick eyebrows, the one with a slash in it drawing her eye as he obeyed and disappeared from the kitchen. She'd seen a lot of scars on his body last night but hadn't wanted to ask about them. And honestly, had more important business to attend to besides dredging up old memories that might be unpleasant for him, but that didn't mean she wasn't curious.

Pulling on an apron from the rack on the wall, she mentally prepared herself for a rough night. She'd worked her fair share of years as a line cook in restaurants in Chicago and New York, as sous chef and eventually head chef for a famous Manhattan restaurateur, so she knew the toll it took on the body. It wasn't the only reason she'd left the kitchen, but a big one along with needing to be at home for her dad more. She enjoyed not having traditional hours and backbreaking work, but she was excited to cook for people again.

She went back to the prep room where Hugh and the other employee, whose name tag read Doug, were chopping up a mountain of onions.

"You located the prep sheet then?" she asked pointedly.

"No," Hugh drawled, his voice muffled under the red handkerchief covering the bottom half of his face. A pair of oversize goggles covering his eyes, he looked so ridiculous and yet she'd never been attracted to him more. "I just decided to kill myself cutting a million onions for the fun of it."

Her lips thinned in irritation, which made him grin. Turning on her heel, she went to the pantry and he followed.

"Fuck, this is harder than I thought," he said, stopping with her at the door. "I can't believe we have to do this tonight and I wasted all day not being naked with you."

She playfully shoved him out of the way and they entered the pantry. "If you give me sex eyes all night, I'm going to pour hot barbecue sauce on your head. I have work to do. Don't make it any harder than it's already going to be."

Picking through the various ingredients, she piled a few items in her arms.

"That just gives me more ideas. I'd love to lick barbecue sauce off of you and would be more than pleased if you'd do it to me."

She threw the orange she'd been holding at his chest, but he caught it in midair before it made contact.

At her surprised look, he deadpanned, "I was an elite athlete."

Shaking her head, she asked, "So do you have a preference on what specials are served?"

"No, but you don't have to do all that anyway. I just need somebody to run the kitchen tonight. All I've got are a bunch of line cooks who wouldn't know management or fine dining if it bit them on the ass."

"Oh, no, I want to cook the specials. I want to show your customers good food for a change," she joked, to which he responded with a playful scowl.

She shooed him back to the prep room while she checked out the refrigerators, where she found that some fresh fish had come in with the current day's date on it. By the time she'd planned and gathered ingredients for her dishes, it was nearly time to open.

"You ready?" Hugh barked, entering the kitchen with buckets of prepped vegetables. She shook her head, ears virtually throbbing in pain.

"Do you know how to speak at a normal volume?"

"Was that not normal?" he asked with mock innocence. "I'm trying to get you pumped up, Jones. Gonna be a long night, gotta stay alert."

"There's only one quarterback in this kitchen tonight and that's me, Matteson," she reminded him, pointing her thumb at her own chest.

That got him, a wide smile cracking his tanned face as he saluted her. "Yes, ma'am."

"Just go do something useful," she directed, not in the mood to banter with him. She had a kitchen to run.

After introducing herself to the kitchen staff, she started on the waitstaff. She explained her two specials in detail and then got to work running orders for the line cooks, which basically meant making sure the dishes for each table got ready at similar times so that some weren't waiting under the heat lamp and drying out.

When a special order came in, she got to work cooking, and as the night progressed she found herself cooking more and more specials and leaving Hugh to expedite on his own. He was an absolute natural at it since it was basically a management position where he could make sure the dishes were being prepared correctly and sent out on time. Directing and barking instructions all night in that near-deafening voice was driving her insane, but she'd bet money that dishes had never made it to customers so quickly.

He was charming, too, following every direction with a compliment and every instruction with encouragement. By the end of the night, she allowed that she had a healthy dose of respect for him. They'd made a good team in a pinch, but she hoped like hell it was her last night in a kitchen for a long time.

Lights out and everyone gone, she pulled a stool from under the stainless steel island and slipped off her sneakers with a sigh of relief.

Hugh came back into the kitchen and smiled when he saw her. "There she is, MVP of the night."

Leaning back against the table, she looked up at him, too tired to even smile. "How are you still this energetic?"

"I got a lot of breaks in and being back here was pretty cool. I do my walk-throughs and stuff, but

I was pretty ignorant about how a kitchen really works. I had fun bossing people around again."

"You were a good expediter. You have a real future in kitchen management."

He laughed. "Let me take you to my house, Parker. You look hot and sweaty, which we both know I'm into, but also exhausted. My hot tub will get you fixed up."

She didn't have the strength to deny what she wanted so she nodded.

"What are you doing?" she yelped when he scooped her up into his arms as if she were a child and not a grown woman.

"You're dead on your feet. I'm carrying you to the car."

Instead of arguing, her head fell against his wide chest. Her eyes threatened to shut but she came to again when he gently placed her in the passenger seat of his Maserati SUV.

"No McLaren tonight?" she asked when his hand was on the door to close it.

"Had hauling to do."

He shut the door and she smiled. There was no way on earth he was hauling stuff in the back of the leather showpiece that was this car. Compared to her late-model Nissan, it was next-level luxury and he knew it. Up to this point, she'd only been vaguely aware of just how rich he was, but now it was in her face for real. Another reason she was glad this was a two-night stand. Okay, maybe she'd push it to a three-night stand, but that was it. They lived in two completely different worlds. Hers was taking care of her dad and writing a simple magazine column, and his was being king of the world.

Their disparate lives only became more apparent when they pulled into a gated community and then through another gate that guarded his actual home. She'd been around this area of Vegas before—Summerlin was a growing food enclave for Las Vegas locals—but she'd never actually been inside one of the gated developments. Not that she could see much now, either. Once inside, she could only make out driveways and the tops of houses in the distance.

His own house was surprisingly modern. Two spare rectangles, one of smooth gray plaster and the other long, stacked layers of natural stone, were flanked by a higher level behind them that seemed to curve toward the sky. The two sides were separated by a cut-out entryway, but he didn't stop the car in the driveway to enter in the front door, instead following the paved road downhill into an underground garage.

"Oh, so I guess you're rich or something," she joked when they were riding the elevator from the basement garage, which had been filled with cars with names and fancy emblems she'd never heard of or seen.

He shrugged. "You could say that."

She wasn't strapped for cash in any way. In fact, made a great living for an expensive city. More than that, she was proud of what she'd accomplished, but Hugh was clearly beyond wealthy.

She wasn't intimidated, but her respect for Hugh was deepening in a way she didn't necessarily want. Falling for him for real would be an awful idea, not only because she couldn't live in Vegas and take care of her dad at the same time. But because she'd never actually fallen for someone before. She was a love virgin, and letting a playboy football player break the seal would be too stupid for words.

Besides, she was never leaving Chicago. That much had always been clear. Her dad needed her and she wasn't going to be the second female in his life to walk out on him. He was the only family she had in the world and she protected what was hers. So she needed to keep her head on straight and remember that Hugh was just for now, despite how much he made her smile or how light he made her feel. As if he was someone who could carry an equal share of the load for once. She was so used to doing everything on her own that just the idea weakened her knees, unraveling a knotted ball of tension in her chest.

To think that her real life could be as easy as her life on the road. That was the dream she hadn't dared.

"I hope you don't mind, but I had one of my assistants grab you some clothes so you can stay overnight," he informed her as if a discussion about it wasn't needed.

Which it wasn't. She was allowing herself another night with him. If not, she wouldn't be in the elevator at all.

"Thanks," she said, oddly touched. "That's very thoughtful of you."

He nodded just as the elevator doors opened directly into what, given the masculine decor and the enormous bed, was clearly his bedroom.

"Well," she snorted, folding her arms across her chest as she stared out the elevator doors, "that's presumptuous."

His shoulders shook with laughter. "Yeah, I guess if you didn't look like you might tip over any second, it would be."

"You promised me a hot tub," she reminded him, peering up at him from under her lashes.

"The clothes, including a bathing suit, are up here, but we can just sleep, Parker."

"You have some soda? I'll get a second wind." Just sleeping was a no-no. That was way too much like a relationship, and this was sex only.

"Clothes are in the bathroom. Go change into whatever you decide. And I don't drink soda but I'm sure my assistant has some stashed somewhere for parties."

She watched him exit the bedroom. Across from the elevator was a wall of windows that opened to a private terrace. Lights from a pool broke up the black night, the emptiness beyond reminding her that they were in the middle of the desert. The bedroom itself was furnished with dark wood furniture, the walls a deep navy, the bed covered with a puffy white duvet, and the carpet charcoal and plush. A massive television anchored nearly one entire wall opposite the bed and a large blue color-block painting akin to Rothko graced the wall across from the terrace doors. It wasn't overly fussy but it was comfortable and masculine. Also, lacking Hugh's big personality, but she guessed he hadn't really put much effort into decorating his second home.

The bathroom, too, was modern like the architecture of the house would suggest. Clean lines and angles gave order to the space with not a curve or furniture placement out of line. Muted white-and-gray Carrara marble blanketed every surface and made it look expensive but not flashy. Sitting on one of the two vanity counters on either side of the room were two large shopping bags along with a smaller bag from a beauty store, which she assumed were the clothes and toiletries Hugh had been referring to.

Peeking inside the small bag she saw every toiletry she might need, and luxury items at that. There were several pairs of pajamas, a couple of swimsuits that were clearly too small but she imagined that was probably by design, and what looked like jeans, a pair of shorts and some T-shirts for tomorrow. A package of underwear and two bras were also included. It was extremely thorough and she'd pay him for it, but she didn't even know that she could fit all of it in her suitcases to go home. She hadn't left any space for Vegas souvenirs since casino chic wasn't really her style.

Parker stripped down and pulled on the black swimsuit, a two-piece tankini number that basically shoved her boobs up to her eyeballs it was so small, but it didn't matter. With any luck, she'd be out of it soon. Just the thought of getting into that hot tub with Hugh was making her neck tingle in anticipation. Being in his car had been like being inside a Hugh cloud, darkly sensual and smelling like his cologne, and that feeling was only deepening now that she was in his home.

Returning to the bedroom, she noticed that a panel of the window wall was retracted and she stepped out onto the terrace to see Hugh already in the tub with five different bottles of soda and a glass of ice sitting on the ledge.

"I didn't know what you'd want," he explained.

The hot tub wasn't a standalone piece; it was sunken in the ground like a small circular pool, the jets streaming out and the water bubbling around Hugh's massive shoulders.

"Nice suit," he remarked, his eyes sliding lazily over her. He was sitting on the seat that lined the circumference of the tub, his arms propped up on the ledge. She took the two steps down into the sparkling teal water until she was fully ensconced in the rehabilitating warmth with an open bottle of diet soda in her hand.

Sitting across from him, she lay her head back on the ledge, letting the jets pulse on her muscles, and sighed. "This was an inspired idea. Thank you."

Hugh didn't say anything for a second, then she felt him pick up her foot from the bottom. Massaging it, he met her eyes. "I should be thanking you. You helped me out tonight and it really meant a lot to me. I hope you know how much I appreciate it."

Their eyes meeting, she got the sense that not many people did things for him. He was all about giving favors, yet rarely asking for them. The car he'd bought for Jesse as if he'd given her something as insignificant as a piece of gum instead of an expensive vehicle. That's the kind of man he was, and she'd been able to do something for him. It felt good to give him that and she hated it because she shouldn't feel that way.

She wanted to tell him not to worry about thanking her, either, but only a moan of pleasure came out of her mouth because at the same moment he dug his thumb into the sensitive and sore ball of her foot. "Oh my God," she breathed. "You're good at this."

He shrugged, the movement causing his abdomen to literally ripple, and she shivered in response. "The team had a fleet of world-class massage therapists. I learned what I could from them."

He moved to her toes, pulling each one just the slightest bit. By the time he was finished and moving on to the other foot, she thought she might be in a contentment coma, she felt so relaxed.

"Is that soda working or do I need to carry you to bed?" he finally asked, his voice deep and soft in the still night air.

It was hot outside even though it was dark, but the sting was out of it and the air was cool on her bare wet skin. "Working, I think," she admitted, knowing that she might be tired, but she wanted him more than she wanted sleep.

"Your specials sold more than any other dish tonight," he informed her, still holding her foot, though the massage had petered off into a light caress. "People loved them. Especially the barbecued fish tacos."

"Fish never gets enough play in the barbecue world, but it's such a mistake because it picks up whatever flavor you stick on it."

"Have you ever thought of starting your own restaurant?" he asked. "You're a really good chef."

"Thanks," she told him, opening her eyes to meet

his. "I've thought about it, but tonight reminded me of what it was like. I'm not ready to revisit that life again. It's why I left the business in the first place. I'm a much better eater than I am a cook."

He smiled. "That makes two of us." Then he paused, regarding her again. "You know, I wasn't kidding about having chefs who work on menus for the restaurants. I know I lost the competition, but I'd be in your debt if you'd contract as a consultant for me. It wouldn't interfere with the job you already have unless you wanted to help me open new locations, and I'd really like your opinions. Obviously, my sauces could use some work."

Parker grinned at him because he could be so incredibly nice and not a huge bossy-pants at all when he wanted to be. "I promise to give it full consideration. Either way, I appreciate the offer."

"Good," he said with a firm nod of his head. "Now get over here so I can touch something better than your damn foot."

She laughed but didn't move, so he reached out and hoisted her into his lap until her legs were straddling his waist and her arms were propped on his shoulders.

"Why did you even bother wearing those shorts?" she asked, annoyed that they'd have to re-adjust, which was awkward in a hot tub. She was eager to get this show on the road and didn't want the barrier between them.

He shrugged. "Seemed polite. And it gave me somewhere to put the condoms." Her gaze went behind him to where he was pointing. Several condoms lay just under a couple of towels. She appreciated the forethought.

Instead of moving her, he gently lifted up and slid the green board shorts off. His cock was already at full mast and she caught his eyes.

"I've been nursing a semi ever since I saw you bending over to get something out of the oven." His hands ran over her ass again, gripping the backs of her thighs as he readjusted her over his length.

Laughing, she leaned into him until their lips met and it was as if she'd never been tired. Her body was immediately energized and ready to go and got even more so when she felt him pulling at the bottom of her suit. Balancing her on his legs, he held her back as he tugged the stretchy fabric off. Satisfied, he returned her to her previous position and instead of removing her swimsuit top, he just pulled the cups to side so that her breasts were framed right in his face for his pleasure.

Greedily taking a nipple into his mouth, he reached behind him and handed her the condom. Bolts of desire lashed at her core, wanting to take him now and tired of waiting. She was needy and hot and far too eager to feel him inside her, already addicted to the rush of that huge, strong body pumping into hers. Ripping open the condom, she rolled it on him as he sucked a little too hard on her nipple, that massive, swarthy hand all but engulfing the white skin of her breasts.

When she had the condom on, she felt his fingers trail down her abdomen and into her folds. He was checking to make sure she was ready and she knew without a doubt she was. When he was satisfied, he placed himself at her entrance and eased her down onto him.

She sighed and let her head fall onto his shoulder. "We'll just take it easy, baby," he murmured, rocking her hips gently against him. "I got you."

The rise and fall was just that, slow and easy, and when it was over he picked her up and carried her into the house, snuggling against her in bed.

CHAPTER EIGHT

THE ROOM WAS dark when Parker woke up. Stretching out her legs against Hugh's soft sheets, she felt languid but refreshed. Grabbing her phone from the nightstand, she squinted against the bright blue light as she read the time. It was already nine o'clock, which was when she realized that the entire wall of windows had been flanked by blackout shades, so not even the barest hint of sunlight peeked through. A clever idea and just another thoughtful thing Hugh had done for her that was making it harder to keep things casual with him.

Thinking about him, she reached out to the other side of the bed hoping to initiate a lengthier redo of the night before, but instead of a warm Hugh she got a handful of cold sheets. It was a real shame, but the thought that she'd overstayed her welcome propelled her out of bed. She flipped on a lamp and headed to the bathroom, where she brushed her teeth and washed her face before returning to the bedroom just as Hugh was coming in.

He was shirtless again and a pair of gray athletic shorts hung loosely on his hips, highlighting the severe vee cutout at his waist that disappeared beneath the elastic band. Sweat dripped down his chest and his brown hair was damp, pushed straight back from his forehead. He'd clearly been working out already, which made her feel definitely like she should have been out of his house already.

His eyes darkened when he saw her in the pajamas he'd procured, a revealing peach set of silk shorts that barely covered her ass and a camisole that was loose around the waist but choked her breasts. She vaguely remembered putting on the first thing that she grabbed after coming in from the hot tub last night. And she was thankful for the choice because he was looking at her like he wanted to devour her.

"You worked out?" she asked, awkward now and not knowing if she should go back to bed or go change clothes in the bathroom. She should have already changed, but she hadn't wanted to spend a lot of time in there if he needed to use it. Her knowledge of what a restaurant chain owner did on a daily basis was lacking. For all she knew, he needed to go in to an office somewhere this morning.

He nodded, still staring at her, which was incredibly unnerving. "I wanted to let you sleep," he added. "You were really beat last night."

"Thanks," she said. "I was just coming to find you. I guess I'll get out of your hair now."

He didn't respond, just shook his head back and forth, his eyes locked with hers. "You want to leave now?"

"Um, I guess?" she asked. "I thought maybe you had work to do."

"The only work I want to do right now is on you."

She looked from left to right, wondering exactly what that meant, but also kind of knowing.

Hugh pulled off his shorts to reveal an already impressive erection; even in the dim light of the lamp there was no mistaking it. Her eyes closed, remembering how he felt inside her, letting the ripples of anticipation wake up her sleepy body.

In response, she pulled off her pajamas so they were standing ten feet apart, completely naked, staring at each other as if they'd never seen anyone naked before. And honestly, she couldn't remember anyone at this point. Her sex life was already going to be measured by before and after Hugh Matteson.

He nodded to the bed. "Lie down. On top of the covers."

Assuming he was going to join her there, she followed his directive. Admittedly, she would have done anything he said when he talked in that no-nonsense voice, which sent waves of need clamoring for space all over her skin. However, he didn't join her, but stayed rooted to the floor, his eyes taking in every inch of her, from toes to head. Maybe in another life she would have felt self-conscious about being on such blatant display, but the way he was looking at her, his eyes dark and his big hand stroking that ruddy, thick erection, was too erotic for those kinds of thoughts to even enter her mind. She was proud of her body anyway, but being watched was different, more intimate, which he knew and was obviously why he was doing this. It was easy to fuck someone; it was something else to share a moment of need with them.

He was drawing it out for both of them, to strengthen the connection they had. She was kidding herself that this was about just sex because from the moment he'd given that hotel room employee his phone number knowing the possible consequences to himself, she was on her way to being under his spell. After her mom left, she'd gone from being a teenager with a normal, protected life to an adult who had to take care of herself and her dad. After just a few days with Hugh, that protected feeling kept creeping in again, an invitation to lighten her load for a little while. From checking on her at the hotel, to cooling her down in the meat locker, to providing her with a hot tub, to massaging her feet last night. It was the most a man had ever done for her and they'd only known each other for a week.

Her eyes met his, a light of intensity in his, drowning out the good-natured playfulness she'd grown so used to with him.

"Touch yourself," he commanded, still stroking himself.

Her shoulders twitched with the order, but she knew she was going to do it. If this is how he wanted to start the morning, far be it from her to stand in his way, especially since she was dying to have him.

"I was disappointed you weren't here when I woke up," she told him, parting herself with a finger, finding the folds already wet.

"Is that right?" he asked, his voice deeper as his cock grew darker, stiffer in his hand as he stroked lazily, gripping harder every so often.

When she nodded, a corner of his mouth quirked. "So did you already get off?"

"No," she said, her voice catching as a jolt of pleasure kicked through her. Watching him watch her was short-circuiting her brain.

"Too bad." He took a step closer to the bed until he was standing right in front of her, and from that angle he could see exactly what she was doing, her entire core on display to him. Her knees were drawn up, and his gaze narrowed on her finger.

Their eyes met again, but she was distracted by the tip of his cock, glistening now with drops of liquid.

"You're really hot," she blurted, wanting it to be

sexier, but not in any condition to be eloquent. She was so close to the edge, but more than that she wanted him, needed to feel his touch.

"Faster," he demanded, even as his own hand went slower, became more measured. "You're really hot, too, Parker. Look at yourself right now, spread out on my bed for me like my own personal feast. You're the first woman I've had here, and it was worth the wait."

Her eyes flew to his in question but he didn't elaborate, just pointedly looked to the hand at her core that had stopped moving at his admission. "Faster," he reminded.

She obeyed, flying over her clit, her back arching as her whole body ached for release. Her skin was on fire, too tight on a body that was struggling to break free, bracing against a tidal wave of desire so acute she could barely breathe. Air entered and exited her lungs on noisy gasps until with a final arch, she let go, falling into a warm pool of euphoria.

When she came to, Hugh was no longer at the foot of the bed but beside her opening the bedside drawer and pulling out an unopened box of condoms. Tearing into them, he had himself sheathed in record time, meeting her eyes as his finger made a crooking motion. He held out a hand and helped her off the bed, only to bend her over it, his hand sliding up the back of her thigh and squeezing one of her ass cheeks.

He kissed a line down her spine, both hands now kneading her behind. "I've been waiting to have you like this since we met."

Then he was pushing into her from behind as her hands curled into the duvet, her insides stretching at his invasion. He was slow this time, too, just like last night when he'd been so gentle with her in the hot tub, but the urgency was there, just contained. Squeezing her ass, he drew a finger down the seam, and her muscles jumped uneasily. Then before she knew what was happening, he laid a firm smack on her right cheek.

She yelped, her body jolting in surprise, seating him deeper inside her. Her skin smarted but he rubbed it gently away until the throb turned into pleasure, all the disparate sensations he was perpetrating on her body coalescing into a divine madness. Nothing he did was enough. She wanted more of him. She couldn't see him, didn't know what he was thinking, only knew the thick slide of him in and out of her, the softness of the cotton she was clenching in between her fingers like a lifeline. None of it was *him*.

"That's payment for lying to me the first night," he growled, still rubbing the spot he'd slapped.

He pushed in, hitting that magic spot inside her.

"Or rather your reward, since I know you liked it."

She whimpered as he left her almost completely, the big broad tip of him poised at her entrance.

"You want it again?" he prodded, that big hand kneading the other ass cheek.

Her eyes closed, she didn't respond, just arched against him, wanting him to move, to smack her behind, to do anything just so he was closer to her. That's all she wanted, was the connection to the only man she'd ever felt this good with.

"Is that a yes, sir, I'd like to be punished?" he prodded, and she could hear the smile in his voice as he pushed back into her with enough force to make her sigh with pleasure.

"Words, Parker," he reminded, pulling her hips up to adjust his angle of entry as if she were weightless.

"Yes," she finally choked out, her orgasm building by rapid degrees. Her muscles were tensed, eyes squeezed shut, and her hips were moving without any rhyme or reason in an effort to find release.

Just as she was nearing the top, her inner muscles clenching around his invading cock, his hand found her other cheek, this time a little harder, and the sting was bliss. He laid a featherlight kiss over the abraded area and she went over the edge, grasping at the duvet like she might literally fall into an abyss without something to hold on to.

Spent and delirious, she felt him grip her hips, his broad fingers digging into her sides as he let loose, fighting for his own release when he reached around to her clit to fire her back up again. In what seemed like an instant she was careering over the cliff again, only this time he was there with her, bowed over her back, his hot breath on her shoulder as he growled his own explosion.

A final kiss on the middle of her back, then he pulled out of her, running a hand over what she had to imagine were red marks on her ass, and then disappeared into the bathroom. When he returned, she still hadn't moved and his weight compressed the bed as he lay against the headboard and pulled her up into his arms.

"That was next-level," he murmured, placing a soft kiss on her forehead.

She nodded against him, gliding a hand down his chest. "I liked it."

That made him laugh and they fell into an easy silence.

Lying on top of the duvet, an industrial steel ceiling fan moving the air slowly across their bodies, Parker felt completely mindless except that she couldn't stop thinking about how she was the first woman he'd had in his bed. That had to be just a throwaway comment to make her hot because she knew his track record with women; he'd done nothing to hide the fact that he was in demand and had taken what was on offer. Statistically, he would have needed to bring at least one or two back to his house. It just didn't make any sense.

The room was dark and quiet and she was draped across Hugh's chest as he played with her hair, twirling it around his finger as if they had all the time in the world instead of a few short weeks until she went back to Chicago. She could spend all day here in his room without a moment of regret. She was in that deep already. It wasn't good news.

Her phone went off and she grabbed it from the dark wood nightstand. A text from her boss that read, READ YOUR EMAIL.

Parker sighed. Her days might be spent eating and writing, but she still very much had people to answer to. Propping back up on Hugh again, she opened her email and read the one from her boss. Apparently, the barbecue contest with Hugh was a hit with readers and she wanted Parker to write her own story about it coupled with a profile on Hugh.

Frowning, she tapped out a response, hoping that Hugh wouldn't have a problem with it. It felt like taking advantage of him now that they were sleeping together. Most concerning, though, was that if he agreed, it meant she'd have to spend more time with him, which wasn't good for her already-in-jeopardy quest to keep things casual between them.

"What was that sigh about?" Hugh asked, his hand drifting from her hair to trace a line down her back.

"My boss wants an article about the contest and for me to do a profile on you for the magazine."

Hugh's eyes grew ornery. "An entire article just about me? Written by you?" When she just rolled her eyes, his arm tightened around her. "That'll be fun. Maybe too X-rated for *Gastronomic*, but I'm up for it."

She playfully bit his pec. "You don't mind?" she asked. "I don't want it to look like I'm using our relationship for access. I can say you aren't interested, it's not a big deal. I mean, you did lose the contest, so that will already be in the magazine."

"You're asking me if I'd like free press on one of the most-read food sites in the country? Consider yourself in possession of a Hugh Matteson all-access pass," he teased, waggling his eyebrows like the goofball he was.

She face-planted on his chest and she felt it rumble underneath her with laughter. "I'm all nervous now. I've been reading your articles and you've already ripped a couple of my favorite places to eat. I can only imagine what you'll write about me as a person."

She laughed and kissed his shoulder, noting how tense it had gotten. Could he actually be nervous? It seemed impossible that he could have any insecurities at all. "You've been reading my stuff?"

"Of course," he told her. "I read basically your entire archive the day I found out about your review. By the way, what's your deal with pickling anyway?"

She propped herself up on an elbow, peering down into his face. His hair was a mess and he smelled like a man who'd worked out, rich and musky.

"Pickling is great, easy, and adds a completely different dimension to sandwiches. Imagine a hamburger without a pickle. Imagine pulled pork without a tangy coleslaw. You can't—it just doesn't work."

"You wrote an entire article on pickled garlic, Parker. That's messed up."

She laughed, playfully smacking him on the shoulder. "Don't knock it 'til you try it." She tried to climb off him, but he pulled her back into him. Instead of resisting, she fell into his arms.

"You can pickle all of my garlic," he said, grinning. "What do you have going on for the rest of the day? Can you stay here? We can shower together, I'll make you breakfast, we can go swimming, watch a movie, anything you want."

Staying with him all day was a mistake, but as she looked down at his face and the little piece of insecurity visible behind his eyes, it was one she couldn't help but make.

"Race you to the shower?" she asked, hopping up from the bed and running full-on to the shower.

She didn't make it far at all before he caught her, hauling her up against his chest and kissing the back of her neck. "I win," he murmured against her skin as he walked them both toward the shower. "Fucking finally I win something."

Much later, she watched from his kitchen island as he cooked her breakfast. Some kind of omelet that she barely paid attention to because he was wearing just a pair of shorts again, and so not just the immense size of his kitchen was distracting her.

Like his bathroom, it was a large space with even more white Carrara marble.

"Your house is really nice," she told him.

"Thanks," he said, cracking another egg into the skillet.

"Do you like it?" she asked, pulling out the tablet she always kept in her bag. Now was a good a time as any to start the profile.

He glanced at her, a slight frown on his face. "Why do you ask?"

She shrugged. "I don't know, it just doesn't scream Hugh to me."

That made him grin. "You think you know me already?"

"A little," she told him, grinning back.

"Yeah, well, this is just a place to be, and I got it mainly for the big garage. My real home is in Texas at the ranch, but I get to spend less and less time there as business expands."

"You miss it," she guessed.

"Yeah, and I miss my family. I've spent most of my adult life on the road and I bought the ranch hoping to spend more time with them, but it kind of hasn't turned out that way because of the restaurant growing as quickly as it has."

He threw some chopped-up peppers, onions and manchego cheese into the omelet.

"Why Vegas?" she asked, genuinely curious. "I know it's your flagship restaurant, but you couldn't make Texas your home base?"

"The ranch is in the middle of nowhere outside of San Antonio," he explained. "So it's not a place for a restaurant and Vegas is the closest restaurant to home. I can catch a flight and be there in two hours if I need to."

"Why not just open a place in San Antonio then?"

He raised an eyebrow at her. "You want me to enter the ultracompetitive Texas barbecue market? Really? I mean, I might as well set my money on fire."

She laughed. "Am I hearing doubts about barbecue ability from the great Hugh Matteson?"

"Listen," he said, pointing a black plastic spatula at her, "I never claimed to be a chef and if you're going to succeed in Texas, you better be the best. I'm already competing with the Big Top here in Vegas and they're killing it even against the strength of my name."

"So what I'm hearing is that you're scared," she teased, tapping away at her computer.

A hunk of cheese landed on her keyboard and she laughed harder at him. "What the hell?"

"You know, maybe if I had trust in an actual chef who could create a competitive menu, I could move home and tend to my sickly parents," he said, giving her a meaningful glare.

"Wait a second, are your parents really sickly?" she pressed, concern settling her. "Why didn't you say that before?"

He flipped half an omelet over the top of the other side. "No, they're fine," he grumbled. "But opening a place in San Antonio would have to be something new and outside the box."

Looking pointedly at her, he slid the omelet onto a plate and placed it in front of her along with a side of salsa, sour cream and crushed-up tortilla chips for makeshift huevos rancheros. Then he got to work on his own omelet.

"You don't really want me to create a menu for a restaurant you open," she told him. "I'm not even Texan."

He shrugged. "Opening yet another Texas barbecue joint in Texas isn't a smart idea. Like I said, whatever I did would have to be different, something no one there has ever seen before."

Their eyes met and excitement, plain and simple, climbed through her like carbonation from a shaken-up soda bottle. It was stupid and she wasn't going to go into business with him, but just imagining all the awesome dishes she could come up with given carte blanche to make a menu was making her itch to get into the kitchen.

"We barely know each other, Hugh," she pointed

out. "Just because I beat you in a barbecue competition doesn't mean I'm cut out to create a menu for you."

"Do you know how much barbecue I tasted from the country's renowned barbecue cooks when I opened Blue Smoke? Hundreds. Literally hundreds, Parker. None of them compared to your stuff. Hell, I even liked that pickled carrot salad whatever the fuck you put on the side of the brisket and I don't even really like carrots in the first damn place."

"Even if I wanted to, I can't move," she informed him, cutting into her eggs. "Chicago is my home base and I can't leave."

As he dropped more toppings into his omelet, she regarded his back. The lines of his muscles formed wings out to his arms and she let her mind focus on how hard he worked on his body instead of building imaginary dreams of creating a menu for a restaurant that didn't exist.

"Family's there?" he asked.

She nodded, then realized he couldn't see her. "Yeah, my dad. Mom left a long time ago."

That had him turning around. "Sorry about that, sweetheart."

"It's okay, but my dad still isn't really over it. He lives with me, so I kind of have to stick around."

"Gotcha," he said, not pressing her further on the issue, which she appreciated. "But you're able to travel."

"Yeah, of course, it's my job," she said. "He's not sick or anything, just depressed most days."

"Because of your mom leaving?"

"He has always been a little depressed," Parker acknowledged, "but it got worse after Mom left. He couldn't hold down jobs for very long and stopped seeing his friends. It's gotten better in recent years, but I can't leave him all alone in a city without me. Family sticks around."

"Yeah, they do," he said. "Except a lot don't. I didn't, obviously."

She met his eyes in warning. Horning in on her personal life was a no-go area for her.

"Look, I'm not judging your choices," he back-pedaled. "I just think it's a shame you're tied to a town when you could be doing whatever you want."

"I am doing what I want," she told him. And it was true. She wouldn't rather be doing any other job. Creating a menu for Hugh would be great, but she'd never give up her magazine job. And if she got a little lonely because life on the road kept real relationships away, well, that's what this thing with Hugh was for. It generally didn't take more than a week with a guy for her to know that she was better off alone.

Hugh turned to her, accepting her answer with a small smile. "You're a good daughter," he said, then pointed to her plate. "Now eat. It's going to be a busy day for both of us."

"I thought we were just going to hang out and swim," she reminded.

He raised an eyebrow and she realized what he meant. She shook her head because he was insatiable, but it also meant more to her than she was willing to admit.

"Am I really the first girl you've had here?"

His fork paused in the air on the way to his plate. Glancing up, he looked the slightest bit hesitant, but then said, "Yeah."

"How can that be?"

His tongue slid into his cheek like it so often did when he was thinking. "Because I didn't think I'd have to kick you out in the morning."

"Wow," she said, leaning back to stare at him.

"It just means you're the first girl I wanted to stay, Parker," he said, oblivious to her heart falling to his feet. "So it sucks to hear that you're in Chicago for life."

She opened her mouth to say something, but he just shook his head. "Eat."

She did as she was told because sex or no sex, she liked Hugh Matteson. Which meant she needed to cut this Vegas trip short because the truth was that somewhere between ordering her first meal at Blue Smoke and eating an omelet in his kitchen, her heart had been put in danger.

CHAPTER NINE

HUGH WAS HAVING a pretty shitty day, which was a rough kick considering how great yesterday with Parker had been. Having her in his house all day as they'd eaten insanely good food, fucked hard and talked their way through the hours had made the day go by in the blink of an eye. For a fun fling, it was the best he'd ever had.

However, yesterday seemed like a thousand years away as he pulled out of the parking lot of the sports bar where he'd met up with an old football buddy.

His friend had delivered the news that Amanda and Todd's third child had been born. They'd sold the first pictures to some gossip rag, a little girl with Amanda and Todd's blond hair and blue eyes. While Hugh didn't want his ex in his life, it was yet another reminder that he was no closer to the family he'd imagined he'd already have by now. Todd was living the life he'd planned for himself, still playing ball, big family. Today it was fucking him up more than usual. Thirty-five wasn't old, but most of his close friends had a couple of kids and happy families, and he was still alone as always.

He'd stopped playing the field in any real way years ago, too. Building the business and fucking around with whoever was available had gotten in the way of him putting any real effort into finding someone. But he wanted a certain kind of life, hated that his house was so quiet and empty when he came home at the end of the day. Having Parker around brought out the stark truth of how lonely he was. He'd buried himself so deep out of fear of getting hurt again, he'd blocked everything out.

For years, he'd avoided looking at pictures of Amanda, Todd or their family. Today, he'd finally admitted why. Seeing the picture of that little baby made him acknowledge that her betrayal still hurt. He'd given Amanda everything. He'd met her in college and they'd grown up together, gone from young adulthood to adulthood side by side. He'd trusted her like his own family, and she'd screwed him over in the worst possible way.

As he navigated the Summerlin streets in the fading late-afternoon sun, he thought of Parker, wondering what she wanted for her future. Was she content having casual relationships on her travel gigs or did she want to settle down, too? After what she'd told him about her family last night, he wondered if she even knew herself what she wanted.

He took the elevator to his kitchen and when the doors opened the smell of food immediately hit him. He remembered that he had an appointment with Parker for his profile tonight and that he'd given her his code. It was a measure of trust he didn't lend to anyone, not even his assistant, but he wanted her to be here whenever she wanted. He'd just change it when she went back to Chicago anyway.

He saw her at the stove, cooking in only an apron, and his heart pretty much stopped in its tracks, his pensive mood evaporating as if it had never existed.

"You're a miracle, Parker," he growled, stalking toward her.

At his advance, she backed away, waving a wooden spoon between them to fend him off, which was a good move because that apron was exactly one nanosecond away from being a floor rag. "Nope, not yet, everything will burn if you distract me."

"You've got to be fucking kidding me with this," he bellowed, throwing his hands up in the air in exasperation. "You can't dress up in a child-size apron and expect me to be hands-off."

He reached for her again, but she slapped his hand with the spoon.

"Come on, baby, I'll let you smack my ass with

that if that's what you're into," he cajoled, crowding her into the corner of the counter, reminding her of what they'd done yesterday. "You can put me in handcuffs, whatever you want. I'm flexible."

She snorted. "Yeah, right."

Looking over her shoulder, he saw that she was frying up some sausage in a large stainless steel skillet.

"From scratch?" he asked, noticing the meat grinder on his counter.

"Yeah," she confirmed.

"Oh, it's gonna be a good night!" he hooted, rubbing his hands together in anticipation.

She leaned up and planted a kiss on his cheek and he gave her a smack on the ass in return. It was well-deserved after taunting him this way. He was only a man. Who could resist a naked woman in only an apron?

Yelping, she backed away from him. "Go over there," she ordered, pointing to the island where a cold bottle of beer was already waiting for him.

"What's all this about anyway? You actively trying to make men fall in love with you?" he asked, settling into the barstool to watch the naked cooking show apparently. "Because I'm as close to proposing as I've ever been." The words were light and joking, but after his lunch he'd be lying if it hadn't crossed his mind that Parker could be the one, which frankly chilled him to the core. Not only could she not be trusted, she was leaving in a couple of weeks. Two extremely good reasons to keep things casual.

Parker looked back at him. "I've been doing research for your profile, so I saw the news about your ex today. Figured you could use a pick-me-up."

Their eyes met and his gut took another massive hit on the day. No one had ever done something like that for him before. He had tons of people whose job it was to cater to him, but no one was doing it just because they cared if he had a shitty day. Hell, for his birthdays, Amanda usually just bought lingerie for him or booked them both a trip to somewhere she wanted to go. At the time, it'd seemed thoughtful enough, but now he knew better. Maybe he needed to let the lying in the beginning go. Because between caring for her dad, who frankly mostly sounded like a deadbeat, and cooking him dinner in the nude after a rough day, it was time to accept that she was a good person.

"That's really sweet, Parker," he finally said, holding her eyes a little too long probably, but craving the connection. "I appreciate it."

"You're welcome," she said, turning to flip over a sausage link. She tossed a salad with a wooden set of tools he hadn't known he had and stirred some sweet potatoes in a skillet.

He was vaguely interested in the food, but mostly he watched her ass shake as she moved, which was

intentional and downright obscene. He was count-
ing down the seconds until she'd let him go at her.
It was the sweetest kind of torture to sit so close to
her and not touch her. The gold light of the setting
sun streamed through the large plate glass windows
that overlooked his backyard, giving her blond hair
a halo and gilding her pale skin in a dusky glow.

Turning from the stove, she regarded him, but
he was mostly looking at her exposed side boob.
"Do you want to talk about it?" she asked, her voice
hesitant.

"About my ex?" he asked, not following the conversation due to all the naked.

At her nod, his head fell back and he looked at
the ceiling wondering how to navigate this mine-
field. He hated talking about this kind of shit, especially having had to deal with it all in the public eye
at the same time his entire life went down the toilet.

"I don't miss Amanda," he finally offered, figur-
ing he owed something to her since she was cooking him dinner. But hell, he was so tired of the pity.
"She was someone I chose when I didn't know any
better. Young and dumb, you know how it goes. But
I do want a family, and that they're expanding theirs
does remind me that I'm not close to that place yet,
when I thought I'd be well into fatherhood at this
point in my life."

Parker regarded him, turning down the burners
on the food to really give him her attention. "I think

we all think life will look different at certain stages than it does, I guess. My parents had that kind of life. I was already five years old by the time my parents were my age. I can barely imagine having a cat right now, let alone a child."

"I can, though," he admitted. "Imagine having a family, I mean. I've been financially stable since I graduated from college. The hours I work are flexible and designed for a family. I've been ready, just not able, I guess."

"Maybe you're not as ready as you think?" she suggested. "Because you're obviously a man of action, and like you said, you've been in a good position financially to have a family. Obviously something's been stopping you these last six years from having a serious relationship with someone who could be the mother of your children."

She'd hit the nail on the head. He hadn't found or wanted to find a possible mate whom he could truly build a life with. "You're probably right."

"Have you dated anyone since your ex?"

"Not seriously," he told her.

She looked at him like that was the answer.

"Yeah, well, I've got some trust issues."

Parker smiled. "Naturally."

"I might not mind dating you," he said, the words coming out of his mouth without thinking. It was too much truth for the both of them, but he found he didn't regret it.

"You're under the spell of pork," she laughed, her nose crinkling adorably.

He shrugged. "Maybe, maybe not," he told her. "But you're the first woman I've ever even considered dating. And you've already lied to me once, so either I really like sausage or even I'm willing to accept that there's something good between us."

Her eyes widened at his admission, and he thought he'd scared her, but then she collected herself. Difficult to do in a mini apron, all things considered. "The news about your ex is just scaring you into a rash decision."

"Right," he told her, meeting her eyes, trying to figure her out. They had something here; she had to know that. "Except she's had a child before and I didn't run after the first woman available to date."

"I have to go back to Chicago in two weeks anyway."

"You know, I have my own plane," he reminded her. "I can come to Chicago whenever I want."

"You want to be in a long-distance relationship with me?" she asked, a dark brow winging up skeptically.

"I don't fucking know," he growled, irritated that he was getting nothing back from her. It wasn't every day he asked women to date him. In fact, it was never. "I don't do this shit, but I know we're having a lot of damn fun, so maybe, yeah."

Her brown eyes looked startled again, mouth

opening and closing before a popping sound from the skillet distracted her. She turned to give the food a look, and he was pissed that he'd blown the conversation. Hell, it wasn't as if he wanted to get married or some shit.

"Are you not over your ex?" Parker asked, setting the spoon down on the counter and facing him again. "I mean, is that why you haven't dated anyone?"

Hugh nearly choked. "Hell yeah, I'm over her. Her betrayal, well, I don't know if I'll ever get over that shit to be honest. You don't forget it when the person you trust most makes a fool out of you in front of the entire world."

"No one who knows your story thinks you were humiliated," Parker said. "People look up to you even more because it means that kind of stuff can happen to anyone, and yet you got the last laugh. You're a successful businessperson and he's warming the bench."

"That shit doesn't matter to me, Parker," Hugh told her. "When you get to my level of fame, you realize pretty quickly that people don't give a shit who you really are. Story or no story, humiliation or no humiliation, I'm just a walking stereotype or meal ticket to most people. And that's fine, I roll with it, but when it comes to letting people into my life for real, I've been picky as hell."

"That's sad, Hugh."

He shrugged. "It's just my life."

Parker met his eyes and he had no clue what she was thinking about. It also didn't escape him that she'd completely derailed their original conversation about dating, which had him wondering just how damaged she was, too.

Another pop in the skillet broke the silence and her attention was back on the stove top.

"It's ready," she eventually announced, grabbing the white ceramic plates she'd set out on the counter.

"The food looks great, Parker," he told her when she turned around again, "but you have to know that it isn't what I want to eat right now."

She rolled her eyes, but turned the burners on low before hopping up on the counter and spreading her legs. With a raised eyebrow, she leaned back and met his eyes. "Your choice, Hugh."

Grinning, he stalked toward her once again, wondering when the last time was that he'd felt so light, so carefree. So happy. That was the word he was looking for.

Eyes still locked on hers, he sank to his knees in front of her, which put him at the perfect height to see her sleek mound, glistening just the slightest bit with arousal. He loved that he turned her on so much. Her hands went around her back and started untying the apron, but he stopped her.

"Leave it on," he said.

He didn't waste any time finding her. Gently

pulling apart her folds and touching his tongue to the finest thing he'd ever tasted. Her sighs echoed in the empty kitchen and he found her nub, licking and sucking until it came to life under his tongue. Ways to take her flipped through his mind like his own personal sex catalog, but it didn't matter in the end because any way they did it would be the best way. She barely had to look at him and he got hard, and she'd gone to the trouble of making him a meal just on the off chance he might be upset.

Pushing one finger and then two into her as he sucked, he wanted her to know how much that simple gesture meant to him. For a person who spent most of his time working and knowing that when people gave him stuff it was because they wanted something in return, what she'd done was special.

And shit, he didn't have a condom in the damned kitchen. All that time flirting with her as she cooked and he could have been getting a condom. She was literally making him dumb.

"I don't have a condom," he cursed, rising from his knees with the intention of carrying her aproned ass into his bedroom.

Parker pulled a foil square out of the tiny front pocket on the breast panel, meeting his eyes with a smug grin.

He caught her lips in a thankful kiss that quickly turned X-rated, her legs locked around his waist and his hands grabbing up her mass of hair.

He kissed her neck, her exposed collarbone, her shoulder, her elbow, anything he could get his hands on. He wanted to know every part of her so he could find her in the dark if he had to, which was obviously madness, but if it was he didn't want to be sane. In this moment, where old wounds were gaping open, exposed to the light of day, he wanted to be in Parker in all ways.

He noticed that her hand had found one of the wooden spoons in his utensil crock. Their eyes met, hers twinkling with mischief, and he regretted pursuing this in his kitchen. He should have known there'd be revenge for last night. She was going to punish him for liking it so much, and it'd been hot as hell to smack that perfect, ripe ass. The way her flesh wiggled on contact and the soft pink handprint afterward reminded both of them that they were skirting the edge of appropriate.

"Strip me then," he ordered, stepping away so she could maneuver his clothes off.

She bit her lip, unsure if he was being for real. He'd let her do any damn thing she wanted to him—he was that kind of gone, but letting her think she couldn't was just fine, too.

After unfastening the button of his jeans and pulling on the zipper, she pushed them down his thighs until he kicked them the rest of the way off. She lifted up his shirt at the hem, her gaze catching on his chest again, which nearly had him grinning.

Then he was naked and bared before her, waiting for any retribution she might want to enact.

In fact, he turned around for her, looking back and meeting her eyes. What he found there got him in the gut, the curiosity, the hunger, the empowerment. He was a big guy, could bench press her with little to no effort, but sometimes it got old, being that person, the guy always in charge. For once, he wanted to feel what other people, who could let their guard down for a moment, felt. Be who he was for a moment and not who the world needed him to be. To not feel like a beast among men, but vulnerable and not pushed aside as somehow superhuman.

He also liked the pain, almost missed being tackled on the field, letting those bottled-up and suppressed emotions out in a physical way. There wasn't much like it outside of sports, but he was open. But he'd never trusted anyone enough before now to even consider it.

She leaned forward, running a hand down his back, over his ass and down his thigh over where one of his scars stood out in white relief against his tanned skin. "I don't like to imagine you hurt," she murmured, dropping kisses along his shoulders as her hands explored the hard, ridged tissue.

"Those days are over," he told her, voice low because the moment was stretching and he was aching for her and something else he couldn't name.

He'd been so isolated that Parker's caring for him cracked open something inside him.

"But you still hurt," she pressed, and he could barely feel her touch, only registering it when she traced around the edge of the scar that traveled up nearly the entire length of his thigh.

"Not so much, I just wanted in your pants that first night," he admitted, watching as, eyes hooded, she picked up the wooden spoon again.

His cock jerked and she noticed, an eyebrow arching up. He took himself in hand, stroking as she decided what she wanted to do.

White teeth tugged at her bottom lip and he dared her with his eyes to do it, to give him what he'd given her. To cross a line they hadn't with others. He could almost taste the pain, yearning for it almost as much as he wanted to be inside her.

"You deserve it," she told him, her grip shifting on the handle, as if trying to muster up the courage to surrender to the moment, to take them over the edge together.

"I do," he agreed, his hand moving faster over his dick, the rocketing sensations from his toes to his balls making his knees weak.

And then she did it, pulled the spoon back and gave him just a single whack on the meatiest part of his ass cheek. It stung, but barely, but the sly look on her face had his cock jolting against his grip.

Turning back to her, he grabbed the condom

from the counter, their eyes locked as he rolled it over himself, shock and desire on her face as the spoon clattered loudly onto the marble. For his own part, he'd never felt so powerful; that he trusted her with something so raw of himself had him shaken, but also steadied him. He was making the leap to trust her, letting go of the fear he'd been clinging to, and it was exhilarating.

He latched his hands on her waist and lifted her straight up off the counter and slid her slowly down his body and onto his waiting cock, the angle of her body leaving her virtually helpless, their eyes locking as her legs finally caught purchase around his thighs. Carrying her to the wide white living room couch, he laid her down and their mouths crashed against each other as he pushed forward into her. Her cries muffled as she bit his shoulder, clawed at his back, it was all madness, the battle for more, and the race toward release.

"Parker," he growled when she pulled at his hair, urging him to go harder.

"More," was all she said, bucking against him as they rode their way messily and loudly toward pleasure that had him reassessing everything he'd ever known about sex.

When he came, the pleasure hazing his vision, the only thing he knew for sure was that he had to have her in his life.

CHAPTER TEN

PARKER WAS ON her second day of observing Hugh at work, which was taking place in a rented office space in Summerlin. She was crossing the parking lot of his building when she got a text from her dad again asking when she was coming home. A medicine ball of guilt weighted her stomach because she'd been having so much fun and didn't even want to go home. The thought of going back to Chicago, being tied down again for however long until her next trip, had her chafing.

More importantly, she didn't want to leave Hugh yet. It wasn't even worth denying that she had feelings for him anymore. It wasn't casual, it wasn't safe, and she didn't care. Not after the look on his face when the elevator doors had opened on the day he'd found out about his ex's new baby. He'd looked so sad and lost and completely unlike the in-charge badass he usually was. And when he'd talked about wanting a family, she'd felt his longing in every word and knew she'd wanted to be the one who made it better for him. At least for that day. She'd still have to go back to Chicago soon, but not today.

Putting her phone and thoughts about home away, she regarded Hugh's office. It was a nondescript blush brick building on a busy street only a fifteen-minute drive away from her hotel. His front door was glass with white block lettering on it that said Matteson Corporation. The name made her smile. No one could fault Hugh for not being straightforward.

She knocked on the glass office door and Hugh appeared in the doorway behind the small reception area, a broad smile on his face as he waved her inside.

Her heart caught on the fact that he was genuinely happy to see her. Hugh wasn't shy with his emotions. It was crazy to her that he'd been without someone in his life this long. She couldn't help the dark thrill of swatting him with the spoon. All of their sex was intense, but she'd understood then that he'd wanted the pain. Maybe thought he deserved it, maybe it was just an unexplored kink. She didn't know the whole answer, but there was more to Hugh than the confident, wisecracking bro he showed the world. He had rivers of complications beneath the surface and part of her ached for him, wanted to take even a little of his pain away, though she couldn't stick around for the long haul.

"You made it." He smiled, gesturing for her to enter the back office.

"I did." She smiled back, feeling shy because she wanted to be able to hug him, but they weren't that so she couldn't. And it sucked.

He led her into his office, which was pretty standard issue. White walls and a drop ceiling, plain brown commercial carpeting, a sleek glass desk with a silver laptop open on top. Two plastic coffee cups were sitting next to a stack of files.

"You don't keep all your football stuff in here?" she teased, but would actually like to see some of it. There was nothing of Hugh in his Las Vegas house and she yearned to know the real him. The one who got depressed about a picture of a baby and massaged her feet without asking.

"Nope, all that shit is in San Antonio. Got a big ol' man cave for it."

"I'm sure it's quite something."

He held out one of the coffees to her. "Caramel latte, coconut milk, half caff, no whip," he informed her as she took it.

His words caught her up because she'd never actually told him that was her preferred drink; he must have just remembered her ordering it once while they were out. Hugh paid attention and cared for her and it was so lovely that she couldn't speak for a second.

"Thank you." She beamed at him. "I'm impressed that you remembered."

Hugh shrugged. "I remembered because it's the goofiest damn order I've ever heard. What the hell is wrong with plain coffee?"

"Are you an old man?" she joked, sitting at one of the two black armchairs in front of his desk. "That's not plain coffee in your cup," she pointed out. "You even added whipped cream."

"I felt so sorry for the baristas I just ordered two of your drink to make it easier for them."

That got her smiling. "And because you knew it sounded delicious."

"Get out of here," he grumbled as he took an extra-long sip, his eyes laughing. "What kind of person doesn't get whipped cream anyway?"

He scooped up some of his topping with a spoon and ate it, purposely twirling the spoon around in his fingers first. She could feel liquid pool at her core, remembering being in that moment. He'd given her the power over him, reciprocating what she'd felt the night before, and allowed himself to be vulnerable in a way not many men would ever do. It was precious to her that he trusted her enough to be completely open with what he wanted.

It didn't help her state of mind that he was dressed casually today, which should have been less sexy than his normal suits, but wasn't. Instead it revealed more of his bare flesh, which took her from a low buzz of sexual awareness to a "heated skin and crossing her legs" kind of need. A white polo shirt tightened across his massive chest and hugged his biceps, and the small vee at his neck exposed his strong throat and the top of his golden chest.

"Whipped cream is only for special occasions," she scolded, giving him a speaking glance. They had actual work to do today, and while sure, she'd already imagined having sex on his desk and licking whipped cream off his bare chest, it didn't mean they were going to do either of those things. They probably were going to later, she hoped, but not right at this moment. Because, again, work.

"Damn right." He grinned, leaning back in his own chair.

"So just go about your day," she told him, "and I'll ask questions as I have them and take notes."

She'd just leaned over to pull out her tablet when his phone rang. He answered it, watching her as she set herself up on other side of his desk so she could write while he talked.

When he got off the phone, he tossed it onto the desk and met her eyes. "Looks like the buildings in Los Angeles and Charlotte are good to go," he informed her, obviously pleased with the development.

"Los Angeles is a great food town," she agreed. "And Charlotte is getting good, too."

"I hate LA," Hugh admitted with a grimace he'd

be mortified to know she found adorable. "Too much bullshit."

"Is that not where you shot your sneaker commercials?"

He grinned his shit-eating grin that both terrorized and aroused her. Crossing his hands over that sinfully rigid abdomen, he goaded, "You searching my back catalog of commercials?" he asked.

"No," she all but sputtered because she was totally busted. "I just remember it from television. There were palm trees and stuff."

"Mmm-hmm," he drew out, waggling his eyebrows.

"You're the worst."

"You know, you can see this," he said, moving his hand to indicate his body, "anytime you want, sweetheart. Just say the word."

She rolled her eyes.

"So you're opening two new restaurants," she said, changing the subject with another pointed glare. "Will they be the same as the others or a different menu?"

"Similar," he said. "Blue Smoke is Blue Smoke, but we do try to improve and update with each location."

She tapped away, taking notes. "So do you see an end in sight to opening new locations? You now have eleven with these two new ones."

"They say if your business isn't growing, it's

failing, so I'll keep doing whatever that means, but I don't want to grow so big that I lose all control over quality and management. Obviously, I'm very hands-on at this location because it's the first and the biggest, but I visit every restaurant at least four times a year. So I don't want to get big enough where I can't do that anymore."

"Do you like traveling?"

"Yeah, and honestly, I can't imagine my life without it at this point," he answered. "I grew up on the road because of football and I like seeing new places. As we've talked about, I'd ultimately like to settle in San Antonio, but if I had to be there all the time I'd lose my mind."

"Same." Parker smiled. It was how she felt about being at home for too long, as well.

Then he met her eyes, his very serious, almost tentative, which was novel because his confidence was big enough to circle the earth on a loop. "Parker, maybe this isn't my business. Fuck, I know it's not my business. But what happened with your mom?"

Parker shifted in her chair. The trick to being a successful adult was to not think about her mom too much, so these kinds of questions were like picking at a Band-Aid covering an open wound.

"You don't have to answer," he followed up at her silence, "but I feel like all my shit is just out there and I don't know anything about you. Except your coffee order."

He paused again, then held her gaze. "And I want to know more."

She would have made a joke and kept it light if he hadn't said the last, but she wanted to go deeper with Hugh.

"She didn't leave until I was fourteen. And I've actually talked to her several times over the years," Parker admitted, though she'd never told her father as much. It would have only hurt him more. "She lives in Florida working as an assistant for a real estate developer. She's remarried to said real estate developer. I think she's living her best life, to be honest with you. I forgive her for leaving, but I don't know that I need to have a close relationship with her at this point in my life."

Talking about it made her feel unworthy all over again, same as the day her mom had left. People who mattered still had moms. If Parker had been at all important to her, she could have visited over the years, but she'd chosen not to. Not that Parker would have seen her anyway, but still. Some token trying would have been the least a mother could do.

Hugh's face was a careful blank mask. "She ever tell you why she left?"

Parker blew out a breath, the old insecurities from that time seeping out from under the door she'd closed them behind all those years ago.

"Yeah, it was a lot of excuses, but mostly that she hadn't loved my dad in a long time and wanted a new life. My grandmother lived in Florida then, so she had family there. In her defense, she waited until I was in high school and could take care of myself. I don't hate her, but I missed her when she left and that kind of pain doesn't just go away. I can be glad that she's happy, but mourn that she was a shitty mom to me."

Hugh reached over the desk and grabbed her hand, pulling her up until she was walking to his chair. Arranging her so she was in his lap, he met her eyes. "So you're afraid to leave your dad like she did," he guessed.

Parker nodded, squirming on his lap because she wasn't a child. She didn't need to be in his arms to talk about her mom, but hated that she liked it. He settled a big paw on her knee, stilling her.

She sighed and answered him. "I know how it feels, so I know it has to be ten times worse for him." Also, it wasn't was if her mom had even asked her to go with her to Florida, which only re-inforced the fact that she must have been a pretty unremarkable child. Certainly not special enough to catch the heart of a football star millionaire en-trepreneur. Her dad was the only person who gave a shit if she was gone or in Chicago and that meant everything to her, so she'd enjoy the time she had with Hugh, but knew how it all would end.

Hugh's mouth softened as well as his gaze and she had to remind herself of that fact once again. He was not for her.

"She's an idiot," he declared loudly, as if that was the whole story.

"You don't have to do that," Parker told him. "I'm over it. Honestly."

"Yeah, I do, because it's the truth. Any person who doesn't want to know you, your mom or a random person on the street, is an idiot. Even though your coffee choice is shit and you made me the laughingstock of the barbecue world, you're pretty awesome."

Parker shook her head. "Thanks, Hugh. But I worry more about Dad. He's fine, but I know his heart is still broken."

She saw pieces of her dad in Hugh. Not that Hugh was pining for his ex the way her dad was, but that he hadn't moved on with his life since the breakup. It was as if they'd both had a plan and when it hadn't gone their way, they'd just shut down that part of their lives.

"I like you, Parker Jones," Hugh said, giving her a gentle kiss on the forehead. "You're a good egg."

She raised an eyebrow, needing to lighten the mood. "Are you sure you're not a seventy-year-old man? Maybe recite me a parable next?"

"Not yet," he said, waggling his own eyebrows, the slit one making her knees sweat as usual.

"Just do your work," she ordered, pointing to the desk at large and trying to get off his lap.

He let her go, but slowly until their entwined fingers were their last contact, and she returned to her seat.

Then he proceeded to pull out a couple of over-size manila files and placed them in front of her on the desk. "This is what's on my agenda today."

She flipped open a couple of the files and saw a bunch of typed-out sample menus, art boards and summary descriptions for, not Blue Smoke, but several different kinds of restaurants.

"You're going to open another chain?" she asked.

He shrugged. "I don't know yet. I was think-ing about it. These are some of the concepts I've been pitched by either fellow investors or sought out from renowned chefs who don't necessarily have the capital to start restaurants on their own. What do you think of them?"

Leaning back into her seat, Parker leafed through the packets as Hugh did his own typing on the computer. By the time she'd reached the end of the stack, she wasn't sure how much time had gone by.

Hugh quirked an eyebrow when she finally looked up.

"Nothing I haven't seen before," she told him honestly. Some of the food would be good for a small to medium city, but nothing was going to make a splash in the food world. She wouldn't make a special trip to a city to go to any of those places for *Gastronomic*, at any rate.

Instead of being irritated, Hugh looked amused. "What would you do if given carte blanche to create your own restaurant?"

She shook her head at him. "Nooope," she drawled, "you're not gonna get me that way."

"Can't blame a guy for trying," he said, those laugh lines around his eyes already so endearing. "But that's what those people in that folder were told to do, dream big and go for what they wanted. I don't know what the difference is if it's your idea in that folder, too."

It sounded good, she had to admit. She'd love to think of a concept from start to finish and then see it all come together. But she was sleeping with Hugh, which meant that anything less than being an equal partner in a venture like that wouldn't feel right.

But then the idea took hold, her mind unable to let it go. If she got a loan maybe she could invest as a full partner, which was different from being on Hugh's payroll. But then what if it failed and she still had to support her dad? It was too risky.

"The difference is that I don't want to be your employee," she told him. "We're involved."

Hugh opened his mouth to speak, but then changed his mind.

"I hear you," he eventually said. "The way I see it, though, is that you've already told me you don't want to date long-distance so once you leave, what's the problem with throwing some ideas around with me? Apparently we won't be involved at that point."

Parker wasn't an idiot. She heard the underlying frustration in his words, but she also didn't like being backed into a corner. She'd given him reasonable explanations for not wanting to do either thing. No matter how great Hugh was, and he was extremely special to her, there was no way it was going to happen. His life and her life might as well be on two separate planets. Her parents had been together forever and her mom had still cut out for a simpler life. Was Hugh, a millionaire football star and entrepreneur who didn't know what expensive was, really going to stick around for her complicated one? Odds were extremely doubtful.

One of the reasons they got along so well was because they had fun together. But that was only her part-time life. While she was on the road, she got to be the free and easy Parker who only had her great job and awesome food to worry about, but in Chicago it was different. Real life was there. And honestly, not to be trite, she kind of needed everything in Vegas to stay in Vegas.

"The problem is that I don't want to and I actually don't need a reason," she told him, giving him a speaking glance, which had a corner of his mouth lifting in wry amusement.

"You're killing me, Jones, but damned if I don't like the way I'm going out."

Parker gave the folder once last glance before meeting his eyes. "And just think, I still have over a week to go."

CHAPTER ELEVEN

"So you got into restaurants because of your dad?" Parker asked, her pink lips forming words that Hugh was not paying any attention to. They'd been doing this profile thing all week and while he liked having her around most days, he was getting antsy. Only a couple more days and she was gone from his life forever. He didn't know what he was going to do about that when the time came, but the eventuality was driving him nuts.

"Why don't you stay at my place until you leave?" he asked, ignoring her question. "You're barely at the hotel anyway and it'll be easier to finish the profile. Plus, I'll even let you use one of my cars so you can check out restaurants during the day for work."

Parker stared at him. "How is that an answer to my question?"

"I've answered the question before," he complained, irritation rising that she was avoiding the

question he posed that it had been damned difficult for him to ask. He didn't even bring women
to his house period, let alone ask them to basically
live there. "A friend from the league invested in a
bunch of restaurants and he was living easy. But
my dad mentioned that I could capitalize on my
Texas upbringing and start a barbecue place and
so here I am."

He pinned her with his gaze again, gnawing on
the inside of his cheek because he was nervous.
The last time he'd lived with someone it had ended
in him walking in on her screwing somebody else.

"Answer *my* question," he demanded, raising
his eyebrow in a way that used to scare the shit
out of rookies.

Parker hesitated and he braced himself for her
refusal, but instead she nodded.

His head dropped forward in surprise, the breath
he was holding rushing out. "Really?" he asked, his
voice nearly squeaking like a teenager's.

"Yeah," she said, shrugging. "I need to do my
own laundry. The hotel dyed my favorite white shirt
pink. Also, I'm sick of wearing flip-flops in the
shower."

"Someone does my laundry, too," he admitted.
"But go to town on your own if it makes you feel
better, and no flip-flops needed."

He stood up from his desk, the chair making a
clatter as it fell backward in his haste. "Let's go

get your stuff now, then. It's almost eleven and you don't want to pay for another whole day in the hotel."

Looking at him from under her eyelashes, she shook her head as he hastily righted his chair. "Are you okay?"

"I'm just sick of being in the office," he told her, which was true. Usually he went out for more meetings, but he'd pushed everything back so he could spend time with her, and he was getting really damn sick of these four generic white walls. "We can stop at Blue Smoke on the way home. Which place were you going to review tonight?"

"I'm reviewing a place for lunch," she reminded him. "That's why I'm here earlier than usual."

"Good," he said, clapping his hands together. "I'll go, too."

He'd tried to bully her into letting him come on more of her review trips, but she'd argued that she didn't want the service to be influenced by his celebrity presence, blah blah, excuses excuses. But they only had a few days left and he was man enough to admit that he wanted to be with her.

"Let's just get my stuff first, okay?" she suggested, probably sensing his agitation.

He nodded, ushering her out of his office with a hand on the ass he was coming to think of as his.

When he squeezed it, she turned on a dime, her hands on her hips. Just as she was about to lay him out, he took her mouth. And shit, it felt good to kiss her. Within seconds her lips were pliant against his and her arms were around his neck. He let her go, sighing as he touched his forehead to hers.

"We have to stop," he grunted, the words more to stop himself from going any further than to explain it to her, "gotta check you out."

He could feel her nod against him and then he pushed her out the office door, following closely behind her so he could smell the citrus scent that had a Pavlovian effect on his dick.

"Did I get you a little too hard?" he asked her once they were in his car and on their way to the Strip.

Shaking her head, she started typing something on her phone.

"What are you doing?" he prodded.

"Emailing my boss to tell her I'm checking out and to cut you a check for the amount we would have paid the hotel since you probably can't take my work credit card."

He swiped the phone straight from her hands and put it in his pocket where she couldn't reach it. "No fucking way are you paying to stay at my house."

"There's no way I'm not turning in a bill for an entire week of lodging and explaining to my boss that I instead decided to shack up with a restaurant owner I met while technically on the clock," she shot back, glaring at him.

"She'll know that's what you were doing anyway if you ask them to send the check to me!"

"I was planning on giving her your business address and saying that you offered me one of your empty rental units," she explained.

He took in a deep breath through his nose to calm his shit down. Paying for her stay at his house made their time together transactional, as if it was just business, and it pissed him the fuck off. Every single other interaction he had with women since Amanda had been just that. But from the article, to the competition, to the profile, all of it had been personal with Parker.

But they didn't have much time left and he wasn't going to argue with her. He handed her phone back. "Fine," he bit off, "have it your way."

Within seconds she was typing away and his fists closed around the steering wheel, his knuckles whitening.

Pulling up to the hotel, he was pretty much back together. She was staying at his house; that was enough. With any luck, he could get her to spend entire days in bed with him that ended with neither of them able to walk.

Hugh helped her pack up her belongings, which didn't take long, and then they were off to lunch at Marrakech, a Moroccan restaurant, for Parker's review. He'd never actually been there before so he was looking forward to it. It ended up being an exercise in torture because it was basically watching Parker eat, which always made him hard as a rock. He picked at his meatball tagine even though it was delicious and watched as she took two to three bites of five different dishes.

"I think it's good," he eventually said.

She nodded. "Decent."

They finished up lunch and returned to the car. "Do you want to go back to my office to write your review or back to my house?"

"I thought you wanted to swing by Blue Smoke," she reminded him.

"Right," he muttered, for some reason now annoyed with the prospect. It was already four o'clock so the dinner crowd would be on its way. A good time to check in to make sure everything was running smoothly. Not that it usually didn't run smoothly, but it was his job and he normally enjoyed it. But now it just seemed like something to take away from his time with Parker. Which she, on the other hand, seemed to have no problem with.

He didn't like this feeling at all. The unfamiliar desperation that was settling in even as he tried to bat it back. Pulling into the parking lot of his restaurant, he turned to her. "I've got a small office in the back you can use to write your review while I circulate," he told her.

"Thanks," she said, smiling at him in that way that suggested she was grateful to him for being thoughtful. It damn near ripped him apart every time. The fact that no one had done shit for either of them was the problem, and every little nugget of caring was lapped up like they were starving. He knew the feeling all too well, hated that she did, too, but liked that he made her happy. It made him feel less on an island.

He spent the next hour traveling from table to table chitchatting to people like he normally did, except he wasn't into it as usual, his mind on getting back to Parker. When he finally made a full circuit through the whole dining room and checked in with his chef, back from sick leave and ready to go, he went to collect her.

"Finished?" she asked, smiling up at him. Today her hair was in a ponytail and she wore a pair of jean capris with holes in the knees and a black T-shirt with embroidered silver stars. The outfit was not at all suggestive, but the shirt was fitted in all the right places and the jeans embraced her ass like a hug, drawing attention to that tight waist. He stretched his fingers out in an effort not to grab hold of her.

He was struggling overall because this manic feeling just wouldn't go away, pressing down firmly on his chest and not easing up. That he was letting something of extreme importance slip away every minute he didn't tie her to his bed and make her stay with him. He needed to get his shit together and stop being such a wimp. They both knew this was a fling and that's where it needed to stay. He needed a family and a woman who would stick. Parker, who couldn't even mention the word *feelings*, wasn't going to fit the bill. But that knowledge didn't stop him from wanting it all the same.

When they got back to his house, he grabbed a couple of bottles of beer and suggested that they swim. Parker hadn't wanted to change into her swimsuit, but sat on the edge of the pool with her legs dangling in the water and drinking a glass of red wine while he waded in the shallow end. He often swam laps in the pool, but this was one of the only times he'd just hung out there with someone.

"I've been thinking," she told him, "I don't need to be a partner, but I could take another look at those restaurant proposals and tweak the menus a bit."

"Is that right?" he asked. Maybe things weren't as hopeless as he'd thought. She was interested in what he'd proposed, but for whatever reason, she was afraid to take the chance or didn't trust him enough. "I have the proposals in my home office, so we can check them out again tonight."

"I like the one centering on local ingredients in Maine. I think it has promise."

"It didn't even have any lobster on the menu," he scoffed, flopping onto his back to float. "What's the point?"

He didn't need to see the look on her face to know that her lips were thin and she was gazing upward. It was what he'd wanted to happen when he'd made the statement.

"That's the whole point," she told him, as if speaking to a recalcitrant child. He loved it. "Learning what Maine has to offer outside of a lobster roll. I just think the menu needs to be broadened a little so it's less like a hippie commune and more accessible to everyone."

"I could get behind it," he said, still floating. "But is there really anything there to take it outside of Maine, you know? Local is local. We're not taking local Maine ingredients to Montana or something. So we're limited on growth."

"You could make it regional," she suggested. "All of New England. Or that could be your whole new chain concept. Every restaurant focusing on the local fare, but with your fill-in-the-blank."

His head shot up then and he stood up, water sluicing down his chest and back. He met her eyes, swiping wet hair from his face, interest pricking at the back of his neck. "So each restaurant has different food but an overarching concept that connects them all?"

"Yeah," she answered, and he felt the excitement in her eyes in his own veins.

"I like it," he boomed, pointing emphatically at

her as his other hand clapped the water. "I like it a lot, Parker."

She grinned. "It's good, right? And you could start with that Maine menu and go from there."

"It's so good," he agreed, grinning.

Swimming over to stand right in between her legs, he brought her down for a kiss and his legs went liquid at her sigh. Fuck, he was going to miss this. He was going to miss her, period. But he really needed to stop acting like a lovesick teenager because they still had a couple of days and she was living at his house. That was good enough, and then he could concentrate on finding a wife. Because if nothing else, this time with Parker had shown him just how great a real relationship could be. And he was ready to find that again.

"So this is a subject change, but I have another question for the profile."

"Shoot," he allowed, "but then we need to think of an overarching concept."

"Do you ever miss football?"

He shrugged. "I miss hanging out with the guys on the regular, but I see them often enough. Playing ball? Every once in a while, but I always figured I'd teach my kids, and I look forward to that."

"You'd let your kids play football even though you got dangerously injured?" she asked, surprised.

"I'm more talking about just tossing the ball in the backyard, not turning pro necessarily." He'd loved playing ball and even still thought about coaching sometimes when he got bored of just doing business as usual, but he volunteered with enough youth football camps and had his own coming up next month that it was just all the fun without the pressure of winning like coaching would be.

"Do you want kids?" he asked, cursing because it was too soon. And it didn't matter anyway.

She flicked at the water and he kicked himself for asking. It wasn't his damned business; they weren't even in a relationship.

"I've never given it much thought, to be honest," she told him. "My dad is around and I've never had a serious relationship, so it wasn't something I honestly considered would ever happen."

"But you're not against them," he clarified, his heart pounding hard in his chest, as if he had a stake in this game.

Parker shrugged, finally meeting his eyes. "No, I wouldn't say that."

And then when the silence stretched for a moment, he found himself asking, "Do you not want to find someone at all, Parker?"

That shrug again, the one he was coming to realize might be her avoiding talking about a real issue. "I do, I just haven't, and the whole happily-ever-after thing never really seemed like a possibility. I just have to look at my dad to know that sometimes it's not worth the trouble. Plus, my lifestyle has never been conducive to it so it hasn't felt like I've been missing out."

Hugh was no therapist, but the look on Parker's face, the one trying to hide the fact that she wanted to believe she could find happiness but wouldn't take the chance, was telegraphed as clear as day. He didn't know her parents, but they'd really done a number on their daughter. Her dad by convincing her that love was conditional on her staying by his side and her mom by making her think she wasn't worthy enough to accept or demand more.

He understood more than he wanted to admit. The whole world loved him, but the only woman who had really known him had found him highly replaceable.

"You're gone a lot, is that it?" he finally managed, giving her an out from admitting that she didn't think anyone could love her if her own mom didn't.

"Yeah, I had a boyfriend back in college for about two years or so, but nothing serious since then. I'm gone at least two but often four weekends out of a month, and sometimes weeks or months at a time if it's an assignment like this, where we really want to explore the food culture. It's just challenging to get something going."

So she hadn't even tried, is what Hugh was hearing. Parker was too scarred from her mom's leaving to even try. That made him really sad and he

dunked his head under the water to avoid the pity-
ing look that was probably all over his face. He had
a caring woman who was still carrying around a
lot of pain and he was pretty clueless about how to
help her heal. Despair crept over him because he
hadn't wanted to admit it, but he knew that the feeling taking hold of his insides was love. And there
wasn't a damn thing to do about it.

He felt a disturbance in the water and resurfaced
to find that Parker had stripped down to her bra and
panties and joined him in the pool.

"It looked too fun to miss out." She smiled, sending a huge smack of water into his face.

Yeah, it was getting damn near impossible not
to admit.

"You're going to regret that," he warned as he
stalked toward her, but knew once he got his hands
on her, regret would be the last thing they felt.

CHAPTER TWELVE

PARKER LOVED BEING at Hugh's house. Not only was it way better than her hotel, which had been constantly crawling with tourists hell-bent on drinking so much they forgot their entire vacation, but it had Hugh in it. Hugh, who had graduated from her favorite indulgence to a basic necessity.

With only two days left, she was having a mild freak-out because it was the end of their time together and she knew it was probably the last time she'd ever see him in her life. It wasn't as if they lived in the same town where they might run into each other or something. This was it. The melancholia was creeping into her cells slowly but poised to take over her whole being once she stepped on that plane to Chicago without him.

She'd played it all wrong. All the lessons she'd learned over the years with guys about how not to get attached, swerving around any possible feelings, leaving them before they left her. Moving in with Hugh had been the ultimate in foolish decisions, because she never wanted to leave. Waking up alongside his too-warm and yet perfect body every morning was better than the thousand fantasy relationship scenarios she'd constructed in her head over the years when the monotony of living with her dad became too much. In her wildest dreams, she couldn't have come up with a person who seemed so unsuited to her and yet fit her more perfectly than Hugh.

He made her breakfast every morning, handed out massages like candy, left her alone when she needed to work or go review a restaurant, patiently answered the most inane questions about his business, and it went without saying that the sex continued to climb in intensity because they both felt the weight of their imminent ending.

But most of all, he made her laugh, and she hadn't realized how much she hadn't been laughing until Hugh.

The years between now and her mom leaving felt like long, empty years in comparison and part of her felt like going back to Chicago was a return to that. Year after year of only existing and never living. But imagining a future with Hugh, she didn't even have the tools. Couldn't imagine staying with anyone and watching them eventually walk away, or her doing it. A month with Hugh and leaving felt like her heart was being ripped out. Being in an actual committed relationship and having him walk away? Hell no.

Which was why she was finishing up her last review and leaving tomorrow. She'd lied and told Hugh she was leaving the day after because saying goodbye was impossible, and if she told him she was leaving, he'd try to get her to stay and/or go into business with him. Which would break her resolve.

The fact was that she couldn't ever leave her dad alone.

For Hugh or for anybody.

She parked Hugh's silver Audi convertible in his garage and took the elevator to the main floor. Hugh was in the kitchen with his shirt off, blaring hip-hop, a baseball game on mute on the television, and tapping away on his laptop. The man could not tolerate silence.

When he noticed her, he smiled, waving her over to the island where he had a cold beer waiting for her. The same kind she'd said she'd liked at his restaurant that first night. The fridge was stocked with that and tons of other random stuff she'd mentioned liking over the course of their month together. Just like she'd taken to finding out and making his favorite meals on the nights they stayed in and doing yoga with him in the morning even though she hated it. She just wanted to show him how much he meant to her. How much all of this time had meant.

"Last work meal of the trip," he boomed, holding up his hand for a high five. "How was it?"

She slapped his big paw, but instead of letting her go, he caught her fingers in his and pulled her in between his legs as he swung the chair around to face her.

"It was good," she told him. She hadn't tasted any of it even though she'd saved the best restaurant for last. Worrying about leaving tomorrow had made it difficult to do anything but cry right into her eighty-dollar steak. For the past two days, tears were very close to the surface, which was stupid because she literally couldn't remember the last time she'd cried. Maybe that animated movie about the toys? It was hard to say.

"What are you doing?" she asked, breathing in the familiar, brightly musky scent of him.

His smile was huge, the corners of his eyes crinkling with excitement. "I just got off the phone with my lawyer," he informed her, grabbing a small stack of papers sitting on the island beside him. "And he drew up an agreement of what it would look like if we did a restaurant together. So just take this with you, look it over, give it to your own lawyer, no pressure. But I want you to know that there's an offer on the table if you want it. A real one, not just one you think I made because we're sleeping together."

Parker had never hyperventilated before, but she feared she was on the verge of it. Her heart was beating so fast she could barely count the beats in her head like she normally did to calm down, and it felt like she couldn't draw a full breath into her lungs.

She nodded numbly at him and took the papers, pretending to look even though the words were just a blurry mess as she continued to stare blindly at them.

"Hey," he asked, standing up and pressing a thumb under her chin so he could see her, concern etched on his handsome, scarred face. "You okay? This isn't to scare you, Parker. I know you've said no before, but I wanted you to at least have all the details so you could make an informed decision. There are two agreements there. One where you could own part of the business with me and the other to only be a menu consultant, which means helping with the menu and concept like we talked about in the beginning. There wouldn't be as much traveling or financial risk involved."

The pay was ridiculous, she saw that, for the consultant. The investment option wouldn't pay out for a while until the restaurant made a profit, but he was really tempting her with the consultant option and he knew it. This is what she'd wanted to avoid by lying about leaving. So much of her wanted to say yes, but the fact was that when she left Vegas tomorrow she was going to be in pieces. It wasn't a matter of if, but just how awful she was going to feel leaving Hugh. The idea of then turning around and seeing him on a merely professional level was impossible. She couldn't do it, she knew it. Nor could she ever do a long-distance relationship. Saying goodbye on a regular basis? She might as well be tearing off her own arm on the regular. That's what it would feel like if today was any indication.

So instead of answering, she did the only thing left to do and kissed him with everything she had. To somehow burn how she felt into his skin so he would know just how much she cared for him.

Their lips met in a bawdy, openmouthed, angst-fueled storm.

Hugh picked her up and carried her to his room, where the wall of windows was retracted. The sun was setting in the desert, the gradated shades of neon red and purple and gold still lighting the sky just enough for them to see each other. He laid her down on the bed and a light breeze floated into the room as he climbed on top of her, returning to her mouth.

"Stay with me a few extra days?" he murmured against her lips, their foreheads together, their warm breath hovering in the air between them like their own intimate world.

"Maybe," she said, because she was leaving tomorrow anyway. What was one more white lie?

"Say yes instead," he whispered, the words

sounding more like a plea than as the suggestion he'd meant. "Stay."

The words were on her tongue—she wanted to say yes, to just let go and let him be part of her life and actually take a chance on the first person who'd made any effort to be there—but they wouldn't leave her mouth. Maybe she was just that broken. She didn't know, but her heart hurt and that was something she hadn't felt since her mom left all those years ago.

"You deserve to be happy, Parker," he continued when she remained mute. "Choose it."

If her heart was stone, which sometimes she'd thought it was, it was nothing but a soft, doughy mass of love after his words. And yet she couldn't take the chance. So she did the only thing she could, her lips finding his mouth again in a fury of unacknowledged emotions and pipe dreams.

His hands found the hem of her shirt, pulling it up and off along with her pants. The warm desert air hit her skin and she felt exposed physically and emotionally. Hugh's lips were on hers as she tugged off his shorts, impatient and desperate to have all of him. His body was large, blocking out the entire rest of the world from her view, and it didn't matter. She didn't feel claustrophobic or caged in; as always, Hugh just made her feel protected and safe. She did not know how she was going to leave him at all, dreaded it with every contrary fiber of her being. Even now, solidly in his arms, she didn't want to be anywhere else ever. She could live inside the cocoon of his brick house body.

He reached over, grabbing a condom out of the bedside table, and her thighs clenched in wanton anticipation, just pushing the reality that she was leaving away long enough for her to enjoy one last night with the best man she'd ever known and the best sex she'd ever had.

"You make me happy," he whispered against her lips, dropping down to her neck, kissing everywhere he could reach. It was lovely and tender and downright heart-wrenching when he got on his knees, kissing up her thighs, worshipping her skin as if she were the first woman he'd ever known.

Fighting back tears, she pulled him up until he was over her again and wrapped her legs around his back, pulling him into her. He positioned himself at her entrance, his head bent and broken eyebrow just visible, and a wave of longing hit her so hard that she had to score her fingernails into her palms to keep from crying. Raising his head again, their eyes met as he inched slowly into her, letting her feel every bit of him. The playfulness that had become a hallmark of their sex life was gone. They were without the jokes or quips because everything she wanted to say couldn't be said.

"You make me happy, too," she finally breathed as he began to move.

He swallowed then, the lump in his throat bobbing as he accepted the words. Dropping his forehead to hers, their lips barely touching, he moved in her, slowly at first, the slide purposeful and measured, designed to draw out their pleasure and let her know how he felt inside her, as if she could forget. As if she'd ever forget anything about him.

Their mingled breaths sounded in the quiet room, passing through the inside, and eventually moved outside, swept away with the breeze, just like she would leave tomorrow. As if she'd never been there.

She wrapped her arms around him, pressing him closer, as close as he could possibly get as they moved together as one, their bodies grinding and grasping against each other for release. His thick shaft slid in and out of her, drawing over her sensitized flesh. Hot bolts of sensation zipped up and down her skin as he gripped her ass, adjusting her angle so he could go deeper, hitting that spot inside her that had her gasping into his mouth in mindless bliss.

"Parker," he choked out, the corded lines of his neck bulging with the effort of holding back. Reaching between them, he thumbed her clit and she flew into the abyss, arms still clutching around him as if she'd never let him go.

"Just go," she whispered, floating down from space, giving him permission to let loose.

And he did, pumping savagely into her, his fingers gripping hard into the flesh of her ass. She came again, the climb violent and the explosion fierce, eventually giving way to mellow contentment as he groaned his release, his whole body suddenly going slack underneath her touch.

He murmured something against her lips that sounded like *thank you* before he rearranged them on the bed so that she was in the crook of his arm.

She almost promised him that she wouldn't leave, wanted to say the words so badly, but couldn't.

"I really like you, Hugh," she finally murmured, knowing they were a pale substitute for what she really felt.

"I really like you, too, Parker," he returned, squeezing her closer into his warm body.

Snuggling against him, she placed a single kiss over his heart to make up for the words that were too dangerous to say and eventually fell asleep.

Hugh woke up to an empty bedroom, knew it as soon as he opened his eyes. Maybe even before his head hit the pillow last night, he'd known Parker was gone.

The look in her eyes when he'd asked her to stay had given her intention away; the fear he'd seen there hadn't been normal. But it also meant that she felt the same way he did and was scared as fuck. It was a fear he could get behind and relate to, if the pain knocking his chest inside out was any indication.

Bolting out of bed, he checked her drawers for confirmation that she was gone before pulling on some of his own clothes. Then he shot down the elevator into his car.

He went to the airport, which was usually a half-hour drive, but he made it there in twenty minutes in part because it wasn't even seven in the morning yet but also thanks to his outrageous speeding.

Parking his car illegally at the drop-off, he handed the keys to a kid taking luggage whose eyes got huge when he recognized him. "Move it if you need to, pal, I'll pay."

Not even caring that the possibility of never seeing his beloved McLaren again was extremely real, he ran into the airport with no idea what airline Parker might be on. So instead he just bought a ticket to Chicago and ran to gate after gate with flights to Chicago searching for any sight of her.

And then finally, when he'd just about given up hope, she stood up from one of the vinyl beige seats intending to board.

Racing once again, he caught her arm just as she was about to take her place in the boarding line.

Her eyes were huge and she looked as if she was already about to cry, which he had to ignore because there was no time and there were things that needed to be said.

"I love you, Parker," he said, not even playing around. "And I don't want you to go."

She stared at him, her eyes impossibly large and unreadable. There was fear, yes, but something else he couldn't quite put his finger on.

Opening her mouth, she tried to speak, but then just shook her head as if whatever she said wouldn't matter anyway.

They announced for passengers to board again and she took a step back from him. His heart sped up and he felt just like he had that day he'd walked in on his ex and his best friend, betrayed, certainly, but most of all, he just felt alone. Again. And he fucking hated it. Loathed the idea of going back to his empty house without her in it.

"Stay with me, Parker," he told her, giving her an out. She didn't have to lay it all out on the table today; he'd be satisfied with more time. "You know you want to."

"It'll just be harder to leave," she finally said, shaking her head. "I'm sorry, Hugh."

His hands fisted. "I can't believe you're doing this," he gritted, his presence already drawing attention from the other passengers in the seating area. "This is something good. Don't fuck it up."

"We said it was just the month," she reminded him. Her words, a callback to their beginning, were lame to his ears. They'd agreed on a month when they'd known nothing about how great they could be together. It was complete and utter bullshit.

"Yeah, we made those rules, which means we can change them," he tried.

She was the last person left to board in her group, the attendant looking expectantly at her. So he did the only thing he could think of and pulled her hard into his arms, catching her mouth up in a kiss. He gave her everything, the love, the affection, the regard, fear, anger, wasted hope, just let it all go because there was too much inside him to hang on to all of it, praying that she'd accept and believe it.

"I need it to be just the month, Hugh," she choked out when the kiss was over.

And so he wiped away her tears and let her go. The old him would have gone after her, demanded that she listen and they give it a shot, but he knew it was Parker's ball now.

He watched her board the plane and though his heart was shattered, it was no small epiphany that he'd still had one to be broken in the first place.

CHAPTER THIRTEEN

As soon as Parker had left Hugh's house for the air-port, she regretted it. Knew in her bones that she might have just irrevocably screwed up the best thing that had ever happened to her. She'd managed to hold off tears that even she was surprised hadn't shown up when he'd found her in the airport until the car ride back to her place in Chicago. But as soon as she'd gotten inside the same model Acura from the car service that she'd taken that first night with him, they'd flowed in earnest. The driver had wordlessly handed her a box of tissues, and also, inexplicably, a lollipop, which she now held on to for dear life as if it were the one tangible thing sep-arating her from a complete emotional meltdown.

Finally trudging up the cement stairs into her house, sleep was the only thing on her mind. She had no mental or physical energy for anything else.

Except that when she opened the door, dropping her purse straight onto the ground in exhaustion, the first thing she saw was her dad holding hands with a woman on the living room couch.

Jaw in the dropped position, she stared as the two jumped apart as if they'd been caught doing something far more serious than hand-holding, her father sputtering Parker's name in shock.

"I didn't know you'd be home so soon," he croaked, standing up and wiping his palms on his pressed khakis. She hadn't seen her dad wear anything other than sweatpants and jeans for years now. Didn't even know he owned a pair of khakis, in fact.

But she didn't concentrate on that so much before her gaze fell on the woman beside him, who was also now standing. Wearing a pastel-flowered skirt and a denim button-down top, she looked like a kindly aunt who carried wicker baskets full of flowers home every Friday after work and baked cookies every Sunday.

"Dad, are you dating?" Parker asked, finally meeting her father's eyes.

As he shoved his hands into his pockets, Parker felt the tiniest bit of hope open up in her chest.

"I wanted to tell you about Sally, sweetheart, but I thought you'd be upset."

Parker laughed. "Upset? Why?"

Sally and her father looked at each other hesitantly before her father nodded in reassurance.

Then Sally held out her left hand for Parker to see, and on it was a small but lovely diamond ring.

"We're getting married," Parker's dad said, pride in his voice, but with an edge of fear.

Parker blinked in surprise, not quite believing it, but the shock was quickly followed by joy.

"That's wonderful, Dad!" Parker beamed, happiness bubbling up in her chest like a shaken soda. "Why would I be upset about that?"

Her dad's feet shuffled around on the ground, clearly uneasy about his next words. "Well, Sally's got a house in Avondale and all."

Parker laughed. "Dad, I assumed you'd be moving out. And it's okay. I've only ever wanted you to be happy." She crossed the room and pulled him into a hug, motioning for Sally to join. Relief coursed through her veins, the melancholy over leaving Hugh still there, but stronger was the feeling of determination that she could set things to rights. That she could finally leave her past behind and concentrate on her future.

"I want you to find love, too, P," her dad said, squeezing. "You are the best daughter a man could ever have and I owe you everything. Your mom will never know the kind of woman you are in spite of her and that's her loss. Go be happy, sweetheart. Wherever that is. You don't have to worry about me anymore."

"You were never a burden, Dad," she assured him, her eyes wet because for all the complaining over the years, she wouldn't have changed having that time with her dad for anything.

"That's a lie and we both know it, sweetheart," her dad said. "You changed your entire life for me—don't think I don't know it."

Parker shook her head, knowing the real truth. The one she'd been denying since her mom walked out on them. The one that had become blindingly clear when Hugh had begged her to stay with him.

"I was using you as excuse, Dad. I was just too afraid to find someone and move on because of what Mom did to you. So I always had to be the one to leave." Just like she'd left Hugh and every other guy who'd ever tried to get close.

And now just like his ex, she'd left him alone again and heartbroken. Because her fear went so deep, she didn't even think about hurting other people, only worrying about her own protection.

"Parker," Dad said, "that's on me, too. I should have set you straight when you never brought anyone serious home. Don't ever let your mom take away your happiness. She's not an evil person like I've been saying all these years, but don't let someone who has chosen not to be a part of your life have such a negative influence over it. Trust me, I had to learn that lesson the hard way."

Parker blinked back more tears and allowed herself a moment to let it all settle. To accept that her mom had left, yes, but it said more about the kind of person she was than Parker. Her Dad had shown her love in a million ways over the years. Words and deeds that she simply hadn't let be real or penetrate because she'd have to admit she was affected by them in the first place.

"I love you, Dad," she finally managed as his hand gave hers a squeeze.

"I love you, too," her dad said. "But you'll still come by sometimes, okay, maybe cook for us? Sally is a grand woman, but she's no chef."

"Of course, Dad," she told him, giving Sally a watery smile.

Sally left them to go into the kitchen, but Parker's dad kept hold of her hand.

"So I met a guy," she started, because she knew what she had to do now, but was also more scared of what would happen if she did. "But he's wary of relationships, too, and I don't want to hurt him by running away again. I already chickened out and left him once. What if I do it again like Mom did to us? Just cut out if things get too difficult?" And they would, she knew, because Hugh was the biggest pain in the ass in America. Followed closely in line by her.

Her dad gave her hand a shake, giving her a fierce expression, his dear brown eyes like hers, familiar but serious. "You took care of me for the past ten years, Parker, at the expense of your own wants and desires. I don't want you to have to do that for someone else again, but if that doesn't prove you've got staying power, I don't know what does. And any man who lets you go isn't worth it anyway."

"Thanks, Dad," she told him as he pulled her in for another long hug. Maybe she did need to have a little more faith in herself. At the very least, she needed to give herself her own shot at being with Hugh.

"I'm still serious about those meals, though, so you better visit your dad here in Chicago."

Parker smiled, giving her dad another squeeze. "You could always come to Vegas, too, you know."

"You couldn't keep me away," he whispered back, and she knew he was teary, too.

CHAPTER FOURTEEN

PARKER TOOK A deep breath as Hugh made his entrance from the back kitchen into Blue Smoke's dining area. It was so much like the first time she'd seen him, and yet completely different. Then he'd looked confident and warm, without a care in the world, and now he looked drawn and removed, his eyes drained of their signature humor. She'd been the one to do that to him, take away a bit of his shine. And that felt supremely crappy, but she was here to make it better for both of them. She only hoped he'd let her.

Her table, the same one they'd first sat at, was once again loaded up with baskets and dishes as it had been the night they'd met. She'd also included the first iteration of her barbecue sauce, which she'd managed to get straight from the distributor since it wasn't actually available yet. That joint venture between them felt important to emphasize at the moment.

Watching as he made his way through the diners, she got the sense that he was actually actively avoiding looking at her table, maybe because like her, he thought of it as theirs. He was always so aware of his surroundings, but tonight he only paid attention to each table he greeted, never glancing around the restaurant, focused on the immediate task and that alone. He was dressed in a charcoal suit, no tie this time, a couple of buttons undone at his collar. His hair was pushed forward over his forehead instead of back and she saw the glint of a silver earring in his broken eyebrow. She was too far away to see what it was, but was dying to know.

Finally, as if in slow motion, he turned, his gaze floating past her table, clearly avoiding it like she'd thought, before her presence registered and his eyes slammed back to her.

That eyebrow quirked and he simply nodded as if he'd been expecting her, his long legs eating up the distance between them in seconds.

She had an entire speech prepared, of course, but before she could even say hello, he pulled her out of the booth and into his arms, his mouth finding hers as if they'd been apart for years instead of days. Her arms wound around his neck, tightening until she might as well be trying to choke him; his did the same around her waist, drawing her in so tightly to him as if they could meld into each other. And it was fine with her because she never wanted to be separated from him again.

"You good?" he asked, finally letting her up for air, his gaze fierce as he stared down at her.

She met his eyes, seeing that the new earring was a silver ball on the bottom and an orange-and-black flame on top. Made sense. He was no longer a football player, he was in the grilled meats business, so an open flame was much more accurate.

"Yeah," she said, breathing in the familiar, deeply fresh smell of him.

Because she knew she had a lot of miles still to climb, her hands started sweating and her stomach lodged in her throat. All she wanted to do was beg for his forgiveness. Also, just multitudinous floods of tears were burning behind her eyes because she missed and loved him so much her body couldn't even handle all of it. Considering how short a time it had been since she'd seen him, trying to even imagine breaking things off completely had been ludicrous on her part.

"So, hi," she finally said in response to the expectant look on his face.

Hugh peered down at her from his significant height. He shook his head and then repeated the inspection before that scarred eyebrow shot up again, waiting.

"Hi, Parker," he said, some of the humor back in his voice, steadying her nerves. She had not completely screwed this up, so there was hope. The actual hard part, though, committing to Hugh for real, was the treacherous mountain she still needed to climb.

She nodded, words sticking in her throat for just a moment, before she gestured for him to sit down at the table.

Pulling out her leather portfolio, she opened it and put it in his lap for him to look at. Over the years she'd collected all kinds of ideas and recipes and snapshots of interiors she admired because in truth helping him open restaurants was the perfect job for her. Creating something from scratch. Hugh had given her that and it was one of a thousand things she'd never have allowed herself to dream about without him.

"I know we tossed a lot of ideas around and I'd build a menu for whatever kind of place you wanted, but I wanted to start with the ideas I have for a restaurant in San Antonio."

His gaze shot to hers, locking there, the green of his hazel eyes softening to sea green.

She nearly caved then and leaped over the table and dragged him out of the restaurant, but she had something to prove first and she would not be deterred.

Pointing to the menu, and also the food in front of them that she'd spent the day cooking in his kitchen before service started, she informed him, "This isn't traditional barbecue. The only way it even makes sense as barbecue is that fact that it's smoked. But nothing on the table has been smoked with wood and the sauces are also smoked. The proteins aren't necessarily traditionally associated with barbecue, but instead use a lot of local to San Antonio ingredients. For example, I used autumn sage, an edible plant specific to the area that you can either eat as is, or smoke and infuse a sage flavor. I did it here to all the meat and also the vegetables, which isn't something any restaurant is doing as far as I know. At least not in San Antonio. I just happened to be able to find the sage here at the specialty market, but you get the general idea."

When Hugh didn't say anything, instead reaching out to try a piece of lightly smoked and grilled trout, she went on. "I don't claim to know a lot about decor, but the concept is fresh so I think that's how we should keep the decor. And it would separate us from the rustic and dark traditional barbecue places."

After he went through a couple of baskets and plates, trying the food, but giving no indication of how he felt about it, he pulled out the sample board for the interior. Deep chocolate fabric swatches, buttery birch wood samples, and deep blue and green tiles made up the decor, and he touched everything before placing that on top of the menu at his side.

His silence was driving her crazy, but she was happy to endure it if only to be in his presence. "I'm not wedded to the decor at all, I just wanted to give you an idea of what it could be. I also had a logo made," she added, pulling another mock-up from

her file that she'd had a friend do on the fly. She'd
thought it turned out pretty well, though.

"Ember," he finally said, nodding approvingly
at the name of the restaurant. "I like that."

Finally meeting her eyes, he looked expectantly
for her to continue. So she took out the contract he'd
given her before she'd left.

"I signed it," she told him as she handed it over.

Instead of looking at the papers straightaway, he
let the moment stretch, and once again, she thought
she might vomit.

"Consultant or partners?" he asked, his gaze in-
tent on her face.

"Partners." Nothing less. Ever.

That broken eyebrow again, the one she saw
when she closed her eyes at night willing herself
forget him.

"Does that mean we can't be involved romanti-
cally?" he pressed, those bodybuilder arms crossing
over his chest. The white fabric of his button-down
stretched with the movement.

"Um, if that's what you want," she hedged, confused about that kiss if what he wanted was just to
be business partners. "My dad is getting remarried
so I'm putting my house in Chicago on the market. I don't have liquid funds yet to invest as a full
partner, but I will."

The look he gave her was loaded, as if to say
he was disappointed in her for not actually saying

the words that needed to be said. Which was fair. This whole experience was testing her limits, but if being with Hugh had taught her nothing else it was to go balls-out, as he would say.

"I love you, Hugh," she grumbled. "Is that what you want me to say?"

That all-or-nothing smile again, the larger-than-life football player who'd made her feel like she was the most important person in his life and in the world. She would never get tired of seeing it on his face and hoped she could make him as happy as he made her. She'd waited nearly thirty years to tell someone she loved them and it had been worth the wait.

"I'm sorry," he said, putting a massive hand behind his ear, "I didn't hear you."

"I love you!" she shouted, her hands lifting above her head in frustration and complete elation. Just saying the words felt like starting a new and better life. One she shared with Hugh.

"Get over here," he ordered, sticking out his hand. "Now."

She clambered over the bench seat, not wasting any time getting into his arms again. He pulled her down into his lap so she was straddling him, the rest of the diners be damned, their eyes joined, and she could stare at the crooked nose, scars and broken eyebrow forever.

"I like the new earring," she told him, drawing a thumb over the flame.

He grinned. "Yeah, well, the old earring didn't quite make sense anymore and I thought I didn't need one, but then I realized I just hadn't known how to fill the empty space. But turns out I found exactly what I wanted there."

She shook her head at what he was really saying, but also absurdly happy because that's how she felt, too, that he filled the empty spaces.

"And I wish you would have given me more of a heads-up that you were coming back because I already bought a place in Chicago."

Her head dropped in surprise. "What?"

He ran a hand through her hair, dropping a kiss on her temple. That freshly clean Hugh scent invaded her brain like a drug, sending pleasure waves through her entire body.

"Yeah, I'd planned to move my home base to Chicago so we could at least still date if you didn't want to be in a serious relationship."

She pulled back, meeting his eyes, her heart growing into one of those gigantic cartoon hearts. Happiness flowed through her, jubilant and fizzy. Hugh Matteson was the last person she ever thought she'd fall for, but he was also the best person she'd ever met. "But you want to move back home to San Antonio."

"Not as much as I want to be with you," he told her as if she were a child. "I love you, Parker. My home is wherever you are."

She almost had the thought that she didn't deserve him, but that was old thinking because she finally believed that she did.

"I'm sorry I didn't say goodbye. I was in a terror state," she joked. "I honestly don't even know how I left. I didn't want to at all."

His lips met hers in a gentle kiss that settled all the guilt her speech had dredged up. They were together for real and it was awesome. All that time spent thinking she wasn't fit for a relationship, and she'd found the perfect one without even really looking.

"I forgive you, Parker," he said, his eyes serious. "I understand being scared, but you can't shut me out again."

"I won't," she promised, and she meant it. Their future was too precious to screw up. She'd found a partner in life who could keep up with her, propel her even further, and make her laugh along the way.

"Good," he said, "because we have a lot of work to do, including buying a house in Chicago and restaurant space in San Antonio."

Parker smiled and gave him a huge kiss. "I can't wait."

He squeezed her against him and her arms wrapped around him and she never wanted to let go. And if she had her way, she never would.

"Neither can I."

* * * * *